VANISHED

Tattoo My Heart

Stacey Lynn Hafner

Rainmaker Publishing

First published by Rainmaker Publishing 2022

Copyright © 2022 by Stacey Lynn Hafner

First edition

This one is for my mom – who raised me to be curious, who made me a reader, and who has supported all my crazy dreams.

Wishing you sweet days & spicy nights!

Stacey Lynn Hafner

"Our bodies were printed as blank pages to be filled with the ink of our hearts."
~ Michael Biondi

Contents

Prologue

Lucas - three years ago

The bell above the door jingles, signaling someone entering the shop. I look up from the sketches I'm working on and size up the man walking toward me.

He's not our typical client. I know tattoos are pretty mainstream at this point, and I know better than most never to judge someone by how they look, but this guy is totally out of place here. *Twisted Ink* is in a rough, barely middle-class neighborhood in Chicago. We don't usually get business types in fancy suits popping in over their lunch break. Christ, this guy looks like he got his shoes shined this morning.

Although we are starting to get some folks sniffing around as stories leak I've made the list of contestants for the next season of *Top Ink*. Most come to check out my designs, see if the rumors are true (I can neither confirm nor deny for another month) and if they can get time on my chair before I'm on TV and my schedule gets tighter, and my fees higher. At least, that's what I hope happens. Assuming I do well in the competition.

This chance could change everything for me. The prize money, the name recognition, I could finally start my own shop, take Jax and Macy with me. Do it the way we want. The way Jax and I have always talked about.

But this guy still isn't the type we usually see. I'll be shocked if he's here for some ink.

"Can I help you?"

"Lucas Gray?"

A referral? Maybe I'm wrong. I don't know why else this guy would be looking for me.

I stand, stretching to my full height. An asshole tactic? Maybe. Honestly, this guy is no physical threat to me, but I know that isn't the only way to wound someone. I take the advantages I have. "Yeah? I'm Luke."

When he doesn't say anything else, I fill the silence. "You looking for a tattoo?"

That seems to shake him loose, and he holds out his hand, introducing himself. "I'm Ethan Abbott."

Curious, I shake his hand, still waiting for answers.

"I have some personal business to discuss with you. Is there somewhere we could speak privately?"

What the hell is this guy's deal?

Another thought occurs to me. "Are you from the network?"

The confusion on his face gives me my answer before he responds. "No. I'm just - I'm here on personal business."

What kind of business could this guy possibly have with me? Let alone anything he needed *privacy* for.

"Hey, Mace?" I yell back without taking my eyes off the stranger in front of me.

"Yo!"

"Can you cover the front for a few minutes?"

A moment later, Macy appears from the break room. I'm a big guy, but Mace is a hulk. I give the suit credit. He looks at us warily but doesn't back down. Mace looks between us and cocks his head, silently asking me if I need backup. We don't have the history Jax and I do, but I trust him to have my back when things go to shit. He's loyal, and he never feels the need to prove anything to anyone. It's a level of chill I have yet to achieve.

I have a fuck ton to prove to literally everyone.

"I'll be back in a bit. You good?"

"My next appointment is at 2. I'm good until then." He nods at me.

That gives the suit just over 30 minutes to explain his 'personal business'. "I'll be back by then. Thanks, man."

I head to the back room, one of the few with an actual door for privacy and not just a curtain, assuming the suit will follow.

It only takes twenty minutes. Twenty minutes to give me answers that explain absolutely nothing. He tells me his family has been looking for me. He tells me they're my family too. He tells me a lot of things I can't hear right now. He hands me a fat envelope and tells me he'll be in touch. Twenty minutes after he enters, he leaves.

My head is swimming, and everything feels muffled and far away. My chest tightens until I feel like roaring to relieve the building tension. So I do, hardly recognizing the sound escaping. I need to hit something. I'd like to hit *my cousin* Ethan, but he's gone, leaving me with unanswered fury and countless questions. I throw open the door exploding through the shop. I stop cold seeing Jax reclining back on one of the battered couches for waiting clients, casually watching videos on his phone.

"What are you doing here? You're not on the schedule."

"Mace texted."

I shoot him a look. Unapologetic, he just shrugs, "Didn't look good, brother."

This tiny show of support calms my rage just a little. My throat tightens with emotion, and I clear it roughly away. I don't like how I feel right now. Like I'm on the verge of losing control. I'll admit the anger inside me is terrifying. Knowing these two are here to help me deal with it and keep me from destroying anything with it is the security I need right now.

Jax slowly unfolds from the couch, tucking his cell in his back pocket. "Want to head up to the Attic?"

That's exactly what I want to do. I exhale in a rush. My shoulders already feel less tense. I nod.

The Attic is what we call the third floor of the building housing the tattoo shop. It's mainly used for storage and has a ton of crap from previous tenants, but we've set up a makeshift gym in the corner with free weights and a punching bag. That punching bag is going to help me process the information overload just dumped on me.

I strip off my shirt and wrap my hands while Jax pulls up one of the camping chairs we have stashed up there. He listens while I repeat everything I've just been told between jabs. I have no idea how long I work out my aggression, longer than the story I have to tell, and by the time I'm done, I'm drenched in sweat and my arms are humming in exhausted protest. Jax throws me a bottle of water and kicks another chair so it skids across the floor toward me. Gratefully I fall into it and gulp the water down.

"These Abbotts are kind of a big deal, man. Did this Ethan guy mention that?"

"What do you mean?"

Jax glances at his phone again and informs me about my *family*. "Well, they're fucking loaded for one. Like inherited money for generations. And one of them - it looks like Ethan's dad is a Congressman running for Senate next fall." He shows me the articles he's found while I've been *exercising*.

"No. He mentioned something about an estate and possible trust, but I couldn't process what the fuck he was talking about."

"They think his sister, the politician guy, is your mother?"

I shrug. After all these years, finding out who my parents were had stopped being a possibility in my mind. Even with someone right in front of me telling me he might have answers, I was still having trouble believing it.

"I couldn't find much about her online."

"He said she ran away when she got pregnant."

Jax nods. "You said he left you with some papers?"

"Yeah. They're still downstairs."

Jax is silent, letting me work things out in my head for a minute.

"What do you want to do?"

It's different with Jax. He knows who his parents were, knows they were pieces of shit that had no business making a kid. Our foster homes were pretty ugly at times, but he knew home would just be a different kind of hell. I had nothing. No information. No ties. No context. Only questions and constant uncertainty.

"You want to take the DNA test?"

Do I?

Ethan seemed to think it was a formality. They were sure he told me. Used 'every resource at their disposal' to find me.

"I don't know, man. It feels pretty fucking convenient."

"What do you mean?"

"That he comes walking through the door now after all this time. Right before his dad starts campaigning for office, and I'm about to be on national television?"

"You think they were sitting on it?"

I shrug. I have no idea what I'm thinking.

The DNA comes back a match. I'm an Abbott. Biologically anyway.

I feel that same wave of rage I experienced the first day Ethan dropped all this on me as I read the terms of my trust.

It's contingent on my withdrawing from *Top Ink*. There are a lot of legal words all strung together that I basically interpret as I can do whatever I want with the money as long as I don't appear on television this year or any other. I look at the dollar amount, literally counting the zeros to clarify what I'm seeing. It's far more than I'd make winning *Top Ink* a dozen times.

But I have a fuck ton to prove to literally everyone. And now, especially one person.

Uncle Theo. You dick.

I'll take your name. Let you explain to all your country club friends and political donors who I am and what your family did to your too-young pregnant sister thirty years ago.

But I'm not signing anything. Keep your bribe, you fucking asshole.

I rip up the papers and open a beer.

I need a drink.

I'm an Abbott. And when I win *Top Ink*, we'll let the skeletons come tumbling out.

Chapter One

My phone dings with a news alert, drawing my eyes away from the sketches in front of me. The name *Abbott* causes me to drop everything else and open the article, even though I know it's probably a bad idea. I probably don't want to know what it has to say about my so-called family. It's probably only going to put me in a lousy mood minutes before I'm supposed to be a charming and entertaining host to a group of tipsy women celebrating their friend's upcoming wedding.

But some days, I'm just a sucker for torturing myself, and I guess today is one of those days.

This time it's my uncle, the senator, making the news. By the nature of his work, he's in the press more often than the rest although I periodically see cousins on the society pages or in business columns. Photos of him at a groundbreaking ceremony in one of the poorer neighborhoods in Chicago fill my screen. According to the article, he's being given credit for helping earmark federal funds to build a community center that will help provide a safe space for kids. Leaders from community organizations I recognize are quoted in the piece. Organizations I know do a lot of good work.

I hate it when he does something I can actually respect. Even if I know it's all for show and he's a fraud.

It doesn't matter to the people he actually helps along the way that he doesn't give a shit about anything but his image. I know that. I get it. But it matters to me.

He's never publicly acknowledged me as his family, although there's been plenty of speculation, especially after I changed my name. I've never commented on it either, preferring to let it silently simmer between us. The speculation hit its peak soon after I won *Top Ink*, but it reasserts itself periodically and the fact neither of us has officially denied it either ensures it will keep coming back.

Peals of laughter interrupt my dark thoughts, and I force myself to close the article and shove my phone into my pocket.

Time to turn it on and go to work. I stand and stretch, working out the tension thinking of my family always causes. Taking a deep breath, I head down the hall to the front of my dream, *Vanished on Halsted,* my own shop. I don't need the Abbotts. I've got what I need under this roof.

And I'm fucking proud of what I've built here.

"I'm on it."

I pause in the hallway, just beyond the lobby entrance, startled by my reaction to that voice. That smoke and honey voice. Then I hear her laugh, and I have to force my body to relax. What the hell? Walking into the middle of a Bachelorette Party with a chubby is probably not a good idea. I'm annoyed by my response to a woman I haven't even seen yet.

After reciting my grocery list and thinking through my appointments for the next day, I finally feel ready to proceed.

Taking a deep breath, I pull myself together and turn the corner, prepared to greet the Bachelorette and her party.

Three steps in, I stop dead, looking at the most beautiful woman I've ever seen.

Gabriella, or Gabby, stands at the counter, clipboard in hand filling out her intake form. Jax is behind the counter, appearing to half-heartedly flirt with two of the bridesmaids while another two sit on the couches along the window and study the various tattoo images and artwork on our walls.

But I have no idea what any of them look like because all I can see right now is *her.*

She's tall and slender with soft curves covered in dark jeans and a sexy black top with a low back. Her dark hair is touched with sun-kissed strands and falls in smooth, loose waves midway down her mostly bare back. Her skin is flawless, pale and smooth and begging to be stroked. And marked - she doesn't have any tattoos that I can see, a relatively rare sight for me these days. Suddenly I'm insanely glad I get to be the one to ink her.

The front door jingles, indicating another customer walking in, and she turns a wide smile lighting her features. I swallow, stunned, and have the ridiculous thought that I want to be the one to put that smile on her face.

What the fuck is wrong with me? I shake my head, slightly disgusted, attempting to clear it out, but her dark chocolate eyes linger. Fuck, those are gorgeous eyes.

She's your client, asshole. She's about to get her future husband's name tattooed on her hip. Get it together.

Maybe she's interested in one last fling? If that's my only option, I'll make the best of it.

"About time! I need your help with some of these questions," she calls to the woman entering the front door. "And how is Tim?"

"Practically perfect, thank you," responds the tiny Latina as she grabs the clipboard away.

"Well, no more sneaking off for calls with your groom! You're ours for the rest of the night," yells one of the women from the couch.

"Yes, ma'am." This response comes again from the tiny Latina, not the tall brunette. Suddenly hopeful, I step forward.

Jax spots me right away and makes the introductions, confirming my growing suspicion the gorgeous brunette is not the guest of honor. I greet everyone with a smile but turn my attention back to her as quickly as I can.

"Hi. Lucas," I introduce myself.

"Ash." She shakes my hand, her skin soft against my palm. I lose myself for a second as those chocolate eyes focus on me. I'd like to lose myself a lot longer, but the excited voices and laughter around us remind me that isn't possible.

Yet.

"Are you interested in getting a tattoo?" I wait, expectant, knowing only if she is that I will be the one to do it. Not one of my staff. No way am I passing up the opportunity to touch that creamy skin.

Ash

"Gabby!"

I wince at Raquel's high-pitched squeal. Technically the party is just getting started, but Raquel has been pretty aggressively pre-gaming most of the afternoon. She was tipsy when she met us to check in to the hotel, and I don't think she has paused since. That was four hours ago. I'm worried that if she keeps going at this pace, she won't make it back to her room without spraining an ankle. The girl likes her stilettos.

She's currently leaning over the front counter of *Vanished on Halsted* attempting to flirt with the rough giant standing behind it. He's being gracious and engaging with her, but I can tell he's not really that into it. I'm sure he's gotten used to drunken bridesmaids attempting to add him to the Bachelorette party favors on a reasonably regular basis. At least, I'm assuming that's the case based on what I've learned about this place.

Shockingly this is the first time I've ever been in a tattoo shop. It's almost what I expected. I mean, considering I really had no idea what to expect. They've rehabbed one of the old industrial warehouses in the neighborhood. The space also includes a brewery, coffee shop, and a couple cute indie stores. *Vanished* itself is spotless with enormous windows, exposed brick, and explosions of color everywhere. It's a space for people far cooler than I am, but I still like it. I like color. When it's done well. And everything here is done well.

"Gabby," Raquel doesn't even turn as she calls out, keeping her blurry eyes and exposed cleavage firmly focused on her target. "You need to check in with the guy... Jax." She touches his chest, covering the *Vanished* logo on his shirt, and purrs, "Hi, Jax."

I glance around the lobby. They've closed shop for the night, staying open just for our party, so I quickly realize Gabby, my best friend and the guest of honor, is not here. I roll my eyes slightly but can't help my smile, knowing damn well she's slipped out to call her fiancé Tim.

"I'm on it." I step up to the counter and hold out my hand for the clipboard Jax just grabbed. He smiles at me and winks playfully. I return the grin and laugh out loud as he inhales sharply and dodges Raquel's wandering fingers. Jessi comes over to join her, and I see a tiny flare of panic in Jax's eyes as he's surrounded. I focus on filling out the intake form with Gabby's vital information, relieved to have a task to occupy me for a few minutes.

I love Gabby, but this whole night is not really my scene, and – I'd never admit this to her – I'm feeling a little awkward and disoriented. Gabby and I have been friends forever, but half of these women I hardly know. The other half I inevitably lost touch with after college graduation – first with med school and then being out of the country the last three years. Gabby was the one I'd held onto, keeping me connected and grounded.

And laughing. Gabby is hysterical.

I've been back in Chicago, back in the States, for only a week. I'm still crashing at Gabby's and Tim's apartment. The most exciting part about this Bachelorette Party for me was the hotel rooms we rented for the weekend. Two whole nights on a real bed in a room that doesn't double as Tim's home office. Luxury.

I might even take a bubble bath. I'm definitely ordering room service. I haven't taken a relaxing bath in years. Or ordered room service. Neither had been available where I've spent the last few years. I was lucky to have a lukewarm sponge bath or cold shower on a daily basis.

Adjusting back to life in Chicago is trickier than I expected, but it's only been a few days. I do love this city, and I've missed it. I'm excited to be back. Really I am. Besides, if everything goes to plan, this won't be permanent. A year tops.

If everything goes according to plan.

I shake my head and refocus. Tonight is about Gabby and having some fun. Or at least pretending to have fun until I can get into that bathtub.

The bell above the door tinkles, and I turn smiling at Gabby as she re-enters.

"About time! I need your help with some of these questions. And how is Tim?" I tease.

Her eyes are legit twinkling as she accepts the clipboard and pen. "Practically perfect, thank you."

"Well, no more sneaking off for calls with your groom! You're ours for the rest of the night." This from Gabby's little sister Camilla.

Laughing, Gabby agrees. Despite me being the Maid of Honor, the others have done most of the planning for the weekend. I have only a vague sense of our agenda, partly because Skype calls to where I was in Nigeria aren't incredibly reliable but mostly because Camilla didn't trust me not to spill the secrets to Gabby. Which – fair.

Vanished is one of the few events everyone knew about well in advance – a special request from the bride herself. A tattoo celebrating her love. Apparently, the owner is a crazy talented artist and won some reality television tattoo competition a couple of years ago that he managed to parlay into his own reality show, and now he's a celebrity that puts his art on other celebrities. And bridal parties if they pay enough. Which Gabby's family is happy to do.

According to the other girls, he's also insanely gorgeous. I have dozens of emails in my inbox right now from the others gushing about how hot all the artists here are and gossiping about what's happening on the show that now focuses on Lucas Abbott post his *Top Ink* championship, but I hadn't bothered to Google any of it. I figured I would find out eventually, and since I wasn't planning on getting a tattoo myself, it didn't seem necessary to look at their designs. Besides, there's an insane amount of pop culture to absorb after three years, and I'm still adjusting my time zones after my 30-hour journey home. This week I slept. Next week I'll catch up on my celebrity gossip.

I'll be honest if Jax is any indication of what to expect, they weren't exaggerating. He's rough around the edges, not polished like most of the men I work with at the hospital, but the man is gorgeous. And pretty adorable when he's flirting but trying to keep a distance at the same time. Watching him walk that line with Raquel has certainly been entertaining.

Suddenly he straightens, all teasing gone as he looks at something over my shoulder.

"Luke. This is Gabby, the bride-to-be. Camilla, Jessi, and," he checks the papers in front of him, "Sofie are also getting tattoos."

"Awesome."

Luke, Lucas Abbott is The Guy. The reason we're all here tonight. I can tell he's already gotten the attention of all the other women in the room, and I feel myself getting excited right along with them. I turn to face the voice behind me and meet the man everyone has been not-so-secretly fantasizing about over our group email chain.

Holy shit.

His dark blue gaze meets mine for a hot second before he focuses on Gabby, giving his congratulations and discussing his sketches for her design. I stand there immediately debating if I should get a tattoo after all.

Because freaking hell, that man is gorgeous. No wonder he was able to pivot a reality competition win into his own reality show spin-off. I can't imagine any straight woman in America turning off their TV set if he was on it.

"Hi. Lucas." He holds out his hand, introducing himself. Those blue eyes are back focused on me.

Determined to play it cool and not fan girl out – considering I've never seen his show, this seems doubly inappropriate for me to do – I clasp his hand. "Ash."

He holds my hand a beat longer than is polite. Or is that just my wishful thinking? "Are you interested in getting a tattoo?"

"No. I'm just here for moral support."

"Ash is going to let me hold her hand," Gabby interjects, and Lucas finally releases our handshake.

He grins at me. "Let me know if you change your mind. I'm pretty good."

I laugh. "That's the rumor anyway."

His smile deepens, and one eyebrow quirks. My stomach flips, and I realize I am interested in this man in a way I haven't been interested in years – maybe ever. Jax is attractive, any idiot would notice that and I'm pretty smart, but I hadn't really *cared* he was attractive just acknowledged it the way I would note a patient's symptoms. Factually. Impartially. Indifferently.

But my body's reaction to Lucas is the opposite of indifferent.

"Ladies." His voice raises as he takes in the whole group. "You all want a quick tour before you get some ink?"

Cheers go up from around me, and we all follow Lucas and Jax through the shop.

They lead us through the rooms quickly and introduce us to Macy and Logan, two other artists that will be working with us tonight. Macy is even bigger than Lucas and Jax, with tan skin and dark hair pulled into a sexy man-bun. He's intimidatingly fierce until he grins and tells Sophie he'll take care of her tonight. Sophie practically swoons. Camilla will be with Logan, the only female and final member of the *Vanished* team. I briefly wonder if being model worthy is a requirement to work here. Logan is definitely the kind of cool I would expect from the crowd frequenting the shop. She's tall and willowy with wide blue eyes heavily rimmed with black liner - her smoky eye game is on point - and long white blond hair, the tips of which are currently dyed an electric blue. Jax leads Jessi to his station, which leaves Gabby and me to follow Lucas.

"I've got a couple sketches worked up for you to take a look at. Once you decide what you like, we can get started."

Gabby claps her hands excitedly, causing me to laugh. I catch Lucas glancing at me from the corner of my eye and try to calm my reaction to him and his attention. Tonight is about Gabby, I remind myself.

Twenty minutes later, I wince as my best friend squeezes my hand with surprising strength considering the tiny package.

"You're doing great. Let me know if you need to take a break, okay?" Lucas tells her.

She nods, gritting her teeth. For several minutes it's quiet, just the hum of the tattoo machine in his hand buzzing around us and the music pumping through the shop's speakers. At some point, I start distracting Gabby with questions about the wedding and honeymoon. Again, I'm still catching up on all the details I've missed while gone. She and Tim plan to head to Maine for a weekend soon after the wedding but are planning a longer getaway later during winter. I'm secretly excited I'll have the apartment to myself for even a couple of days.

"Hey, Luke. Sorry man, but Krista is on the phone. Says it's urgent." Jax ducks out again, having delivered his message.

Lucas grimaces before switching off the tattoo gun and leaning back. "Sorry, I have to take this. I'll just be a minute."

My eyes follow him out of our little station, watching him curiously. He's been friendly but professional, primarily focused on his design and letting Gabby and I chat around him. I wonder idly who Krista is. I hear laughter from the station next to us and smile, wondering if Raquel is having any luck with her flirting. What is it like to be that brazen and outspoken about what you want? I wonder -

My thoughts are interrupted by Gabby's harsh exhale. Guiltily, I turn my attention back to her.

"How are you holding up?"

"I'm good. Thanks for sitting with me."

"Of course! It's actually been really cool even if I didn't have any idea about this place."

She smiles brightly, and I feel a slight pang realizing how much I've missed her the past few years and how grateful I am we've managed to stay close. How lucky I am to be included in her wedding. I don't know how I would have gotten through junior high, let alone med school, without Gabby's perky enthusiasm.

"Lucas is nice," she says pointedly.

And I'm also reminded that Gabby knows me better than anyone on the planet. She's probably noticed me... *noticing*...him. I feel my cheeks heat and know from experience the pink blush giving me away. *Damn.*

"He is," I agree, hoping she'll drop it.

Knowing I'm probably not going to be that lucky.

"You should invite him to come join us after this."

"What? Why?" I'm shocked she would even suggest such a thing. Not because I'm a prude who doesn't think women should be able to pick up men if that's what they want. Note my earlier thoughts. But because it's her Bachelorette Party. I'm not going to ditch the girls, no matter how tempting the guy may be.

Incredibly tempting.... Sinfully tempting.... Once in a lifetime kind of tempting....

I shake my head, dismissing my thought and her suggestion.

"You are so clueless. He can hardly take his eyes off you. If my tattoo is messed up because the tattoo artist was making googly eyes at you the whole time, I'm going to be totally pissed, bitch."

I burst out laughing at this ridiculousness. But my best friend isn't done.

"You deserve to have some hot stranger sex. And with a celebrity! That's even hotter. You should totally invite him. I bet he's an excellent dirty talker. He seems like he'd be really vocal."

I feel my blush kick up another couple of notches, both embarrassed and, I'll admit, a little intrigued by her assumption. "Gabriella! How could you possibly know that?" I can't help the little giggle that escapes.

"You don't think so?" she asks, eyes wide with fake innocence.

"I have no idea." I'm sure I'm an insane shade of red at this point, and pray Lucas doesn't choose now to return.

"Invite him."

"I'm not going to invite him to join your Bachelorette party!"

"Then I will."

She nods slightly and presses her lips together as if that settles the issue.

"No, you won't!"

"If you don't, I totally will. You need to get laid. And not in a boring way like you usually do."

I look away, trying to hide my cringe as her remark hits home. I don't have a very exciting romantic history. My last "relationship" was so lackluster it fizzled out and faded away without either of us even really noticing. I console myself with the reminder that I've just been focused on other things. I'm happy. I have a good life. I'm excited about my future. What's the big deal about sex anyway?

"I've had good sex," I half-heartedly protest, not quite willing to give it up. "I mean, it's not always boring."

"Ashland Grace, I have known you since we were thirteen and for every one of your boyfriends. You have *not* had good sex. Lucas would definitely be gooooooood sex." She draws it out, wiggling her eyebrows suggestively.

"I'm good, Gabby. Really." But I can't help laughing at her antics.

Her face settles into serious best-friend mode. "Just because Will ended up being a dud doesn't mean you're doomed for mediocrity for the rest of your life, you know. Lucas Abbott would know what to do with a naked Ash."

Totally mortified and sure the man of the hour will walk back in any second, I hiss, "Gabby! Be quiet!"

"Well, he would," she grumbles but seems to finally be backing off.

Just in time, too, because no sooner does she settle back in her chair with a tiny huff than Lucas is back, pulling on a fresh pair of gloves. I don't know if it's because we were just talking about him or because I'm having very non-boring thoughts about him, but the room suddenly feels smaller, the air a little thicker than it did before.

Oblivious to the tension I'm experiencing, Lucas slides onto the stool next to Gabby and smiles. "Okay. Sorry about that, ladies. Ready to finish this?"

"Let's do it," Gabby agrees.

His eyes meet mine, and he winks playfully before returning his attention to my best friend's hip. I can't help my little thrill and wide grin in response. He's so pretty. Is that an offensive thing to say about a man? But he is. He has perfect pale Irish skin and thick auburn hair long enough to brush his neck as it meets the collar of his black t-shirt, repping the *Vanished* logo. It looks a more and deeper red depending on the light. And he has the darkest blue eyes I've ever seen. They seem more serious than the chill vibe he gives off.

It makes me curious about his story. Would watching his show appease my curiosity or only make it worse? I could see an unhealthy obsession forming.

Gabby catches my eye and looks deliberately at his bent head. *Ask him*, she mouths silently.

I shake my head stubbornly. She doesn't know the thoughts in my head. I doubt I could just enjoy Lucas Abbott's skill and attention for a night. I would want to know more about him. He wouldn't just be a way for me to blow off some steam, as she seems to think. He would be a distraction. One I doubt I can afford right now.

Ask him, she repeats.

As if on cue, Lucas asks, "So, what else do you all have planned for the night?" And Gabby narrows her eyes at me as if trying to Jedi mind trick the words into coming out of my mouth.

I startle as Camilla pokes her head into our room. "Hey, Gabs! The others are all finished, so we'll head over to the hotel and make sure everything is ready for the evening's entertainment." She grins, loving to have secrets she can hold over her older sister. "You need anything? Want any of us to wait for you?"

"No, we're good. You guys go ahead. I don't think we'll be much longer. Luke?"

"Twenty minutes. Unless Ash changes her mind."

I look over to see him smiling at me. Less professional and more friendly now. My stomach flips. I know he's talking about getting a tattoo, but my earlier conversation with Gabby has all sorts of dirty thoughts springing to mind. His eyes slip to my mouth, and I realize I'm biting my lip nervously.

Am I changing my mind?

Incredibly tempting...

"Perfect! That'll give us plenty of time to set up the games." Camilla winks, giggles, and ducks out to rally the rest of the girls back to the hotel suites.

I exhale slowly, relieved the moment was broken.

Gabby looks at me expectantly but, thankfully, is still focused on her sister's comments and not the unspoken tension between her tattoo artist and me. "Games?"

I shake my head and give her a little shrug. "They didn't trust me not to tell you," I admit.

"So you don't know either?" I feel the tiniest bit of satisfaction at the slight panic in her expression. Serves her right for giving me such a hard time.

"No. Although I did veto the private showing of an all-male revue. You know how obsessed Jessi is with Magic Mike."

I swear I hear Lucas snort, although he stays focused on his work.

"Well. Thanks for that anyway," Gabby sighs.

Jax enters a few minutes later, studying the design on Gabby's hip over Lucas's shoulder. He gives her a grin that is somehow both flirtatious and respectful. "Beautiful. I think your man will love it."

I feel another pang, seeing the expression of joy spread across Gabby's face. "Yeah?" she asks, a ridiculous smile in place.

"Hell yeah. It's hot when a woman is that sure of you, you know?"

A warm feeling settles in my chest, witnessing how happy my best friend is. She and Tim really are a fantastic couple. They complement each other well, support each other's goals, and have so much fun together. Again, I'm no expert on relationships, but the ability to have fun together seems… significant.

"Macy and Logan packed up and headed home. I'm going to take the trash out back and start to lock up. You good?" he asks Lucas.

Nodding, Lucas responds, "Just finishing up. Go for it." He rubs some gel on Gabby's finished tattoo and gives her aftercare instructions. She's practically bouncing on her toes, she loves it so much. He turns away slightly as she pulls her jeans back up, fastening them carefully over her hips and the bandage he applied.

"Let me clean up a couple things here, and I'll meet you guys up front to settle up."

Gabby slips her arm through mine, and we head down the short hallway back to the lobby.

She nudges me with her elbow. "Last chance. Are you sure you want to spend the rest of the night playing games and answering quizzes about what Tim and

I fight about, what was our first date, or who's the better cook when you could be spending some quality time with Lucas Abbott?"

I mean, when she puts it that way.... I picture Lucas sharing that amazing hotel bathtub with me and bite back a smile.

Really though, there's no chance that's happening tonight. Tonight is for Gabby. But maybe another night?

No, Lucas Abbott probably has women throwing themselves at him all the time. Do I really want to join those ranks? Could I handle a one-night casual encounter? That's never been my thing, but then again, I've never had a man like Lucas as an option.

We step into the spacious lobby, and suddenly I stumble forward as Gabby is yanked away from me. I see a man wrap one arm around her torso, clamping his hand over her mouth and cutting off her cry of surprise. I stifle my own response seeing the gun in his other hand, terrifyingly close to my best friend's ribs. A movement over his shoulder captures my stunned gaze, and I see he isn't alone.

And his friend's gun is pointed at me.

Automatically I raise my hands to my sides, palms out, trying to demonstrate I'll cooperate.

"Okay. It's okay." I keep my voice calm and steady.

Gabby is struggling, trying to pry away the hand still muffling her screams. Based on his pupils and breathing, I'm guessing the guy is high out of his mind. The other *gentleman* seems calmer, at least. Not as jumpy.

"Who else is here?" Mr. High-As-A-Kite demands, trying to look around me and see if anyone else is in the hall. I am incredibly grateful the rest of the girls have already gone.

Before I can say anything, his friend snatches my wrist and puts a similar hold on me. Gabby makes a high-pitched squeal and then settles down, breathing erratically. He's digging his gun into her side, warning her to be quiet.

"Who else!" He yells again.

My captor's arm squeezes me tighter.

I hate it when people pull guns on me.

Damn it.

Chapter Two

Lucas

*D*amn.

I thought for a minute there my gorgeous girl was going to take her friend's advice and invite me to join the party. *Ashland Grace.* I smirk. Even her name is fucking perfect. Representing both Chicago and beauty - two of my favorite things. It was probably an asshole move eavesdropping on their conversation, but when I hear two beautiful women talking about sex, I'm going to listen.

Krista's definition of 'urgent' and mine differ wildly. Jax may not feel like he can hang up on our producer, but I have no problem telling her I'll call her back. Don't get me wrong, I appreciate the job she does for me, for all of us, but if I have someone in my chair, they always come first. My producer can wait until morning to run through whatever logistics she needs to check off her list. Krista's big on lists. We're not even filming right now. I'm sure some days she hates me, but the show's ratings speak for themselves. She'll deal with my cranky ass, especially because she knows I'll get the job done when she needs me to. I'm not stupid enough to blow this opportunity - I've had too few of them in my life to get lazy about one this amazing.

Three years ago, when I was cast on *Top Ink,* I thought that was as good as it was going to get - a chance to show my work to a national audience, a chance to win, a chance for a prize. Money and exposure that would enable me to start my own shop, be my own boss, and take my best friends with me. That seemed like an insanely bold dream for someone who grew up like me, but my life now? I never would have dared imagine it. So, yeah, I may prefer to work on my timeline and not Krista's, but I'm also not going to shirk my responsibility, and she knows it.

Getting her off the phone only took a couple minutes and left me wandering back right into the middle of Gabby and Ash's very... *enlightening* ... conversation. I'd love the chance to prove Gabby right - that I would know, do know, exactly what to do with a naked Ash, but I kind of like the fact she's not jumping at the chance to jump some random 'celebrity'.

Because, let's face it, that's all I would be to her right now. A celebrity screw she could brag about to her friends.

It's weird realizing people think of me that way now.

I'm not sure why that seems so unappealing with Ash. It's not like I haven't enjoyed my new status over the last couple of years. I haven't had to chase a woman since my first appearance on *Top Ink.* Although I didn't have to work all that hard before then either. My "family" may be assholes, but they have good genes. Females have always liked what they've seen. At least long enough to jump on and take a ride.

I finish tidying up my station and head up front where the girls are waiting. I wonder if I can still charm my way into an invitation to join them or if I should tread lightly with this one and just try charming her phone number out of her. The idea of her walking out when I have no way to see her again isn't an option.

It might not be tonight, but soon I will prove to Ash that Gabby knew exactly what she was talking about.

And I promise she won't get bored.

I grin at my thoughts.

I sense something is wrong just before I turn into the lobby. It's too quiet. And I swear I hear a whimper.

On high alert, I turn the corner, once again stopping dead just inside, but this time for very different reasons.

Fuck.

I take in the scene in front of me. Ash and Gabby are both being held at gunpoint. Two young guys, fuck, practically kids, using them as shields in front of them. The dude with Gabby has a hand over her mouth, and I realize it was her whimper I heard as she cries again, gripping the arm at her throat ineffectively. The guy is practically vibrating, he's jonesing so hard.

Not good.

The guy with Ash seems calmer. At least his eyes can focus. Surprisingly, she looks reasonably calm too. Her dark chocolate eyes are wide as they meet mine, but despite the gun against her side, she's keeping it together.

I hold my hands out from my sides and try to appear as unimposing as possible. Considering I've got six inches and probably forty pounds on these kids, I'm not sure how successful I am.

"There's money in the register. Just stay cool," I offer.

"Get it!" the one holding Gabby yells.

I move behind the counter to the register, trying to figure out how to diffuse the situation without anyone getting shot. Most people pay with cards these days, and we make a deposit every day we bring in more than $500 in cash. I doubt he's going to be happy with this take.

"Open it! Hurry the fuck up!"

I grab one of the canvas bags with our logo and use that as a money bag. Maybe if he doesn't know how little it is, he'll take it and go. As I'm moving back around the counter to give it to him, he pushes Gabby away from him, his gun swinging wildly between the two of us.

"Don't move! Stay right there. Give it to the girl."

Clearly, my attempt to look non-threatening is not fooling this guy.

Gabby sniffles and moves to take the bag. I try to reassure her with my eyes. *I'll get you out of this.*

"Hey, man. You done yet? Let's get out of here and grab a drink." Jax obliviously wanders into the lobby, looking down at his phone.

Somehow time starts to unravel in front of me, both in slow motion and too quickly to process what's happening. I just react.

Obviously rattled by the appearance of another person, the first gunman starts swinging his gun erratically between the three of us. I tackle Gabby to the ground as the first gunshot rings out, and the frosted glass behind where she was standing shatters. Immediately another shot rings out. Shielding Gabby with my frame, I look up and try to spot Ash in the chaos. Another shot. Ash is wrestling with the guy who had been holding her. Distantly, with removed fascination, I realize she seems to be holding her own. The shooter starts to take aim again, firing another shot as I lunge and take him out at the knees. He goes down hard, but I'm not in a very good position, and he kicks out, connecting with my jaw.

Pain explodes across my head, and the gun discharges again. Leaning up, I swing, punching him square across the face causing him to *finally* release the gun. It clatters across the floor, and I swat it farther out of his reach and turn back to Ash and her attacker. I'm breathing hard, pinning down the body beneath me.

Ash is standing ten feet away, radiating leashed tension. Her now unconscious attacker is at her feet. Awed, I watch as she deftly removes the clip of his gun and empties the chamber.

"Don't pull a gun on me. Stupid fucking kid," she's muttering.

I can't help the grin pulling at my lips. Releasing the adrenaline.

The shooter beneath me keeps trying to wriggle out of my hold. Turning my attention back to him, I fist his t-shirt pulling his torso slightly off the floor, and punch him again. He slumps, unconscious.

Ash meets my gaze as I get to my feet. Her eyes are serious and a little sad as they hold mine, something unspoken arcing between us.

"Ash!"

The moment broken, Ash immediately turns her attention to Gabby who is scrambling across the floor.

Across the floor to an immobile Jax and the pool of blood slowly spreading around him.

I sprint to his side.

Ash

Shit.

My training immediately kicks in. I shoulder Lucas out of my way so I can kneel next to Jax, and I start barking orders. "Gabby assess his leg. I'll work on his chest wound. Lucas, call 911 and find us some towels."

He stalls behind me. I glance up and note how pale he is. "Lucas!" My voice is sharp as I call him out, jarring him out of his stupor. He blinks, his eyes meeting mine. "Towels. 911." I keep my voice level now. He's experiencing some shock; I've seen it before. Clear specific instructions. I nod at him.

He nods back, breaking loose and returns quickly with an armful of towels, then he dials 911.

I hear an odd groaning sound, but it's not coming from Jax. Out of the corner of my eye, I see the shooter, the kid I'm sure is high on something, scrambling to his feet and bolting out the door. Lucas moves as if to go after him but refocuses when the operator picks up.

I hear him giving our location and explaining the incident to the person on the other end of the line.

"Lucas, can you put it on speaker so I can talk to the dispatcher?" I speak without looking up from Jax and his wounds. He's losing a lot of blood, and I don't like that he's been unconscious the entire time.

He holds the phone next to me and I start relaying instructions.

"This is Dr. Ashland Carrington. Male victim, 30 to 35. Three bullet wounds, one a through and through on his upper thigh and the other upper right chest, no exit wound. Third bullet grazed his head. I think there may also be a head wound from when he fell. I'll assess that now. Please make sure the ambulance is routed to Memorial Hospital.

"Lucas? Can you apply pressure here? Press down as firmly as you can. I have to check his head. Gabby? How's the leg?"

Lucas sets the phone, still on speaker, on the floor next to Jax and takes my place, holding a clean towel against the bullet wound in his chest as Gabby reports her progress.

"Paramedics are five minutes out," informs the voice on the phone.

Five minutes. I inhale deeply, maintaining my calm. *Shit,* I hope that's quick enough. The wound in his chest isn't immediately fatal, but blood loss could be. And the bullet is still in his chest somewhere.

"Are you able to contact Memorial for me?" I ask the dispatcher.

"Yes, Doctor."

"Please instruct the Emergency Room to page Dr. William Parker and inform him I'm bringing in a trauma patient with a head injury and would like him to scrub in with me."

"Right away."

After that, there isn't much to say. Five minutes in these situations feels like five years. We've managed to control some of the blood loss. His breathing is raspy but seems steady. We won't know more until we get to the hospital and see what's going on inside.

"You're a doctor," Lucas states quietly, his eyes focused on his hands and the bloody towel he has pressed against Jax's chest, hopefully preventing his best friend from bleeding to death.

"I'm a trauma surgeon."

"Is he going to make it? He can't die."

I swallow. *He can't die. She can't die.* I've heard that plea formed as a fact too many times to count. Tragically, people do die. People who shouldn't. I do what I can to reverse that messed-up twist of fate, but I'm not always successful. Jax shouldn't be here, bleeding on the floor. He should be walking out the door on his way to get a drink after work with his friend. Instead, some addict looking to make enough for his next score walked in.

I hesitate before responding. Professionally, rationally, I know I can't ever make that promise. But something in the tortured pain in his whispered words is affecting me more than usual. I suspect this wouldn't be the first person he lost so cruelly. I study him, waiting for him to raise his eyes and meet my gaze. "We're not going to let him die."

He stares into my eyes for a minute, then nods slightly.

The kid I fought with, I realize now he's probably only sixteen, starts to rally, pushing himself to a sitting position. He stares frantically at the bloody scene before him. When he starts to stand, Lucas spears him with a glare and growls.

"Sit. The Fuck. Down."

Shockingly, the kid does.

The police arrive first and take him into custody. The paramedics arrive soon after, and there's a flurry of activity as I rapid-fire updates and instructions. They load Jax onto the stretcher and jog back to the ambulance. I go with them.

Lucas

Police and paramedics arrive, and I feel like I'm in the way no matter where I stand. I watch as they load Jax onto the ambulance, and Ash climbs up beside him. I go to follow but feel a hand on my arm tugging me back.

Glancing over my shoulder, I see the hand is attached to Gabby. Her expression grim, worlds away from the giddy Bachelorette of, shit, it wasn't even an hour ago I finished her tattoo. I rub a hand over my face. *Christ.*

"We need to talk to the police," she tells me softly. "And then I'll go with you to the hospital. He'll be in surgery for a while. Is there anyone I can call?"

I watch the lights of the ambulance pull away, Jax and Ash inside. Sighing heavily, I focus on the scene in front of me. My shop is swarming with cops, lit in alternating shades of red and blue from their cars parked in front. The frosted glass wall separating the lobby from the first set of stations is gone, shattered pieces over the floor. My best friend's, my brother's, blood is staining the wood floor.

Not quite yelling, but loud enough to make sure I'm heard over the chaos, I demand, "Who do I need to talk to so I can get the fuck out of here?"

I feel Gabby shiver beside me and realize she's still terrified. That despite her fear, she worked right alongside Ash to try and save my friend. I place a gentle arm around her shoulder and urge her into my side.

"You okay?"

She nods but her lips quiver, giving away the lie. She hugs me back, though, her slim arm wrapping around my waist.

One of the officers finally approaches to take our statement. Ash's attacker is now handcuffed and sitting in the back of one of the squad cars. Based on our description, they put an APB out on the other.

I'm uncomfortable and irritable as I recount the events. I'm still uneasy around the police. It's hard for me to believe they're on my side, considering my childhood. Too many run-ins when they assumed because I was poor and hanging out on the street corner that I was causing trouble. That I was just some criminal in training.

Finally, a familiar face, one I've come to respect over the years, appears by my side.

He nods at the uniformed cop. "I'll take it from here. Thanks."

I lift my chin in greeting. "Melrose."

"Luke." He never uses my last name. I'm unsure if it's because he knew me before I changed it or because he knows I hate what it represents, but I appreciate the unspoken respect. "Fucking mess, man." His expression sober, he takes in the scene.

I grunt. *That's an understatement.*

He asks me a few additional questions before also talking to Gabby.

Dylan Melrose is a homicide detective with the Chicago PD. I'm assuming he's here because we go back years and the press is going to be all over this, not because the cops plan on Jax dying. *He's not going to fucking die.*

"Officer Hernandez will give you a ride to the hospital. Keep your phone handy. I'll keep you posted on our end." Melrose motions one of the uniformed officers over.

"Thanks, man. I appreciate it." We clasp hands, and he smacks my shoulder.

On the way to the hospital, I can't believe I'm willingly sitting in the back seat of a police cruiser, I contact Macy and Logan. I can't deal with the questions I know they'll have so I take the coward's way out and just text them Jax has been shot and to meet me at the hospital. I can tell they know it's serious because both respond immediately they're on the way and don't bother to call and quiz me. Gabby is sitting next to me, murmuring into her own cell, quiet tears sliding down her cheeks. I assume she's talking to her sisters or fiancé, but I tune most of it out, instead silently watching the city I love roll on. I don't know what it is about skyscrapers that have always soothed me. Some people find it in nature, I guess, but for me looking up at the city skyline has always brought me a little peace. Something I could really use right now.

I try not to think about what is waiting for us at the hospital, try not to 'borrow trouble' as one of my old case workers was fond of saying. I'll know when we get there.

Chapter Three

Lucas

"What is taking so long?"

Forty minutes later, Gabby found a private waiting room in the hospital. I stop my frantic pacing and collapse into the chair next to her. I spear one hand through my hair, trying to settle my impatience.

"This is normal," Gabby reassures me. "Ash will come update us as soon as she can. I left messages with the nurse's station and one with the OR staff. She'll know where to find us."

I blow out heavily, still trying to reign it in.

"Thanks. For waiting with me. Not much of a Bachelorette party." I meet her eyes with a grim smile.

Her smile is kinder. "You're right. I should be at the hotel playing games like 'Pin the Penis on the Man'."

Unbelievably, I feel myself chuckle at her description, appreciating her presence even more.

She places a hand on my knee, making me realize I've been bouncing it like a jackhammer since I sat down. "This isn't a place anyone should be alone."

I grab her hand and squeeze in silent gratitude and then stand to resume my pacing. I make it to one end of the tiny room when Mace enters.

He pulls me into a quick, tight bear hug and slaps my back. Christ, this fucker's strong. I'll take his strength. I suspect Jax will need all of it we've got for him.

"Any news yet?" he asks softly, glancing at me and then at Gabby.

She shakes her head and stands as he approaches, giving her a much gentler hug. I swallow back the lump in my throat.

"Sorry it took so long, brother. Cubs game just getting out. Traffic is a mess."

"Logan is on her way." He nods as if he knew that.

I resume my caged-in prowling as Macy lowers himself onto the tiny couch across from Gabby. He looks ridiculous, dwarfing the hospital issue furniture, but manages to stretch his legs out and find a comfortable position. Immediately I feel a little calmer. Macy must be the chillest guy I know. He lives his life with this contented confidence I envy at times. Knowing he has my back is reassuring, and I breathe a little easier with him here.

He's also an excellent balance to the fiery *screw-you* attitude Logan brings to the team. I get a kick out of her sarcastic wit and blunt commentary, but I suspect it's because I relate to the chip on her shoulder. If traffic is messed up because of the game, then the 'el' will be ridiculous too, and Logan only takes public transit, claiming that's all she can afford. I have no idea what she does with her paychecks, but the girl is always broke. She's not spending it on drugs though, that shit doesn't fly in my shop and she knows it; other than that, it's not my business.

My cell phone starts vibrating on the coffee table, making an obnoxious sound as it clatters across the glass. I snatch it up. *Krista calling.*

Shit.

Sending the call to voicemail, I shove the phone in my pocket and continue pacing. Immediately it starts buzzing in my jeans. Then again.

Finally, I press accept. "Not really a great time, Krista," I snap.

"Luke, I just heard. How is he? How are you?"

"How did you hear already? Logan hasn't even gotten to the hospital yet."

She sighs on the other end of the line, and I can almost picture her grimace. "Paparazzi listen to the police scanners. It's already on *TMZ* and local Chicago affiliates. Reports are still vague. I actually got a hold of Logan, that's how I knew it was Jax."

"Fuck." I squeeze my eyes shut, annoyed. Press is the last thing I want to deal with right now.

"Look, Rob is already in Chicago, and I'm sending Tanya out on the first plane available to help you deal with the media and fans," she tells me, referring to one of the assistant producers and a member of the PR team. "She'll help make sure you get whatever you need, okay? She'll handle the press and try to give you guys a little more privacy."

"Sure. Whatever." Then because I don't want to seem like a totally ungrateful asshole, I say, "Thanks, Krista."

"Call me with updates. Or if you need anything. I'm here."

Logan rushes in as I hang up, muttering something about stupid drunken frat boys. She stops short just inside the door. "Is he okay? Have you heard anything?" she demands.

I shake my head. "Not yet. No."

She sucks in a deep breath, and I see her bracing herself, pulling herself together. I've seen that look in my own eyes before. I know she's barely keeping it together. We stare at each other mutely for a long minute. When her lip starts to quiver, Mace stands with a gruff sigh and pulls her to him. She resists for a second, her slim arm flung out, attempting to ward off any gentleness that could weaken her and shatter her tough image.

But Mace just gives her hand a soft tug. "I won't tell anybody." And with that permission, she collapses into his arms with a sob.

My chest aches watching them, but I know I'm in no shape to offer any ... softness. If I try, I'm likely to end up exactly where Logan is.

Eventually, they move to a different couch, one as far from Gabby as possible in the small space, giving Logan the illusion of privacy.

Some indistinguishable amount of time later, an African-American woman in pink scrubs tentatively enters the room. She's a grandmotherly type with gray hair, plump cheeks, and a kind smile carrying a tray of sandwiches and cookies.

"Dr. Martinez?"

Gabby glances up from her seat, still on vigil with the rest of us.

"The cafeteria is closing soon. The girls and I thought you all might need some food yet. I'll leave them here." She places them on the table in front of

Gabby and gives her a quick hug. "I'm here all night. You let me know if you need anything else."

"Thanks, Rose."

Rose nods, and her eyes land on me. I get the distinct impression she would hug me too if I asked, but instead, she just smiles graciously and leaves again.

More to distract myself than because I'm actually hungry, I sit down next to Gabby and grab a sandwich. Macy and Logan join us. She's pale but calmer and even manages to say a few words and nibble on a cookie.

Trying to fill the silence, I ask Gabby, "So, Doctor, how did you get stuck babysitting this ugly bunch instead of going into surgery with Ash?"

Gabby shakes her head while she finishes chewing. "I'm a pediatric surgeon. Kids. Dr. Parker specializes in head injuries. Brain surgery."

Brain surgery.

We all sit silently as that sinks in. My best friend is having brain surgery.

Some of what I'm thinking must show on my face because Gabby grabs my hand again. "Will and Ash are the best, seriously. He could not be in better hands right now."

I nod and clear my throat, ignoring the lump that's formed once again.

"Have you called Lori?" Macy asks.

"Shit. I didn't even think."

He nods. "I think she's in Costa Rica or something for the summer. I'll track her down."

"Thanks, Mace."

The hours go by. *Drag* by. *Limp* by.

Eventually, I see Ash, now in green scrubs, walking through the door followed by another doctor. My breath locks in my chest.

Ash

I'm exhausted.

But still a little juiced from all the adrenaline. My body is humming as these two things battle it out. Now that we're finally out of surgery, the release of tension, I suspect it won't be long until the exhaustion wins out.

Lucas jumps to his feet as soon as I open the door to the private waiting room he's been assigned. I take in the whole *Vanished* team plus Gabby and their expectant faces.

"This is Dr. Parker."

Will steps forward with the updates. "He's in critical condition, but he's stable for now." The energy in the room immediately shifts as everyone exhales in hopeful relief. "We were able to quickly deal with the bullet wound in his leg. The concern, of course, is the wound in his chest and his head injury. Luckily, Dr. Carrington and Dr. Martinez were on the scene and able to respond quickly."

I pull Gabby aside as Will continues his explanation and answers questions from Jax's people.

"You still here?" I give her a little hug.

"Yeah. I didn't want to leave them. Now that he's out of surgery, I'll head to the hotel to be with my sisters."

"Did you talk to Tim?"

She nods. "He wanted to jump on a plane and come home, but I told him Sunday was still fine. I've got all my girls here. You heading back to the hotel at some point?"

I sigh, glancing at Lucas. "I'm not sure when I'll get out of here. But I'll text you." In addition to getting my patient, Jax, settled, there's also an officer here to take my statement.

"Head injuries are unpredictable," Will is explaining as we rejoin the group. "Right now, he's sedated and we'll monitor him closely overnight. Hopefully, he'll regain consciousness tomorrow, and we'll know more."

I can tell from the grim expressions around the room they aren't happy with this answer but know it's the best we can do. For now.

CHAPTER THREE   29

Will shakes hands and leaves the room. The tension in the room is palpable as they process all the information. Gabby gives a round of hugs as she says her goodbyes with assurances she'll see everyone soon. Although I know I shouldn't, I linger, waiting to see what the rest of them have planned.

Finally, Lucas speaks. "You guys should go home and try to get some sleep."

"I'm not leaving," Logan bursts out. "No way." She looks at him like he just suggested she sacrifice kittens or something equally abhorrent.

Looking as exhausted as I feel, Lucas stabs his hand through his hair and opens his mouth, prepared to respond. I interject before he can, hoping to provide a little calm.

"I know how terrifying it is to have someone you care about here." I move forward into their circle a bit and try to sound soothing but not condescending. I'm not sure I'm successful. "And that the idea of them feeling like they're alone here is unthinkable. But I also know him waking up to you all looking scared and beat up isn't going to help him. It will make him feel guilty and self-conscious and distract him from focusing on his recovery. Best case, he's here for a week and a half, maybe two. He's not going to wake up for hours at least. Use this time to get some rest and take care of things at home so you can be here when he needs you."

Logan still looks prepared to protest, and I place a gentle hand on her shoulder. "I promise. If he wakes up before you get back, I'll call you."

Eyes bright with unshed tears, Logan finally nods her acceptance.

"Come on. I'll give you a ride home," Macy offers.

Logan nods again and the two of them leave, heading to the elevator.

Very aware of Lucas standing beside me, I watch Logan and Macy leave, knowing he is watching me.

Without looking at him, I ask, "You're going to stay, aren't you?"

"Yep."

"Can't change your mind?"

"Nope."

His response manages to get a little chuckle out of me as I turn to face him. "Follow me."

I stop at the nurses' station and manage to get Jax, who is still in recovery, moved to a family room so Lucas will have a pull-out couch to sleep on. I discover someone has already taken care of security - I'm assuming that's because of his public position and the press. We can't have random people wandering the halls hoping to get a peek. I give the uniformed officer my statement. Luckily with one of the thieves in custody and both Gabby and Luke having already given statements, the officer doesn't have that many questions for me, and we are able to wrap it up quickly.

I help Lucas set up his bed for the night. I suspect probably for the next several nights based on his commitment to his friend.

"Who was it?" he asks out of the blue.

I glance up sharply from stuffing a pillow into its case. "Who was what?

He sits on the edge of the bed, done with his own setup, and lifts his chin gesturing towards the hallway and waiting rooms beyond. "The person you were talking about. When you were talking to Logan."

Oh. I swallow before speaking. "My mother."

His face softens with sympathy, and I need to look away, thankful I can refocus briefly on my pillow. His pillow. You know what I mean.

"Sorry. Is she okay now?"

"She died when I was thirteen." I place the now fully dressed pillow on the pulled-out bed and steel myself before turning back to him. It's been years, almost two decades, but every once in a while, especially when I'm emotionally and physically tired like now, the pain is still fresh and raw.

"I'm sorry."

I nod to show him it's okay, sitting on the opposite side of the makeshift bed.

He looks over at the still empty hospital bed. It'll be another hour or two before Jax is brought in.

"I never knew my mother. Or my father." His voice is softer than I've heard it before. "Jax and I ended up in the same foster home when we were eleven. He's my family."

We sit there in silence for a stretch, both absorbed by separate thoughts. The mattress bounces as he shifts position. "We're not going to let him die, right?"

Fear and guilt streak through me. I shouldn't have made that promise. I knew it then, and I know it now. Jax is stable, but he's got a long way to go and a lot of unknowns yet.

I don't respond but squeeze his hand briefly.

Jax better not make a liar out of me.

Chapter Four

Ash

F ar too soon after my head hits the most glorious fluffy pillow I've touched in years, my wake-up call does its job. I groan and lift the receiver, mumbling hello. I'm never sure if the hotel staff expect me to chat with them in these situations, but it feels rude to just hang up without acknowledging there may be a live person on the other end. I'm greeted with a cheery announcement that my chosen time has arrived. I murmur a thank you and fumble the phone back together. Rolling over onto my back, I study the ceiling above me, appreciating the comfortable bed I now have to leave.

Despite my attempts to focus on the physical here and now, images from last night come filtering back in, preventing me from falling back to sleep. I stayed and chatted with Lucas last night until Jax had finally been brought in from Recovery and used that as my opportunity to exit. I contemplated going back to Gabby and Tim's, but a combination of not wanting to be in an empty apartment and my still-burning desire to test out this hotel room brought me here instead. Our original plan was to have brunch downstairs this morning before taking an architecture cruise, picnicking on the beach, and then enjoying another night out, but I'm not sure if any of that is still happening or not.

What a shitty Bachelorette party. Poor Gabby.

Immediately I feel stupid for grieving a Bachelorette party when Jax almost died. And still could. When Lucas is probably sitting beside his unconscious best friend.

Groping for my cell, I finally locate it and text Gabby. Then I drag myself to the shower. By the time I finish my morning routine - the fancy shower every bit as glorious as that bed - I have a response from Gabby. She and the others are meeting for brunch in ten minutes which gives me just enough time to call the hospital and check in before heading to meet them.

"Ash!" Camilla jumps up as soon as she sees me and rushes forward to give me a hug. "Oh my god. Gabby told us what happened. It's still so hard to believe. Are you doing okay?"

Camilla is such a sweetheart. She's like a mini-Gabby but with a little less stubbornness. I've known her just as long, obviously, and she's like a little sister to me too.

"I'm fine. It was a long night. Jax is stable but still unconscious."

She leads me over to the table where Raquel and Jessi are already seated. Raquel has her hair piled on top of her head in a messy bun and is wearing sunglasses despite the fact we're inside and sipping on a Bloody Mary.

I grin at her and can't resist a little tease. "Little hair of the dog?"

She groans and waves her hand in front of her face dismissively. "Turns out my questionable decisions were not the most interesting thing that happened last night."

I look around and lean in, "Before Gabby gets here, what's the plan for today? Is she still up for...."

I don't even really know how to ask what I'm asking.

Grimacing, Camilla nods. "We talked about it a little last night when she got back. We still want to do it, but...."

"It feels weird."

The others all look at each other somberly.

"But it's also Gabby. She's getting married in a month and deserves a fun weekend."

"Maybe we could also do something for Jax and Lucas and the others?" Jessi suggests.

"Like what?" Raquel asks.

"I don't know. Walk their dogs? Clean up the shop? Bring them food? I have no idea what to do in this situation."

"I doubt they'll allow visitors right now," I explain.

She shrugs. "But you could get in to see them, right? Bring them some food. See if there's anything else we can do."

So, it's decided I'll skip the cruise to check in on Jax and meet up with the girls at the beach after. Gabby arrives, and I cringe inwardly at the overly enthusiastic greetings we all deliver, unsuccessfully trying to ignore the dark cloud lingering from last night.

When I arrive at the hospital, I have to show my staff ID to get by the security guard at Jax's door. Inside I see Lucas uncomfortably sprawled across the chair in the corner. His legs are stretched out in front of him, fingers laced together and resting on his stomach, his head tilted precariously to the side as he sleeps. These chairs aren't really made for people his size.

I can't help the soft smile on my face as I watch him. He must have gone home at some point, or someone brought him a change of clothes because he now has on a clean pair of jeans and a faded navy Cubs t-shirt. The short sleeves reveal his muscled forearms and the colorful tattoos covering them.

I'd been a little flustered by his presence during the tattoo and then distracted by getting held at gunpoint and trying to save Jax to really take my time looking at him yesterday. But now, I look my fill. He's gorgeous. I remember his blue eyes, dark blue, darker than any I've seen before, with surprisingly dark lashes. And his shoulders... his shoulders are... big. Strong.

Delicious.

My stomach flips, and I shake myself loose abruptly putting an end to those thoughts. I fumble a bit as I set down the box of gourmet cupcakes in my hands, courtesy of the girls. The coffee tray balanced on top pitches slightly, and I swear under my breath, catching it before it can do more than slosh a little over the side. My clumsiness apparently is noisy enough to wake Lucas.

He inhales sharply and blinks rapidly until his eyes focus on me.

"Hey." His voice is scratchy from sleep. Sexy.

Pull it together, Carrington.

"Hey. I thought you could use a decent cup of coffee," I say, handing one over to him. "And the girls sent cupcakes." I nod at the box.

Sitting up straight, he smiles sleepily and accepts my caffeine offering.

"Thanks." He takes a fortifying sip and exhales heavily. "How'd you know I was here?"

I grin. "You're kidding, right? Even if I hadn't seen your refusal to leave last night, the hospital gossip line is ringing off the hook. Celebrities and all. You even have a guard at the door. It attracts attention."

Lucas snorts and runs one hand roughly back and forth through his hair, leaving it mussed and even more sexy. "That was the show's idea. Press is all over."

"It's probably a good call."

He shrugs, studying Jax, and sips his coffee.

"Has Dr. Parker been by yet this morning?"

"Not yet. Nurses through the night."

Feeling awkward, I call up Jax's chart, checking his stats. Some of the numbers make me concerned, but Will is the neuro expert. I shoot him a text, hoping to give Lucas some good news.

"Can I ask you something?" I'm jolted out of my thoughts by his question.

"Of course."

"Where did you learn to fight like that? Disarming that guy last night? It was pretty badass." He grins crookedly.

"I teach self-defense. I trained during med school." My dad had been pretty paranoid about raising a daughter on his own. Initially, he'd insisted on the classes, but I continued well beyond basic self-defense. I saw far too many women brutalized working in the ER during residency. "And I've spent the last three years operating in refugee camps near war zones. The insurance company even required us to take a kidnapping survival and prevention class."

"Is that why you didn't freak out when he had the gun?"

I shrug and confess. "Not the first time a gun was pulled on me. Luckily, even in armed conflict, both sides usually see the value in medical personnel."

"Wow." Lucas looks impressed. "I'd love to hear those stories someday."

"Maybe someday I'll trade you for some of yours."

He stands, stretches, and makes a face. "Eh. You can watch all of mine on re-runs."

I study him carefully, wondering if he's being falsely modest or really believes that's all he has to offer. I've known him less than twenty-four hours and I already know that's not true. "Somehow, I doubt that."

His eyes land on mine and stay there, locking my breath in my chest.

"Thank you. For saving him." He looks away first, glancing at Jax.

"Thanks for saving Gabby. If you hadn't tackled her, she would have been shot too."

My cell dings, and I see Will has responded to my text. He's on rounds and should be here shortly. Good.

I'm about to let Lucas know when Jax's monitor starts beeping and he starts convulsing in his bed.

Oh no.

Lucas

"What's happening?" My heart kicks and I freeze, unable to process the scene in front of me.

"He's seizing." Ash darts around me and pounds on a button on the wall. Jax is jerking on the bed and machines are beeping loudly all around us. I watch, weirdly detached, as several hospital staff flood the room seconds later. I realize the button must have been some kind of alarm.

"Page Dr. Parker!"

The team moves seamlessly, lowering the bed, attending to the machines, passing Ash equipment.

She flashes a light into Jax's eyes. "His pupil is blown. We need to get him into the OR."

Once again, I feel useless as others move around me with purpose and efficiency. One of the nurses places a hand on my arm and escorts me back to the private waiting room.

Fuck. Fuck. FUCK.

My stomach heaves, and I worry for a second I'm going to hurl. The way Jax looked on that bed is an image I doubt I'll ever be able to burn from my brain. Please don't let that be the last sight I have of my friend. I sink into one of the chairs and bury my face in my hands. I'm so fucking useless right now. I know all I can do is wait, but the waiting itself is unbearable.

I should call Macy and Logan and tell them what is going on. They're both at the shop, cleaning up. I stare at my phone, unable to dial. What the fuck do I say?

"Luke!"

I look up, heart in my throat, expecting someone in scrubs, but it's Tanya from the show. I vaguely remember a text that her plane had landed a couple hours ago.

"What's going on? I was going to see Jax, and they directed me here."

Clearing my throat, I force the words out. "He's back in surgery." I don't even recognize my voice. I cough again.

Tanya rushes over and gives me an awkward hug, her breasts in my face as I stay seated, not bothering to return her gesture. Straightening, she takes in my phone, still useless in my hand.

"Do Macy and Logan know?"

I shake my head.

Ever efficient, Tanya nods and informs me, "I'll call them. And Krista. And then I'll get a statement out to the press, so they stop speculating. Do you want to see it before I send it out?"

I shake my head again. I don't give a fuck what she tells the press.

She pulls out her phone and crosses to the other side of the room, getting to work. I start pacing, unreasonably annoyed by her calm and professional manner. Doesn't she know my best friend, the only person who gave a shit about me *before,* may be dying? When she takes out her laptop and starts tapping away, my hands fist at my sides. I really should have taken Macy up on his offer to meet me at the boxing gym this morning. It probably would have helped to pound some of this stress and aggression out. But I didn't want to leave the hospital for longer than a quick shower and change. And now I'm going to lose it on this poor woman who is just trying to do her fucking job.

I'm not sure if my pacing is starting to get to her or if she senses I'm a walking powder keg, but Tanya excuses herself to make the rest of her calls outside. Where I don't know. Elsewhere.

My phone vibrates with another text from Mace. I told them not to bother coming. They couldn't do anything here. And I'm not really in the mood for company. Even silent, supportive company. I really don't want to explode at the two people I have left. Safer to keep a little distance.

It's hours before I hear anything. Tanya pops her head back in periodically, sees my continued prowling, and ducks back out. Once, she dropped some food and coffee on the table. It sits there untouched. She replaces the coffee with a fresh cup at some point. I ignore her.

"Lucas."

I spin abruptly at my name and see Ash standing just inside the door. She's in scrubs again, her dark eyes calm and kind and soothing. I force the words out, the terror of knowing overwhelming. "Is he -" I have to clear my throat, unable to continue.

"He's stable," she assures me, crossing the room to stand in front of me. I go limp with relief, literally bending over to brace my hands on my knees. I squeeze my eyes shut tightly and repeat her words silently over and over while I struggle to take a breath.

Fuck.

She places a comforting hand on my shoulder, her touch becoming an outlet for all my pent-up *feeling*. Without really deciding anything, I straighten abruptly, gathering her against me, burying my face in the curve of her neck. She stretches up along my frame, her arms holding me firmly. I inhale deeply, my breath shuddering through me, and allow her to soothe me, use her to soothe me. I've always been a pretty physical guy, but I've never been very comfortable with more *tender* touches. Probably because I had so few as a kid. I never had a mom kiss me when I scraped a knee or a dad who put an arm around me while reading a bedtime story. I don't cuddle after I fuck. I don't hold hands walking down the street. I don't do forehead kisses or wipe tears away.

But *damn*. This feels nice.

There's just something about this woman. She's all soft curves and soft skin and soft eyes. But I've seen her strong. And right now, standing here, feeling her soft and steady in my arms, is somehow releasing all my rage and fear.

Thinking I hear the door opening, I lift my head and glance over, but there's no one there. I turn back and meet Ash's gaze, arms still wrapped around each other. I'm about to loosen my hold when I hear her breath hitch and her eyes drop to my lips. She pushes up on her toes, her eyes returning to mine for a brief second before she kisses me.

Ash is kissing me, and her being in my arms takes on a whole new context. One I'm much more comfortable with and frankly psyched about.

So damn sweet. Her lips are soft like the rest of her.

I tighten my arms around her waist. She fits perfectly. I deepen the kiss, exploring. Everything else is pushed to the back of my mind, and all I know is her.

She sighs into the kiss and suddenly my cock is rock hard and raring to go. My groan seems to startle her back to reality. Not what I was going for. She leans away, palms flat against my chest, a horrified expression on her face.

"Oh my god! I am so sorry. I shouldn't have done that." She shakes her head, pink tinting her cheeks. "I should not have done that."

Frowning in confusion, because what the fuck is she talking about?, I try to stop her spiral. "Ash."

Her wide eyes meet mine.

"Are you seriously apologizing for kissing me?"

Shaking her head slightly, she breaks our gaze, but she still hasn't stepped out of my arms. "I'm sorry. It was inappropriate and unprof-"

Not wanting to hear this nonsense, I cut her off with another kiss. Unprofessional? Is she serious?

I have never had a woman apologize for kissing me, even though I can think of a couple from the past few years that probably should have. You'd be surprised how many people, "fans", think they can touch celebrities without any encouragement, let alone permission. I can't decide if I like it or not. Ash apologizing, I mean. I definitely don't like the panic and alarm in her eyes. Or the fact that somehow she has no idea exactly how okay I am with her kissing me. Kiss away, woman. I'm here for it.

My kiss as a distraction seems to work. She's no longer apologizing. Instead, she presses against me, as eager as I am. Damn. I could do this for hours. I don't actually remember ever just kissing, exploring, enjoying.

Finally, the need for oxygen forces me to break the kiss. I watch as Ash's eyes slowly blink open, their chocolate depths clearly dazed, and lust rages through me knowing I did that. Meeting my gaze, she takes a shuddering breath that only serves to press her breasts more firmly against my chest. I close my eyes against the temptation she presents but can't help tightening my hold around her waist.

"Lucas," she murmurs my name, her voice smoky. Sexy. Still with that dazed look in her eyes, she raises one hand and gently traces my lips with her fingertips. I smile into her touch.

She lifts onto her tiptoes and presses her lips against mine once again.

The door opens, and Ash abruptly jumps away, quickly putting distance between us. Dr. Parker hesitates in the doorway, clearly not fooled. Ash subtly tries to turn away, hiding her flushed cheeks and obviously well-kissed lips. I don't like the fact that he's probably seen her like this before. I'd figured out pretty quickly 'Will the Dud' Gabby had talked about while in my chair was this guy. I straighten to my full height, refusing to feel embarrassed. He had his chance with her and obviously couldn't hack it.

His eyes flicker, taking in the scene, but his professional mask stays in place as he enters, prepared to give me the update.

"Mr. Abbott," he nods. "Mr. Hall is in Recovery. He should be moved back to his room within the next two hours."

"So, he's going to be okay?"

"We'll know more when he wakes, but Dr. Carrington and I are optimistic. His head injury caused a small hemorrhage, which triggered the seizure. We were able to relieve the pressure on his brain and stop the bleeding." He continues his explanation using words like *aneurysm, hematoma, stroke*. Words that terrify and overwhelm. It's a lot to take in, and finally I interrupt him, trying to focus on what matters.

"But he's going to be okay?"

"He's young and strong and had no health problems before the injury. We have to prepare for possible complications, but I see little reason to think he won't make a full recovery."

I exhale like an inflated balloon, scrubbing one hand over my face. Dr. Parker excuses himself.

When I turn back to face Ash, she's pulled herself back together. I'm both fascinated and a little annoyed. This isn't really how I imagined our first kiss. And it's definitely not how I imagined our first kiss ending. She's studying me carefully as if trying to decide how to escape.

"Should *I* apologize?" I ask.

Hoping like hell the answer is no.

Ash

Should I apologize?

I'm still struggling to get my breathing back to normal, and his question knocks me off balance once again.

I have no idea what possessed me to kiss him. I have never acted so inappropriately with a patient or a loved one. I'm mortified that Will walked in and witnessed my behavior. But despite everything, it's hard to regret sharing that kiss with Lucas. *Kisses.* A sexy shiver racks my frame out of nowhere. Aftershocks from Lucas Abbott.

When I first walked in and saw him standing there looking so... untethered, I'd been unusually drawn to him. There was no way I couldn't reach out to him, offer him some kindness. Then, the desperation and fierce relief when he'd grabbed me to him had only seduced me further. Apparently, I'm a sucker for sexy tattoo artists with dark blue eyes that exhibit vulnerability.

I'm pretty sure those brief moments being kissed by Lucas had started an addiction, and I wouldn't be able to wait long for my next fix.

He's watching me with a guarded expression on his face, still waiting for my answer to his question.

"I won't if you won't?" I smile uncertainly.

His eyes heat at my response.

Before either of us can say more, a woman I haven't seen before hurries into the room. She's wearing all black, business pants and a chic black blouse. Her curly chin-length hair is cut in an effortlessly styled bob and she has a pair of funky black glasses perched on her nose. She looks incredibly put together in contrast to my disheveled hair and scrubs. She also seems urgently distraught. "Luke, I saw the doctor leave. Is Jax out of surgery?" Her gaze flickers over me quickly, then, apparently dismissing me, returns to Lucas.

I think I see a flash of irritation cross his face at the interruption, but that may be my wishful thinking.

"He's okay. He'll be back in his room soon."

She peppers him with questions and I excuse myself. I need to text Gabby explaining my delay and meet up with her and the girls.

Will is still in the hallway when I emerge, and I hesitate, still embarrassed he witnessed my unprofessional behavior. But I stand there too long. He looks up and sees me, our eyes meeting. He crosses the hallway until he's in front of me.

"I didn't realize you and he -" he trails off.

I rush to explain. "We're not. I mean... we just met. He was upset and..." Realizing I'm only making things worse, I stop talking.

He studies me carefully, his eyes sad. Will and I have been over for a long time, but once I tried imagining a future with him. He's a good man. But we didn't... fit right. We were boring. Gabby likes to make me feel better by blaming the boring on him, but that's because she's my best friend and she loves me. We were boring *together*. The problem was he was okay with boring. I wasn't.

"Ash," Will starts and then pauses, a pained expression on his face. I stand, fidgeting back and forth, just wanting to leave and put this awkward situation behind me. Finally, he sighs heavily and tells me, "Just be careful. This guy, he's ... complicated."

I feel my skin prickle with annoyance. "Complicated? What does that even mean?" Then I shake my head dismissively. "No, never mind." I start to walk away, then turn back abruptly. "I appreciate your concern, but this isn't any of your business, Will."

"I still care about you, Ash."

Silently, I stare at him because what is there to say to that?

He smiles sadly as we stand there. Thankfully the woman from earlier exits the waiting room and approaches him with questions. I am much more appreciative of her interruption this time. While they discuss Jax, I attempt to slip away.

"Excuse me, Doctor?" she calls out before I'm successful in my escape. "Can you wait a moment? I need to speak with you as well."

She returns her attention to Will, not waiting for my response.

I tune out a little as he gives her what information he can. She seems unhappy with Will's answers and frequent suggestions she needs to get that information from Lucas, Jax's in case of emergency contact. I learn she is from *Vanished's* PR team when she explains why she should have access to confidential information. Will doesn't budge, which I appreciate.

But it means when she focuses again on me, she is already obviously in a bad mood.

Great.

"Tayna Richardson. I'm with *Vanished.*" She extends her hand as she introduces herself.

"With the show's PR team?" I clarify. I don't know why. She irritates me. I've met the *Vanished* team. I saw them working together in real life and rallying together in tragedy. She's not one of them. Not in the ways that matter. Not that I can see.

Her eyes flash with irritation at my subtle, maybe not so subtle, dig.

"Yes. And I am here to take care of their publicity and their privacy until this is resolved." She pulls a piece of paper out of the file in her hand. "If you are going to continue on Mr. Hall's medical team, I'll need you to sign this non-disclosure agreement. I'm sure you understand how sensitive this is, and the team wants to be assured that no one will leak any information without their consent."

I glance briefly at the legal contract I've taken from her out of politeness or habit.

"I'm required to protect my patient's privacy by law and professional ethics. As are all the staff here. I don't see why this should be necessary."

"Well, this is a unique situation. Few of your patients have this level of notoriety. There are news agencies that would pay significant money for private information. A temptation most are not usually faced with." She holds out a pen.

She really irritates me. I'm torn. What she says makes sense. Kind of. But I'm also insulted she thinks I would betray my patient and myself for a payoff.

"I'll discuss it with Lucas and the hospital attorney. If they both agree, then I'll sign."

Tanya smiles tightly. "That isn't necessary. I'm here representing Mr. Abbott's interest and this document has been reviewed by several lawyers."

"Then those conversations should be straightforward and Lucas can return it to you after I've signed."

As if speaking his name conjures the man himself, Lucas emerges from the waiting room.

"If that would make you more comfortable," Tanya concurs and abruptly rushes to his side. Off balance, I study them for a few minutes and glance again at the document in my hand.

Then I leave to meet Gabby and the girls.

Chapter Five

Lucas

"Lazy asshole. Wake up."

Jax doesn't respond. Just like he hasn't responded for days. It's taking too long. The doctors haven't come out and said so, but I can tell each day he stays unconscious, the tension and concern grow. I sit in the chair next to his bed, holding my head in my hands. I'm so sick of this fucking chair. This hospital. This waiting.

I miss my friend.

And I'm terrified this is all I get. Missing him forever. I clear my throat, attempting to dislodge the lump constricting it, and pound a fist against my chest.

A nurse enters and smiles at me sympathetically. While she does her routine check of the machines, I stand and try to stretch out some of the stiffness.

I wonder when Ash will visit today.

The only pleasant part of my days right now.

Ash.

Every interaction only intrigues me more. She seems to like talking to me. She laughs at my stupid jokes. She's comfortable just sitting with quiet when I don't feel like joking. But she doesn't like it when I get too focused on her. Since our kiss three days ago, she gets flustered and backs away when I flirt. She's been very careful not to get too close or be alone with me for too long.

This is a reaction I am not used to, and can't quite figure out how to respond. Even before the show, women had come pretty easily to me. At least on the surface.

Because she'd been out of the country, she's never seen the show. It's been years now since I've met a woman who has absolutely no idea who I am. And I like it. A lot.

I like that she seems to want to get to know me. That she asks me questions and actually listens to my answers. She doesn't presume to know me because she's seen edited clips of my life on television. To her, I am a blank slate.

So we talk. While I wait for Jax to wake up.

And I've discovered Ash is infuriatingly, intriguingly, attractively... skittish.

But she always asks what time I'm coming to visit Jax the next day.

And she always comes.

There's a knock on the door, and I look up to find Melrose at the entrance.

"Hey, Luke. You got a minute?"

I grimace and nod at the other empty chair, then glance at Jax, still unconscious. "Right now, I've got nothing but time. What's up?"

He folds into the seat next to me, responding, "I wanted to let you know we got the shooter in custody."

I inhale grimly. *The shooter.* Damn. I hadn't really even thought about that since getting to the hospital. All I had been able to think about was Jax. But suddenly, I'm pissed. Jax is here because of him. The shooter. He's not fighting for his life because of some random accident. Or sudden illness. He's here because of another person. Someone, *something,* I can blame. I can fight.

"Good," I bite out.

Dylan acknowledges my comment with a nod but makes no move to leave.

My helplessness has morphed into rage, and I now have a target to release it all on. "I want to see him."

"That's not a good idea, Luke." He looks pointedly at my fists, clenching and unclenching on the arms of my chair.

"Melrose -"

"No. Not going to happen."

"Detective-"

His exasperated sigh clearly indicates how ridiculous he thinks I'm being. I refuse to concede I know he's right, but drop it for now.

Instead, I say tightly, "Thanks for the update."

Silence falls between us but he still makes no move to leave.

"How is Jax?"

I shrug and give my now standard response. "Doctors are optimistic, but we won't know any more until he wakes up." *Fucking wake up, Jax.*

Dylan nods again. I appreciate that he doesn't try to bullshit me with any platitudes, reassure me how strong Jax is, that he's a fighter, how great the doctors are, blah, blah, blah. He knows just as well as I do that people die. Sometimes violently. Sometimes suddenly. And often the ones who deserve it least.

"There's more."

I suspected as much. I meet his eyes and wait.

"The other kid, the one arrested on the scene...."

"Yeah?"

Inhaling deeply, Melrose shifts forward in his seat, resting his forearms on his knees. I can tell by the expression on his face either he doesn't like what he's about to say or he doesn't think I will. "He wants to talk to you. All of you."

"You just said-" I'm confused. Why would he suggest this when he denied me time with the other one?

"He wants to apologize."

"What?"

"He's a stupid kid. Got dragged into this by an older cousin. His gun wasn't loaded, and he claims he didn't know his cousin's was. He's got no priors, has managed to stay in school, even has a shot at college in a couple years."

I digest all this information and try to remember the robbery. Four nights ago. *Shit, is that all?* It feels like I've been here for weeks. I try to remember the one with Ash, who didn't seem to be high, who stayed on the scene even though he had a chance to run while we were helping Jax.

"How old?"

"Fifteen."

I sigh. "Fuck."

"Yeah."

I rub my hand roughly through my hair, considering. I was such a fucking screw-up at fifteen. Both of us were. Jax and I. We were smart enough to stay away from guns, but I can't say we never stole anything. I can't say we never made stupid decisions, never listened to, *followed* people we shouldn't have.

Damn it. My rage, so welcomed just moments ago, is seeping out of me, leaving me tired. Exhausted. Resigned.

"All right," I finally agree.

Dylan nods and there is something about it that convinces me he knew that would be my answer. And he approves. He has more faith in me than I do, apparently.

"When?"

"Can you come by the station tomorrow? We can bring him over around 10am."

"I'll be there."

Ash

"Dr. Carrington!"

I glance up and see Will approaching, a strange well-dressed man at his side. His suit screams money, as does his impeccable haircut and the expensive watch on his wrist. He studies me silently as they close the distance between us, making me feel a little uneasy under his hazel-eyed gaze. I stand straight, refusing to shift and give away my nerves.

"Ash, I wanted you to meet someone. This is -"

"Ethan," the other man interrupts, holding out his hand to shake.

I grasp his hand and nod in acknowledgment. "Ash."

Will continues the introduction. "Ethan's family has been long-time bene-factors of the hospital. His mother is currently on the Board of Directors. I was just filling him in on your work in the refugee camps and ideas for expanding that program."

"I'd love to hear more about it. My parents are always interested in supporting important work. Especially when you come so highly recommended by friends and people we admire. The Chief of Surgery has also mentioned how excited she is to have you back."

A bubble of excitement grows in my belly. Having major donors of the hospital behind my project would dramatically increase the chances of additional funding. My smile widens, genuine, not just polite. "That's wonderful. I'd love to tell you more about it."

He grins and suggests lunch next week.

"Absolutely. That sounds great."

He quickly hands me a card. "Call my office and we'll schedule a time."

"I'll do that. Thank you." I hope the giddiness inside me isn't showing. He needs to see me as competent and capable. Squealing while jumping up and down would not be the right impression.

Even if that is precisely what I feel like doing.

"Will, thank you for your time today. I appreciate the tour and overview of your neurology department. My mother is very proud of the work Memorial is doing."

The two men shake hands. "Anytime. Your mother has done a lot to support our work." Will glances at his watch. "I should get back to rounds. I have a couple patients I need to check in with."

"Jackson Hall is one of your patients, isn't he? How is his recovery going?"

"That is none of your fucking business! What the fuck are you even doing here?"

I jump, hardly recognizing the angry roar coming from Lucas as he storms down the hall toward us.

He stops a few feet from our little circle and glares over my head at Ethan. His chest expands with his harsh breath, fists clenching at his sides. I have no idea what is going on, but suddenly I am very sure between these two men is *not* somewhere I really want to be. I no longer feel like squealing. I have come crashing down.

"You have no business here," Lucas growls.

I hear Ethan sigh before responding, "Actually, business is exactly why I'm here. Dr. Parker and Dr. Carrington and the hospital have some very ambitious plans we're interested in possibly supporting."

Lucas flicks his eyes at me briefly, the first time he's acknowledged my presence in any way. But his expression holds none of the warmth I've come to expect. This Lucas is a stranger. An angry, aggressive stranger, and I am reeling and off balance at the change.

"Then I suggest you keep it to those 'plans' and off Jax. Keep *your* family the fuck away from *mine*."

Ethan remains silent, his face an impassive mask that does nothing to calm Lucas.

Will breaks the silence, "Mr. Abbott, I suggest you go back to your friend, or I'll need to call security."

"That won't be necessary," Ethan assures Will.

"No. Not necessary," Lucas sneers. "*Mr. Abbott,*" he places a strange emphasis on his name, almost like a warning, "was just leaving."

I notice Tanya for the first time, standing a few feet behind Lucas. She steps forward and grips his arm, tugging him back. He shakes her off, and for a second, I think he's going to resist leaving but then, with a final glare at Ethan, he turns and walks away, following her back to Jax's room.

I stare after them, confused by what I just witnessed. I'm clearly missing something. Ethan and Lucas clearly have history, but how? And why is it so obviously hostile? My feet are frozen as I watch the hallway he disappeared down. Despite my training and ability to manage urgent and critical medical situations, I am not good when faced with personal conflict. My mind tends to just go blank until the moment passes.

I'm brought back to the present as Will apologizes to Ethan, who seems to be shrugging it off as nothing. He seems unruffled. I feel very... *ruffled*. Still.

He turns to me and shakes my hand once again. "It was lovely to meet you. And I look forward to hearing from you soon for that lunch."

Forcing myself to return his smile, I assure him I would call and schedule something soon.

Will offers to walk him out, Lucas's hostility putting a damper on their productive morning. He shoots me a glance over his shoulder as they leave a clear *I told you so* in his expression. *I told you he was complicated. I told you it was a bad idea. I told you he wasn't the guy for you.* I hear it all without him saying a word.

I'm left standing in the hallway, Lucas in one direction, Will and Ethan in the other, with no clear idea what had just happened.

But still very sure between those two men is not somewhere I want to be.

Distractedly I look down at Ethan's business card, flipping it between my fingers. I read it for the first time.

Ethan Abbott

Abbott Enterprises

Abbott?

What the hell?

"When the *Top Ink* season with Lucas first aired, there was all sorts of speculation that he was some illegitimate love child of one of the Abbotts. I don't know where the rumors came from, but apparently, he changed his name to Abbott right before filming the show," Gabby informs me over lunch. I told her about the surprisingly hostile run-in as we waited to pay for our selections from the hospital cafeteria. Settling into an empty table, she tells me what she knows.

"The Abbotts are everywhere in Chicago, business, politics, philanthropy. And Lucas being so public about growing up in foster care...," she shrugs, "people love a scandal. The stories went wild, but he's never commented on it. I kind of just assumed it was stupid gossip, but clearly, there's something going on there."

I'm uncomfortable, feeling somehow disloyal or disrespectful, discussing this behind Lucas's back. But I'm also uncomfortable with the angry version of Lucas I saw upstairs. Gabby is the only one I can ask about it. "He mentioned foster care the first night. He said that's where he and Jax met as kids."

Gabby nods, chewing a bite of her sandwich before responding. "They're very public about it. They both do a lot of volunteer work with foster kids in the city."

My heart warms a bit with that information. That seems more in line with the Lucas I was beginning to know. Or at least the Lucas I wanted to know. I'm hoping I haven't romanticized broad shoulders and dark blue eyes into seeing someone that doesn't exist. I don't like people with volatile tempers. I know many people shrug it off, calling it passion or intensity. Some that even find it exciting but not me. I need stable ground beneath my feet. It's why I think I'm good as a trauma surgeon. I take the injuries created by chaos and stabilize them. I don't like chaos. It doesn't rattle me the way it does other people but only because, at least in an operating room, I am confident I can fix it, control it, calm it. Professionally anyway. Personally, I don't want to constantly be wondering when the next explosion will come.

Maybe I am boring.

"You're not boring." Gabby rolls her eyes at me and I realize I muttered my last thought out loud. "You just don't like stupid drama. I love that about you."

I blow her a kiss across the table. "Love you, too, Gabs."

She throws a wadded-up napkin at me and I laugh.

"I don't know. Lucas was furious. I really thought he was going to hit Ethan." Gabby grimaces but doesn't say anything else, letting me process.

She knows I don't like conflict in my personal life. It's probably why my past relations have been kind of boring. I saw my mom die; I saw what that did to my dad. Not just during but after. In the weeks after she was gone, he was angry at everyone and everything. That instability and uncertainty, on top of grieving my mom, caused me to shut down. Eventually, my dad pulled himself together. After a screaming match with my aunt, his sister, he finally agreed to go to grief counseling. I didn't tell Lucas the whole story when we talked about my self-defense classes. My dad was nervous about raising a teenage daughter on his own, but his counselor also suggested them as a way to help me deal with my 'freeze' response. She thought if I felt I had more control in situations I found frightening, it would help me engage. And it worked. Mostly. But there's still a difference between "soldiers" demanding medical attention, strangers with guns and people I've invited into my personal life. People I care about.

I'm probably overthinking this whole thing. I mean, really, we've just had a couple conversations and a few kisses. What do I care if he's volunteering with kids or starting fights with wealthy, maybe relatives? I'm not looking for a relationship right now. I should be focusing on my career and getting funding for more trauma training and staffing at the refugee camps. I should be spending my lunch thinking about how to get Ethan Abbott to support my proposal, not how to get Lucas Abbott to tell me all his secrets. You don't need distractions right now, remember Ash? Even incredibly sexy ones.

Definitely not angry or violent ones.

Decided, I smile at Gabby. "It's fine." I shake my head, releasing the rest of my confusing thoughts. "We'll get Jax back on his feet and send them back to their reality show. I'm perfectly happy keeping the drama on my television screen."

Clearly skeptical, Gabby asks, "Oh yeah? You going to start watching their show now?"

Memories of our kiss flash through my mind, and I imagine sitting at home while watching him flirt with customers on television every week.

No.

Definitely not.

Lucas

I shouldn't have lost my shit like that. But I can't seem to help it around my *family*. Especially him. My cousin. Smug bastard.

Back in Jax's room, I attempt to pace in the confined space, but it's too small to provide much satisfaction. I collapse into my usual chair instead. Tanya shoved me back in the room and went to get me a coffee. I'd rather have a beer, a common reaction after interacting with Ethan, but I suspect that goes against hospital policy.

Forcing myself to relax, I replay the scene in the hallway. Fucking Ethan. Always sticking his nose in my business. Afraid I'm going to do something to damage the family name. Not for one second do I believe his interrogation came from a place of genuine concern. If so, why not text me? He has my number. But I've not heard one peep from any of my so-called family about my best friend lying unconscious in the hospital.

I really wish Ash hadn't been there to see that shitstorm. When I'd first spotted Ethan, I hadn't even processed who he was talking to, and then I heard him say Jax's name and just...exploded. And then it was too late. Damage done.

The quick look I had of her face proved I definitely inflicted some damage to whatever it was happening between us. She looked shocked and uneasy. I've gotten a lot better at locking down my temper. Have coping mechanisms to channel it. When I was a kid, it was always art. Well, when it wasn't fighting. But eventually I figured out that even if I was the one left standing, I never really won a fight. So I joined a boxing gym. Seemed like a harmless but still very physical way to release some bad energy.

I've also learned over time a lot of the people that ended up in the fallout zone didn't deserve my anger.

Except when it comes to the Abbotts. But they deserve all the rage I have for them.

One of the machines in the room gives a loud beep shaking me out of my dark thoughts.

Jax makes an odd gurgling sound, and one of his hands jerks against the blanket. I'm at his side before I even realize I'm moving, but I just hover there, too afraid to touch him. His eyelids flutter, and he makes that sound again. I repeatedly press the button for the nurse as his eyes open. One of the machines starts beeping loudly, and he thrashes, his eyes wide. I move over him so he can see me and grab his hand.

"Easy, brother. Easy." He focuses on me and settles, continuing to cough and choke. A nurse materializes on the other side of the bed, speaking calmly.

"Mr. Hall, you are in Memorial Hospital." She presses a button on one of the monitors and the irritating beeping subsides. She explains he has a tube in his throat and instructs him not to try to talk. "The doctor will be here in a moment."

Jax is calmer now but wheezing as he struggles to breathe on his own around the tube.

Dr. Parker enters, introducing himself to Jax as he quickly reviews the chart and notes the readings on the machines surrounding the bed. My breath gets stuck in my chest as I wait, once again helpless. He pulls out a penlight and shines a light quickly into both of Jax's eyes, his expression serious. Once, twice…three times. My vision starts to narrow, and finally, my breath bursts out, and I drag in another ragged lungful.

An eternity later, Dr. Parker straightens and smiles professionally. "Welcome back, Mr. Hall. We're going to remove the tube. I'm not going to lie, it's going to be extremely uncomfortable. Try to cough as we go." Quickly the medical team does as instructed. Jax gasps and collapses limply back on the bed. "Your throat will be a little sore for a couple days."

"Can you tell me your first name?"

"Jax…Jackson." His voice is scratchy and faint but hits me hard. He's back. He's awake.

He's back. I quickly send a text to Macy and Logan, letting them know.

"Do you remember what happened?"

His brow furrows a bit, then he says, "I was shot? I remember being at the shop and walking in and," a flash of panic crosses his face until his eyes find me again, and if possible, he wilts even more, sinking deeper into the hospital bed, "two guys with guns. The girls?" He's asking me.

"They're fine. You were the only one hit," I answer.

He nods weakly.

"Turns out 'the girls' were doctors," I attempt a joke.

Jax gives a shaky laugh. "My lucky day."

Dr. Parker smiles, "It was. They likely saved your life. You were shot in the leg and in the chest. Another bullet grazed your head. The impact caused you to fall and hit your head...."

I tune out the rest of the explanation as Dr. Parker updates Jax on his injuries and the treatment he's already been subjected to.

He's back.

As Dr. Parker finishes his summary, the door opens again, and I see Ash walk in. She scans the room, her eyes briefly landing on me before moving on.

Shit.

"I heard you finally opened your eyes," she smiles at Jax and places a gentle hand on his shoulder. "Welcome back."

I watch Jax attempt a grin, but even that seems to require too much energy.

"It's going to take some time, and you'll likely require some Physical Therapy, but you'll be back hosting Bachelorette parties soon enough," she teases.

"No more Bachelorettes. They're dangerous." He croaks out.

"I'm going to let you rest, but I'll be back to check in on you tomorrow. If you need anything, push the nurse's call button."

She barely looks at me.

"Guests are fine but limit it to two at a time and short visits, okay? The best thing you can do for the next couple of days is sleep." She smiles again and excuses herself.

Fuck. I blew it.

Chapter Six

Lucas

"Y ou look like shit, Luke."

"Yeah, well, you don't look too pretty right now either."

Jax had fallen asleep soon after the doctors had left and just woke up again a few minutes ago. I've been keeping an uneasy vigil at his side for hours. Worried it was a fluke and he wasn't going to wake up again. But he's now back to insulting me, so I guess that's progress.

"I was shot. What's your excuse?"

"Drugs and hookers."

He snorts.

"Logan and Mace are down the hall. You want to see them?"

"In a minute." His voice is still hoarse, and he closes his eyes wearily for a moment before blinking them back open. I pour him a glass of water with a straw and wordlessly hold it for him as he sucks it down.

"'Bout time you woke up, asshole."

He grunts and relaxes back into the bed. "Sorry for taking my time."

"Don't do it again."

"Not part of my plan, brother."

"Good."

"Better tell Logan she can come in. I'm sure she's terrorizing someone."

I laugh because he's probably right. Most likely Tanya right now. She's still too grateful to the hospital staff to give any of them much grief. I send her a text and give her the all-clear.

Almost instantly, she's at the door. I hear her snap at our security guard about being on the list and grin. Must be a new guy on duty if he didn't recognize her.

"Jax." She hesitates just inside the room.

"Hey, Streaks," he croaks out.

"I told you not to call me that." But she doesn't sound angry. She sounds a little choked up and Logan hates to show any weakness. Slowly she crosses over to his bed, stopping next to me. She punches me in the shoulder.

"Ow! What the hell?"

"Well, I can't hit him!"

It's so ridiculous we all burst into laughter.

"Shit," Jax groans. "Don't make me laugh. Too soon."

"Sorry." She grips one of his hands lightly. "I've been worried about you."

I step outside, giving them a few moments alone. Tanya is in the hall, standing next to the security guard. She looks up from her phone when I approach and smiles. "Hey. Can I see him after Macy? Such a relief."

I nod, "Of course."

Macy turns the corner and comes walking down the hall. "Good news," he says simply. He gives me a half-hug and back slap in greeting.

"Yeah. It is."

"You want to get out of here for a little while? I can stick around."

"Probably a good idea. Thanks. I'm supposed to go to the police station in the morning. Meet with Melrose." I don't mention I'm also meeting with one of the robbers and his court-appointed attorney.

Tanya's phone chimes. "Excuse me, guys, I have to take this. Let me know when you're done, Macy, so I can say hi."

He nods and watches her walk away. "I think she's got a thing for our boy."

"Really?" I shrug. "Hadn't noticed."

He grabs my shoulder and squeezes, not hard, just a show of support. "Go on. Get out of here. Get some rest. I'll stick around and keep Jax company. If anything happens, I'll let you know."

"Thanks, Mace."

"Lucas Abbott? I'm Olivia Peters. Thank you for agreeing to meet with us."

The following day I'm at the police station as promised.

I shake her hand. Wondering for the millionth time if I'm doing the right thing. She hands me her business card. "I'm representing Mateo Ortega." She motions me toward a small interview room, and I grab a seat.

"I'd like to discuss a few things with you before Mateo is brought in if that's alright."

I nod, eying her skeptically.

"Like I said, I appreciate your willingness to meet with us. I know this is unusual, but I really believe that Mateo deserves a chance. I don't think justice is served by sending him to jail for the next 20 years of his life."

"My best friend nearly died."

Her professional mask softens as she responds. "I understand that. How is Mr. Hall recovering?"

"He's awake," I admit grudgingly.

"That's good. I really am glad to hear that."

We're silent, staring at each other across the table for a moment.

I hear her inhale deeply as she opens a file folder in front of her and continues. "I've managed to get Mateo's case severed from his cousin's-"

"The one who shot Jax?"

She nods. "He is moving forward in the criminal court with his public defender."

"You're not defending him too?"

"No, Mr. Abbott-"

"Just Lucas," I interrupt.

"Lucas. I'm not a public defender or a defense attorney."

I'm confused. "You said you were representing him?"

"I'm a Child's Advocate. Detective Melrose contacted me about Mateo and asked me to review his file."

Fucking Melrose. Christ, that guy plays by his own rules. Although to be fair, that's probably why I like him.

Most of the time anyway. Whether or not I like him today is still up in the air.

"I'm trying to keep Mateo out of criminal court," she continues to explain.

"You don't think he deserves to be there?"

"No, Mr. Ab-Lucas," she corrects herself, "I don't."

I lean forward, ready to argue, but she holds up her hand asking me to give her a minute. "Let me explain what I am proposing. Then meet Mateo. Talk to him yourself. And if you disagree, if you think he belongs in jail, well, I'm not likely to get very far with any judge without you and Mr. Hall and..." she glances at one of the papers in front of her, "Dr. Carrington and Dr. Martinez supporting the motion."

"You're going to talk to all of us?" Shit. I better talk to Jax. He doesn't even know I'm here.

If I agree to any of this.

"I managed to get Mateo a bail hearing for tomorrow afternoon. I'm asking for him to be released into my custody. We work with a group home here in Chicago; it's a good place. Well run. He'd be on a strict schedule and closely monitored. But he'd be able to continue in school. He'd be required to partici-pate in extensive community service. And, if you agree, to work off the damages to your place of business."

"You want me to give this kid a job?" I ask incredulously. The balls on this woman.

"I think being required to interact with you and Mr. Hall on a regular basis, to work until he's repaid some of the damages, would force him to confront what it is he became a part of. A constant reminder how different this could have turned out. But if you refuse, we can propose a different work scenario."

"And the cousin goes to jail?"

"Again, I'm not involved in that case, but Mateo has agreed to testify if it goes to court. I think it's likely his Public Defender will advise him to take a plea deal. No trial."

"He'd testify against his own family?"

She regards me steadily across the table, her jaw tight. "It isn't much of a family," she informs me, voice flat.

I get that. That, more than anything else she's said up to this point, convinces me to hear him out.

"Okay. Let's meet Mateo. Then we'll talk."

Chapter Seven

Lucas

I'm still distracted by everything that happened this morning, wondering how I tell Jax I think we should help one of the kids that is partly responsible for him being in the hospital when I open the door to his room. I blink, not believing the cozy scene in front of me.

"What the hell are you doing here? How did you get in here?"

My *cousin* Riley pops up guiltily, glancing between me and Jax lying in bed.

"I told the guard it was okay. She's not some crazy fan," Jax explains, but I'm not having it.

"Did Ethan send you?" I demand, focused on her. My blood boils at the thought he would send a woman to spy for him. "I told him to stay the fuck away."

"Luke-" Jax tries to interject.

"No, it's okay. I'll go. I just wanted to see if either of you needed anything." Riley grabs a giant purse from the chair she vacated and gives Jax a wobbly smile. She comes within inches of me as she crosses to the door. Her pale face almost makes me regret my aggressive tone. She's a middle school teacher, for Christ's sake, not some master manipulator.

She hesitates at the door, and I stiffen, ready to battle, despite my thoughts. "Ethan didn't send me," she informs me softly. "Neither did Uncle Theo. I just -" she trails off and eventually opens the door and walks away without finishing.

"KitKats!" Jax yells at the closing door.

I give him a *what the fuck* look because, seriously, what the fuck?

"You didn't have to be such an asshole to her. She brought me Duk's."

I'm still in fighting mode, "Are you serious right now? She turned you with a hot dog?"

"Chill out, Luke. What is up with you right now?"

I exhale heavily and collapse into a chair. "I'm sorry. They are just fucking everywhere lately."

"Duk's isn't just any hot dog, and you know it."

Leave it to Jax to make me laugh when just seconds ago, I was ready to fight. "Fine. I didn't mean to insult your favorite dawg."

"Damn right." He settles back into the pillows propping him up. "So, what's going on with you and the hot doctor anyway?"

I grimace and admit. "Not as much as I'd like."

Fucker laughs at me, then groans, clutching his chest.

"Serves you right. Laughing at my pain."

He snorts. "Going to do anything about that?"

Shrugging, I respond. "We'll see. There's a lot going on right now."

"Tell me about it."

I snort.

"No, seriously. Tell me about it. I'm not doing anything but sitting here in bed all day. I'm bored out of my mind."

"Well, don't get shot again, asshole."

"Believe me, it wasn't part of my plan this time."

"Melrose asked me to stop by the station this morning. That's why I wasn't here earlier."

"And left me vulnerable to the undoubtedly evil intentions of your tiny teacher cousin? I thought you were my friend."

"Jackass." But I chuckle. He's made his point. I probably overreacted to Riley's visit. Doesn't mean I'm going to apologize. Not to her anyway. Not to any of *them*.

"They've got the guys who did this in custody. How much do you actually remember of what happened?"

His face serious, Jax studies the ceiling while he considers the question. "Bits and pieces, really. It happened so fast. I remember walking in and seeing Ash and Gabby. I barely had time to realize there was anyone else there before all hell broke loose. And then I remember the pain. That's it, really. There's some other stuff in there, but I'm not even sure it's real and not a dream."

When he's done, he focuses on me again. "What did Melrose want? For you to identify them?"

Shaking my head, I lean forward and rest my forearms on my knees. "No. No need. One of them stayed. While we were ...." I don't know how to say 'while we were trying to stop you from bleeding out' to my best friend. I don't want that image in his head. "While we were...scrambling and calling 911, he stayed. Sat there and waited. And when the police came, he gave up the other one, the one who actually shot you. It took a little while to track him down, but they found him high and hiding out at a girlfriend's apartment and arrested him."

Jax is watching me steadily, waiting for me to get to the point.

"His name is Mateo. The kid who stayed."

"You soft-hearted bastard. I don't want to know his name!"

"He's fifteen, Jax."

"Fucking marshmallow, you know that?"

"Remember what we were doing at fifteen?"

"We weren't pulling guns on women!"

"He didn't know they were loaded."

"Where the hell is Macy? I'll have him kick your ass until I can do it myself," he mutters.

"Look, I was pissed too, believe me, but I met him-"

"You what? Fucking hell, Luke."

"He made a stupid choice. One I don't want to define the rest of his life. I want to give him a chance, man."

Silent, Jax leans back and again stares at the ceiling. Sighing, he asks me, "Why?"

Why?

I don't really know why. I guess I just don't want to be yet another reason this kid's life gets off track. Meeting him and talking to his children's advocate, I learned a little more about how he ended up stupidly following his cousin into my shop. And if someone had just... not let things go bad. If one teacher had noticed his bruises before his mom ran off. If one social worker had bothered to find out his cousin was repeatedly busted for drugs before placing him with his aunt. If his school counselor had helped him get a job....

"We can help him land someplace better, Jax. Before he's too gone to save." He knows, just as I do. We'd lost friends moving through the system. Drugs. Violence. Depression. It's so fucking hard to get out once you start to spiral.

Jax shakes his head, running a hand over his face. "Fuck." His voice has lost all its heat from moments ago, and now he just sounds tired.

"What do you want to do?" he asks.

"That's up to you. I'll back your play on this, whatever you decide. But hear her out, okay?"

"Hear who out?"

"His advocate. She's a lawyer for kids in shitty situations, I guess. Melrose found her."

Jax snorts. "Right."

"You up for this or not?"

"Bring it on, you fucking wuss."

I snicker and move to open the door and let Olivia in. She's much more convincing than I am.

Ash

"Dr. Carrington?"

"Yes?" I look up from my charts and see a lovely brunette in a suit and glasses standing in front of me. "Can I help you?"

"My name is Olivia Peters. I'm representing Mateo Ortega in the shooting and robbery that took place at *Vanished on Halsted* last weekend. You were one of the witnesses, correct?"

I stiffen, flashes of Friday night bombarding me. "I was a little more than that. I had a gun pointed at my head."

"That must have been terrifying," she says softly. "I'm relieved everyone is okay. I was told Jackson Hall is awake and expected to fully recover."

Now I'm suspicious. How would she have heard that? Maybe Tanya's paranoia is well deserved. "I can't discuss my patients with you."

"Of course, I understand. I met with Lucas earlier, and he mentioned it." She pulls a card out from her bag and hands it to me. "I'm about to meet with Mr. Hall and discuss options for my client. I was hoping to speak with you and Dr. Martinez as well as the other two on the scene."

I'm still so off balance by this whole encounter, it's taking me a minute to catch up. "What did you say his name was? Your client?"

"Mateo Ortega."

"Which one was he?"

"Mateo was taken into custody on the scene. My understanding from his recounting of events was that he was the one that," she hesitates briefly, "held the gun to your head."

Oh.

"I've discussed alternative options to criminal charges for Mateo with Lucas, and he's agreed to my proposal, contingent on the rest of you also agreeing. Mr. Hall in particular."

"What kind of 'alternative options'?"

"I'm hoping to get him released into a group home with mandatory therapy and community service. He'll also be required to work off damages at *Vanished*."

"Lucas agreed to this?" I'm skeptical. Lucas is devoted to Jax. I can't imagine him being okay with one of the people that put his best friend in the hospital, nearly dying, getting off lightly.

"Contingent on the rest of you signing off on the proposal. Having all of you supporting the motion would go a long way with the judge."

I'm silent, processing all this information. She's digging through her bag again and comes up with an envelope.

"Before you decide anything, please read this. Mateo wrote each of you a letter. And then talk to Lucas. He was able to talk to Mateo this morning. I think it changed a lot of his thinking."

"Oliva?"

We both turn and see Lucas leaning out of Jax's room. He hesitates when he sees me.

"Ash."

I wave like the awkward idiot I am.

He turns his attention to Olivia. "Jax is ready to talk." She nods and hurries to his side. "Ash, can you wait a minute? I'll be right back."

"Sure," I agree.

He flashes me a quick smile, and I feel a flutter in my stomach. Ugh. The man is lethal. It's really not fair.

While I wait, I open the letter Olivia had given me.

Dr. Carrington,

My name is Mateo Ortega. I'm writing to tell you I'm sorry for what I did. Ms. Peters just told me your friend is going to be okay. That's good. Ms. Peters is going to talk to you about trying to help me, but it's okay if you don't. I just wanted to let you know that I'm sorry. I didn't mean for anyone to get hurt.

"Hey."

Lucas is back, interrupting me from the rest of the letter. He's got his hands shoved deep in his pockets and an almost sheepish expression on his face.

Ash, you are a rock. No distractions, remember?

"Sorry, I was hoping to talk to you before...," he gestures, indicating Jax's room and Olivia.

"Yeah. I'm still processing. She said you talked to him? Mateo?"

"This morning."

"And you agree with this idea? Trying to get him off?"

"He'd be on probation until he was eighteen. I checked out the group home and the guy running it is decent. Assuming Jax is okay with it, yeah. I'd like to support Olivia's idea."

I study him carefully. "Can I ask why?"

He smirks. "That was Jax's question too."

"And? What did you tell him."

He shoves one hand through his hair, leaving a few strands sticking up at odd angles. It does nothing to diminish his appeal or my reaction to him.

"That he's just a kid that made one stupid mistake. And yeah, it was a big one, but I don't want this one choice to define the rest of his life."

I glance at the letter in my hand, contemplating.

"What if you're wrong? What if he does something stupid again?"

"Then at least it won't be because I didn't give him a chance."

My chest tightens at his answer. The rock has melted. It's now a puddle.

Crap.

I inhale slowly. "You believe him? He's sorry? He learned his lesson?"

"I do. He's smart. Despite evidence to the contrary," he grins crookedly, but it shifts into a grimace. "His family fucked him up. It's why I think this group home could be good for him. I looked into it. And I trust Olivia. She's going to fight for him. Make sure he's given every chance."

Lucas Abbott *is* complicated. Will was right about that. But I've never been afraid of complicated.

"I'll talk to Gabby."

His eyes light up. "You're in?"

I nod. "I trust you. If you believe in him."

I can't quite read the expression on his face.

Unable to help myself, I reach out and grasp his arm. Then piling on the stupid, I step forward, stretch up on my tiptoes and give him a quick kiss on the cheek.

His eyes flash with emotion when I lower back down. We're standing so close I can feel the heat radiating off him. For a moment, I'm mesmerized, unable to move. But then someone bumps into us, and I'm abruptly reminded we're standing in the middle of the hospital hallway.

"I'll talk to Gabby," I promise again and rush away.

Chapter Eight

I *trust you.*

I pound the punching bag, that short sentence echoing in my head.

Two weeks later, and I'm still gut-punched every time I remember Ash's softly spoken words. I don't know why it hit me as hard as it did. But it means something that she trusted me.

It feels good to be back in the gym. I've been spending every possible minute at the hospital, which means my typical method of stress relief has not been happening as often as usual. I could feel the tension piling up, so this morning I made it work.

Olivia managed to keep Mateo's case in juvenile court and got a judge to agree to probation and community service. She'd had a statement from the four of us confirming he'd had a chance to run during the chaos and hadn't. She'd even gotten his track coach and a couple teachers to act as character witnesses. I'm impressed by her fire. He's supposed to start 'working' at *Vanished* next week.

Next week, after Jax is released from the hospital. Finally.

He's still got some physical therapy ahead of him, but soon he'll only have a couple scars to remind him this ever happened. To remind any of us.

My arms are starting to burn, which is exactly what I was going for. I take the gloves off and instead grab a jump rope.

Things seem to have shifted between Ash and me. There's been no more kissing, unfortunately, but at least she's not avoiding me anymore. I'm hoping that means future kissing is back on the table. But I'm not entirely sure how to make that happen.

Macy appears at my side. Usually, Jax is the one to join me for these morning workouts at the boxing gym, but while he's been in the hospital, Mace has shown up once or twice a week. I appreciate the support especially knowing he prefers to go running in the morning. He's not a boxer. He doesn't have the same aggression to work out.

"Early start this morning?" he asks, grabbing a rope of his own.

"Couldn't sleep," I huff out, not missing a jump.

He starts his workout a few feet away, starting slow, warming up.

"That Peters chick called with Mateo's schedule. She wants us to let her know what hours we could have him at the shop."

I nod.

"You sure you want to do this?"

I don't respond right away, thinking. I go back and forth. Will Mateo get his shit together, or is this whole thing just a sucker's waste of time? Will having Mateo in our space keep it too fresh in everyone's minds? Will Jax be okay with it? He agreed to this plan, but that was when it was just an idea. The reality of seeing Mateo's face every day may be something very different.

But ultimately, I come back to what I told Ash. I don't want to be another person who lets this kid down. If I bail, if I just let someone else deal with him, that's exactly how he ended up in this situation.

I pump my arms, feeling my legs burn as I jump high, finishing strong.

When I stop, my breath is harsh. I wipe my forearm across my sweaty forehead. I gulp a lungful of air and feel my heart starting to slow down. Mace has stopped jumping as well and is waiting for my answer.

"Yeah. I'm sure."

"Okay," he nods. "Let's do this."

I hold out my arm, and he grips my hand like we're going to arm wrestle. "Thanks, Mace."

"You got it, brother."

Ash

"I saw Meg Curtis at the hospital today. She was excited to hear you were back in town."

I glance up from my food at Gabby, sitting across the dining room table. I feel a pang of guilt at her words. I've done an awful job reconnecting with folks since I've been back. Meg coordinated the self-defense classes I had volunteered with during med school. She had been a significant presence and mentor in my life since high school when I first walked into one of the courses she taught. And I haven't called her.

"You know, there's no rule that says you can't have a real life here just because you want to go back to Nigeria someday."

"What are you talking about?"

"You. Sitting here with me and Tim every night. When you could be volunteering again. Teaching classes. Or enjoying this amazing city we live in." She pauses, then looks at me pointedly. "When you could be having fun with Lucas."

I shake my head. "No. Remember? We discussed this."

She shrugs. "Have you seen him lose his shit like that again? Because I haven't. In fact, I've seen him be a pretty amazing guy. Taking care of his friend. Nice to the nurses and staff. Helping out that kid."

I blink at her, saying nothing. There's nothing really to say. She's right.

"I get that your career and this project are important to you. But it doesn't have to be everything to you, does it? Try actually *living* here, Ash. Not just passing time."

She's right, I realize. I've been back nearly a month and have hardly been anywhere other than the hospital and her apartment. I haven't even started looking for my own place.

"You *like* him, Ash. He makes you smile."

I do like him. I make a point of visiting Jax when I know Lucas is there just so I'll have an excuse to see him. I'll admit I was a little freaked out seeing his explosive temper that day with Ethan. But I've seen nothing of that since then. Clearly, something is going on with him and the Abbotts. Something pretty ugly. Does that mean I should ignore all the good things I have seen?

"The two of you have something. It's obvious. Why not see what could happen?"

Why not?

"Jax is being released in a couple days."

I am well aware of this fact. Jax will go home. And Lucas will go with him. I won't have an easy excuse to see him, chat with him, *look* at him every day.

Shit. That's depressing. Those ten, fifteen minutes I'm "checking" on Jax has quickly become the highlight of my day.

"I'm supposed to meet with the Chief next week, so he can review my plan and estimated budget."

"And I'm sure you'll be ready. I can even help you if you need it. But I will be very, *very* disappointed if, between now and then, you spend every night on my couch working."

I grimace. "I should probably start looking for my own place, huh? You and Tim have been so generous letting me stay here."

"That is not at all what I meant. After so many years away, I love having you here. But I want you to love it here too, and I don't see that happening if you never really get out of the hospital."

Silently, I ponder her words.

She's not wrong.

After dinner, I slip into my bedroom and call Meg. An hour later, we've caught up on three years of life, and I've committed to helping teach two self-defense classes a week. I'll shadow her tomorrow afternoon, and likely next week, I'll start having my own sessions. It feels...like an accomplishment. I'm surprised by how good I feel, how excited. Gabby was right. I haven't let myself have much of a life here.

Time to change that.

Chapter Nine

Lucas

*D*amn it.

I crumple the drawing I just finished in my fist and toss it into the basket at my feet. I'm working on a pinup style for a regular client, which should be a relatively easy and fun assignment. Unfortunately, all I can think about is Ash. Which means the sketch I just did looked disturbingly like a particular doctor I know.

Like hell I'm tattooing her face on some other guy's bicep. Even if I'm the only one who would probably ever know.

I'm man enough to admit she's got me totally twisted up. We've been dancing around each other for two weeks now, and I can't figure her the fuck out. That kiss we'd shared, brief as it was, was one of the hottest experiences of my life. I'll also admit that memory has been the jumping-off point to some seriously sexy fantasies while I take care of my morning wood in the shower. More times than is probably healthy.

Jax is coming home tomorrow. And while I'm relieved as fuck my best friend is healed enough to leave the hospital, it's like a glaring countdown clock is now hovering above my head. Because when he gets discharged, I'll have no reason to see Ash again, let alone every day.

Movement in the corner of my eye catches my attention, and I look up, expecting to see Logan entering my space. She's the only one working right now and usually alerts me to any clients before sending them back. But I'm wrong. It's not Logan.

Instead, it's like I've conjured my beautiful tormentor because Ash is the one poised in the doorway.

Looking gorgeous, as usual. Her hair is down around her shoulders like that first night. At the hospital she always wears it pulled back in various styles. She's wearing a simple white sun dress with an uneven hem, giving teasing glimpses of bare leg between her knees and ankles. Tiny straps show off her shoulders and peaks of cleavage. Christ, her breasts are perfect.

The caveman in me is howling. It's like she's waving a red flag in front of a caged bull. And yet, she obviously has no idea how sexy she is.

"What are you doing here?" My voice is harsher than I intended, my thoughts annoyingly raw. And now I'm fucking turned on.

The sparkle in her eyes dims a bit at my tone, and she glances behind her towards the exit. I half expect her to bolt, but instead, she squares her shoulders and steps farther into the room. Having her get closer to me may not be the best idea right now.

"Ash, what are you doing here?"

This time my stay-the-fuck-back bearing does give her pause.

Her momentary courage crumbles. "Sorry. This is probably a bad time. I didn't mean to interrupt."

She starts to back away. *Shit.* I'm being such an asshole. It's not her fault I want her more than she wants me. Or that I freaked her out when I lost my shit at Ethan. She saved Jax's life and has been nothing but good to me, confusing maybe, but kind.

I sigh roughly and shake myself out of my dark mood.

"Wait." I reach out, gently tugging on her hand to stop her backward retreat. "I'm sorry. You're not interrupting anything. I'm just sketching while I wait for my next appointment."

She's stopped moving, which was my goal. Seemingly mesmerized by my hand holding hers. Which is when I realize not only haven't I released her, but I've moved closer, and my thumb is now tracing soft circles against her wrist.

Her breath hitches in her chest, causing her breasts to jiggle. Fuck, she's killing me.

"What are you doing here?" I ask again, this time much softer, smoother.

She tears her eyes away from our entangled fingers and finally looks up at me. I watch her throat flex as she swallows. She licks her lips nervously.

"I - ah - I just -" she takes a deep breath; it takes every ounce of discipline I have to keep my eyes on hers and not sneak another peek at her boobs. "I didn't want this morning to be the last time I saw you."

My inner caveman is now beating his chest in victory. I want to throw her over my shoulder, find the nearest bed, and show her how much I appreciate those words.

But what I do is take our entwined hands and move them to her lower back, using them to pull her snugly against me. My other hand raises to her shoulder and caresses down the length of her arm. Her shiver reassures me she's equally affected.

"Yeah?" I whisper.

She nods, her chocolate eyes dilated with arousal.

Keeping my impulses tightly leashed, I press a soft kiss to her lips. Exploring. Asking. Wanting.

Over and over again, I brush my lips across hers, deliberately never taking it further. She makes a small sound in the back of her throat and lifts to her tip toes, trying to deepen the kiss. Her free hand fists my t-shirt as she strains against me.

I lift my head up, out of her reach, and wait until her eyes slowly blink open. "I'm really glad to hear that, Ash."

She smiles softly and arches one eyebrow. "Yeah?" she repeats back to me.

Chuckling, I confess, "Hated that idea."

We just stare at each other for a minute, silly grins on our faces.

"God, you're beautiful."

Her smile widens, and she tugs that hand still gripping my shirt playfully, pulling my lips back to hers.

This time I increase the pressure and use my tongue to tease her lips apart so I can deepen our kiss. She responds immediately, tangling her tongue with mine. I groan into the caress.

This woman. She goes right to my head. And my cock, which is currently throbbing against my zipper.

Recently I've started doing my drawings in one of the empty stations we have in back, the ones waiting for our expansion plans to take place, and I thank fuck for the extra bit of privacy this affords us. Because unless she pulls back, there is no way I'm stopping.

Ash

I can't believe I did it.

I've never been much of a risk-taker in my personal life. Professionally maybe, but even that is debatable. But definitely never in my personal life. These last couple weeks, spending time with Lucas, getting to know him, flirting with him, it has become increasingly clear that Gabby was totally right that first night. My dating history is boring. With a capital B.

The idea that the last conversation we would ever have was about Jax's post-care weighed on me all day as I finished my shift. It was clear that Lucas wasn't going to push the issue, not after I'd shut him down, thrown off by his violent reaction to Ethan. That whole situation still confuses and concerns me, but I've spent enough time with him to believe that's not who he is. But today, it was obvious that the ball was in my court, as they say.

If something was going to happen between Lucas and me, I was going to have to be the one to make it happen. Which meant taking a risk and saying out loud what I wanted. What I really wanted. Gabby's pep talk helped. She's been spending nearly as much time as I have checking with the *Vanished* crew and thinks Lucas is great. And still thinks he'd know exactly what to do with a naked me. Her suggestion was to just drop my dress and see what happened.

I'm really glad that wasn't necessary.

Telling him I wanted to see him again was nerve-wracking enough.

Probably I should examine that further. Should this be such a big deal for a thirty-year-old woman? I don't know, but I kind of doubt it.

I still can't believe I did it.

But obviously, I did because Lucas Abbott is currently kissing me more thoroughly than I can remember ever being kissed.

And if kisses from Lucas Abbott are the reward, then sign me up for risky behavior every day. Every. Damn. Day.

He releases my hand, using both of his to grip my waist and pull me unbelievably closer to him. My eyes closed, my arms twine around his neck as I stretch against the muscled length of him, desperate for more of these brain-melting kisses. Suddenly, I'm weightless, Lucas lifting me up and hitching me higher against his chest without breaking our kiss. Instinctively, I wrap my legs around his waist to secure myself.

Holy shit.

I don't remember him moving, but he must have because suddenly I feel a wall at my back, and Lucas pressed tightly along my front. Proof of his desire is notched between my thighs, separated only by his jeans and my thin underwear. His kisses turn demanding, devouring. I realize one of my hands is fisted in his gorgeous hair as I return his kisses with equal urgency.

"Ash," he murmurs my name against my neck, nuzzling the skin below my ear. Skin that is, apparently, incredibly sensitive. The combination of that caress and his husky voice makes my stomach flip, sending tingles through my core and to all my limbs. I'm sure my underwear is soaked with my arousal. And I love it. I squeeze him tighter, wanting to be as close as possible, impossibly closer.

His teeth gently tug on my earlobe, and I can't contain my cry of pleasure.

"I'm so fucking hard right now."

God, his *voice*. His voice alone could make me come.

I arch my hips against him, rubbing my core along his length. His lips are now tickling along the V-neckline of my dress. I want his lips on my breasts, my nipples.

"So beautiful," he says again.

He makes me feel beautiful. He makes me feel sexy and almost bold. He makes me feel *good*.

"Can you get off like this?"

My eyes lazily blink open as I register his question. Can I? Should I? Reality starts to nudge its way in. Is that what I want?

His dark blue gaze is studying me, practically leaving a trail of heat everywhere it touches. He rocks his hips against me, giving me some delicious added friction between my thighs, and my eyes flutter shut again, reveling in the sensation.

Yes.

I want. It's been forever since I've had sex, and this man...this man is exposing all those previous experiences to be mere warm-ups. I've *never* had sex like this.

"I - I don't know," I admit in a whisper, meeting his eyes again.

As if sensing my momentary hesitation, Lucas gives me a sweet smile and presses a series of soft kisses along my collarbone. Somehow, without losing any of the contact between us, he manages to hook a leg of a stool they use for tattooing, and the wheels allow him to pull it to us. He shifts his hands to cup my ass. I gasp at the contact, and he eases us down until he's sitting with me straddling his lap. Then he pushes until his back is against the wall, using his feet to brace us.

He returns to kissing me, and I settle into this new position. Shifting until his erection is exactly where I want it. He groans as I arch my hips against him, and the sound is empowering. He's feeling everything that I'm feeling, and the knowledge makes me bold.

"Do it. Rub against me. Take what you need and make yourself come."

Oh god.

My eyes fly to his. He's wearing a naughty, sexy grin that causes my heart to pound. The tingling in my core intensifies, and suddenly that is the only thing I want to do.

Gripping his hair, I pull his head back to mine, demanding more of his award-winning kisses. They should be anyway. I'll give him all the awards.

I giggle against his lips.

He pulls back, eyeing me curiously. "Something funny, gorgeous?"

I shake my head almost frantically, not liking his mouth not on me.

One of his hands is under my skirt, so, SO glad Gabby convinced me to wear a pretty dress before coming over, his rough fingers tracing gentle lines along my outer thigh. His eyes slowly touch every part of me, and I wonder what he sees. They linger at the tiny bit of shadow revealed between my breasts.

Slowly, tortuously, his other hand traces over the curve of my breast, pausing for a beat over my erect nipple, jutting against the fabric of my dress. "Anything else you want to show me?" His husky voice, and his request, sends a shiver through me.

I know what he's asking. Can I be that bold? Take that risk?

If Lucas Abbott's kisses are my reward...

I loosen the zipper on my side and the bodice of my dress gapes open. His fingers slowly pull one strap over my shoulder, letting it hang off my arm, revealing one naked breast. I watch his reaction, the way he closes his eyes for a moment before returning his hot gaze to my skin.

"Fuck." His voice is almost reverential. My skin feels tight and tingly.

He snaps the tension between us. And suddenly, I feel him everywhere - kisses on my mouth, his muscled chest rubbing against my breasts, one hand caressing my thigh, the other gripping my ass, his hard thighs clenched beneath me, and his erection throbbing against my core.

I can feel the pressure building as I strain against him, hips grinding against him. "Oh, god!" I want this so badly. He feels so good.

"Do it," he growls against my lips, pulling my hips down against him.

"Lucas!" My cry is sharp between us as I splinter, shuddering in his arms with the force of my release. He holds me tightly through the aftershocks, his own breathing unsteady.

My heartbeat slowly returns to normal, as do my thoughts.

Did that really just happen?

Lucas

Fucking perfect.

Watching Ash orgasm is perfect. I did that. I made her feel that good. And I want to do it a fuck-ton more.

She's slumped against me as she recovers, her face tucked into my neck. I can feel tiny huffs of air against my skin, and the little tickles combined with her curvy body in my lap keep me on the edge of arousal. I hadn't meant for things to go quite so far, but she's so sweetly responsive that I couldn't help myself. I'm running one hand up and down her back, perfectly content to stay here for the foreseeable future. But after a few minutes, she takes a deep breath and lazily pulls back to look me in the eyes. The sated expression on her face causes my cock to pulse.

I see a flash of uncertainty enter her expression, and I know reality is setting in. I'm going to have to move quickly, or she's going to bolt.

So I kiss her. That seemed to work out well the last time. But this time, I keep it soft and slow. Savoring. I kiss her like that until the gathering tension is once again gone, and she's practically a soft puddle in my lap. Then I pull back, squeezing her to me and place one last kiss along her neck.

"Damn. That was fun. Hot."

I feel tremors wracking her frame, and a flash of panic spears through me until I realize she's giggling. Thank god. Good tremors then. I exhale in relief.

A familiar chime sounds throughout the shop signaling the front door opening. I suspect it's the client I was waiting for when Ash arrived. *Damn it.* I know Logan won't send him back, especially knowing I'm with someone, but I'm going to have to separate from Ash for at least a few hours.

My dick is howling his disappointment at this development. He's a greedy little shit. The rest of me isn't that psyched, either. But screwing Ash in the back room was never part of my plan. Not that I'd planned any of this but hell if I was sorry it had happened.

This time when she pulls back, her cheeks are flaming, and she won't quite meet my eyes.

Oh, hell no.

I cup her face, thumbs brushing her cheeks. "You okay?"

Eyes on my collar, she nods.

"Hey," I jiggle one knee, causing her to bounce and gently request, "Look at me?"

When her eyes meet mine, I hate the questions in their depths. She has no idea what she does to me.

I watch, fascinated, as she pulls herself together and shrouds herself in a little of the bravado that brought her through my door just a little while ago. "Better than okay. Not sure I can stand up, though."

I don't push it. For now. Eventually, she'll have no doubts where I'm concerned.

Reluctantly I inform her, "You're going to have to. I think my next appointment just arrived. And my hard-on isn't going to go down with you sitting on it." And then both to soften my words, and because I can't help myself, I press a swift kiss to those sexy swollen lips.

"Oh. Right. Of course." Her cheeks are flaming as she scampers off my lap.

I stand, quickly pulling her back into my arms. There's something about this off-balance, nervous Ash that's tugging at all my protective instincts.

"Can I see you later tonight?"

"What?" A bright smile spreads across her face.

"Tonight, when I'm done here, can I come over? Spend some time with you out of the hospital?"

She nods, eyes sparkling. "I'll text you the address."

I lean down for another taste of her. My erection, which is still strong, pokes her in the stomach.

She reaches for the button of my jeans. "I could...I could help...with that."

Realizing what she's offering, I snatch her hands away. She has no idea how badly I want her hands on me.

There's a rap outside the doorway, and Logan yells, "Three o'clock, Luke!"

"Shit," I mutter. Then loud enough for Logan to hear me in the hall, "Five minutes!"

Ash is looking at me expectantly, that same uncertainty and bravado warring in her eyes. I lift her hands, kissing her fingertips.

"No way I'm going to be satisfied with a quick tug if it's your hands on me." I try to keep my voice light and teasing, but I'm not sure how successful I am, considering the lust raging through my body right now. I've got to calm down so I can go back to work.

"Oh." Her blush deepens, but her breath speeds up, eyes dilating. She's turned on. *We'll have to explore that more later.* "But you're - you're going to...?"

"Yeah," I admit with a grimace. "Probably."

"What will you think about?" Her eyes get wide, jaw dropping. "I'm sorry! Never mind. I shouldn't-"

"Are you kidding?" I interrupt, chuckling, and nod at our stool. "After that, all I'm going to be thinking about is you. The sexy sounds you made. How gorgeous you looked. And all the things we didn't get to do. Yet."

She inhales sharply. "Lucas."

The door chimes again and I hear what sounds like Macy's low rumble out front.

"I should go. You have work to do."

I nod reluctantly. "Text me the address."

Ash smiles. She hesitates briefly, then reaches up, quickly giving me a kiss on the cheek, and bolts out the door, yelling goodbye over her shoulder.

And I stand there like a chump, touching my cheek with a stupid grin on my face.

Chapter Ten

Lucas

By 9:30 that night, I'm knocking on her door, having wasted no time closing the shop. Well actually, I let Macy take care of most of the closing routine, too eager to see Ash again. *I'm such a sucker.*

I even stopped and picked up a bottle of wine.

Ash lives in an elevated first-floor apartment of a house that's been converted to three units, obviously recently rehabbed. It's a quiet tree-lined residential street in West Town, an easy walk to public transit. I'm about to knock again when the door opens.

But not by Ash. Some tall, lanky guy with reddish-blond hair is standing in the doorway. "Hi. Can I help you?"

"Yeah. I'm here to see Ash."

The stranger raises his eyebrows expectantly. "Oh. Why?"

Irritated, I give him a once-over. "Who are you again?"

"Ash's boyfriend."

I feel like I've just been gut-punched. I take a step back. "You're her what?" How does she have a boyfriend? This makes no sense.

Suddenly Gabby appears at this guy's side and shoves an elbow into his stomach. "Knock it off, Tim. Don't torture the guy. He saved my life." Her expression exasperated, she ignores his grunt of discomfort and turns her attention to me. She makes a cute *harrumphing* sigh and smiles. "Hi, Lucas." She quickly waves me inside. "This is Tim. My fiancé. Sometimes he tries to be funny even though I've explained to him, *multiple times,* that he's not." She shoots him another glare. He just grins at her and rubs his side.

Right. Tim.

I realize Ash must be staying with them while she gets settled back in Chicago.

"Sorry, man," Tim apologizes, holding out his hand to shake. "C'mon in."

Gabby takes the wine from me and leads me through the apartment to the kitchen in the rear. "Ash should be home soon. She stopped to grab some take-out. Do you want to wait for her to open the wine? We've got some beer in the fridge."

"Uh, yeah. Sure. That would be great." This is awkward. I feel like I'm in some weird meet-the-parents scene.

Gabby has just handed me a bottle when I hear the front door open and Ash calling from the front room.

"Hey Gabby, I'm back so you and Tim can make yourselves scarce. Lucas will be here any second-"

"Lucas is already here," Gabby interrupts in a cheerful sing-song voice as we leave the kitchen.

Ash spots us and her steps falter, cheeks going pink. "Oh. Hi." She's changed into a pair of jeans and a simple black tank top.

She's so fucking cute; I can't help my grin. "Hi."

We stare at each other for a heartbeat, and I can't help but remember a few short hours ago, she was coming apart in my arms. My jeans get snug.

"I...ah...brought sushi, but it occurs to me now I don't know if you actually like sushi."

"I do."

"Oh. Good."

"Ash, you look flushed. Are you warm?" Tim asks with fake innocence.

Gabby jabs him in the side again. "Okay, we're off! We'll be late, so probably won't see you until tomorrow! Night!" And with a fierce tug on her fiancé's arm, they are out the door.

Smirking, I walk over and grab the take-out bags out of her hands. Then, because I can't seem to help myself, I lean down and give her a soft kiss. She smiles into it and makes a tiny sound that makes my jeans impossibly tighter.

Pulling back, I whisper, "Hi."

"Hi." Her smile punches me in the chest.

She turns away, breaking the tension. I expect her to head back to the dining table, but instead, she settles onto the floor unpacking our order on the low square coffee table. I lower down next to her on one of the giant pillows strewn around, I'm assuming for this very purpose. Spotting my beer, she jumps to her feet.

"Do you need another?"

"No, I'm good." I've barely started this one. "I brought some wine, though. Gabby put it on the counter."

Ash disappears down the hallway, reappearing minutes later with the opened bottle and two glasses, and returns to her spot next to me.

"How were your last appointments?" She asks before taking a bite.

"Good. Actually just one long appointment. Guy whose father just passed away and wanted a portrait of him."

Her eyebrows raise, surprised or impressed, I'm not sure. "You do portraits?"

"Gotta do everything if you're gonna win *Top Ink.*" She snorts, making me laugh. I like that she'll call me out when I'm cocky. Giving her an honest answer, I explain, "It's not my favorite or what I'm known for, but I can hold my own."

"That's sweet. That he wanted something for his father."

I nod. "We get a lot of that, actually."

"So, what do you *like* to do?"

"Neo-Traditional. Gabby's was a simple version of what I do."

Ash grins a little smugly. "I can report back that Tim really liked it."

I laugh. "Good for them."

She fills me in on her day. I'm a little intimidated by how smart she is. The abandoned foster kid I can't quite shake whispers I'm not good enough for her. But I want her. Enough to ignore that voice, even if part of me suspects it's right.

Done with the sushi, I lean back against the couch behind us, stretching my legs out. She does similar but twists on her side, facing me like a little mermaid, and sips her wine with one hand, the other propped on the couch seat.

"Tell me about *Top Ink*."

I stare at my feet, unsure where to start. "What do you want to know?"

She thinks before answering, which I like. Although it's becoming increasingly obvious, I like everything about this woman. But her taking a minute to think about it makes me feel like she's actually curious about my experience, not just the *fame* part of it.

"Why did you want to do it?"

Wow. Nobody has ever asked me that. Most assume the answer is obvious, television, money, exposure. Those were only part of my reasons. I'm silent for a bit, struggling with how honest I want to be. I'm well aware she pulled away seeing my reaction to Ethan and the Abbotts, and I really don't want to screw it up again now that we're here.

"At first, it was mostly about the recognition. Nobody expected Jax and I to make much of our lives growing up. They assumed we'd be in jail by the time were twenty, I'm sure. But I always knew I had this one thing, you know? I always knew I was good at this. Art. I guess part of me wanted to prove it."

I glance at her and grin. "The money was nice too."

She smiles. "Did you always plan to use it to open your own shop?"

"Yeah. That was the plan, win or lose. Winning just made it faster."

"So you and Jax have known each other since you were kids. What about Macy and Logan?"

"Mace worked with Jax and me at *Twisted Ink*. Pretty quickly, we started talking about having our own place so we could do it our way."

"Your way?"

I shrug. I don't like bashing Nik, my old boss. He gave me a shot and taught me a lot, but....

"The owner was kind of old-school. Kind of an ass."

"How so?"

I stall, finishing my beer and setting it on the table. "He wouldn't hire women. Gave a lot of shit jobs to Mace; made cracks about his mother. She's Hawaiian, so he's half Polynesian. One of the other tattooers was dealing, and he just looked the other way. May have even been taking a cut, I don't really know."

"That's awful."

I don't respond but pour some wine into the still-empty glass. I glance at her, and she nods, letting me top her off.

"I'm glad you guys made it happen. Your own place. Is that why you hired Logan?"

"Partly. I knew I wanted to have a woman on staff. Sometimes customers, women, feel more comfortable. But also, after being on *Top Ink,* talking to some of the female competitors there, I realized Nik wasn't the exception, you know? So after I won, I started asking around for recommendations."

I smirk, remembering that first run-in. "I asked her if she could take a break and talk, and she looked me up and down and told me I could talk all I wanted, but she wasn't going to suck my dick no matter how many competitions I won."

I laugh at the expression on Ash's face, quickly reassuring her. "That was not even a thought in my head. I swear."

Shaking her head, she stammers, "No. I didn't - I ..." at a loss for words, she finally lands on, "Logan is tough."

"Yeah. She is. But she rounds out our team pretty well. For now."

"You think she'll leave?"

"I hope not. I just mean, eventually, we're hoping to add more artists."

"You said at first it was about the recognition. What else was it about?"

Maybe it's because people's lives depend on her not getting distracted, but when you're the focus of Ash's attention, you feel it. She is wholly and unwaveringly focused on you. I'm surprised it doesn't make me uncomfortable, that focus, but instead, it makes me feel like the luckiest son of a bitch in the city.

Because I can't seem to stop myself from touching her, I brush her hair over her shoulder and stay there, rubbing the soft strands between my fingers.

"My family. The Abbotts."

She doesn't say anything, just watches me with those melted chocolate eyes encouraging me to spill all my secrets.

"I found out about them after I'd made the show but before I left for LA to film it. They offered me money to drop out and not appear on television. I basically told them to go fuck themselves."

"Are you serious?"

I wince. I knew I shouldn't have brought them up. "Yeah. That...run in... you saw with me and Ethan? That's ... pretty standard."

She waves her hand around in the air dismissively. "I don't mean that. I mean they tried to bribe you not to do the show?"

Nodding, I run my hand through my hair.

"That's...so thoughtless."

A warm feeling spreads through my chest at her words. Despite that, I try to make a joke, starting to feel uncomfortable with the serious turn the night has taken. "It was a strong offer. Lots of zeroes."

"But not the point," she states and I nod in agreement. "Recognition."

She gets it.

Ash

Wow. No wonder Lucas had been so pissed off at the hospital. I'd be pissed, too, if virtual strangers tried to control my decisions without bothering to understand my motivations. And then to feel like they were keeping tabs on you more than supporting you....

I'd seen what loyalty and support meant to Lucas. He'd practically lived at the hospital with Jax. Logan and Macy were also there as often as they could be. The *Vanished* crew were family by choice, something that obviously meant a lot to all of them.

"What about you?"

I jolt at the change in topic. "What do you mean?"

"Why did you decide now was the right time to come back to Chicago?"

"I didn't, really. Funding kind of decided that for me."

"What do you mean?"

"Most of the clinics, those projects are funded through grants and donations. The fellowship I took was a three-year fellowship, so...." I shrug. "I'm back."

"Do you miss it?" he asks.

"Sometimes. But I sometimes missed Chicago when I was there, so it all evens out, I suppose."

I divide up the rest of the wine, feeling a pleasant warmth in my stomach from what we've already consumed.

"I'm actually hoping to raise more money so we can expand the work we do there. Abeni, the woman I worked under in Nigeria, she does amazing work, but they just don't have enough resources. And so many of the local staff have limited training. It costs money, and they'd have to leave where they're needed in order to get the training. I'd love to set up an exchange where doctors from there come here and work in the hospital. And some of our specialists go there to help with the more difficult cases and provide on the ground training. It'd be great experience for everyone and would supply a needed influx of doctors to these communities."

"That's amazing."

I shrug. "It's just an idea right now. But the Chief of Surgery likes it, which will help a lot. Now I just need to find some funders."

"Where were you based? When you were in Africa?"

"A few different places, actually. I was in Cameroon and Nigeria the longest."

"What was it like?"

I smile softly, remembering. "Overwhelming at first. Sad. Inspiring. Chaotic. Quiet. I loved it most the time, hated it once in a while."

I tell him about Abeni, a fantastic mentor to me. How inspiring it was to see her do so much with so little with such passion and strategy. Her strength and conviction. Some of the more challenging cases. Some of the scary days. The joy you can find there.

He asks more questions and really listens to my answers. Next thing I know, it's nearly one in the morning, and I'm yawning in the middle of a story.

"I should probably get going." Lucas stands, pulling me to my feet and into his arms.

Disappointment and a tiny bit of insecurity hits me at his words.

"You're leaving?" I rub my cheek against his soft t-shirt, hiding my face in his chest. "I thought maybe... you'd want to stay."

His arms tighten around me, pressing me closer. I shiver feeling him nuzzle the sensitive spot between my neck and shoulder.

"I do. I do want to."

I pull back just far enough to peer into his face.

"So?" I smile expectantly.

He won't quite meet my eyes, his expression conflicted.

"Lucas?" Uncertain now, I step back out of his hold. "Is something wrong?

He sighs roughly, jamming a hand through his hair, face inscrutable, and takes a few steps away.

"What? What is it?"

"I don't want this to be a one-off."

"A what?"

"A one-off. A one and done. I got the feeling that first night with Gabby, she was suggesting you hook up with me to scratch an itch, you know? A one-night stand."

My stomach sinks, mortified. "You heard all that?"

He shrugs. "Some."

Oh my god. I have no idea what to say. That was weeks ago. I'd known him for two hours then. So much had happened since that first meeting, I'm shocked he would think that's all this would be.

"So yeah," he continues. "I want to stay, but I don't want this to just be a one-off. If that's all you want, if that's all you're ready for then I should probably go."

I can tell my face is flaming. "Lucas, I - that's not what I want. Even then." I gesture helplessly. "I'm not really a one-night stand kind of girl."

He nods as if he knew that. "But I'm not the type of guy you're normally with. Right?"

I cock my head, studying him. "Am I *your* usual type?"

Grimacing, he confesses, "I don't really have a type."

"Oh." I'm a little insulted.

"Oh?" He sounds a little defensive.

I scrunch my nose up in distaste. "Man-whore?" I'm really hoping that's not the case. But I suspect it is. I knew even that first night I wouldn't be unique in Lucas Abbott's world. That doesn't mean it's not disappointing.

Lucas is shifting uncomfortably under my gaze. "Maybe. But that's not what this is. I mean-"

"I'm special?" I cut him off, the sarcasm in my voice obvious.

"Shit," he mutters, looking up at the ceiling. But then he looks directly at me, his blue eyes intense and molten. "Yeah. You are." He pauses. "I really like you, Ash."

Suddenly I can't breathe. Because I believe him. And it occurs to me that saying yes to this, whatever this is, is probably more than I can handle. In the past, I've avoided this flip in my stomach. I stayed away from the men who could turn me on with a look. Has anyone ever made me want like Lucas? No one had ever made me come like he had this afternoon.

And no one had ever looked at me the way he was right now.

"I like you too," I hear myself whisper.

"Yeah?"

The smile on his face... *damn.* This man is so beautiful. Each interaction we have convinces me more it's not just on the surface.

I nod, returning his grin.

"How 'bout you come over here?"

"Since you asked so nicely." I giggle and move to stand just a breath away. I tilt my head up, meeting his eyes. Waiting.

He slips his arms around my waist and lifts me off my feet, pressing me tightly against him. A surprised squeak escapes before I can stop it, and I wrap my arms around his neck, holding on. I can feel every inch of his hard frame against my softer curves and I love it.

"I like you a lot," he whispers into my neck, his warm breath causing shivers to dance down my spine.

And then he's kissing me and I'm desperate to get closer to him, but we're already wrapped tightly around each other and he's in no hurry.

God, he's a good kisser.

Chapter Eleven

Lucas

"Hey, there he is." Jax looks pointedly at the clock as I walk into his hospital room. Hopefully, for the last time. "Running a little late this morning? Wonder why that is.... Late night maybe?" He smirks at me.

I roll my eyes. "Macy's got a big mouth," I muttered. But I can't help the smile that's been plastered on my face all morning.

"Finally got to spend some time with the hot doctor outside the hospital, huh?"

"Her name is Ash."

Jax is loving this, I can tell by the wicked gleam in his eyes. "I know her name."

I had managed to pry myself away and go home last night. The amount of willpower that took was insane, but I meant it when I told her I wanted more than just one night. So after a few more kisses, well, after thirty more minutes of kissing, I said good night.

And alternated patting myself on the back and kicking my ass the entire trip home.

"You going to see her again?"

"Hell, yes."

He nods knowingly, still with that smirk on his face. "Well, at least me getting shot worked out for *you*."

I laugh. "You ready to get the hell out of here?"

"Hell yes," he repeats back to me.

"It's Eviction Day!" Logan shouts, entering the room, hands in the air.

Jax rolls his eyes at her making me laugh at both of them.

Tanya is right behind her, carrying a large vase of flowers. She crosses the room and sets them on the table by the windows. "'Congratulations, You're Getting Out of Here' flowers," she explains with a shrug.

Raising his chin in thanks, Jax asks, "Where's Mace?"

"He's getting his spare room set up for you." Macy is the only one of us that has a place that won't require Jax to use stairs for the next couple of weeks while his leg heals. He's pissed he's not going home, pissed he needs help, pissed he's still in pain. Macy is probably the best one to deal with him in that mood anyway. "And he's getting stuff together for the barbecue tomorrow."

Tanya suggested we do something to celebrate his release, and Mace is always up for manning the grill. I insisted we keep it small, knowing Jax isn't going to want anyone else to see him until he's back on both his feet. So it's just going to be us. Although I'm hoping Ash will want to come.

Just then, Ash walks in and her eyes meet mine. She smiles shyly, her cheeks going a little pink. I fucking love it. I grin at her and wink. Her blush deepens, and she ducks her head, turning to Jax.

He's got that annoying, knowing smirk back on his face.

"Dr. Ash! How was your night last night? Did you get a lot of rest? You've been working hard."

I can tell she tries to keep a straight face, but Jax's over-the-top greeting, not at all subtle, makes her laugh. I'm still wearing that same stupid grin.

Logan is looking from Ash to me and back again, a scowl on her face. "Seriously?"

I shoot her a look. "Mind your business."

She rolls her eyes but doesn't say another word.

Ash checks Jax's blood pressure, his pupils, his stitches.

"Have you got your physical therapy scheduled?" she asks, poking gently at his leg wound.

"Yeah," Jax mutters. "That guy's a sadistic bastard."

She laughs at him. "He's a good doctor. He'll get you back to one hundred percent in no time." She straightens and places a hand on his shoulder. "You should never like your PT doctor. It means they aren't working you hard enough."

"If you say so. He doesn't have to enjoy it so much, though."

She laughs again.

"One of the nurses will come in and take you for some last minute tests. Just to make sure everything is still looking good. And then we'll get you out of here."

"'Bout time."

Smiling, she looks up, and her eyes find me again. "I'll see you later."

It encompasses all of us, but I sense she's asking me. I nod.

She most definitely will.

Jax is wheeled away, and the rest of us scatter. I need to get some food or I'm going to pass out. Logan needs a caffeine fix, and Tanya is on her phone, as usual. I grab something quick in the cafeteria and scarf it down, not sure how long Jax will be gone and not wanting to keep him here any longer than necessary. In less than thirty minutes, I'm hurrying back.

I jerk to a stop just inside his room. It's currently empty, but it looks like a bomb went off. The flowers from this morning are strewn across the floor in a puddle of water and shattered glass. All the cards he's gotten have been ripped or crumpled, and they litter the bed and floor like sad chunks of confetti. What the hell?

I back away and stride over to the nurse's station.

"Where is Jackson Hall?"

One of the nursing staff glances up, a pleasant smile on her face that does nothing to calm the edges off my anger and fear.

"He's still upstairs. He shouldn't be much longer."

Well, that's good, at least.

"Who went into his room? It's been torn apart."

Her smile twists into a frown. "What do you mean?"

"Someone destroyed all his shit." I'm making a conscious effort to keep my voice somewhat calm.

She comes around the desk in order to see for herself. I follow her down the hall.

"Oh my word," she gasps. She turns back to me, her face alarmed. "I'll call security." She scurries away.

Logan appears at my side, two coffees in hand. I spot Tanya coming down the hall over her shoulder.

"What the hell happened?" Logan asks, spotting the mess through the doorway.

"I don't know. I came back and found it like this."

"Shit."

Tanya stops beside Logan and looks up at me, a smile on her face. "I just talked to Kristin. We've got some great ideas -" she stops when she realizes the tension coming off us.

"What's the matter?"

I nod at the open door, and she peeks around me to see inside. Her eyes are wide when she turns back to us.

"Is Jax okay? Has he seen this?"

"No. He's still getting looked at."

"Where the hell was security?" Logan demands.

Good point. I frown. Where was security? I've gotten so used to their silent presence I didn't even notice the lack of it today.

"I - I canceled it," Tanya admits in a whisper. Tears spring to her eyes. "I just figured with all of us here and Jax leaving today...."

Well, that explains that.

"It's not your fault," I tell her.

The nurse I spoke with returns. "Security will be here in a minute. In the meantime, I called up and let them know to find Jax a room on the third floor. We can do all his release paperwork there, so he won't need to come back and see this."

I murmur thanks. She shuts the door to his room and ushers all of us to the waiting room once again, this time to wait for security.

Ash

I can tell something is going on by the hushed whispers of the nursing staff all around me but I refuse to get distracted. I'm trying to finish my charts so I can get out of here at a reasonable hour.

Gabby comes rushing up to me. "Oh my god. I just heard. Have you talked to Lucas? What happened?"

My stomach drops. Has something happened to Lucas? Charts forgotten I stand up. "What are you talking about? What happened?"

She blinks. "Oh no. I was just talking to Cleo upstairs, and she said security was called to Jax's room for some kind of disturbance. I guess there was some vandalism or something."

"What? That's insane. How...?"

Shaking her head, she says, "I don't know. Cleo just heard because they needed to find him another room."

"Crap," I glance at the pile of work I still need to complete.

"Do you want me to go check on them?"

"No, I just need a minute, and then I can go. Unless you want to come with."

She nods. I finish the patient file I was in the middle of and wait on the rest. And then we go to find Lucas and the others.

The door to Jax's room is closed when we pass, but I peek in the window and see the mess left behind. *Holy shit.* I hurry down the hall to the waiting area, Gabby close behind. We open the door and find the *Vanished* crew, minus Jax and Macy, as well as one of the nurses and two security guards. One of the guards is speaking with Tanya, serious expressions on each of their faces. Lucas is leaning against the wall off to the side, arms crossed across his chest.

"Hey," I rush over to Lucas. "What happened? Is everybody okay?"

He gives me a small smile. His hair is messed up like it gets when he's been running his hands through it. Like he does when he's uncomfortable or worried. I'm learning these little things about him.

"Yeah. Pissed off and confused, but physically we're all fine." Despite his answer, he doesn't seem pissed off, showing none of the rage he did the other day with Ethan. It reassures me I was right to give us another chance.

"What happened?" I repeat.

He shrugs. "When Jax went for tests, we all took off. I went to get food, Logan went for coffee, Tanya had to make a call. I got back to the room first and it was totally trashed."

I place a hand on his arms, squeezing gently. "I'm sorry."

He glances over his shoulder at the others, but no one is paying us any attention. He leans down and gives me a quick kiss.

"Thanks for checking in on us."

"Of course. Can I do anything?"

His voice lowers sexily, and he leans in. "I can think of several things that would make me feel better, but most of them would get us arrested if we did them here."

I shove his shoulder away playfully. "I'm serious," I protest, but I'm smiling. And now I'm imagining what some of those things might be.

He groans. "Those pink cheeks kill me."

I feel my blush deepen.

"I can't believe this. I've never heard of something like this happening." I hear Gabby murmur to the others. I squeeze Lucas's bicep, partly to show support, partly because...any excuse to touch him, and we move to join the others.

"Are you contacting the police?" I ask one of the security guards.

"Is that necessary?" Tanya asks. "That's public record. The press...."

Logan snorts. "Screw them."

"Yeah, well, it's not exactly that easy," Tanya hedges.

"Whatever, Tanya. It's your job to manage the press. Manage them. I say we call Melrose. This is bullshit. That," she waves her arm towards the now trashed hospital room, "isn't normal and I don't want whoever did it walking into our shop."

Lucas turns his eyes to me. "What do you think?"

I swallow nervously as everyone's attention is suddenly on me. I see Logan roll her eyes again. But I focus on Lucas, letting him calm me. "I think Logan is right. I would get the police involved."

He nods, considering my words.

"Lucas, the press will go insane if this gets out. Especially so soon after the shooting. I know you hate to be in the spotlight like this, and it will just prolong the frenzy. Not to mention the more time you are a story, the more someone is going to get curious, and those rumors will all resurface."

There's a flicker of anger across his face before he squelches it. I'm guessing she means rumors about his family and connections to the Abbotts. Without thinking, I slip my hand into his and squeeze reassuringly. I want him to know he has my support. He startles, his eyes sliding back to mine. "Does that matter as much as you all being safe?"

He takes a deep breath before turning to the security guards. "I'll be contacting Detective Melrose with CPD. He'll get in touch with you."

The senior guard nods and the two of them leave. Tanya immediately pulls out her phone and makes a call, crossing to an empty corner of the room. Logan watches me carefully, not quite glaring but definitely not with a friendly expression.

"We should probably get back to work," I say, including Gabby. "Text me if you need anything, okay? I'll call you when I get off tonight."

Despite the cloud in the room, a naughty smirk spreads across Lucas's face, and I can feel myself blushing when I realize what I inadvertently said. I shove him playfully. "You know what I mean."

He laughs. "I'll talk to you later. Thanks, Gabby."

She gives him a quick hug. Mine is a little less quick. But I manage to pull myself away and return to my files.

Chapter Twelve

Lucas

We manage to get Jax released from the hospital without any more problems. I have the shitty honor of telling him what happened to his room and why he wasn't taken back there. Typical Jax, he shrugs it off. That room was never his space, never someplace he wanted to be, so it feels less like an attack. But I still don't like it. Logan packed up any personal stuff that *wasn't* destroyed. And Tanya's been on the phone 'strategizing'. As promised, Ash called when she got off work to check-in. I was having a beer with Jax and Macy, so didn't get to see her last night. But I did manage to get her to agree to come to the barbecue this afternoon.

Melrose sounded annoyed when I called him about someone trashing Jax's room but promised he'd 'look into it.' Whatever that means. Hopefully, the hospital has security tapes. Maybe he can get something off them. I'm not holding my breath.

"Incoming!" Mace yells and tosses me a bag of hamburger buns. I snatch them easily and add them to the insane amount of food on the picnic table. Macy has a great old house with a fenced-in backyard. His dad's family has lived in Chicago for generations, and while most of his relatives live in the Pilsen neighborhood, he bought this house on the edge of Bucktown from one of his uncles a few years ago. He got a massive family discount.

I check the time. Jax sees me and smirks. He loves this.

I'd offered to pick Ash up, but she insisted on meeting me here. She was teaching a self-defense class this morning and will have to leave relatively early this afternoon. She and the other bridesmaids have organized a mini 're-do' of Gabby's Bachelorette and are going out dancing tonight. And 'other stuff', whatever that means.

I pretend to ignore Jax and grab a beer from the cooler. "Anybody need anything?"

"I'll have a 312," Logan calls out her favorite. I root around the cooler for a minute before successfully pulling one out. Jax requests an IPA and Tanya asks for the same. Macy lifts his beer in my direction, indicating he's good for now.

My phone buzzes in my pocket, and I grab it, finding a text from Ash.

I'm here. I think.

We're in the back. Go around to the right - I'll meet you.

Shit. I'm actually nervous. This is different than when it was just the two of us. These are the most important people in my life. What if Ash doesn't like them? What if they don't like her? What if she thinks I'm different with them and not in a good way?

I'm so wrapped up in my ridiculous teenager with a crush thoughts Ash's sudden appearance startles me.

"Hi." She smiles, and immediately, I feel calmer. She hesitates for a second and then leans in to give me a quick hug. I squeeze her tight for a second when she starts to pull away before releasing her. I want her to know she can hug me anytime she wants.

"Find us okay?"

She nods and brushes a stray piece of hair behind her ear. "No problem." She's wearing a long flowing summer dress. It's dark blue and strapless, the elastic around her breasts holding it up. Which means she's either not wearing a bra or is wearing one of those strapless ones. My cock really likes this train of thought, and I have to quickly shut him down. I will not be finding out what her underwear looks like tonight. She holds up a container. "I brought my famous brownies and some peanut butter, chocolate rice krispie treats."

I take it from her hands. "You didn't have to do that."

Ash shrugs, her cheeks get pink, and I feel a tiny kick in my chest.

Juggling the treats, I place a hand low on her back and guide her the rest of the way.

"Hey, Doc!" Jax calls out.

She lifts her hands and wiggles her fingers in a little wave, then she grabs a seat at the picnic table with everyone else.

Mace is quick to offer her a drink and lists off all the options.

"Um. I'll have a 312. Thanks." She smiles as he sets a beer down in front of her.

"Time for grillin'!" Mace grabs a set of tongs and snaps them in the air around him.

"Do you need any help?" she offers.

"Ash," Mace looks at her gravely and explains, "You've never attended one of my little soirees, so I will forgive you this time. Grillin' is what I do. Stay seated."

I shrug and inform her, "It's his thing. We let him have it."

Her laugh is light and fills the space around us. "Got it."

"Whobroughtthemarshmallowtreats?" Jax asks around a mouthful of... marshmallow treats.

"Ash did. And some brownies."

"Gimmee!" Jax yells, snatching the desserts from Tanya's hands.

Logan rolls her eyes and throws a chip at him. "Please don't forget to chew. I'm not visiting you in the hospital if you get there because you're stupid."

Taking the time to swallow this time, Jax argues, "That's not true, Logan. You love me. You know you do."

She sighs. "Once in a while."

Ash is laughing and turns to me, her eyes shining. I slide a little closer to her on the picnic bench, feeling relaxed for the first time in weeks. Maybe longer.

It's an awesome afternoon.

Ash

I think Logan hates me.

She's tough to read, though, so I'm really not sure.

I'm pretty sure.

Everyone else has gone out of their way to make me feel welcome. Although Jax seems to take a lot of pleasure in giving Lucas a hard time about 'his special guest'. But Lucas seems to be taking it in stride, which I appreciate. I like Lucas's friends. I like their dynamic. They're relaxed and at ease with each other, with lots of good-natured jabs and laughs. It's nice seeing them like this after so many weeks seeing them tired and worried. Jax coming home is something they all needed to celebrate, and I'm glad I was able to join.

I check my watch and realize I need to head out if I'm going to make it on time to meet Gabby and the others. Reluctantly I stand to say my goodbyes.

"Time to go?" Lucas asks, his smile fading a tiny bit. I nod.

"I'll walk you out." Lucas stands and waits while I hug Jax goodbye and wave to all the others.

We walk slowly to the front of the house and pause on the sidewalk.

"You okay from here?" he asks me.

"Of course. The 'el' is only two blocks from here. I'm good."

"I can walk you."

"No, I'm fine. Stay with your friends."

"Thanks for coming. I know it was short notice."

"I had a lot of fun." Silence falls between us as we stand facing each other. "So," I'm not sure why I'm so nervous. He likes me. That's obvious, right? He just asked me to spend the day with his closest friends. That has to mean something.

He cups my shoulders and runs his hands lightly up and down my arms, distracting me. That's nice. The small, tender smile on his face also doesn't help my concentration. I'm getting lost in those dark blue eyes.

"Mmmhmm?" his slight sound shakes me out of my haze.

"Gabby's wedding is next week."

His face shutters, going blank. Nerves are back.

"Right." His voice is equally flat, revealing nothing.

"I, um, was wondering if you would want to go with me," I say in a rush before I can lose my courage. "It's okay if you're busy. And I know weddings can be intense, but Gabby would love to have you and I...."

His eyes are starting to twinkle a bit, reassuring me a little. "And you would like to have me too?" he asks, a teasing grin on his face.

I smack him gently on the chest, leaving my hand covering his heart. He pulls me closer, lacing his hands behind my waist, and places a quick kiss on my nose. I wrinkle it after, really wishing he had kissed me somewhere else.

"You want me to be your date? To Gabby's wedding?" he clarifies. I nod.

"Sounds great. I'm in."

My wide smile almost makes my cheeks hurt. I stretch up and place a quick kiss against his lips. As I pull away, he makes a sound of protest and tightens his arms around me, kissing me thoroughly. I wind my arms around his neck, pressing closer. His kiss is slow but intense, like him. I feel the tip of his tongue trace the seam of my lips and I part them without hesitation, inviting further intimacy. In the back of my mind, I know this isn't really the time to get carried away. Half a dozen of his friends and coworkers are just a couple yards away in the backyard. Not to mention we're on a public sidewalk. He seems to recognize this at the same time and reluctantly ends the kiss. Kisses.

"You have to go." I'm unsure if he's reminding me or himself, but he's right. I need to leave.

Which kind of sucks. Even though I'm excited about a night with Gabby and the girls.

Lucas is a different kind of exciting.

"I do." I agree, although neither of us moves.

He groans and buries his lips against my neck. I'm quickly discovering I love it when he does that, sending little shivers down my spine.

Abruptly he releases me and steps away.

He shoves his hands in his pockets. To keep from touching me? I like to think that might be the case. That he has shaky self-control around me.

"Have fun tonight."

"Thanks."

"Strippers?" he asks, eyebrows raised. I think he's kidding. But I also think I see a slight frown on his face.

"I don't think so?"

"You don't think so, huh?"

"I'm not kept fully in the loop on things they want to keep from Gabby."

He smiles at that.

"Have fun."

"You said that already," I tease, smiling.

"I guess I did." His eyes darken as he watches me and my stomach flips. That look can make me forget all my responsibilities and inhibitions. That is a dangerous look.

"You have to go." But he steps closer, closing the distance between us.

"You said that already, too," I whisper, looking up and getting lost in those blue eyes again.

He cups my face and gives me another slow, sexy kiss. I feel the heat of his palm on the small of my back. As he finishes the kiss and slowly pulls away, I swear I feel his hand lightly skim down my side and graze my butt.

Shit, my knees are jelly. He jellied my knees.

"I'll talk to you tomorrow?"

I nod, still dazed. His grin is cocky now, seeing the effect he has on me.

Feeling oddly uncoordinated I start down the street.

"Have fun!" he calls again, laughter in his voice.

Lucas

I watch Ash walk down the sidewalk for a few minutes and then return to the backyard.

Jax and Macy start whooping and cheering and heckling as soon as I turn the corner behind the house.

"Shut up, you assholes," I mutter, fighting the smile on my face. I snag an empty seat next to Logan and grab my beer, taking a swig.

They burst into laughter but are quickly distracted. Thankfully, Macy's parents stop by to see Jax. He's the only one of us that has a solid family unit. Logan has a decent relationship with her parents, but they're down in Arizona and rarely get back here. But Macy grew up in Chicago, and his folks still live in the house where he and his siblings grew up. It took me a while, but eventually I got comfortable with how they seemed to take us all in. They cluck over us like actual parents. It's equal parts bewildering and endearing.

I make eye contact with Jax across the table and see him watching me steadily. He nods, acknowledging me. He knows me better than anyone. Can probably see right through me and knows how gone I am with this woman. I tip my bottle in a wordless toast that he returns.

Fuck, I'm glad he's home.

Tanya appears at his side with a slice of this chocolate pie that Mace's mom makes that's freaking delicious. She's been all up in Jax's business all day. Maybe Mace is right, and she does have a thing for Jax. I frown, wondering if I should talk to him about that. Hooking up with our PR rep seems like a particularly bad idea.

Logan plops down next to me with a slice of pie for each of us, startling me from my thoughts.

"Thanks."

She shrugs. "No problem."

I shove a giant bite of the creamy chocolate and coconut goodness into my mouth, making a humming sound of approval. Freaking delicious.

After I swallow, I turn to Logan. "You want to lay off of this one?"

She turns to me with a wide-eyed, fake innocent look. But I'm on to her. She was particularly brutal this afternoon. I'm borderline pissed, but I know Logan.

Despite her bitchy tongue she's got a good heart. She's just picky about who she lets see it.

"Don't deny it," I shut her down. "You could be nicer to Ash."

Sighing, she looks down at her fork and plays with her slice of pie. "You sure this is a good idea?"

"She's different than the others. She's never even seen the show." I'm referring to all the women constantly throwing themselves at Jax, Macy, and me since the show started. We're not saints and sex is fun. We've taken more than our share of them up on what they've offered. But it's always clear what it is. It's just a hook-up. Nothing real or long-term. And Logan isn't exactly celibate. She gets hit on regularly, and I've seen her take dudes home more than once. Although she's also got some long-term, on-again-off-again thing with some douche she's known forever. It seems pretty casual, mostly because he's never around. He blows in and out of town whenever the whim strikes and expects Logan to just be available. Which she always is. I don't like it, but she seems okay with it, so I try to mind my business.

"It's not just that, Luke. She's a doctor. You know how much school that takes? She's lived in multiple countries, and you've only left the US what, once? And her best friend is from a family that can afford to rent out *Vanished* for a private party."

She's right. We charge a shit load for that.

I'm silent as I take in her words. When it's me and Ash, it's easy. Those differences don't seem to matter. But would they long term?

Because I think I might want long term with her.

"I just don't want you to get hurt. What if this is just some fun fling for her, and a few months from now, she's back dating doctors and shit?"

I get her concern. Just now, when Ash mentioned Gabby's wedding, I was expecting her to explain she already had a date or why she couldn't take me. The relief and surprise I felt when she asked me to go with her....

I wrap her in a fake choke hold and mess up her hair. The fact that she hardly protests is a good indication of how worried she actually is about me.

"I've got this. If she dumps me for some doctor, you can be as mean as you want, okay? But until that happens, give her a chance."

She raises an eyebrow as she meets my eyes. "Oh, like you give Bodhi a chance?"

Bodhi's the disappearing and reappearing douche.

"I don't like how he comes and goes whenever he wants," I admit. "You never even know when he's going to show up."

Logan is uncharacteristically soft when she replies. "I know it looks bad. Maybe someday I'll explain it. But Bodhi is doing exactly what we both need him to be doing right now."

Logan has her own shit she's dealing with, I know that. She hasn't shared much, but it's pretty obvious when you spend a lot of time with her. This might be the most vulnerable I've ever seen her.

"Okay. Fair. I promise you lay off Ash, and I'll invite Bodhi for a beer next time he's in town. Deal?"

"Fine. But if she breaks your heart, I'll kick her ass back to Africa." And she's back to normal.

"Whose ass are we kicking?" Macy asks, interrupting.

"Your's if you ate the last piece of pie," Logan snipes. But she's grinning.

Hours later, I'm sprawled on my couch, flipping through shows. After the last few days, I'm too keyed up to sleep, but I'm not interested in anything I'm finding on the screen. My phone beeps and I grab it off the cushion next to me. It's later than I thought, nearly one in the morning. I shift into a slouching seated position when I see Ash's name appear. Stupidly eager, I open her text.

Texts. She's sent two back-to-back.

The strippers weren't nearly as hot as you.

You're a really good kisser.

I grin and type my reply.

I'm glad you think so. :) I really like kissing you.

I shoud have kissssed you more this afterNonAnd done over things.

This is interesting. We haven't done a ton of texting, but enough for me to know she's a pretty deliberate texter. She doesn't use any of the shortened words or tons of emojis. She even tends to use correct punctuation. I suspect she and the others have been downing a few cocktails.

You a little drunk, beautiful?

Those three little dots appear so I know she's responding.

Maybe little...Raquel ordered ussshots.

While I'm thoroughly entertained by a tipsy Ash, I'm also a little concerned there's no one sober with them.

You all have a ride home right?

Betcha. Gabs = limo.

Damn. She's a mess. Despite my concern, I can't help but laugh.

Will you text me when you get home?

U cold come over...ifyowant.

That's tempting. Not because I want to fuck her, I mean, I do, obviously, but not tonight and not when she's clearly drunk off her ass. I'm not a total asshole. Or a criminal. But it would be nice to go to bed knowing she's safe. Although she's with Gabby, they'll go home together. I'm overreacting. I'm not used to feeling protective, but that's definitely the feeling I'm having right now. It's new and I'm not sure I'm handling it well.

I press call.

When it connects, I hear weird knocking sounds and something like fabric rustling. Then I pick up a muffled voice I don't recognize speaking in the background.

"...I will...yes...Raquel, get in the car, please!"

"Hello?" a voice finally speaks into the phone.

"Who is this?"

"This is Cami, one of Gabby's sisters. Luke?"

"Yeah, is Ash okay?"

"Well, she's drunk, but so is everyone else. I'm attempting to herd everyone into the limo."

"You guys are okay? I can come meet you if you need me to."

"That's very nice - Raquel, please get in the car! - but the limo driver is dropping everyone at home, and I'm staying with Gabby and Ash, so I think we're all set. Thanks, though. Really."

"Okay, if you're sure you've got it."

I listen as she talks to the driver, giving him an address.

"We're all accounted for," she assures me.

"Can I talk to Ash?"

"Sorry. She passed out mid text. I'll have her call you tomorrow, though."

"Okay, thanks, Cami. Can you do me a favor?"

"Sure."

"Just... text me when you all get home okay?"

"Oh my god, you're sweet. Of course."

I hang up, not at all sure about how I feel being called 'sweet'. Probably it's a good thing if her friends think that? I just hope Jax and Macy never hear about it.

It's nearly an hour later after I've moved from the couch to my bed, I get Cami's text.

She's sent a picture of Ash safe and sound under a pile of blankets, so only her face and dark hair are visible. She's sound asleep, her lips slightly parted.

I feel a tiny kick in my chest. She's so beautiful.

Home safe. Good night. <3 Cami

I go to sleep smiling.

Chapter Thirteen

Ash

My head hurts. My mouth feels grainy it's so dry. I try to swallow but it doesn't seem to do much good. Reluctantly I open my eyes, blinking against the late morning sunlight. I don't really want to get up. But my bladder is aggressively protesting, and I do want some water. Ugh. I shut my eyes again, two conflicting desires battling it out. Those shots were a bad idea.

Shots are always a bad idea. I know that. I've learned that, like most people, the hard way.

Ultimately my bladder wins the debate, and I slowly roll myself out of bed and head toward the bathroom.

After taking care of business and splashing some water on my face, I fumble towards the kitchen and, hopefully, some coffee. I find Tim and Cami singing loudly off-key as they make breakfast together. Gabby is sitting at the table, head in hands, staring into her mug.

"Good morning, Ash!" Tim bellows. I wince and manage to pour myself a cup of coffee.

"You are inappropriately chipper this morning," I mumble and flop into a chair next to Gabby.

Without looking up, Gabby tells me, "They are cruel and I hate them."

Cami twirls over to us and places an omelet in front of her sister.

"I take it all back. You are an angel and I love you." Gabby picks up a fork and takes a bite.

"Ash? Omelet?"

I nod. "Please." Closing my eyes, I rest my chin on my hand and pray for the caffeine to kick in.

"So, Ash, you and Lucas are getting kind of serious, huh?" Cami asks over her shoulder, working at the stove.

My eyes spring open. "What? No. I mean, we've only gone out a couple of times." Serious? It's way too soon for that, right?

"Really? He seemed pretty concerned last night."

Who needs caffeine when Cami keeps dropping these bombs?

"What do you mean?"

"He called when I was getting all of you drunkards into the limo."

"He did?"

She nods and continues, "You passed out mid text, and next thing I know, your phone is on the floor ringing with a call from Lucas Abbott."

Oh shit. I squeeze my eyes closed. I don't remember texting. "Oh, no," I groan.

Omelet finished, Cami sets my own plate in front of me and joins us at the table. "He asked if you were okay and offered to come meet us if we needed him to. And then he asked me to text him when we all got home safe, which I thought was really sweet."

"You were sexting with Lucas from the limo?" Gabby asks.

"No!"

I wasn't, was I? Oh my god, that would be so embarrassing. I look at Gabby, sure my face reflects all the panic I'm feeling at the moment. Faster than I would have believed possible just five minutes ago, I bolt for the guest room and find my phone. I cringe inwardly, reading my messages from the night before. They aren't too bad. I guess. I mean, they're only a little bad.

Oh, this is so not good.

Slowly I return to the kitchen table.

"I texted Lucas last night."

Gabby and Cami exchange a look, their expressions a mix of concerned and amused.

"And?"

"I was pretty drunk."

Gabby holds out her hand, "Let me see." She scans my texts from the night before and giggles. "These aren't bad. Relax. You're cute. And he seems to be into it."

I groan, collapsing into my chair. Cami takes the phone so she can see for herself.

"Oh, please. This is nothing," she dismisses and hands me my cell.

"Really?"

"Seriously. Nothing. Text him good morning; you'll see."

I hesitate and Gabby nudges her fiancé. "Tim? Let's get a guy's perspective."

Tim doesn't even look up from his plate of food. "Nope. Not going anywhere near that."

I groan again.

"Seriously, Ash. It's not that bad."

Okay, suck it up. This isn't a big deal. You got a little drunk and you sent him a couple sloppy texts.

"You're right. I'll just tell him I'm sorry." Before I can lose my nerve, I fire off yet another text.

Morning. Sorry about last night.

I put the phone, screen facing down, next to my breakfast, and try to ignore the fact that I desperately want a response. I force myself to finish eating before checking for a reply.

You really need to stop apologizing for doing things I enjoy.

I can't help the grin that breaks across my face any more than I can the blush I feel staining my cheeks.

"See? Told you he was into it," Cami says smugly. I make a face at her and put my phone away. She sighs dreamily. "I can't believe you're dating Lucas Abbott."

"Okay, let's not get carried away. We're just getting to know each other."

Gabby and Cami roll their eyes at the same time and Gabby says, "Whatever. He likes you."

"I'm just glad I didn't say or do anything too stupid last night. No more shots for me."

Cami snorts. "Stay away from Raquel." And all of us laugh.

"I wonder how she's feeling this morning."

"Probably better than you two. She's at least used to it."

Tim stands, clearing the table. He stops to give Gabby a quick kiss. "Even when you're a mess, I love you," he tells her.

"I can't wait to marry you next week," Gabby says.

Cami and I exchange a look. "And on that note, I'm out of here."

"I should take a shower and get ready," I say, jumping up.

And we leave the love birds to their over-dirty-dishes-flirting.

Lucas

Morning. Sorry about last night.

I grin. Bet she's feeling rough this morning. But I don't want her to feel embarrassed about being less than perfect around me. I like her messy, silly, loose sides too.

I shoot off my reply.

You really need to stop apologizing for doing things I enjoy.

Usually, I take Sundays off, but I'm still trying to catch up on appointments I canceled or had to reschedule while Jax was in the hospital. He decided to come in with me and hang out for a bit. I figured it's probably a good idea for him to get back in here as soon as possible. Find out how he's going to react to being back where he was shot. And Mateo is coming in today so I can show him around when it's not very busy. Probably good for them to meet face to face again without much of an audience.

"Must be Doc. You only get that dopey look on your face when she's around."

"Fuck you." But I'm grinning as I say it, so I don't think it carries much weight.

"You're pretty into her, huh?"

I shrug, shove my phone back in my pocket and head back to finish setting up my station.

"You can't run from me, asshole," he yells at me from the couch in the lobby. Except right now, I can totally run away from him. He's recovering well but needs to use crutches to get around. Which he bitches about on a regular basis.

"Luke! They're here!" I hear Jax shout. Assuming he means Olivia and Mateo, I head back to the front.

Olivia walks in the door, Mateo following behind her. It's weird. Being here with Mateo and Jax. And if it's weird for me, I can only imagine how uncomfortable it is for them.

"Hey, Olivia. Mateo." I try to break the ice.

He nods behind her, looking down and shuffling his feet nervously.

Jax is still seated on the couch. He tries to lean forward but winces when his leg protests.

Olivia turns to the side and places a hand on Mateo's shoulder in a show of support. "Thank you both for agreeing to this." Mateo nods his agreement, still studying the floor.

I look at Jax. He's studying Mateo carefully. "You Mateo?" he calls out. Another nod, but he looks up briefly at Jax. "I got your letter." That gets him to look up again. "You mean what you wrote?"

"Yes, sir." His voice is surprisingly strong, considering his obvious nerves.

"I heard your mom took off a few months ago."

"Yeah." Now Mateo is watching him with a suspicious look in his eyes.

Jax nods. "My mom used to do that shit too."

"Yeah?"

"Yeah. No excuse for that shit you pulled, though."

Mateo nods again and shrugs. He looks at Olivia nervously, then back to the floor.

"You mess with guns again, you're out, got it? Or drugs."

"Yes, sir." This time when he looks up, there's a tiny bit of hope in his eyes.

Jax settles back into the couch. "Luke will show you around."

Well, that went as well as it could.

Mateo and Olivia stayed a couple hours. I showed him around, discussed his 'job'. For now, he's mainly doing cleanup. Eventually, we'll likely train him to answer the phones and schedule appointments, but we'll see how it goes for a while. He seemed to relax a little after Jax's talk. He'll be here two afternoons a week after school and for a few hours on Saturdays unless he has a track meet. When my first appointment arrived, they left and gave Jax a ride back to Macy's. I texted Mace to check in and see how Jax was doing with everything but haven't heard back from either of them.

Four hours later and I'm ready to head home. My phone buzzes.

Melrose cell.

Christ, I hope this is anything but bad news. I press accept.

"Yeah."

"Thought you'd want to know, I was able to get security tapes from the hospital."

That was pretty fast. I'm surprised but relieved to know he did actually follow up. "And? Anything?"

"The entrance to Jax's room is in a blind spot, of course. But we do have a clear shot of the hallway. I'm going to go back through and review them more closely, but at first glance, there doesn't appear to be anyone that doesn't have a legitimate reason to be there. Most of the people are hospital staff. Some visitors, of course, but they seem to be going to specific rooms. I'm compiling photos and going to talk to the nurses on the floor; see if there's anyone they can't ID."

"And if they can't?"

"Then we have to consider that whoever did it was in the hospital."

"You mean someone working at the hospital."

"Or someone actually visiting another patient on the floor. Did you ever interact with any other visitors?"

"No. We were either in Jax's room or in that private waiting room. I mean, we were around, vending machines, the cafeteria, whatever, but I never had anyone bother me. I'll ask Logan and Macy, but neither has mentioned anything like that."

"Okay, ask them and let me know. I'll keep you posted."

"Thanks."

Melrose disconnects.

I text Logan and Mace right away, asking if either of them had any weird interactions with any staff, patients, or visitors at the hospital. While I wait for a response, I finish locking up and call Ash.

She picks up on the second ring.

"Hi." Her voice is a little sheepish like she's still embarrassed about last night.

"Hey. Feeling better?"

She laughs lightly. "Much. Thanks."

"That's good. So, what do I need to know about the wedding this weekend?"

"Oh, right." She goes quiet for a second, and I have a sinking feeling, worried she's changed her mind and doesn't want me to come after all. "I probably should have mentioned when I invited you the wedding is in Milwaukee."

I exhale roughly in relief. I can handle a trip to Milwaukee. It's only an hour and a half away. Easy.

"Gabby said a room was still available in the hotel block they reserved, so she put your name in. That way, you can check in without me. I'll need to be there earlier for maid of honor duties."

"Gotcha. So I'll meet you there?"

"If that works for you?"

That definitely works for me. We'll discuss the room situation when the time comes. I'm hoping one of our rooms will go mostly unused, but I'll leave that to Ash.

I mean, I'll try to be persuasive, but will follow her lead.

"That works for me. This isn't a black-tie kind of wedding, is it? I'll need to take care of that."

She laughs. "No. Luckily it's just a normal fancy wedding, not a ballgown fancy wedding. I'm sure some guys won't even be in suits."

"Good to know." I'm wearing a fucking suit. I'm going to look like I'm supposed to be on Ash's arm. Luckily, I have a couple from events around the show. Premieres and that kind of shit. "Can you text me the address and times and everything?"

"Yep. I... I'm really glad you can come." Her voice is soft and my chest does that weird tightening thing again.

"Me too. I'll talk to you tomorrow, okay?"

"Okay. Good night, Lucas."

"Night."

Ash

I'm embarrassed to admit it took most of Sunday for me to fully recover from the Bachelorette shenanigans. I swear, for the hundredth time, I will never again do shots. But by Monday morning, I'm feeling back to normal and ready to meet with the Chief of Surgery and the hospital's PR rep to discuss my ideas for expanding my fellowship and providing more medical support for refugee camps around the world. Gabby helped me practice over breakfast.

I'm ready.

That doesn't prevent me from being nervous as hell, but I'm as prepared as I can be.

I think.

I take a deep breath and enter the Chief's office.

My initial pitch goes well, just as Gabby and I rehearsed. My nerves are settling a bit. Now comes the hard part.

I already know the Chief likes my idea in theory, but theory is a long way from reality. Funding is going to be a huge hurdle. And her support isn't going to be enough. Public Relations, Legal, the Board of Directors, all of them are going to have to be on board if this has any chance of moving forward.

Jennifer Johnson, I don't know why it strikes me as so amusing that our PR rep has such an average name, closes the folder I've provided, and sits forward. "This is very ambitious. And I can see a need for a program like this but, forgive me for being blunt, what is in it for the hospital?"

I'm ready for this question. I launch into an explanation of how this will elevate us as a premier teaching hospital and trauma center in the Midwest. The additional training our doctors will receive in practical hands-on skills, not to mention increased experience working with different cultures and how that will benefit their ability to work with our community in Chicago, a diverse and multicultural city. When I'm done, she says nothing, just looks to the Chief.

"Thank you, Dr. Carrington. You've included a proposed budget in the materials?"

"Yes. Very rough, I'm afraid."

Chief Haywood nods. "Can you give us a minute, please?"

"Of course. Thank you." I stand, heart pounding. I hope I did enough. Outside the office, I pace restlessly, waiting. Thinking of all the other things I could have, *should* have said. The wait feels endless but the clock on the wall tells me it's been less than ten minutes.

The door opens, and Jennifer Johnson exits. She nods as she passes me but her expression reveals nothing. My stomach drops.

Damn.

The Chief pops her head out. "Come on in, Ash."

I sit down, trying desperately not to fidget and broadcast my nerves.

Sitting across from me, she folds her hands on her desk and smiles widely. "Well done. Ms. Johnson thinks this has multiple opportunities for the hospital to generate positive publicity and raise our profile. And I think it could help a lot of people. And help us train better doctors."

I smile in triumph.

"You're going to need funding. I think you're underestimating the costs, but we can meet with someone in accounting and budgeting to get more specific numbers. In the meantime, you need to start securing donors. The hospital is having a fundraiser in two weeks, and you should be there. Several of our current donors and other well-known philanthropists from the Chicago area will be there."

I nod.

"Plant some seeds. Set up some meetings. Getting a few large donors on board will go a long way to moving this forward and winning over the Board of Directors."

"Yes, Chief."

She stands and holds out her hand. "Well done, Dr. Carrington. I'm excited to see what we can do with this."

"Thank you. I am too."

I send a text to Abeni, celebrating and scheduling a time to go over everything with her. She's been on the ground for years, coordinating camps across northern Nigeria, and knows precisely what is most needed. She's excited about my idea but also skeptical. Too many disappointments over too many years. Too many promises broken.

But I am determined.

I don't get an immediate response, although I didn't expect to. Time zones and all.

Taking a deep breath, I allow an excited, triumphant smile to break across my face.

Holy shit. I did it.

Chapter Fourteen

Ash

L ucas is a fantastic wedding date.

I'd been worried he'd end up bored and mostly hanging out alone while I attended to my wedding party duties. Other than the girls from the Bachelorette, all of which are with me, he doesn't know anyone. If the situation were reversed, I'd probably hate it, lurking on the edges while putting on a smile. But Lucas has been amazing.

Gabby introduced Lucas as 'the man who saved my life,' and all her *Tias* have been fawning over him all night. Shoving cake into his hands, pinching his cheeks, I swear I saw one pat him on the butt. But he's handled it all in stride, even getting out on the dance floor for a rousing Chicken Dance surrounded by his gray-haired fan club. The groomsmen aren't much better, eager to discuss his show, celebrity, and tattoos. He promised the best man to help him with a cover-up - apparently, Darren once made a spring break 'mistake'. The bridesmaids are even more enamored of him now than they were at the Bachelorette but knowing he's here as my date keeps the flirting friendly and harmless.

Despite all the attention, Lucas makes sure I never feel ignored. He includes me in conversations, checks in frequently to make sure I have a fresh drink or just to touch me in some small way. His eyes find mine across the room often, communicating his amusement. He's friendly with everyone, including the women obviously flirting with him, but he never makes me uncomfortable. He never looks at any of them with the same heat in his blue eyes I'm lucky enough to experience.

It's easy for me to feel a bit awkward and end up on the fringes in large social situations like this, and usually, the guys I date either end up on the sidelines with me, obviously bored, or disappear into the crowd and find me at the end of the night. It's only now, seeing how seamlessly Lucas is able to engage with everyone while still making me a priority, I realize how lame and one-sided those past experiences have been. After dinner, when the majority of my Maid of Honor duties have been fulfilled, we spend most of the night on the dance floor. Dancing has always been an easy way for me to disguise my shyness. I can stay in the middle of the party without having to actually make any of the dreaded small talk, which I'm so bad at. The slow dances are particularly enjoyable. Lucas pulls me close, a naughty grin on his face, and spends most of each song whispering sexy compliments in my ear.

"You look fucking gorgeous in that dress."

"Thank you. You're looking pretty sexy in your fancy suit."

His eyebrows go up as he smiles at me. "Oh, yeah?"

I giggle at his expression. "Yeah." He does. He looks sexy as hell. He's wearing a navy suit with a crisp white shirt. He's skipped a tie, though, and glimpses of colorful tattoos peek out occasionally at his cuffs and the edges of his collar. His hair is brushed back from his forehead, and the ends also brush against his collar. I play with the hair at his nape, enjoying our bodies moving together to the music.

"Had to look good to be on the arm of the Maid of Honor, you know." He winks at me playfully.

I smile at his compliment. "I'm glad you came," I whisper.

"Me too."

He watches me with a calm look in his eyes I haven't seen often, and it warms me he's so comfortable here. I know the last month has been hard for him, for the whole *Vanished* crew, and I like that I can provide a distraction from all that. I like that he seems relaxed with me. None of the tension he shows when talking about the press or the Abbotts or Jax's treatment plan. Because he makes me comfortable too.

The music changes, picking up the pace.

He spins me playfully and I burst out laughing. We dance for hours taking breaks to gulp water and sip champagne. Eat wedding cake. Eventually, the band announces the last dance, another slow song, and Lucas moves close.

"Tired?" he asks. I shake my head. Gabby's family has rented a large suite for the wedding party to continue celebrating if we want. And I know a couple others plan to go to a club and continue dancing.

But that's not what I want to do.

"I think you should share my room tonight," I whisper. I can't quite meet his eyes and instead stare at his chin. I've never boldly propositioned a guy before. Well, except for maybe the other day in *Vanished*. Does that count?

He's silent for a long time. Long enough I'd be worried or insulted, but I can feel certain *parts* of him clearly liking that idea. I press against him teasingly. His reaction gives me enough confidence to look up into his eyes.

"How drunk are you?" he asks.

I stretch up and cup his face in my palms, kissing him slowly. He responds immediately, deepening the kiss until we're both breathing heavily.

"I'm not drunk," I whisper. I'm not. I've had enough champagne to feel good, but I know exactly what I am doing and who I am doing it with.

"That is excellent news."

His expression, a combination of relief and eagerness, makes me laugh even as my body starts to tingle with nerves and arousal.

"You wanting to make that happen anytime soon?"

I smile. "Ready when you are."

The fire in his blue eyes flips my stomach. He pulls me impossibly closer. "Go say good night to Gabby. I'll meet you at the elevators."

And my smile slowly widens before I go and do exactly that.

Gabby is also happily tipsy, drunk on both love and champagne. She hugs me hard and tells me how much she loves me while Tim watches on with a happy smile. I hug him, too, before saying good night. And then, stomach fluttering with nerves and excitement, I exit the ballroom and find Lucas at the elevators. He looks up when I approach and grins crookedly, pressing the up button.

Unfortunately, a group of three guys and another couple get on the elevator with us. I keep sneaking looks at Lucas, and eventually he catches me peeking and smiles. I bite my lip to keep from giggling nervously. Finally, we reach my floor, and I step into the hallway, feeling Lucas behind me. I risk another look at his face when I move to unlock the door and the heat in his eyes takes my breath away. The green light flicks on and I press down on the handle.

The second my hotel room door closes behind us, Lucas has me pressed against it, kissing me thoroughly. Have I mentioned I love his kisses? I really do.

And tonight, we're not stopping at a few kisses.

Yay, me.

Lucas

Christ, I'm all over her. But I can't seem to help myself.

Her breath catches as I kiss her, pressing her into the door. I want to be as close to her as possible. My hands are caressing her everywhere, unable to decide where to focus my attention. She sighs brokenly, which only ramps me up. Fuck, I want her. My dick is already standing at attention, and we've barely just begun.

Kissing Ash is like nothing I've experienced before. I don't know what it is about this woman, but I can lose myself in her in ways I never have before. All night, this has been in the back of my mind. Being alone with Ash. Finally finishing what we started that day in *Vanished*. All the ways I want to touch her.

I feel her hands pressing against my chest and force myself to reign it in. Breathing heavily, I pull back, giving her space. Her eyes blink open and gaze up at me, their chocolate depths dazed. All I want to do is kiss her again, but I make myself wait and follow her lead. She inhales slowly, and her eyes drop to my chest as she reaches up and begins unbuttoning my shirt.

I stand still in front of her as she works the buttons, her eyes hot on my skin. I shrug out of my suit jacket as she untucks my shirt to get to the final buttons. Her nails gently flow over my abs and chest up to my shoulders and she tugs my open shirt off and down. I stand rigid, hands clenched into fists at my sides as she tentatively traces the patterns and lines of my tattoos. I want to give her this, a chance to explore, but I'm not sure how much longer I can hold out.

I get my answer when I feel her hands at my waist, starting to undo my pants.

I grab her hands and stop her movements. Eyes wide, she glances up at me once again. Damn, she's beautiful. Probably more beautiful than I deserve, but I'm hoping I can be what she needs.

"Let's even things out."

Her smile makes me feel like a god or a superhero or just a really, really lucky bastard. Turning, she presents me with the zipper at her back. I take my time sliding it down, appreciating the softness of her skin. She shivers and the dress falls, a dark red pool at her feet. The sight before me causes my cock, already painfully hard, to press insistently against my fly. Eager fucker.

Damn. That's pretty.

Ash is like a fantasy come to life. She's wearing this fancy lacy underwear that reveals her ass cheeks, and I can't resist cupping them in my hands. They fit perfectly. She makes this breathy moaning sound and it is now my mission to hear her make that sound as often as possible. Gripping her hips, I pull her back against me, giving me better access to kiss along her neck. One of her arms lifts up and back, winding around my neck. I feel the sting of her hand pulling at my hair. Fucking hot.

I continue to spread kisses along her neck and shoulder, one hand finally moving to cup her breast.

"Lucas," her sigh tells me everything I need to know. I explore until she's breathing heavily, squirming in my arms, pressing her ass into my thighs and arching her back, thrusting her breast into my palm. With a full body shiver, she pulls away, but before I can protest, she turns in my arms and squeezes tightly against me.

"Kiss me."

That's one thing I'll never say no to. Our kiss escalates quickly, tongues stroking, exploring. I can't get enough of her. Wrapping my arms around her waist, I lift her without breaking our kiss and feel her legs raise and tighten on my hips. I move us to the bed and set her down carefully in the center. She looks up at me, her eyes wide and soft.

"Take your pants off."

I give her a cocky grin. "Impatient, beautiful?"

She nods.

I do as she asks, ridiculously eager, toeing off my shoes, removing my pants and underwear as she watches. Naked, I can't take my eyes off her as she looks at me. She inhales sharply, and her eyes widen as she takes in my erection. I stroke my hand over my dick as she watches, her breath quickening.

"See what you do to me," I murmur. Her eyes flick up to mine briefly but return to my dick. I fucking love the way she looks at me.

"Take your bra off," I order. Fair is fair. She doesn't hesitate, turning me on more. And then her perfect tits are bare and begging for my attention. I groan and practically pounce on her, pressing her into the mattress.

She giggles and teases me back. "Impatient?"

"You have no idea. You're even more gorgeous than I imagined. You should be naked all the time."

She laughs again, her hand stroking my cheek as I settle half on, half off her. "That could get awkward. Besides, you're much more beautiful to look at."

I raise an eyebrow, "Beautiful, huh?"

Nodding, her cheeks pinking, and moves her eyes down my body. God. Superhero. Lucky bastard. Her hands softly follow the path of her gaze, moving along my arms, chest, abs, finally stroking my cock. I groan and press against her hands.

I fucking love her touching me.

"Feels so good, Ash." I close my eyes and rest my forehead against hers. I let her explore as long as I can before taking control. I slide down her body, settling myself between her thighs so I can reach her breasts. Those incredibly perfect breasts. I cup them in my hands, kneading gently, and press a soft kiss between them. She sighs, melting into the bed beneath us. Unable to resist, not even trying, I place a hot kiss over her nipple, sucking gently. She gasps and arches her neck, urging me on. I need little encouragement. I scrape my teeth over her tight nipple. She's straining against me, her hot core pressing against my stomach. I switch to her other nipple, not wanting either side to feel neglected. Ash is breathing heavily, her hands fisting my hair and I freaking love it.

I continue my exploration down her body, shifting so I can trail more kisses down her flat stomach. I reach the edge of her insanely sexy underwear and press an open mouth kiss just above the band. Ash stiffens beneath me, and not in a good way. I look up so I can see her face. Fuck, that's pretty. She's splayed out, her chest rising rapidly with her breaths, breasts flushed, nipples tight. But there's a hint of uncertainty in her eyes that wasn't there before. One of her hands tightens on my shoulder, the other still gripping a fistful of my hair.

Without breaking eye contact, I press my lips against her stomach once again. And I see it. A flash of heat but still that uncertainty.

"You still with me, babe?"

She nods, her teeth sinking into her bottom lip as she watches me. I move back up her body, settling on top of her, pressing her into the mattress, and kiss her. She relaxes beneath me, wrapping herself around me, holding me tight.

I suspect what's making her nervous and make a mental note to explore that further. Later. Not now.

While we're kissing, I move my hand down her side, feeling lace at my fingertips, and I shift to make room for my hand to slip between us and cup her sex. I groan against her lips, feeling how hot and wet she is even through the material separating us. She makes that sound again and my cock twitches against her thigh.

"You remember that day you came to visit me at *Vanished*?"

She nods, making a sound of agreement, and shifts her hips, pressing her core into my hand. I move my fingers, tracing her through the lace.

"Watching you come was so hot."

"Lucas," she groans.

"I really, really want to watch you come apart again."

When she looks at me, her eyes are dazed. She grabs my hand and shifts it against her, showing me how to touch her.

"You going to let me do that? Make you come again?"

She nods and pulls my head down for a hungry kiss. I give in for a moment, our tongues caressing.

I tug gently on her underwear. "Can I take these off, beautiful?"

Ash lifts her hips eagerly, giving me access. "Yes. Lucas. Please."

She sounds desperate, which is exactly what I was going for. I can't remember ever wanting inside a woman this badly. I need her to want this as badly as I do.

Together, we work her underwear down her legs and she kicks it away. I return to kissing her, my fingers exploring her sex this time with no barrier between us. Fuck. Ash is naked. In my bed. Needy and eager.

I slip a finger inside her core and she cries out, her head back. My lips find her nipples again, alternating my kisses as my fingers continue to slide through her wetness. The sounds spilling from her throat are so sexy, keeping me on the edge. I need her to come. My thumb presses against her clit, rotating in tight circles as I curl my fingers. Ash comes on a loud groan, her body shaking. I hold her through it, my palm tight against her. She shivers against me and sighs, a small smile on her lips.

I press a kiss against her cheek and whisper in her ear. "You're not done for the night, are you?"

She blinks up at me, that sated smile still on her face. That smile does something to me.

"I sure hope not." She grins wider, and I respond with my own.

Unable to resist, I kiss her again and then turn my attention to our clothes all over the floor. "One sec..."

She leans up, watching me as I stand. "Where are you going?"

She takes my breath away; she's so beautiful. For a second, I'm distracted from my mission, staring at her.

"Condom. I have one...." I trail off, looking again for my pants and wallet.

Ash leans over and reaches into the bed stand, pulling out a few foil packets. Blushing, she explains, "I put some in here earlier."

Unable to stop the grin on my face, I jump onto the bed next to her. My landing causes her to bounce and her boobs to jiggle invitingly. "Look at you. So prepared."

Giggling, she wraps her arms around my neck and pulls me down on top of her. "I wasn't going to let you get away again."

"That right?"

"Couldn't let that underwear go to waste."

My cock pulses at the reminder. "That was sexy." I kiss her, my hand caressing down her curves. I squeeze her knee, pulling her leg up until it curves against my waist. I settle into the juncture of her thighs, my dick happily nestled against her sex. We rub against each other, teasing. She's arching against me again, pulling me tightly to her.

"Lucas?"

"Yeah?"

"You should put one of the condoms on now."

I'm not an idiot. I kneel and do as I'm told, smoothing one of the condoms down my length. Ash watches with lust-filled eyes keeping me on the edge of coming. When that's done, she sinks back into the bed, raising and spreading her knees, giving me a deliciously filthy view. I squeeze the base of my dick, willing myself to calm down.

"You ready for me, beautiful?"

She nods, reaching out to pull me close. For a moment, I still just enjoying this feeling of Ash in my arms, skin against skin. But then I feel her grip my dick, positioning me at her entrance. I raise up on my arms, bracing them on each side of her head, and watch, hypnotized, thrusting home.

Gasping, Ash's fingers dig into my hips. I give her a minute to adjust and then slowly withdraw before easing back inside. Fuck, that's hot. Watching her take me. She tilts her hips and sighs. I continue my slow thrusts. She feels so good. Her palms smooth along my abs, up to my shoulders. Finally, she cups my cheeks and urges me down for another kiss. I fold my arms, collapsing on top of her. After a few slow kisses, I shift so I can slide my tongue across the stiff peak of her nipple, her core clenches, squeezing me so sweetly. I groan against her skin, my thrusts increasing. I need her to come. I'm not going to last much longer. She arches her back, offering her other breast, and I take it. Her breathing catches but it's not enough.

My hand slips between us, seeking out her clit again. Circling, paying close attention to her body and what she likes. She cries out. *There.*

Eyes wide, she looks at me and squeezes my shoulders. "Lucas. Oh god." She groans again.

I feel tingling shocks gathering at the base of my spine. My hips thrust, growing frantic, I'm practically mindless with pleasure. So good.

"Ash," I groan. "Come for me." I pinch her clit and bite down on her neck, and *finally*, I feel her shudder beneath me. Her hips jerk and her core squeezes me tight, pulling me deeper. She groans my name and I lose my shit. I grip her ass and pull her tight against my hips, grinding myself against her until I feel the building tension explode. Pulsing through my body, leaving me drained. I collapse on top of her, face buried in the crook of her neck as I attempt to catch my breath.

That was intense.

When I'm finally able to lift my head, I press a soft kiss to her shoulder. Her hands are soothing along my back, soothing and arousing. I shouldn't be able to get hard again for hours after that, yet her soft touches are doing just that. I groan, forcing myself to twist away from her so I can deal with the condom. When I return, she's climbed beneath the sheets. She reaches for me with a sleepy smile that hits me in the chest. I pull her into my arms and listen to her breathing as it evens out as she falls asleep.

I'm a little too amped to sleep but enjoy having her in my arms.

Maybe too much. I'm beginning to see what Logan was so worried about. I'm in deep with this woman and it's only been a month since she walked in my shop. I stare at the ceiling processing my thoughts. This is going to end badly for me. But the idea of ending it to save me from rejection later isn't appealing. I want her as long as I can have her.

She stirs when I pull away and lifts her head up, eyes blinking heavily with sleep. "Are you leaving?"

"No," I whisper, "I'm just grabbing some water."

"Oh. Okay." Ash smiles contentedly and snuggles into her pillow, eyes closing.

I feel that growingly familiar tightness in my chest and lean over to press a kiss against her forehead. *I am in so much fucking trouble with this woman.*

Ash

It's the heat that wakes me. I sigh and stretch, feeling smug and satisfied. Last night was incredible.

I feel Lucas still snuggled tight against my back, the source of all that heat. I shift, pressing my ass against his groin. I can feel him getting harder, his erection growing as I tease him. I've got no complaints in that department. Lucas Abbott is both a shower *and* a grower. I try to stifle a giggle in my pillow.

I feel him shift behind me, one arm wrapping around my side and pressing into my stomach, pulling me tight against him. His erection nestles into my ass cheeks. I wiggle into him.

"You need a good morning orgasm, beautiful?" His voice is hoarse and scratchy with sleep. He's so sexy. Everything about him. I look down, studying his arm at my waist. Admiring all the colors and designs. It distracts me from his question.

I feel a kiss against my shoulder and I shiver. He's so sweet. How can someone so tough on the outside be so sweet?

"Tell me about your first."

He stiffens and shifts away from me. I roll over so I can see his face. He looks wary and a little confused. "My first."

I grab his arm again and trace along the designs. "Your first tattoo." I grin, feeling lighter than I have in ages.

He relaxes, and I giggle, enjoying teasing him. His eyes narrow and he rolls until I'm trapped beneath him. "You feel like playing this morning?"

I nod and laugh as he nuzzles his face into my neck, pressing tickling kisses along my skin. I bury my fingers in his hair, tugging gently. Eventually, he raises his head and kisses me thoroughly.

"Morning." He smiles sleepily, and even that makes my pulse speed up.

"Morning," I whisper.

He leans over and grabs his phone, checking the time, then settles back on top of me. "So," he's back to nuzzling again. I'm not complaining. "What's the plan for today?"

Really, I just want to enjoy this, him pressing against me, allowing me to touch him all I want.

"Gabby and Tim are hosting a lunch for everyone before people need to travel home. I should probably make an appearance."

"What time?"

"Noon."

He pops his head up, grinning at me. "Lots of time."

He ducks beneath the comforter, pressing kisses between my breasts.

I laugh and then sigh, feeling his lips tugging on my nipple. I run my fingers through his hair, somehow even more turned on, not being able to see him as he moves beneath the blankets. I feel a hot, wet kiss on my navel and I shiver. I can feel my cheeks flaming, knowing Lucas is basically face-to-vagina at this point. I try to relax and enjoy his attention, but...I can tell I'm not entirely successful. I'm tense as his hands grip my thighs, making room for his wide shoulders between them. He places a slow kiss low on my pelvis and I shudder out the breath I've been holding, squeezing my eyes shut.

Lucas throws off the hotel comforter and surges up my body until he can look into my eyes.

"Ash?"

I'm confident Lucas is far more experienced than me and the other men I've been with. They never cared much if I didn't want them to spend much time down there. But something tells me Lucas... something tells me Lucas knows his way around and doesn't like to settle.

"Ash?" he asks again, interrupting my increasingly unhelpful thoughts.

"Mmm?" I can't quite meet his eyes, instead focusing on his lips and chin. Luckily he has a very sexy mouth. And chin.

"I'm just going to ask, okay?"

"Ask what?"

"You tense up. You don't like it? You don't want me to go down on you?"

Oh god. My cheeks are so hot. This is so embarrassing.

"No, it's not that. I like it okay, it's just...I don't...I can't come that way. I don't want you to think...."

I brave a peek at his eyes. Their blue depths are molten his gaze is so hot.

"I don't want you to think there's something wrong when I can't.... It's not you," I explain. Could this be any more awkward? It's hard to imagine.

He's silent for a minute and I fidget, annoyed I somehow managed to mess up our sexy morning. I just want to go back to that.

"But you like it? It feels good?" he finally asks, breaking the silence.

I nod, cheeks still flaming.

He grins and presses a kiss against my lips. "I want to make you feel good."

But he doesn't go back down, returning to his position before this conversation. Instead, he rolls to his back with me on top of him and holds my face still while he kisses me breathless. It's not long before I'm sinking into him, rubbing my core against his erection, pressing kisses across his chest. His hands are everywhere, tickling my spine, cupping my breasts, squeezing my ass. I reach for a condom, ready for those good morning orgasms he mentioned.

We're interrupted by Lucas's phone. He groans, pressing his lips to my skin, not moving.

"Ignore it," he growls, his voice sending shivers through me.

I groan as well but don't move. Eventually, the phone quiets, and I breathe a sigh of relief, refocusing on Lucas beneath me.

The annoying peals start again and he swears.

I move my fingers through his hair, lightly scoring his scalp. He hums appreciatively. "You should get it," I whisper.

He growls again but rolls away and reaches for his phone.

"This better be good, Tanya."

I can't help feeling a little satisfied by how annoyed Lucas is at being interrupted.

"What?" I immediately sense his change of mood. He's tense in a totally different, not good way. My first thought is of Jax, and I scramble out of bed, slipping into a hotel robe. "Is she alright?"

She? Not Jax, then. I relax a tiny bit but am still uneasy. I wait, trying to be patient as Lucas holds his phone with one hand and starts pulling on his clothes with the other. I hand him his shirt, and for a moment, his eyes meet mine as he grabs it from me.

"I'll be there as soon as I can. It'll be a couple hours, though, at least."

He disconnects, turning to face me. He shoves a hand through his already messy hair. "Logan was in a bike accident this morning."

"Is she okay?"

He shrugs. "It sounds like it's not too bad. She didn't want Tanya to call, but it happened when she was on her way to open this morning." He sighs. "I need to get back," he says reluctantly.

"Of course." I nod, squeezing his arm.

He pulls me close, nuzzling the curve of my neck. I can feel him press a warm kiss to my skin.

"This isn't how I wanted this morning to go."

I hug him, stretching to press a swift kiss against his cheek. "I know. But I understand." His obvious reluctance to leave warms me. It reassures me that last night meant something to him too. It gives me the courage to ask him something else I've been thinking about.

Staying plastered to him, I rest my chin on his chest and look up at him. "Any chance you want to put that suit back on in a couple weeks?"

He gives me that crooked cocky grin I love. "We don't have to wait two weeks to relive last night."

I roll my eyes but can't help grinning back. "Not what I meant. The hospital is having a fundraiser in two weeks, and my boss thinks it would be a good place to talk about my idea to expand the fellowship I had. I was wondering if you would want to come with me."

His face is inscrutable, all the flirtatious teasing gone. "You want me to be your date at a work event?"

I nod. "It's that Saturday night. Will you need to work or...?"

He bends down and gives me a slow kiss.

"I'll check my schedule. I might have to rearrange a couple things, but I'll be there."

"Yeah?" I can't stop the smile spreading across my face.

"Yeah." He smiles. Our moment is interrupted by his phone ringing again. Lucas swears under his breath. I squeeze him briefly before reluctantly moving away.

"You should go. I hope everything is okay."

He answers his phone and snaps, "One sec." Then looks at me. "I'll call you later, yeah?"

I nod. Swearing, he gives me one last, desperate kiss. It leaves me breathless and unsteady on my feet. His eyes are hot as he pulls away and turns to the door. "Yeah?" he barks into the cell. I watch as he walks out the door.

Hours later, when I'm at the lunch, I get a text.

Next time I'm going to spend hours making you feel good.

Jesus. Even across state lines he can make my thighs clench.

Lucas Abbott is dangerous.

I love it.

Chapter Fifteen

Lucas

Logan is fine. A few scrapes and bruises, but relatively unharmed. She's more annoyed than anything. And her bike is busted up, which pisses her off. Her brakes jammed or some shit, and she swerved into a parked car to avoid the moving ones. Tanya forced her to go to the Emergency Room, but luckily none of the injuries were serious. I don't think I could have handled another one of us in the hospital for any length of time. I'd prefer we all stay far away from now on. I mean, except for Ash.

I hated leaving her, but I appreciated that she understood why I needed to go. She respects the other people in my life, something other women I've dated haven't always done. Those women have never lasted long. For multiple reasons.

Fuck, that was a fantastic night with her. One I'm eager as hell to repeat. Just remembering it is enough to get me hard. Unfortunately, it seems like it may be a while until our schedules can sync up. I'm still working my ass off to catch up on all the appointments I canceled because of the shooting, and Jax still isn't back full-time. Soon. Can't be soon enough for that asshole, he bitches and moans on a daily basis about how slow his recovery is going. He's even driving Macy fucking nuts.

Melrose stops by midweek.

I tense as soon as he walks through the door. I can't remember him ever coming by just for the hell of it.

"Luke." He nods.

"Melrose. What's up?"

He shrugs. His casual attitude isn't fooling me.

"How's Mateo working out?"

"He's fine." I think he's fine. He shows up on time, does what he's told, never complains. But he's still obviously uncomfortable, rarely says a word. Olivia assured me he was going to therapy as required, so I try to leave it alone. Sometimes words aren't what people need and I'm sure as hell no therapist.

"His cousin took a plea deal. Ten years."

I'm silent, absorbing this information. Ten years. Is that enough? What would be enough for what he did to Jax?

"You tell Jax yet?"

Melrose shakes his head. "Going to see him next. He's still staying with Macy?"

"Yeah, for now."

He could have let me know about Mateo's cousin with a phone call. Why is he here, in person?

"I'm still going through the people from the hospital tapes. So far, I haven't come up with much."

"I get it. I'm sure it's not a priority right now. No one was hurt."

"Anything else out of the ordinary happen?"

I take a minute to consider his question. "No. Nice and quiet."

"Heard Logan had some trouble this week."

I shrug. "Bike accident. She's okay."

"Pretty common. Glad she wasn't hurt."

We fall silent, eying each other. This whole visit is weird, but I can't quite put my finger on it. Melrose and I go back years, we're not friends, but he's definitely the one I call if I need to interact with law enforcement. He's a good cop but also willing to ignore 'protocols' if they get in his way. He's always struck me as one of the cops that are actually trying to help people. I've never seen him on a power trip. And while I suspect his moral code doesn't always align with the law, he applies it consistently, and that I can respect.

"She around?" he asks, referring to Logan.

"Working on a tattoo right now."

He nods. "She gonna be long? I can wait a little while."

I check the time. "Maybe another 20 minutes?"

"Cool. I'll grab a coffee and be back. You need anything?"

"I'm cool. Thanks." I watch him walk out, heading to the coffee shop two doors down. What the hell does he want with Logan? Just making sure the accident is legit? It's not like someone ran her off the road. I shake myself out of my thoughts. Melrose can spend his time however he wants, I guess. He returns a few minutes later and settles on the couch to wait. My next appointment shows up, and I take him back to my station. On the way, I pop my head in and alert Logan that Melrose is waiting for her.

She pauses her machine and looks up at me. "What's he want?"

"Heard about your accident."

Logan makes a face. "We're just about done." She smiles at the guy in her chair and turns her machine back on.

The rest of the day is uneventful. Thankfully. During closing I check in with Logan.

"You and Melrose get squared away?"

She shrugs, packing up her stuff.

I pause, an uncomfortable feeling in my gut. "Logan? You'd tell me, right? If you were in some kind of trouble? You know we'd have your back."

Logan stills, staring into her bag. "I know. I'm good. I just...." She stops and slings her bag over her shoulder.

"What?"

Sighing, she admits, "It just feels like a lot of bad stuff has been happening lately. And we still don't know what happened to Jax's room that day. I don't like it."

I jam a hand through my hair, surprised she's admitted even that much. "I've been meaning to add more security since the shooting. I promise I'll get it done, okay?"

She nods but doesn't seem any more relaxed.

"You heading to the 'el?"

"Yeah. Going be a couple days at least to get my bike fixed."

"Me too. I'll walk with you."

We part ways at the station, heading in different directions. Before she walks away, she says one more thing.

"Just be careful, Luke. I have a bad feeling there's more coming."

Ash

The fundraiser is just as extravagant and overwhelming as I had pictured. Chicago's elite has shown up in their black-tie-best to show their support, drink fancy cocktails, see and be seen. The Chief had given me a few suggestions, people I should meet over the course of the night. She's offered to introduce me when possible, but I know she has her own conversations to have.

Once again, having Lucas at my side makes the evening much easier and more pleasant than I anticipated. I'm awful at small talk and that's a huge reason I'm here tonight. To schmooze. To shake hands. To make connections with donors. I'm surprised how many people, even in this crowd, recognize Lucas from his show. Instead of me having to chase everyone down, a fair number of people approach us, wanting to meet Lucas, a local celebrity. But he doesn't monopolize. He's incredibly adept at turning the conversation to me and my work, giving me openings to make my pitch and discuss the refugee doctor swap - I have to come up with a better name for this. When I comment on it, he grimaces and admits he's had media training because of the show.

"Tanya and Krista wanted to make sure I knew how to avoid the topics I wanted to avoid without seeming to avoid any topics," he explains.

Whatever the reason, I'm grateful for it, and these conversations boost my confidence so the big donors I do need to chase down, well, it's less intimidating and uncomfortable than I expected. I'm riding high, flushed with accomplishment, when I feel Lucas tense next to me, his arm under my hand has gone stiff.

"Dr. Carrington, how nice to see you again."

Ethan Abbott is standing in front of us, and I am frozen with uncertainty. Politeness forces a smile to my face and I shake his hand, murmuring hello. After the blow up in the hospital, I'd never contacted him again. It's probably a professional mistake not to follow up, but... it feels like I'd be betraying Lucas to recruit his family's financial support.

Ethan turns his attention to my date, "Lucas."

I dare to glance up at him. He's glaring at Ethan, ignoring the other man's proffered hand. My stomach drops. I can feel the rage sliding off of him, pooling at our feet, rising to drown us all. Oh god. I swallow painfully. I should pull him away, something, anything, but I'm again frozen in the face of this violent emotion.

Lucas's arm beneath my hand is rigid. The silence stretches painfully. Eventually, Ethan lowers his hand back to his side and sighs. "Still refusing to give, huh?"

"Fuck you. I don't owe you anything."

I sense people around us starting to pick up on the tension. I glance around and see several eyes on our small group. Whispers as people see Lucas and Ethan together in public.

"Basic courtesy apparently too much to ask?" Ethan's voice is dry and unaffected.

Before Lucas can respond, I manage to squeeze his arm, reminding him where we are. Creating a scene will only feed the speculation that's finally starting to die down after the shooting and the incident at the hospital. Most of it circles around Theo Abbott and his two brothers, assuming one of them must be Lucas's father from an affair. Their only sister, Lucas's actual mother, has been all but forgotten in the family narrative. Which I suspect only adds to his pain and fury.

He hesitates and I can see his internal struggle, wanting so badly to respond. But instead, he makes a sound similar to a growl and storms away. His exit cracks the ice that had me frozen, and I exhale in relief. Inhale as the air returns to the room.

I'm left standing awkwardly in front of his cousin, who also happens to be one of the hospital's most significant benefactors.

"I apologize," he murmurs. "Lucas and I don't ... communicate very well."

Without thinking, the words spill out. "It doesn't seem like you communicate at all." My eyes widen in surprise. Shit. Probably shouldn't have said that.

But Ethan actually laughs. "Fair enough. I'm better with computers than people."

"People are more complicated." *Ash, stop while you're ahead,* my inner voice screams.

"That is very true," he agrees. "I'm sorry if I spoiled the evening for the two of you. I'll let you get back to socializing."

I murmur a goodbye as he walks away and subtly try to look around for Lucas. Finding him, I make my way to the bar in the back of the ballroom and approach Lucas where he stands, forearms resting along the edge, staring into a glass of amber-colored liquid. I'm guessing bourbon.

Sliding up next to him, I stand close but make sure we're not touching. Touching Lucas tends to distract me, and I can't afford to be distracted right now.

"Lucas, I need you to talk to me about this." I'm proud of how steady my voice is. Inside I'm shaking with nerves. It's not like me to push an issue like this, but he's more important than my comfort. I need to know how to navigate these situations. I can't freeze every time Lucas has an angry interaction with his family.

He sighs heavily and downs the rest of his drink.

"I know this is complicated and I know this is hard for you. But I will continue to run into these men, and if you don't talk to me, I'll never really know how to handle this situation."

I watch his jaw tighten and his chest expands with a rough inhale.

"Lucas." I wait until he finally looks at me. I'm struggling with what I want to say. I want him to know I'm on his side. I want him to trust me. I want these interactions to not cause him such obvious pain. I want to understand why he deals with his pain with anger. I want, somehow, to make this easier for him.

I want the words I choose to communicate all of that.

"I'm with you. You know that, right? I'm on your side."

His eyes flash with tortured emotion. "I'm sorry. I know this night is important for you."

I cup his cheeks in my hands, just for a moment, but long enough to whisper, "You're important to me too."

"Every time I look at him, all I can see is him trying to bribe me not to do *Top Ink*. And the fact that none of them have publicly acknowledged my mother but would rather deal with rumors they cheated. Like it's more offensive to be a pregnant teenager than a cheating asshole. I just lose my shit," he offers, confirming my earlier thoughts.

"Have you ever thought about...talking to Theo? On your terms. Maybe it would help if you got some of this out of your head and out between you."

He shakes his head, dismissing this suggestion. "I don't think I could. I'd lose my shit. Besides, I don't know what he could say to explain...."

"Do you want to leave?" I have a small knot in my stomach, hating everything about this situation. But if he can't be here, I understand.

He frowns a bit. "Can you leave? I thought you needed to be here."

"I do. But you don't. If it's too uncomfortable for you-"

His blue eyes soften as he presses a tender kiss to my lips. "No. I'll stay. I can handle it." I start to protest, but he presses a finger to my lips, silencing me. "I'm not leaving you. I've got it. Promise."

I smile, the knot in my stomach releasing a bit. It means something that he's willing to do something hard and uncomfortable to support me. It means a lot.

Lucas

I'm still practically vibrating I'm so pissed off and tense. It's not helped by the fact that in addition to Ethan, I've spotted several other Abbotts in the crowd. My uncle the Senator and his wife. His brother Edward and some of his spawn. I keep them in my peripheral vision so I can avoid whatever part of the room they happen to be in. I can't tell if Ash is on to what I'm doing or not. For the most part, she stays by my side, although once in a while, she's called away to meet another colleague or donor. I assure her I'm fine, trying to make up for my earlier freakout.

Will I ever be able to interact with them without losing my shit? Part of me, deep down, doesn't really want to. My rage and hatred are the only things that even try to punish them for what they did to my mother. In the three years since Ethan barged into my life and flipped everything I didn't know upside down, I've learned virtually nothing about the woman who gave me up. Back then, there was no social media, there wasn't the same media attention; it's like she never existed. I haven't even been able to find any articles about her running away, going missing. No attempt by the family to find her, offer a reward, anything. Nothing. So I hold onto my anger. At least it's something.

Other than Ethan, none of the other Abbotts have ever reached out. I wonder if things would be different if I'd agreed to their terms and never done the show, but I doubt it. I'm not a guy they want at their family dinners.

Ash's boss comes over to 'steal her away'.

"I won't be long," she assures me.

I squeeze her hand. "Take your time. I'm going to get a drink and check out the silent auction."

"I'll find you." She smiles and crosses the room, talking with her boss. I follow her with my eyes appreciating Ash all dressed up. Tonight, she's got on a sleeveless black dress ending just below the knee. It's simple but looks stunning on her, of course. Her ass looks amazing, and I'm eager to get her home and explore. It's been way too long since our night in Milwaukee, and I still need to fulfill my promise. I pull my eyes away, those thoughts are only going to embarrass me, and a flash of red hair catches my attention.

I inhale slowly, a stab of guilt hitting me as I spot Riley standing on the edge of the crowd watching me. I guess one other Abbott *has* tried to reach out, although I wasn't very welcoming. Jax's verbal ass-kicking has made me regret how harsh I was during that interaction, so I attempt to at least be polite and acknowledge her presence. I lift my chin and silently toast her with my empty glass. Which reminds me, I need another drink.

I'm only a little surprised when Riley appears next to me at the bar. She's persistent, I'll give her that.

She orders a sparkling water with lime before she finally turns her attention to me.

"I - I didn't know you were going to be here tonight," she says and attempts a smile.

I shrug and swirl my class, watching the golden liquid swirl. "I was invited."

She glances in the direction Ash had gone but doesn't pry, which I grudgingly appreciate.

"What about you?" Ash and I had gotten in free as hospital staff, but I know the open bar and fancy meal are being paid for by the massive charge per plate the hospital is charging for this fundraiser. "Quite a price tag for a teacher, isn't it?"

Riley glances away and shifts nervously from foot to foot, reminding me I'm an asshole. "My, uh, giving back was important to my parents."

Right. I suspect this is her way of explaining that she also has a trust fund without coming right out and saying it. I am an asshole. Her parents died when Riley was a kid. Car accident. Her father was the third and final Abbott brother. She had the advantage of being born when her parents were married and at an acceptable age, so when her folks passed away, she was taken in and raised by Theo and his wife. But, I remind myself, none of that is her fault.

The bartender sets her glass in front of her and Riley thanks her, picking it up.

"Not much of a drinker, huh?" I'm grasping for a topic that won't make me want to hit something, particularly my uncle. Or Ethan.

Although I would really like to hit Ethan at some point. Not tonight. Some time it won't make Ash look bad.

"No, not really," Riley chirps brightly. "Photographers are all over these things. I don't think the school board would like it if I was in the paper with a bunch of drinks in my hand."

I snort, understanding what she means. Even if she nursed the same drink the entire night, shady people could make it look like whatever they wanted to in the press.

"I heard Jax is doing well."

Nodding, I offer, "He is. It was nice of you to check on him."

She smiles brightly and her eyes light up at even this small gesture.

Shit. Jax was right. She's just ... fucking sweet, isn't she?

Ash slides up to my side, and without even thinking about it, I slip an arm loosely around her waist. Having her close calms me down.

"Hey, you. I thought you wanted to check out the silent auction?" She grins at me.

I smile down into her face. "Haven't made it there yet."

Riley is sipping her water, shifting side to side again and trying not to look at us.

Fuck me. I'm really going to do this, aren't I?

"Ash, this is Riley." I nod and Ash, still smiling, holds out her hand to my *cousin.*

"Hi, Riley. Nice to meet you."

Eyes wide, Riley looks nervously at me, then back to Ash and takes her offered hand. "Nice to meet you."

"Riley Abbott." I clarify.

I feel Ash stiffen next to me and squeeze my hand on her hip, trying to communicate that I'm okay. At least, I think I'm okay. An awkward silence falls on our group until Riley, obviously trying to pretend everything is perfectly normal, pipes up.

"So, how do you two know each other?" Her voice is that same overly bright chirp as earlier. I think this is a tell for her nerves.

"Uh," Ash hesitates, looking to me.

"Ash was at the shop when Jax was shot. She's a doctor at the hospital."

"Oh! Oh my gosh! I heard there were doctors there. I didn't realize... Thank you for helping save him," she finishes sincerely.

Shit. Her seemingly genuine concern for my best friend makes it harder to hate her. Even though I want to hate her. Lump her with all the others.

Persistent little pixie.

The lights dim twice, indicating the meal and program are about to begin.

Sounding slightly disappointed, Riley says, "I guess we should take our seats. It was good to see you, Luke."

I press my lips together and nod.

"You okay?" Ash asks softly as Riley moves away. She's sitting with the rest of the Abbotts at a front table. I watch as she smiles and hugs everyone before settling into her seat, a strange pang in my chest.

"I think so." I tear my attention away and focus on Ash's concerned brown eyes. "She's not so bad," I offer.

Ash slips an arm around my waist and hugs me quickly. And just like that, I feel better, a gentle warmth spreading through me.

"Want to speed through the silent auction before we eat? See if there's anything worth bidding on?"

I shrug, "Sure."

She takes my hand and pulls me behind her. And I follow.

I'd follow her anywhere.

Chapter Sixteen

Ash

A t the end of the evening, Lucas invites me back to his place. It's the first time I've been to his condo, and I'm enjoying this peek into who he is. It's cleaner than I expected from a guy living on his own. It's in a new building, so everything is modern and sleek. He's personalized it with colorful artwork. That's the only thing he's really added, though. The furniture is sparse and basic, almost like he's just moved in though he said he's been here a couple years. After he signed on for his own show.

I slip my heels off, and he removes his suit jacket. He pours us each a glass of water and leans against his kitchen counter listening as I process the night out loud.

"The Chief even told me someone scheduled time to meet with us on Monday afternoon," I finish.

He gives me a crooked grin. "Sounds like you nailed it, babe."

Warmth spreads through me at his words. "Thanks. Thanks for coming. It was...nice having you there."

His eyes start to smolder, and he crosses the room to stand in front of me.

"So, I was thinking," he wraps his arms loosely around my waist and pulls me against him, "tomorrow we should spend the day together. Whole day."

I raise my eyebrows and smile up at him. "The whole day, huh?"

He nods and rubs his nose down along mine. "Mmmhmm."

"I didn't bring a change of clothes."

"I don't see a problem with that," he grins playfully. "I can come up with lots of things for us to do that don't require clothes."

His enthusiasm makes me laugh. "I guess we'll figure it out." I smile up at him.

Lucas leans down and gives me a soft kiss, but it escalates quickly. I'm still riding the adrenaline of the evening, and suddenly all of it is channeled into him and what he makes me feel. His lips are firm as they press against mine and I sigh, melting into him. He tilts my head back and moves closer until I can feel every hard inch of him. God, he's so big and hard *everywhere*. My hands dive into his hair, gripping tightly as our tongues meet and explore. I feel the heat of his hand on my ass, and I shiver with pleasure. He pulls his lips from mine and explores along my jaw and down my neck.

"You remember what I promised you after the wedding?" he murmurs against my ear.

I shiver in reaction, both from his hot breath tickling my skin and from the memory of his text. I nod.

He nibbles the column of my neck, causing tingles to spread throughout my body. I wore my hair up for the party tonight, giving him plenty of access.

"What did I say?" he asks.

Oh god. My stomach flips and the tingles go lower settling at the juncture of my thighs.

"Ash?" he prompts. "What did I say?"

"You," my voice cracks and I pause to clear my throat. "You said you were going to make me feel good."

"For hours," he growls.

It can't be normal to be this turned on by just a few kisses and the sound of his voice. It's not. It's not normal. At least not for me. Not before Lucas. But he's changed everything, raised every bar I've had before him. My breath is unsteady as he pulls back and leads me to his bedroom.

His bed is a giant king. Plenty of room to play. I'm almost more nervous this time than I was our first time together. Which is crazy but there it is. My heart is pounding erratically. I'm standing staring at his empty bed, and he moves behind me. His hands span my waist, and he presses a kiss to my shoulder.

"Have I told you how beautiful you are tonight?"

I turn in his arms so I can look him in the eyes. Their earlier smolder is still there, his blue eyes hot and needy. It's such a turn-on knowing he wants me. I trace the line of his jaw with my fingers and reach up to kiss him. Without breaking the kiss, he finds the zipper at my back and tugs it down. His fingers slip under the straps of my dress and slides them down my arms. I tremble as the material falls to my feet, leaving me only in my underwear.

Lucas groans. "No bra, beautiful? You're killing me."

"It's built into the dress," I murmur, loving the way he looks at me. I reach up, pulling pins out of my hair which has the added effect of lifting my chest.

His eyes on my breasts, he tugs off his shirt, not even bothering with the buttons. And then he pulls me against him, his hard chest brushing against my breasts, teasing the tips into hard points. This time when he kisses me, it's more demanding and I love it. His hands cup my ass, caressing, kneading, turning me on even more. He walks us until the back of my legs hit the bed and follows me down. His weight settles on top of me, pressing me down into the mattress. My hands move restlessly over his back, finally settling on his shoulders. God, they're massive.

Lucas settles between my thighs and shifts down my body, so he's at eye level with my breasts. The material of his pants is rough against my inner thighs. I moan as he takes one nipple into his mouth, sucking gently. Then not so gently. I arch against him, silently begging for more. He chuckles and shifts his attention to my other side. One hand grips a fistful of his gorgeous hair, the other squeezing his shoulder.

"Look at you, so beautiful, spread out on my bed." He plays with a piece of my hair, running it between his fingers.

I smile softly, feeling my cheeks going pink.

He groans. "You know I love those blushes. Makes me want to corrupt you."

I giggle. "I'm not that innocent."

"Maybe not. But you're sweet. I like it." He kisses me again until I lose any ability to think.

"You have too many clothes on," I groan.

"I can fix that." He rolls to the side and undoes his pants, lifting his hips to push them down until he can kick them away. And then he's back, his hard body pressing into me, kissing my neck, across my collarbone, down to my breasts. I'm shifting restlessly beneath him, trying to find a more satisfying contact. But he teases me and moves down my body, soft touches of his lips along the way.

He presses a wet kiss to my stomach, just above my underwear. I feel his fingers pressing into my hips as he pulls the material down and off.

"So pretty."

I glance down and see Lucas, eyes hot as he finds room between my thighs. He presses another kiss just above my mound, and his blue gaze meets mine.

"Feeling good, baby?"

I nod as my stomach flips with arousal. *Oh god.*

"Are you wet for me?"

I nod again, feeling my cheeks heat even more. And then I feel his breath hot against my core and instinctively raise my hips, arousal spreading through my limbs.

"Lucas."

"Yeah, beautiful?"

"Oh God." The anticipation is killing me. I don't normally *want* like this. My entire body straining against his. "Please."

"Shh. Just relax." And then he finally lowers his mouth and *feasts*.

My back arches as I cry out. I meant what I said last time. I've had boyfriends go down on me before, and it's always nice, but I've never been able to come this way, and usually, over time, they would do it less and less. And I know he took it as some kind of challenge, even though that's not what I intended. I don't want him to think he's... I don't know... lacking somehow or something. It's not him; it's me.

But everything is so much *more* with Lucas. It's never felt like this before. I'm writhing beneath him, pressing my heels into the mattress. It's so good.

I grip his hair with one hand, grasping at sheets with the other. My back arches as I strain against the building tension.

"Lucas. Oh god."

"Shhh. Relax."

I can't stop my legs from shifting restlessly, my whole body tightens chasing relief. I'm so close. This never happens. *Oh my god.*

"Please." I don't even know what I'm begging for, I'm just mindless with *want.*

Lucas slides two fingers inside me and gently sucks my clit, and I splinter. I don't even recognize the sound that comes out of me as my body quivers and I thrust my hips against him, chasing more.

He stays with me, holding me through my orgasm. But he doesn't give me much time to recover, instead moving up my body and entering me in one smooth stroke. My back bows and I grip his hips, adjusting to his size. That hungry moan? That came from me. I inhale shakily, still trying to catch my breath.

"Fuuuuuck," Lucas groans.

His hips are tight against me, his arms on each side of my head, holding him above me. He looks into my eyes and kisses me softly before looking down our bodies to where we're joined together. He shifts his hips, watching, and slowly enters me again. And again.

"So good, Ash."

Incapable of words, I pull him down to me for a kiss. His thrusts come faster, less controlled, and unbelievably I feel another orgasm building. Inhaling sharply, I move my hips in rhythm with his. He collapses on top of me, still thrusting, and cups my ass, adjusting the angle. And I break apart again, calling his name. Seconds later, he jerks in my arms, groaning his own release.

I feel him shudder a final time, and he rolls to the side, taking me with him, keeping me close. When our breathing returns to normal, he twists away briefly to deal with the condom. When had he put that on? Man has serious skills.

He smacks my thigh lightly. "Up," he instructs. I shift so he can pull the covers down, and we slide beneath them. Tucking me into his side, Lucas sighs contentedly.

"Feeling good, beautiful?"

I look up and see his eyes are closed, a smug smile on his face. I pinch him lightly on the side, and he laughs, squirming away.

"Fishing for compliments?" I tease.

"From you? Always."

My stomach flips. I smooth a lingering kiss to his chest where I'm pressed against him. And suddenly I'm nervous again, although I don't know why. But this man is changing everything, and I'm equally amazed and scared. Because I never intended to stay in Chicago, but I can't imagine giving him up.

I hear him sigh again and shift against me, rearranging us until he's curled around me with one hand squeezing my breast. I fall asleep with a smile on my face and Lucas Abbott sneaking into my heart.

Lucas

I groan as I'm pulled from sleep. Something is tickling my chest. Not unpleasant exactly, but unusual enough to wake me up. Slowly I take stock. I breathe in the pleasant flowery scent that is Ash, and I smile remembering last night. I can feel her heat and softness next to me. Where she should be.

I can also feel my dick getting hard. It's not unusual for me to wake up with some morning wood, especially not when I wake up with thoughts of Ash but having her in bed next to me? I'm rock-hard and ready in seconds. I open my eyes and discover what's been doing the tickling.

Ash is leaning up so she can look down my body, the tips of her hair brushing across my chest and abs. I can't see her face but can practically feel her eyes watching my cock grow. My eyes follow the curve of her spine. I'm kind of fascinated by all her pale skin. The same way she seems into my tattoos. I wonder if she'll ever let me tattoo her. Nothing massive. My name on her pelvis would be a good place to start. Christ, I'm an asshole. If she could hear my thoughts, she'd probably punch me in the junk.

I'm not used to feeling possessive of anything, let alone women. Growing up like I did, I got used to nothing actually belonging to me. Anything I had could be taken away without notice, relocating to a different foster home without warning. My shop is the only thing I feel is mine, and that's only been the last few years. Even this condo doesn't really feel like a permanent home. Not yet. It's hard to feel settled when you're used to the ground constantly shifting beneath you.

But being with Ash somehow calms me. Maybe it's because she seems so content to just be with me. She's never waiting around for paparazzi wanting to get her photo taken. Or looking over my shoulder to see if a more famous client is walking through my door. Even last night, when the whole point of us being at that party was for her to talk to other people, she made me feel like a priority. I could tell she was a little anxious at the beginning, and frankly, it makes me feel awesome that I was able to help her relax. She's so fucking brilliant. Listening to her explain her experience and ideas to some of the city's wealthiest and most well-connected people was both intimidating and filled me with pride.

I'm really fucking glad I didn't blow it when I ran into Ethan. Man, I want to hit that guy.

My thoughts have distracted me from far more important things, and I pull myself back to the now. A naked Ash and a ready dick. She's been studying me a long time, and I'm curious what she's going to do. It's killing me to just lie here and do nothing, but I'm trying to be patient.

Eventually, I'm rewarded, and I feel one of her soft hands wrap around my length. Unable to stay quiet any longer, I groan my appreciation. She looks up at me, her hair tickling across my skin again, and smiles.

"Morning."

"Morning, beautiful."

"Sorry if I woke you." Her smile is anything but.

"You can wake me up like this any damn time."

"That's good to know."

Now that she knows I'm awake, she shifts and takes a firmer grip on my dick, stroking slowly. I grin and do some touching of my own anywhere my hands can reach her smooth skin. But I'm mainly focused on what she's doing. Because it feels freaking amazing. She squeezes my shaft and caresses its length. Her hand smooths over the tip and back down. I groan and thrust against her hands. My heart is pounding, and my breathing unsteady. What this woman does to me.

My body tenses as I feel tell-tale tingles at the base of my spine. Shit. As much as I'd love to let her continue, this isn't how I want to come.

I stop her hands and grab her waist, shifting her on top of me. I settle her on my thighs, so I have full access to her gorgeous body. And I start my own exploring.

She groans when I cup her breasts and tease her nipples with my thumbs. Her chocolate eyes are half closed as she watches me. I skim my hands along her thighs until I reach her hips and squeeze. I need to get inside her, but I need to make sure she's ready first.

"Come here. Kiss me."

Her smile makes my cock twitch. She rests her hands on my chest and leans down until I can reach her lips. I slip a hand between us, so I can explore her core and groan into her kiss when I discover how wet she already is.

"Ash," I moan her name. "Did touching me turn you on? You ready for me, beautiful?"

She makes that noise I'm quickly becoming addicted to and shifts lower until her core rubs against my erection and she starts grinding. Her breath hitches as she finds the friction she needs, her hips jerking.

I sit up abruptly but keep her hips pinned to mine. "Condom," I groan. She nods, moving against me frantically. Blindly I reach out and grab one from the nightstand. Her tongue teases my lower lip and then moves along my throat as I fumble with protection. Fucking hot feeling her lose control.

When the condom is taken care of, I lay back down. Squeezing her hips, I ease her over me. My jaw clenches against the pleasure when she lowers herself onto my shaft. I move my hands to her perfect ass, kneading, urging her on. Her shaky exhale is hot against my neck when she takes me all the way, as deep as she can.

"You feel so good."

So does she. Shit. Those pulses at the base of my spine are back. I'm not going to last long.

"Are you close?"

She nods frantically.

"Touch yourself, Ash. I need you to come."

She stills above me, eyes wide with a mix of hesitation and desire.

"Show me," I urge and take one of her hands with mine to her core. "Show me how to touch you."

She's a little tentative at first, but lust quickly overrides her inhibitions, and she moves our fingers, chasing her own orgasm.

"Lucas." I love the way she says my name. Her hips are moving, finding a rhythm she likes. "There. So good."

My other hand caresses down her back, urging her down to me so I can suck on her nipples, and she comes apart. I feel her core pulsing around my dick, squeezing so sweetly, and I thrust up into her, groaning my own release.

I wrap my arms around her, wanting to keep her close. And I feel her start to shake with laughter.

"What's so funny?"

Lifting her head up, she meets my confused but sated stare.

"How are you so good at that?" She giggles again.

I'm sure my smile is the definition of 'smug bastard'. "Me? This is all you."

She settles into me, still stifling giggles.

"You're sex-drunk," I tell her. And I want to pound on my chest with pride.

"That right? I like it."

I press a kiss to her forehead. "I like it, too."

I like it a hell of a lot.

Chapter Seventeen

Lucas

We do spend the entire day together. Most of it in my bed, which suits me fine. We spend the time touching, talking, teasing, and I'm into every minute of it. Eventually, we emerge for food. I order delivery so Ash can remain mostly naked. She pulls on one of my t-shirts but nothing else while we eat, and it's hotter than hell.

As evening approaches, I'm reluctant to let her go, so during our delivered-to-my-door dinner, I work on persuading her to stay another night.

"I have to work in the morning. And I definitely can't go to work in your shirt," she teases.

"That's perfect. I'm taking Jax to his physical therapy appointment tomorrow, so we can give you a ride."

Ash shifts from her seat onto my lap, and I wrap my arms around her. "You've been giving me rides all day." She's silent for a beat and then bursts into laughter.

"Why stop now?" I murmur, slipping my hand under the hem of my shirt and teasing the skin of her thigh.

She gets this look on her face I now recognize as a thinking look. I try to tip the scales in my favor and brush her hair to the side so I can nibble her neck. I've discovered over the last twenty-four hours how much she likes that. Her breath hitches, and she grips a fistful of my hair. I continue spreading kisses over her neck and behind her ear, and my fingertips tickle her inner thigh. She spreads her legs slightly, inviting me higher, but I keep my hand where it is. I'm on a mission and I'm not going to be distracted.

But I underestimated how determined Ash was. She whips her, my, shirt over her head, leaving herself gloriously naked, and shifts so she's now straddling me. She wraps her arms around my waist and plasters herself against me. I only bothered to throw on a pair of sweatpants that do nothing to hide my reaction to her. She kisses me, our tongues tangling, breaths mingling. And then I feel her busy little hands slide down my chest, tease my abs and slip under my waistband. I groan as she squeezes my length, my head tilted back in pleasure. Her lips press against my throat. She pulls my waistband away, freeing my cock and continues her exploration. Unable to wait, I dig into my pocket and pull out a condom.

"Where did that come from?" she giggles.

"Are you kidding? You're not wearing underwear. I'm keeping at least one with me at all times." She laughs at my explanation but snatches it out of my hand and smooths it down my length.

After we're done defiling each other, I return to making my case for her to stay another night.

"Okay," she agrees.

"Yeah?" I can't stop the grin spreading across my face.

"Yes. I want to stay. But I need to swing by my place and grab some things."

"Done. I'll drive you."

She smiles sweetly. I try to find her a pair of sweatpants she can tie at the waist, but the effort is laughable. Eventually, she just puts her dress from last night back on and pulls her hair into a messy ponytail. We luck out with a parking spot right in front of Gabby and Tim's. I follow her inside, not wanting her out of my sight for even a few minutes.

And yes, I realize how whipped that makes me.

Tim emerges from the kitchen as we enter and pretends to be surprised to see her.

"Ash! Good to see you! I wasn't sure you still lived here. Gabby's going to be so excited."

"Ha ha." Ash makes a face at him and continues back to the room she's staying in.

He shakes my hand and offers me a drink, but I'm not sure how long Ash needs, so I pass. Gabby's not home, so the two of us hang out awkwardly until Ash reappears with a bag over her shoulder. She's also changed into jeans and a long-sleeved t-shirt.

"All set?"

She nods and says goodbye to Tim. "Tell Gabby I'll see her tomorrow."

I grab her bag and slip it over my shoulder.

We head back to my place, where it takes me approximately 2.5 seconds to take her clothes off again.

The next morning, we swing by Macy's, so I can pick up Jax, and the three of us head to the hospital. He's cranky as ever about his slow recovery, but I'm too mellow after morning shower sex with Ash to give a shit. With our audience, I can't give her a proper goodbye. Instead, I just get a quick kiss and a promise to check in later. He's the first appointment of the day, so he is led right in. I settle into the waiting room and pull out my phone as a distraction while I wait.

Ninety minutes later, he's back, hobbling a little as he tries not to use his crutches.

"Weight-bearing as tolerated," he explains.

Back in my car Jax announces he's starving.

I shrug. "My first appointment isn't until noon. Want to grab some food?"

We head to a diner not far from *Vanished* and grab a table.

"You and Doc are spending a lot of time together."

I shrug. Jax knows me better than anyone, but I'm still not sure I'm ready to talk about what is happening between me and Ash. Even with him.

But he's a persistent bastard.

"I like her. She's cool."

I grunt, focusing on my coffee.

"Logan still being a little bitchy?"

"She promised to give Ash a chance, but they haven't hung out since the barbecue."

Jax nods, studying me silently.

"What's up?" I finally ask him.

"You getting serious? I don't remember the last time you spent the whole weekend with someone."

Am I?

We haven't known each other for long, but I feel... good... when I'm with Ash. I feel... settled. She's sweet and tough. Smart and makes me laugh. And the sex is off-the-charts hot. She doesn't care about the show except to support my career. She doesn't care about the Abbotts. Has never once implied I should try to get my hands on their money. She makes me want to be better. But also that I can be myself. That I'm enough.

"Yeah," I admit. "I guess I am."

He shovels in a massive bite of pancakes, so I do the same.

"She know about your family?"

"I told her about them, yeah. We actually ran into Ethan and Riley at the party Friday night."

"Oh, yeah?" He raises his eyebrows. "How'd that go?"

"Ethan? 'Bout as you'd expect. But Riley was okay. Even introduced her to Ash."

"No shit?"

I shrug. "You were right."

He smirks. "Usually am."

Ash

"Oh! I've been wanting to see this! You're famous."

"What are you talking about?"

Gabby and I are eating lunch in the lounge at the hospital. I've already suffered through her ribbing and a series of questions only a best friend could get away with asking about my weekend.

"You haven't heard? There's a whole spread in the paper about the fundraiser. I heard there's a photo of you and Lucas," she teases.

Gabby snatches the newspaper clipping off the table, and unfolds it to get to the photos. I see her stiffen. "Uh, Ash?"

"Do I look awful? I didn't even notice the photographers that night." I roll my eyes and shrug. Oh well.

"No, it's not that." Gabby looks up at me, a concerned expression on her face.

Puzzled, I reach for the article. She hands it over a little reluctantly. And finally, I see what has thrown her. There are several photos of the attendees. The Abbotts feature prominently, including one of Lucas and me in a conversation with the Chief. But only my face has been scribbled out with a black marker.

I frown a little off balance. It's unsettling. I try to shrug it off and hand it back.

"Someone's jealous, I guess."

"I guess," Gabby mutters, obviously still concerned.

"It's not a big deal, Gabs."

She folds it again, hiding the offensive image. "I don't know. It feels... wrong. Angry. What if it's the same person that trashed Jax's room?"

"I'm not dating Jax. And none of the flowers and cards were from me. I'm sure this is nothing. Just someone doodling."

"Only over your face?" She sounds skeptical.

My beeper goes off, ending the conversation. "Gotta run. I'll see you tonight." Thankful for the distraction, I rush out of the room and force the newspaper article from my mind. I have rounds to do, and then I have a meeting with the Chief to discuss my project and one of the donors that seemed particularly interested. I don't need to be worried about some stupid high school jealousy. Focus.

That afternoon I take a deep breath and knock on the Chief's door. She calls me in immediately. There's a man already in the room, sitting in the chair across from her desk. I'm assuming he's the one I'm here to meet. Chief stands and greets me warmly and the older man does the same. I step forward, hand outstretched to introduce myself, and falter, recognizing who it is.

Senator Theo Abbott stands before me, a warm smile on his face. He's in his late fifties. Distinguished and very handsome, with the same chiseled jaw and thick hair as Lucas, although his is mostly gray.

If he notices my hesitation, he ignores it like a professional, which I guess he is. He shakes my hand, which is still just hanging out there between us.

"Dr. Carrington. I've heard wonderful things about you and your proposal. I'm excited to learn more."

"Th-Thank you. Senator Abbott -"

"Theo, please."

"Please sit." The Chief gestures at the chairs across her desk. I glance at Theo's face, unsure exactly what he's thinking.

"Theo was just telling me that his wife and son are both very excited about expanding the hospital's commitment to trauma centers around the world."

"Yes, Ethan, in particular, feels very passionately about it."

He does? I'm skeptical that's true. At least that it's true without any ulterior motive.

"Can you tell me more about your work overseas? Your personal experience?"

I shake myself out of my stupor and pull myself together. I pretend he's any other potential donor and go through the details of my idea, sharing stories of my time in Nigeria. He asks several questions, all of which indicate he likes the idea. If it was anyone else, I'd be thrilled with the meeting. But instead, I'm left with an uneasy feeling in my stomach. This feels...wrong. Like getting offered precisely what I want but with strings attached. I'm just not entirely sure what those strings are.

It feels a lot like what he did to Lucas all those years ago.

I lurk just down the hall, casting frequent glances at the office door. After a seemingly endless wait, he finally emerges, and I make a beeline for him, intercepting him before he can get to the elevators.

"Senator Abbott!" I call out.

He turns with a smile, spotting me rushing up to him.

"Dr. Carrington. Is there something else I can help you with?

"Senator Abbott -"

"Theo. Please." He smiles kindly, and I steel myself against his charm and my own nerves.

Inhaling deeply, I continue. "Senator Abbott, I appreciate your interest in the work we're hoping to coordinate in Africa. And I very much appreciate your offer to help with the other Board members and building their support. I am happy to discuss it with you at any point."

He nods, a small smile playing around his lips, but his eyes are intent.

"But I will not be an easy access point for you to get to Lucas. If that is what this is."

His eyes widen slightly, but other than that, he doesn't react to my statement.

Uncertainly I hold my ground. There isn't really anything else I need to stay, but leaving it this way feels... unsatisfying. I want him to acknowledge my statement in some way to assure me he understands and will respect my wishes. The silence stretches unbearably until finally, I nod and start to turn away.

"You must care about him very much." His statement pulls me back.

"I do," I concede. That's not a secret, right? I'm risking a massive career setback, pissing this man off. But I can't, I won't, let him use me to manipulate Lucas.

"He's never had that before. I'm glad he has you now."

I am so confused. Every interaction I have with an Abbott that isn't Lucas - it's like there are two versions of them. The version they present to the world, even me. And the version Lucas knows. It would be easy to assume that Lucas is wrong, that he has misunderstood, that he should give them a chance. But I know what they did to him. I know what they did to his mother. And he is my priority. Whatever, however, he decides to move forward with them, I am on his side.

"I know you have no reason to believe this, but I only want the best for him. And when he's ready, I want him to be part of our family. I know the information Lucas has is painful, and I understand why he doesn't trust me. But there's always more to a story, isn't there?"

"That's between the two of you. It has nothing to do with me."

He smiles at me knowingly. Annoyingly. "If you say so."

He presses the button on the wall, calling the elevator.

"But if you prefer, I will limit our interactions to professional matters only. Until you or Lucas decide to change that."

"Thank you."

The elevator doors slide open, and he steps inside. "You've got a good vision for this project, Dr. Carrington. I would want to support that even if you weren't dating my nephew."

I'm so stunned hearing him directly acknowledge his relationship with Lucas I can't reply, and the elevator closes. My impression is that he's never publicly admitted Lucas is part of his family or how. Does his doing so now, to me, mean anything? Or is he assuming I'm safe? That because I'm with Lucas, I'll be discreet? Is that why he's never made a public statement? Discretion?

God, no wonder Lucas gets so twisted up about his family. My interactions with them leave me spinning with questions and uncertainty and I have way less invested than he does.

Who the hell are these people?

Chapter Eighteen

Ash

The next Sunday, Macy once again decides to host a barbecue. Jax is recovering well and planning on returning to his own place soon, and there are only so many weeks until the weather turns in Chicago and outdoor activities require multiple layers of clothing. Gabby and Tim join me now that they aren't worried about wedding preparations. Lucas and I have both had a busy week, and this is the first time we've managed to see each other in person. I haven't told him about my meeting and conversation with his uncle. It feels wrong keeping it from him, but it wasn't something I wanted to talk about over the phone either. I'm hoping I can fill him in tonight when we're alone.

"Hey, Doc." Jax greets, grinning at me. He's the first to spot the three of us come around the corner of the house. Lucas turns and smiles, seeing me. He crosses the yard, says hello to Gabby and Tim before pulling me to his side and giving me a quick kiss.

His eyes are warm when he looks down at me. "Hi."

"Hi back."

Gabby and Tim move on to say hello to everyone else and grab a drink. I hardly notice.

He's wearing a pair of faded jeans and a blue t-shirt that sets off his eyes and shows off his tattoos and muscles. And suddenly, I'm counting the hours until we can get out of here and be alone. His next words imply he's thinking along the same lines.

"It's been too long since I kissed you for real."

"I agree." I smile. God, I'm like a teenager with a first crush around him.

"Think we can fix that tonight?"

I nod. "I even packed some clothes."

"That implies you'll need them. You didn't last time."

I push him away playfully, laughing. "I have to work tomorrow."

"Right." He sighs exaggeratedly. "Work. I guess I have to do that too. I was thinking next weekend I could take you on a date. Real date."

Confused, I ask, "Haven't we been doing that? What do you mean real date?"

"I mean, just you and me. No big event. No backyards with my friends. A real date."

"Oh. Well, in that case, I'm in." My smile is even bigger.

"Come on, you two! Stop being anti-social!" Macy yells out.

I feel myself blush, and Lucas's eyes smolder at my reaction.

We grab drinks and sit at the picnic table with Jax and Logan.

"Is that Macy's date?" I ask, nodding at the curvy blond standing with him, Tanya, and Tim at the grill.

"No, she's an old friend. Tends bar at his parent's pub," Logan answers. Her phone beeps, and she glances at it, reading a text. "My date, on the other hand, is twenty minutes out."

I feel Lucas stiffen next to me. "Bodhi's in town?"

"Just about." She's still holding her phone but stares at Lucas, this challenging look in her eye.

I can tell he's still tense, but he shrugs. "Invite him over. Plenty of food."

She smirks and shoots a text off. I assume doing just that.

"I'm going to grab another drink. Anybody need anything? Ash?" Logan offers. She doesn't seem nearly as annoyed by my presence this time, although I think it helps having Gabby and Tim as a buffer.

I shake my head with a smile. "No, thanks. I'm good."

"I'll go with you. See what the options are." Gabby hops up.

"I'm going to get an ETA on the burgers. I'm starving. You two good?" Lucas asks. Jax and I grin at each other and nod.

Lucas steps away, and Jax's expression turns serious, eyes still intent on me. I squirm under his scrutiny, wondering what he's thinking.

"You love him?" he blurts out.

Startled, I glance quickly at Lucas's retreating back and then return to Jax, my mouth opening and closing soundlessly in shock.

He grins crookedly. "You've been spending a lot of time with my boy the last couple of months."

"I have," I agree.

"You don't really seem like the casual hook-up type."

"I'm not," I agree again. My head is spinning and my stomach is fluttery with nerves.

"You saved my life the night I was shot. I know that. But I would have been dead years ago if it wasn't for Luke."

He shifts around in his chair, straightening and repositioning his injured leg. I remain silent. I have no idea what to say to this line of questioning.

Comfortable again, he continues. "People think he's tough because of how he looks, how he carries himself. Because they've seen him angry once," he snorts. "But he's not. Not really."

"He's told you a little about when we were kids?" He takes a sip of his beer while I nod. "I was a stupid little shit. So cocky and pissed off. I was looking for any possible shortcut to make my life easier. I'm lucky as hell I never ended up in prison, some of the stunts I pulled."

This is news to me.

"He was never really tempted, though. He was stronger than me. The really bad times, he'd just turn it in, you know? Focus on his art. Wait it out. Never crossed those lines. Pulled me back over the line more than once."

I stay silent, letting him talk, taking it all in.

"So, yeah. He's stronger than me. Probably the strongest guy I know. But he's not tough. And he's into you in ways I've never seen him into anyone. So, if you're not in this for real, if he's just some celebrity fuck for you, end it. Walk away. Before you break him."

I glance at Lucas, joking around with Macy at the grill. As always, I'm struck by how handsome he is. He smiles, and even now, my stomach flips. He laughs at something Logan says, and I can't help smiling a little.

"Well. I guess that answers that," Jax says, pulling my attention back to him. "What do you mean?"

He shrugs, but before he can say any more, Tanya comes up carrying a plate of food for him and one for herself. The burgers are ready. Saved by the bun.

Lucas

Bodhi does actually show up. I still don't like it, like him, but Logan seems to be making an effort, so I try to do the same. He's a serious guy and doesn't say much, but he stays and hangs with us for a few hours at least. Still don't get what Logan is doing with him.

People start to head out around ten. Finally. I love these guys, but I've been waiting to get Ash home and naked for fucking hours now. God, she's beautiful. She's wearing jeans that mold her perfect ass and a black tank top, her hair in a bouncy ponytail. I want to get her home, bend her over something and watch that ass as I take her from behind.

And see how her week was, of course. We haven't talked much this week. But priorities.

Gabby and Tim left an hour or so ago. They're waiting for the weather to get cold before they take their honeymoon. Smart. February in Chicago is the worst.

Tanya says goodbye to everyone and stands awkwardly at the side of the house. I see Jax stand and realize what's going on. Shit.

"I'm out. Tanya is going to give me a ride home."

I frown and tilt my head, indicating I want to talk to him.

"You moving home tonight?"

"No time like the present." He's flippant, clearly not interested in this conversation. Too bad.

"You sure that's a good idea?"

He slaps me on the shoulder. "All good, Luke. Seriously. It's just a ride." He smirks.

"You need help moving stuff back?"

Jax shakes his head. "I've got a load with me. I'll grab the rest later."

I still don't like this whole scenario, but they're both adults. I stare at him for a moment. "Be smart."

He grins. "That's your job. I'll see you tomorrow." He squeezes my shoulder and waves to the remaining group. And then he and Tanya leave. Shit.

I turn back to the picnic table and catch Ash's worried eyes. She can already read me pretty well. Surprisingly, it doesn't bother me. I like that she cares how I'm feeling.

Fuck, I am a wuss.

I cross back to her. "You ready to take off?"

She nods and smiles. That smile punches me in the chest. She slips her hand in mine and stands before saying her goodbyes.

Back at my apartment, I immediately set out to fulfill my earlier fantasy.

Before the door fully closes, I've got her in my arms, kissing her. I feel her hands cupping my cheeks as she kisses me back, humming her appreciation. Those little sounds she makes get me harder than even the dirtiest porn. Who needs porn when I've got Ash tightly pressed against me?

"Lucas," she sighs into our kiss. "Wait, I need to talk to you about something."

"Later," I mutter. "We can talk after, promise." I press my mouth to the pulse in her neck and inhale deeply. I feel her shiver against me and grin against her skin. I love how responsive she is with me.

Her hands slip into my hair, gripping fiercely, and she pulls my face back to her for another kiss. I slide my hands down her back and cup her ass, pulling her firmly up against my erection. She moans and moves to pull my shirt off. The smile on her face as she explores my chest and abs only amps up my lust.

I move us to the edge of my couch and turn her around. Then I pull off her tank top, my hands immediately moving to cover her breasts. I tease them through the lace of her bra, watching her breath speed up with my touches. When she's mindless in my arms, I shift directions, undoing her jeans and smoothing my hand over her stomach, cupping her mound. She gasps, one hand reaching back to grab my hair and pull me down for a kiss, the other gripping my wrist as I touch her. My middle finger lightly brushes over her clit before moving back and sliding inside her heat. The heel of my palm presses firmly against her clit, doubling her pleasure.

"I love how wet you get," I whisper against her lips. Her eyes blink open slowly, and she gives me a smug smile.

"I love how hard you get," she teases. Only Ash could make me laugh while I have my hand buried between her thighs.

I play for a few more minutes until her stomach starts to clench, and she's panting unsteadily. Her ass brushes against my painful dick every time she moves; eventually, I can't take anymore and pull my hand out of her underwear. She starts to protest but quiets when I peel her jeans and underwear down her smooth legs.

"Bend over the edge of the couch," I urge while freeing my cock from my jeans.

She does, looking at me over her shoulder with half-closed eyes glittering with heat. Fuck, I could come from that look alone. From the sight in front of me. I squeeze the base of my cock, trying to gain some control and smooth my other hand over her ass.

"So pretty, Ash."

She arches her back, pressing her ass cheek more firmly into my palm. "Lucas," she groans. "Hurry."

Screw control.

Frantically I dig the condom out of my pocket and smooth it on. Then I line us up and slam home.

"Oh!" she cries out, and she rotates her hips feeling me inside her. She's bent over, her elbows on the back of my couch, and I've never seen such a pretty sight. She's hot and tight and... I need to move.

Gripping her hips, I slide out, watching as my dick nearly exits and then thrust to the hilt back into her soft warmth. I groan, loving how her ass shakes as she takes me. I lean over, pressing a hot kiss to her spine. My thrusts increase in speed, and I feel her inner walls clenching, indicating she's close. Thank god.

I move one hand so I can get to her core and play with her clit. Her breath hitches, and she screams my name as she comes. I still, and just feel her as she explodes around me, squeezing me tight. But then I have to chase my own orgasm and pound into her as I spill into the condom.

Breathing heavily, I kiss her shoulder blade and feel her shiver beneath me. I straighten, can't resist squeezing her ass one more time, and pull out so I can deal with the condom. When I return, she hasn't moved, a dreamy smile on her face. I pull her into my arms and press a kiss against her lips.

"Shower or bed?" I ask.

"Bed," she murmurs.

Once in my room, we remove the rest of our clothes and settle under the sheets. She doesn't hesitate to tuck into my side, sighing in contentment. I wrap my arms around her to keep her close.

We just enjoy the quiet after for a few minutes. I feel her finger tracing lines across my chest, along my tattoos.

She sighs again, but not one of her happy-best-sex-ever sighs.

"I do need to tell you something," she murmurs.

I stiffen. Nothing good ever follows those words. "What's up?"

"Remember how I told you about the donor who scheduled a meeting with the Chief to discuss the trauma centers?"

I nod. Where is she going with this?

She sighs again and sits up, wrapping the sheet around her nakedness.

I really don't like that.

Looking down at me, I see the worry on her face.

"What is it, beautiful?" I sit up, too, tracing her bottom lip with my thumb.

"When I got there on Monday, the meeting was with... your uncle."

My stomach drops. "Theo?"

She nods, her eyes wide and concerned.

I'm trying really hard to keep it together. Which means I shouldn't say anything right now. So I don't.

My silence clearly concerns Ash, though, because she rushes to explain. "I didn't know it was him, Lucas. I-"

"Hey," I interrupt, "hey, I know that. I know that."

She nods but her eyes still reflect her concern.

I clear my throat and look away, head spinning. Rage building. Why can't they just stay the fuck away from me? Now they're using Ash? I feel better listening to her continued explanation. My chest aches at the way she stood up for me. When she's done, I still can't find words to respond. But I lay back down, pulling her with me. Having her in my arms helps.

She's quiet and still a little stiff in my arms while I process this Abbott bomb.

"If he can help you, Ash, you should take it. But be careful, okay? My experience is that his help comes with strings attached."

I feel her nod against my chest. "There's more." She tells me about him calling me his nephew, claiming he wants me to be part of the family. I squeeze my eyes shut, annoyed those words have any effect on me.

"Should I not have told you that?" she asks softly.

I squeeze her. "No, you should. I just...." I don't know how to explain the mess of my thoughts and what is in my head right now. But she doesn't seem to need an explanation.

Instead, she stretches up and presses a sweet kiss to my cheek, settles back into my side, and wraps her arms around me.

Chapter Nineteen

Lucas

The following weekend I keep my promise to Ash and take her out on an actual date. I had to work on Saturday, we're finally getting back to our regular schedule after the shooting, but I had the entire night and all of Sunday alone with Ash. I even managed to leave her with clothes on for a good portion of it. We went to a movie in the park on Saturday night, and Sunday afternoon, I took her bowling. We went for a long walk through the city streets and talked. And we made a good dent in my supply of condoms. All in all, an awesome weekend.

Even a crazy hectic Monday can't kill my buzz from this weekend. Jax has been needling me all day, trying to piss me off, but even he can't ruin my good mood. He's back on full-time. I'm worried he's pushing too hard, too fast, but whenever I bring it up, he shuts me down. We're all keeping an eye on him, though. Quick to jump in if he seems to be tired or in pain. He's the cranky one, annoyed by the rest of us babying him.

But not me. I don't think anything could ruin my mood today.

My phone buzzes, and I grab it, hoping for a text from Ash.

What the fuck?

Guess I was wrong about nothing ruining my day.

I immediately recognize the image of Ash on my phone, despite the fact her face has a skull over it. Before I can react, another text comes in. This time the photo is accompanied by a message: **You should stay away from her.**

I respond: **Who the fuck is this?**

Another photo, this one taken in front of the hospital, her face similarly covered. My confusion is quickly being replaced by anger. Why is some sick fuck following Ash around?

Stay away from her. They warn again. Another picture from our date two days ago. There are more messages spewing bullshit that I scan through quickly.

"'Sup Luke? You look like your head is going to explode."

I ignore Jax's question and try to call the number, but not surprisingly, it doesn't go through.

But they send one last text. **Stay away or next time it will be her that gets shot.** This time they've edited the photo to make it look like she's dead.

My blood boils. This fuck has no idea what I will do to him when I find him.

Taking a deep breath to try and calm myself, I bring up Ash's contact and press call. Jax is watching me, surprisingly patient. Thank god, she answers on the second ring.

"Hi!" She sounds happy to hear from me, and I can picture her bright smile. Despite my concern and rage, her voice soothes me.

I try to keep my voice normal so I don't freak her out. "Hey, beautiful. What are you doing right now?"

"I just got back from teaching a class, and now I'm just making some dinner."

"Are you cooking naked?" I'm stalling, wanting to hear her smile and laugh a little bit longer before I drop this bomb on her.

Her husky laughter comes through the line. "Sorry, no. Fully dressed in leggings and a green hoodie. Not sexy, I know."

Green hoodie. I stiffen, on high alert. Fuck, one of those pictures was just taken.

"Ash." I clear my throat, heart pounding as I grab my jacket and head for the door. "I need you to do something for me, okay? No questions asked. I am on my way, and I promise I will explain everything when I get there. Okay?" I hear Jax calling after me, but I'm too keyed up to stop and explain. I need to get to her and see she's okay. He'll have to wait.

"I thought you had to work tonight?" she sounds confused.

"Something's come up. I'll explain when I get there." I unlock my car and slide inside. Thank god I drove today.

"What's wrong? You sound weird."

So much for trying not to freak her out. My phone is beeping; I'm sure Jax is texting me to find out what the fuck is going on. At least, I hope it's him and not more creepy photos.

"Are Gabby and Tim home?"

"No. They're doing a date night. Why?"

Shit. She's alone. With someone following her. Taking pictures of her. And I'm twenty fucking minutes away.

I'm wracking my brain, trying to figure out what to do.

"Lucas?"

"Ash, I'm on my way. I'll be there in twenty minutes. As soon as I can. I need you to go to the Starbucks across the street, okay? Leave right now and go."

It's the closest thing I can think of to make sure she's not alone until I get to her.

"What? Why? I just got home."

"Please, Ash. I promise I'll explain when I get there. But do this for me, okay?"

I hear a rough sigh and sense her frustration. I just hope she trusts me enough to wait for a reason.

"Okay. I'll go. But you'll have to be creative in how you make it up to me."

I force out a fake laugh and promise.

"I have to make another quick call. But I'll call you right back. I'm on my way. Starbucks," I remind her.

"I'll be there. Oh, but-"

Shit, I ended the call and missed whatever she was going to say. But I'm going to call her back as soon as I get reinforcements.

I dial again, relieved when he picks up. Fuck, I've practically got this guy on speed dial lately.

"Melrose."

"Melrose, it's Luke. I need your help."

It's just a few minutes later, after I've quickly explained the situation and gotten Melrose to agree to meet us, I call Ash back.

It goes straight to voicemail.

Shit. I press down on the accelerator.

Ash

The barista calls out my name and sets my drink on the counter. I grab it up, trying to let go of my irritation. I just want to be home, in some comfy clothes with my dinner and a glass of wine. I keep running through my conversation with Lucas in my mind, trying to figure out what could possibly be going on. It's not like him to be so vague and cryptic. At least, I don't think it is. I guess I haven't known him that long.

But I feel like I'm getting to know him well. And as far as I can tell, other than discussing his mother and her family, he's been nothing but upfront. Even with that, he's always been honest; it's just obvious he'd rather not talk about it.

So even though it felt like a ridiculous request, and I'm irritated to be here and not on my couch, I'm choosing to trust him.

I hear my name bellowed behind me and feel myself yanked around and slammed into a wall of man. Luckily, I figure out pretty quickly that it's *my* man.

"Lucas, what is-"

The rest of my question is cut off when he presses a hard kiss against my mouth and then holds me tight enough breathing becomes uncomfortable. Worry starts to prickle my senses, eliminating the last of my irritation. Something is obviously not right. I squeeze him back, trying to reassure him. I'm learning with Lucas physical contact is the form of communication he understands best. He's almost always touching me when I'm within arm's reach. Most of the time, I don't think he even realizes he's doing it. But it seems to calm him, and that's clearly what he needs right now.

And I don't find touching him to be much of a hardship and vice versa.

For a moment, he just holds me, one hand tangled in my hair, pressing my face against his chest while he seems to breathe me in.

"Thank God you're okay. Your phone kept going right to voice mail."

Why wouldn't I be okay?

But instead of asking that question, I respond with, "The battery died. I tried to tell you it was going to, but you hung up too fast. My work cell was on."

He chuckles roughly into my hair. "I guess I need to get that number, huh?"

He finally pulls back so I can see his face. As always, his handsome face spreads warmth through my belly. I smile up at him, trying to reassure him everything is going to be fine.

Even though I still have no idea what has got him so worked up.

He turns to the side slightly and I realize for the first time he's not alone. Standing back slightly, allowing us some privacy is a strange to me man. He has no visible tattoos, save an image I can't quite make out on his forearm. He's in jeans and a simple black t-shirt stretched across a broad, muscled chest. He seems to be taking my measure with his steady hazel eyes. His black hair was probably carefully styled several hours ago, but now the curls are starting to get a bit unruly on top. His square jaw is sporting an evening shadow. And if I wasn't totally convinced Lucas was the hottest man in Chicago, I would notice that this man has a very kissable bottom lip. But I don't notice that. At all.

Why are all of Lucas's friends ridiculously attractive? It's really not fair. I really should have more single girlfriends.

Lucas makes introductions. "Ash, this is Dylan Melrose."

Dylan smiles warmly, his eyes serious, and shakes my hand. His name rings a bell, but with everything going on right now, I can't remember where I've heard it before.

"Ash, I'm a Detective with the Chicago PD."

What?

I shoot a confused and slightly panicked look at Lucas. "What - what's going on?"

And then it clicks. He was the one Lucas planned to call after Jax's room was vandalized. And he was the one that found Olivia for Mateo. Instinctively I move closer to Lucas. Has something else happened?

Detective Dylan Melrose nods to one of the back tables and suggests we take a seat. I take a deep breath, realizing that going along is probably the fastest way for me to get answers. Once I've settled into my seat, Lucas folds into the chair next to me, pulling my chair closer to him. Despite my confusion, I'm warmed by his desire to be close to me. Dylan sits across the table.

"Lucas, you're really freaking me out. What is going on? Are you okay?"

My eyes flit between the two men. The ragged expression on Luke's face makes me nervous, while Dylan's seems more assessing.

Lucas sighs heavily, bringing my attention back to him.

"I got some threatening text messages today."

My stomach sinks, and I suddenly feel chilled. "Threatening how?" Needing to touch him, I place my hand on his forearm, squeezing reassuringly. "Are you okay?"

"They weren't threatening me, Ash. They threatened you."

I'm stunned. What the hell? Why would anyone threaten me? And why would they send the threats to Lucas? It must be some bad joke. My confused thoughts are pinging rapidly around my head.

"Me? I don't understand."

Lucas is watching me intently, his eyes clearly communicating his concern. And that is what finally starts to really freak me out.

"Show her," Dylan states.

Lucas shoots him a glare but then attempts to school his features and hands me his phone.

I steel myself and then begin to scroll through the texts and images on his phone. There's a series of photos featuring me from various times throughout the last few days. I don't spend much time reading the texts, the images were enough to convince me this wasn't good, but I do spot one that informs Lucas he doesn't have to be so nice to me just because I saved his best friend and offering to take care of it if I'm bothering him.

I'm starting to feel nauseous. My hands are shaking as I identify the photos for Lucas and the Detective. "That's from my lunch break today. I ran to the farmer's market. And that's as I was leaving the hospital. I don't understand."

I feel Luke's warm hand on my knee, silently offering comfort.

"This happens sometimes. I mean, I've gotten weird fan mail and threats before. Not much but some. But this is different. This is someone who was able to get my personal cell. And knows about you."

This is so creepy and gross.

The Detective, Dylan, I don't know what I should call him, leans forward and tries to be reassuring. "It might be nothing. Just some weird prank and this is the end of it. But I think we should take it seriously until we know for sure. That's why Luke called me."

"Right. Of course."

"Do you feel up for answering some questions for me?"

I feel myself nodding. Lucas leans back in his seat and rests one arm along the back of my chair. I'm doubly thankful he'd pulled me closer to him when we sat down. His body heat and scent are helping keep the chill at bay.

"Did you notice anyone out of the ordinary today around the time these were taken?"

I rack my brain, trying to remember if anyone had given me a weird vibe but ultimately come up with nothing. "No. It was a perfectly normal day."

"How many people know about your relationship with Luke?"

"I mean, hospital staff know I was on Jax's case while he was there. And Lucas came with me to my best friend's wedding. And a hospital fundraiser. There was a photo of us, but others were in it too."

"Any idea who could be doing this? Has anyone been giving you a hard time?"

"No. No one." I'm starting to feel incredibly unhelpful. But honestly, this is coming out of nowhere for me. I'm too stunned to think clearly. It's possible Gabby told some of the girls Lucas and I had started seeing each other more seriously, but I doubt it. Not once it became obvious this wasn't going to be a one-night stand. And frankly, even if they did know, why would they do this? It makes no sense.

"Any ex-boyfriends?"

"No. I was in Africa and Asia for almost three years. I've only been back a little over two months and haven't dated anyone. I mean. Until Lucas. I mean, not that we're dating exactly. We've just been hanging out." I'm blushing furiously, self-conscious discussing this with a man I don't know in front of Lucas when Lucas and I haven't even had the conversation. It's only been a little over a month since Jax was released from the hospital. It seems early to have the relationship talk. Isn't it? "But there hasn't been anyone else dating or hanging out," I rush through the rest of my explanation awkwardly.

Lucas grunts next to me, and my eyes flash over quickly, noting the scowl on his face. He crosses his arms over his chest as he watches me. I immediately miss his warmth at my back. "We're not 'just hanging out'. Words aren't going to scare me, Ash."

Then he looks directly at Dylan and says, "We're together. She's my girl-friend."

This is such an inappropriate time for me to smile. I manage to squash it, just barely. But I can't help the giddy rush spreading through me at his declaration.

Is that the most important thing happening right now?

Probably not.

Is that the most important thing I've heard at this table?

Yes. Absolutely, yes.

He's so getting lucky tonight.

Focus, Ash.

I turn my attention back to Dylan, whose expression seems grimly resigned to some new fact. "No one who might want to rekindle something from before you left?" he continues without missing a beat.

Yet again, I shake my head unhelpfully. "No. There wasn't anyone serious enough they'd still be pining after me three years later."

I feel Lucas shift positions beside me but try to stay focused on Dylan.

"What about at the hospital? Could there be anyone who resents your position? Someone denied a promotion because you got the job or thinks they deserve the spot more than you?"

I consider this for a moment but inevitably come up with nothing. Shrugging, I explain, "Maybe, but I doubt it. The position only exists because of a grant the hospital got based on the work I was doing abroad. If it wasn't me doing it, the position probably wouldn't exist at all."

"Okay." Dylan nods, pulls a business card out of his pocket and pushes it across the table to me. "Here is all my contact information. Put it in your phone and memorize it. I'll want you to come into the station in the next few days to make a formal report. In the meantime, safety in numbers, okay? Don't go anywhere alone. I'll see about tracing the texts. If you see anything or think of anything else, call me. Even if it seems silly. I'm here to help."

"Thank you."

Dylan and Lucas share a look.

"You be okay here for a second, beautiful? I'm going to walk Dylan out."

I exhale, trying to release the tension in my shoulders. Will I be okay? My first instinct is to panic, not wanting to be alone after all this. But this seems like a perfectly safe place for me to be, and Lucas will be back in a second.

"Yeah, of course."

Lucas lifts my chin with his finger until I raise my eyes enough to meet his. Warmth spreads through me at the concern in his gaze and I offer a shaky smile. He kisses me, slow and sweet.

"I'll be right back."

Lucas

Well. That fucking sucked.

I follow Dylan back outside to the sidewalk. The cooler night air feels good against my skin, and I take a deep breath, trying to chill the fuck out.

I'm not remotely successful.

"You think you'll get anything from the texts?" I ask.

"Doubt it. Anyone savvy enough to pull this off is going to know enough to use a burner or cloak it somehow. We'll try, but...." He shrugs, signally his doubt.

"Right." That's what I expected.

"You want to tell me what's bugging you?" Dylan's a pretty sharp guy, and like I said, we've known each other a long time. I'm not really surprised he can sense I've got some *thoughts* or that he indicated he wanted to talk to me alone.

I don't like leaving Ash alone, though. Even though I suspect she's about as safe in this moment as she can be. And I feel weird ratting her out to Dylan, but something she said didn't sit quite right. It didn't feel right calling her out in front of Dylan, and I doubt she'd appreciate what I'm about to do but *fuck*. I also really don't like someone following her or threatening her.

"Besides my girlfriend being stalked?"

"Besides that," he agrees.

I take a deep breath and look back inside the cafe, finding Ash. Why *didn't* she say anything? Did I read the situation wrong?

I don't think so.

But also, so what if I'm wrong? Dylan will check it out and come up with nothing. No harm, no foul.

"There's a guy at the hospital. Dr. Will Parker. I don't know why she didn't mention him. I'm pretty sure they used to date."

He doesn't respond, so I continue. "We haven't gotten to the 'tell me about your exes' phase, but I overheard a couple conversations. I don't know how serious it was. But they still work together, and he didn't seem pleased when he walked in on us kissing once."

"I'll look into it," Dylan promises, and I immediately feel better.

"You said you've had a few threats before?"

I shrug. "Yeah, weird letters, gifts, that kind of thing. We've got a P.O. Box for fan mail, but it's not hard to find the shop."

"Can you send me whatever you still have? I'll see if anything stands out."

"Thanks, man. I appreciate it." I clasp his hand, pulling him in slightly to pound him on the back. "I'll have Tanya drop stuff off."

"I'll keep you posted."

"Thanks."

I nod goodbye and walk back inside. To Ash.

She's staring into space as I walk back to the table. I suspect deep in thought processing everything that's happened. Usually, I like watching her work things out in her head, dissecting whatever problem is in front of her. I like that she's so smart. And that I've never seen her use that intelligence to make others feel dumb.

I like a lot of things about her.

But knowing what is on her mind right now, I only want to distract her. Try to make her smile.

As I approach, she straightens and focuses her attention on me. She looks up at me, a forced smile on her face. Not the smile I want to see.

"Ready to head out?" she asks.

I nod. "You okay with going back to my place?"

I don't know why. None of the images had been of her at home, but I feel safer with her in my space.

She stands. "Let me just go back and grab some stuff."

I text Jax and give him a brief rundown on what's going on while Ash packs a bag. He seems just as furious. I appreciate that he has her back too. He offers to let Krista and Tanya know so I don't have to deal with them until tomorrow. I hadn't really thought about it, but I guess they do need to know.

Less than an hour later, I'm unlocking the door and letting Ash into my apartment. I head to the kitchen, asking if she needs anything over my shoulder.

"Some water?"

I'm back momentarily, a glass of water in each hand. She's still standing awkwardly in the entry, a fierce grip on the bag she'd brought with her to stay the night.

"You okay? Want some food? I'll order something for us."

Silently she shakes her head. I gently take her bag and set it in the hall.

"Hey. What's going on in that brilliant head?" Her behavior is starting to concern me. I take her hand and move us together to the living room.

She shifts away as we settle into the couch, half turning so she can face me.

"You, ah, you called me your girlfriend. Before. With Dylan."

I almost laugh with relief that's what has got her so off balance. Not a potential stalker. I manage to keep a straight face, though. Even I know laughing at a time like this will likely not go over well.

"Is that a good thing or a bad thing?" I ask her, unsure what she's getting at.

"We haven't really talked about," she gestures between us, "*this.*"

I grin at her. I can't help it. She's so fucking cute.

"This?" I mimic her hand gesture.

"Luke!" She huffs adorably, and she scowls at me. Oh, she's serious. She never calls me Luke. Okay.

"So, let's talk about it. What's on your mind?"

"Did you. . .mean it?"

"I try not to say things I don't mean, Ash."

"Okay, well. What does that mean to you?"

Oh. No one's really asked me that before. Isn't it obvious what it means? Shit.

I've been silent too long. Ash starts to fidget and glances away.

Say something, asshole!

"I guess it means we'd be a couple." Shit. Now I'm being awkward. I shove my hand through my hair, exhaling roughly. "I'm sorry. I'm not very good at these kinds of conversations."

My admission seems to relax her. She shifts closer and grabs one of my hands.

"So, does that mean you want us to be exclusive? I just, I want to make sure we're on the same page."

"Ash. I wouldn't ask you to make a commitment I'm not willing to match." I feel like I'm missing something. Instead of getting any clarity, these questions are just confusing me more.

"It just...with the show...I mean, I've seen how people, women...."

Suddenly it clicks what she's worried about. "That's not what I want, Ash," I tell her. "I won't lie and say I haven't...but," I shake my head, unsure how to finish the thought.

"I need the words, Lucas. I need you to say it."

"I don't want to see anyone else. And I don't want you to either."

She starts to smile, then bites her lip to stifle it.

"Hey." I crowd into her space, pulling her close, and kiss her lightly. Then I kiss her again. "You can be happy about this. I'm happy about this. The idea of you with another guy shreds me. And I can't imagine wanting another woman. All I see is you."

Her soft palms cup my cheeks, and she kisses me sweetly.

"Lucas?" she whispers against my lips.

"Yeah?"

Eyes shining, she teases, "You're better than you think you are with 'these kinds of conversations'."

I laugh and kiss her again. And then I do other things to keep her from thinking about anything but me. But us.

Hours later, with her sated and safe in my arms, I bring up the question that's been bugging me since our conversation with Dylan. I'm staring at the ceiling, one hand lazily teasing up and down her back.

"Why didn't you mention Will when Dylan asked about your exes?"

I feel her cheek brush against my chest as she shifts. She raises onto her elbow, staying glued to my side as she looks into my face.

I don't meet her eyes, instead continuing my study of the ceiling. This conversation makes me uneasy, and I'm not entirely sure why. Except that I don't want to piss her off hours after she's agreed to be my girlfriend. She's never mentioned dating Will; it's just something I suspect based on overheard remarks and awkward interactions.

Finally, she breaks the silence. "I guess I just didn't think about it. We were never serious, barely dated. I can't imagine he'd do something like that."

"People are capable of all kinds of things you wouldn't suspect."

I think of my family. The upstanding Abbotts. Chicago's golden family. And what they've done to me. Did to my mother.

As if she can read my mind, Ash kisses my cheek and settles back down against me. Her leg shifts, settling between mine, and she lays her arm across my chest.

"Do you...have questions? You can ask me about Will if you want. You can ask me anything."

I shake my head but then realize I do have questions.

"Why did you break up?"

"We just kind of ended. There wasn't any drama or anything. He's a good guy. We have our work in common. It made sense on paper, but in practice, we just weren't... what I wanted, I guess. And then I got the fellowship in Africa, and I went."

"Did he want to get back together when you got back?"

"Not that he mentioned. And then, a week later, I met you. So...." She shrugs.

"What did you want?"

"What do you mean?"

I move quickly, rolling so I'm leaning above her, able to see her face. "You said it wasn't what you wanted. With him. What did you want?"

Her eyes soften as they roam across my face. "I wanted to laugh more. To feel more. To be heard, not just listened to. I wanted something that felt right, not just sounded right."

She lifts her head and gives me an easy kiss. "This," she whispers. "I wanted this."

I'm not sure what to do with the gentle pain in my chest. Not for the first time with her, I wish I was better with words so I would know what to say to that. How to let her know what that means to me. But she doesn't seem to expect or need a response. Instead, she just smiles and rolls to her side, pulling me down beside her, so we're spooning. She tugs my arm around her and tucks her ass against me. I press a kiss to her shoulder and hear her sigh in contentment.

I can do this. If this is what she needs, this I can do every single night.

As soon as I find the asshole threatening her.

Chapter Twenty

Ash

I can't sleep. I appreciate the warmth and comfort of having Lucas holding me, but even that can't calm the thoughts racing through my head. Why is this happening? Who would want to threaten me? Why send threats to Lucas and not to me?

Not that I want them. I'm just saying.

Lucas shifts behind me, squeezing me tight for a brief second, even in sleep. It makes me smile.

I hear my phone buzz, and since I'm awake anyway, I grab it off the nightstand.

Just making sure you're alive.

I grimace at the text from Gabby. Unintentionally freaky considering everything else that's happened today.

And that's when I remember.

Oh shit.

Ever attuned to my body, Lucas immediately asks me, "What's wrong?" His voice is scratchy with sleep.

Sitting all the way up, I turn to face him.

"I totally forgot. Remember the photo of us that was in the paper?"

He levers himself up onto one elbow, rubbing his other hand over his face to wake up. "The one from the fundraiser?"

"Yeah. The day after that ran, Gabby and I found a copy of the article in the doctor's lounge. My face had been scratched out."

Now I've got his full attention. "Are you serious? Why didn't you tell me?"

Shrugging, I tell him, "I honestly didn't think it was that big of a deal. Just someone jealous of my hot date."

My attempt at a joke falls flat. He's turning away, reaching for his own phone. "I don't suppose you kept it, did you?"

Damn. "No. Like I said, I didn't think it was anything. But now...."

He looks up at me from his phone. The light from his screen reveals his grim expression. "I'll tell Melrose."

I nod, not sure what else to do. But that sounds like a good idea.

I respond to Gabby's text, confirming I am, in fact, alive. And tell her I'll talk to her tomorrow.

Finished messaging with Dylan, Lucas climbs back into bed, and I move immediately into his arms.

"He wants you to call him in the morning and tell him what you remember. He might want to talk to Gabby too."

Sighing, I say, "I guess I should tell her what's going on."

"She should know, Ash. She can help keep an eye out for anything weird. Anyone sketchy at the hospital or in the neighborhood. The more people keeping you safe, the better."

I shiver and burrow closer to his warmth.

"What?!" Gabby shrieks.

The next morning, we meet for breakfast near the hospital at her favorite little cafe so I can update her on the chaos my life has become.

I glance at the table next to us. "Sorry," I apologize to the couple sitting there, staring at us wide-eyed and startled.

"Sorry," Gabby throws out dismissively and lowers her voice. "Are you okay? This is crazy."

"I'm a little freaked out," I admit.

"Of course you are. I'm so sorry."

"Well, and it reminded me of that scratched-up photo we found."

"Do you think that's related to these texts?"

Taking a sip of coffee, I debate my answer. "I don't know. Maybe? But it doesn't really matter since we don't have it."

Gabby stares at me and blinks.

"Gabs? You okay?"

"I still have it."

My fork clatters to the plate, and I lean back in surprise. "You do? Why?"

"I thought it was weird. I told you then it didn't feel like nothing. They destroyed your face! That's weird, Ash."

I grab my phone and text Lucas, letting him know.

"I can't believe you kept it." Tears spring to my eyes out of nowhere. "I love you."

She gets up so she can hug me. "No one messes with my girl."

I awkwardly squeeze her back from my position, blinking back my tears. "Thank you."

Settling back into her chair, she asks, "What else can I do?"

I shrug, shaking my head. "I have no idea. This doesn't even feel real, you know?"

"Well, I'm calling Tim. We'll get a security system installed at the house as soon as we can."

"I'm sorry. That's so much trouble. I'll pay you-"

"You will not! We probably should have done it a long time ago."

Shit. She's really trying to make me cry this morning.

"Let's talk about something more pleasant."

"Sounds great. Honeymoon?"

Gabby purses her lips, pretending to consider her options. "I was thinking more like, you've spent a lot of nights not at home the last couple of weeks."

My standard blush makes an appearance, but I laugh. "You're ridiculous."

"Well? I've heard next to no details, which is totally breaking the best friend code. Was I right?" She raises her eyebrows suggestively.

I am sure I am bright red at this point. I glance at the couple next to us again, hoping they can't overhear any more of our conversation. They don't appear to be paying any attention to us.

"Hello? Waiting...."

"I've got no complaints," I inform her with a satisfied grin. "And I'm never bored."

"Mmhmm," she nods approvingly. "Dirty talker?"

I refuse to answer but can't seem to squelch the tiny smile on my face. I try to hide it behind my mug of coffee, but Gabby sees right through me.

"I knew it!"

Lucas

"Jax is doing good? Tanya says he's back on full time," Krista says.

"Yeah, he's good. Shop's back to normal finally." I shift back in my chair, making myself more comfortable. I had several messages waiting for me first thing this morning from Krista. She'd gotten a quick update from Jax but obviously wanted to check in with me about everything. In addition to all the drama we've been dealing with, we have to finalize our upcoming shooting schedule, and she's got ideas for marketing and press she wants to discuss. As soon as I dropped Ash off with Gabby - I'm not leaving her alone until this asshole is found - I opened *Vanished* and returned Krista's call.

"That's great, Luke, really."

I mutter an agreement.

"Tanya was planning on returning to LA at the end of the week, but Jax told me about the weird messages you received yesterday. Do you want her to stay a bit longer?"

"I mean, I'm hoping to keep this out of the press," I point out.

"You're working with the police, right?"

"Yeah. They're on it."

"It seems like more of a police matter than a PR matter, but I'll ask her to stay if you want additional backup. We can obviously help from here if anything does come up."

I think about it. Tanya has definitely helped the last couple of months, but what I really want is for things to go back to normal. That seems unlikely until we find the person who sent those threats and figure out how serious it is. Melrose hasn't ruled out that it was just a sick prank. I hope he's right, but I'm not willing to take that chance. Not with Ash.

But Krista's right. That's for the police.

"No, it's fine. She should go home."

"And the new addition to the team? Mateo? How is he doing?"

I shrug even though she can't see me. "Good. Always on time, does his work. Pays attention. Sharp kid."

"I know this isn't why you did it, but it will be great for ratings."

I roll my eyes. No, that's definitely not why I did it. "He's not going to be on camera, Krista."

"Think about it. Could be-"

"No," I interrupt.

I hear her sigh on the other end of the line. I know she gets frustrated with my narrow commitment to publicity. But I'm not using a kid to make myself look good. That's bullshit.

"Okay. Well, at least consider including him in some of the season premiere events. That's months out."

I grunt, non-committal.

We agree on a date to start filming, and she goes over some minor staff changes to the crew. She also gets me to agree to a set of special interviews to 'tell our side' of the shooting and Jax's recovery. RJ, who is based in Chicago, will start next week.

"I have two more things." She must sense I'm getting restless. I know this is important, stuff we need to decide and finalize, but I've never been that good at sitting still unless I have some kind of canvas in front of me. "Tanya mentioned Jax has some ideas for creating a line of merchandise. I think it's a great idea and would like to have him put together an actual plan and proposal. We can have someone polish it up if we need to."

"He does?" This is the first I'm hearing about it. Why didn't he say anything?

Because he almost died, and you've been spending all your time with Ash. Shit. I shove a hand through my hair. I'm being a shit friend.

"I mean, yeah. That sounds great. I'll talk to him about it."

"Awesome." She pauses, and I have a suspicion I'm not going to like what's coming next. "So, this woman, Ash? I'd like to talk to her about signing a release and doing her own testimonials."

She wants Ash to be on the show. Fuck. See? I knew I wasn't going to like it.

Ash

"Ash!"

I glance up from my lunch and see Will rushing over. He grabs the empty chair next to me.

"I just talked to Detective Melrose. He told me about the threats you received."

Shit. Melrose works fast. I feel a pang of guilt I didn't warn Will. "I'm sorry, I-"

He interrupts me. "I don't care about that. I know he's just doing his job, talking to everyone. Are you okay?"

I shrug. "Physically, sure. Yeah. I'm fine."

The expression on his face is skeptical. "We're still friends, right? You can tell me if something is going on."

Are we friends? I care about and respect him, yes, but to confide in him? That feels wrong.

"I know. It just happened, and everything since has been moving so fast."

"Of course. I'm just glad you're okay. Have you talked to the Chief? Maybe she should alert hospital security."

"I haven't. But you're right; that's a good idea." Everyone seems better at this than me. Lucas, Gabby, and now even Will - they've all come up with ideas to keep me safe, to try and figure this out. What have I done? I'm just in a fog, going through the motions of the day, trying not to think about it too much, so I don't freak out.

His expression changes. "I hate to say it, but I told you this guy-"

"Don't, Will." I don't want to hear any accusations against Lucas. "This is not his fault."

He looks away, exhaling roughly. "Alright. You're right. I just hate to see you...."

"I'm fine. Gabby's installing a security system. The police are looking into it. I'll talk to the Chief. I'll be fine."

He exhales again and finally turns back to me. "Okay, let me know if you need anything. If I can help in any way."

"I'll be fine. Thank you." I reach out and squeeze his hand, releasing it quickly.

I appreciate that he wants to help me, I do. But I know I won't ask him for help. Asking him would feel wrong, like betraying Lucas. I do, however, take his advice, and after I'm finished with lunch, I go to see the Chief. She's understandably concerned and gives me a contact for hospital security to coordinate with Detective Melrose.

The rest of the day is uneventful in the best possible way, although Gabby insists I wait until she's ready to go home, not wanting me to go anywhere alone. I don't put up much of a fight, honestly, this whole thing and everyone's reaction to it has me appropriately freaked out.

I'm okay traveling in groups for a while.

Gabby insists she's tired and wants to splurge on a taxi home instead of taking the subway like usual. I know what she's doing but go along with it. I appreciate she's worried about me. As soon as we're through the door, Tim announces someone is coming in two days to install an alarm and security camera. Tim also works fast.

I'm starting to feel like a burden. These two have totally disrupted their lives for me, first by letting me stay with them at all, and now this. I was just starting to look at apartments, and now I... well, I really don't want to live alone with all of this going on. As much as I hate causing them trouble, I appreciate having their company and support.

I know Lucas would let me stay with him, but I can't move in with a guy I've only been dating for a couple of months.

Can I?

No. That's crazy. Besides, Lucas may invite me over often for sleepovers, but it's not like he's asked me to move in permanently, and I can't exactly invite myself. Not that I'm ready for that.

I'm not. We're not.

So, I guess I'll continue to intrude on my best friend and her new husband. That's what best friends are for, right? Letting you crash at their apartment when you are maybe being stalked and don't want to live alone?

I skip dinner and shut myself in my room. I have a call with Abeni in the morning so we can strategize, and I can give her all the updates. But I'm too uneasy to focus on work. I need something, though, so I grab a book, hoping it will be good enough to distract me from my depressing thoughts.

Chapter Twenty-One

Lucas

I lean back and stretch, loosening my shoulders after finishing up my last tattoo for the day. I'm pretty excited about it, though. A starting player from one of Chicago's local baseball teams has come in for an arm piece. It's a multiple-day, several-appointments kind of tattoo, but if he likes it, and I'll make sure he likes it, it will mean some dope exposure and even more professional athletes coming into the shop.

Tanya is standing out front, frowning into her cell. The energy coming off her is all wrong; she's tightly coiled. I can tell she hasn't exactly been patiently waiting for me to finish up with my last client. I glance at Logan, working behind the counter, but she just shrugs and rolls her eyes. She doesn't know what's going on.

"What's so urgent?" I ask, bringing her attention to me, off whatever task she's absorbed in on her iPhone.

She exhales dramatically and rushes to my side. Now I'm the one frowning. Tanya isn't usually dramatic. She and Krista are incredibly competent professionals. They know their shit, and they don't try to manipulate my 'image'. As annoyed as I can get with this aspect of my job, I recognize everything they do for us and how lucky I am the show found her to do our PR.

She hands me her phone. I can tell she doesn't like what she's about to show me. I steel myself. Fuck. But I'll fight to keep what I have. Whatever this is, it won't take the life I've worked so hard to build.

"We've got a problem."

"What the fuck?!" I burst out. Because staring back at me is a video of Ash and me...together. It's from months ago, the day she came to *Vanished*, right before Jax was released from the hospital. I'm tempted to throw the phone and its offensive video across the room but manage to reign it in and hand it back to Tanya. I slam my hand against the wall instead.

"What the fuck is that? How do you have that?" I growl. Furious.

"I don't have it. *TMZ* has it. They've posted it to their website."

Logan snatches the phone up, her face pinched with anger when she realizes what it is. "*Lucas has a Lover*," she reads the headline. She quickly puts the phone screen down on the counter. "Such bullshit. Can't we sue them for that or something?"

Tanya nods, "We can try if that's what you want to do. I've already contacted Krista. She wants to set up a call with you to discuss options and how you want to handle this."

"There's nothing to *handle*," I grit out. "Get the fucking tape off their website."

She nods again. "I'll do everything I can."

Shit.

I pull my phone out and text Ash, praying she hasn't seen it yet. Although I'm not looking forward to it, I should be the one to tell her.

Tanya is still talking 'strategy', but I'm not paying any attention until I hear, "stop seeing each other for a while-"

"That's not going to happen," I snap. But then I realize it could. She could, I mean. She could end it. I still have a lot to learn about Ash, but I know enough to know this kind of attention is not something she would ever want.

"It's the easiest way to kill the story," Tanya insists. "If you're not seen together, there is no gas for the flames."

I'm going to lose it. This is too fucking much on top of everything else that's happened. It's been barely a week since those weird text messages, and now someone is spying on us? Sending videos to the press? "How the fuck did this happen?" I demand.

Tanya looks at me with wide eyes. "I don't know."

Still no response from Ash.

"Damn it!" I yell, causing Tanya to jump. Logan watches me with steady eyes and a scowl on her face.

"I'll call RJ and have him check the cameras. See if he can figure out what's going on," she suggests.

I nod my thanks.

"I need to go see Ash."

"First, we should -"

I cut Tanya off. "No. No first. She's first." I turn back to Logan and ask, "Can you call Macy or Jax to help you close up?"

"Yep. Go ahead. Take off."

I do. Still no response from Ash. It's possible she got called back into the hospital with an emergency, but I'm hoping she's still at home. And just not reading her texts for some reason. Or not answering my texts because she's heard about the video. Shit.

Wanting to waste no time, I flag down a cab.

Shit. She's still on edge after the creepy text messages, and now we've got this to deal with. What the fuck is going on? I throw cash at the driver and jump out of the cab as soon as it pulls up in front of Gabby and Tim's place. When I get to the front door, I force myself to take a deep breath and ring the bell instead of pounding on it like I want. I see her peek out the window and then, a moment later, open the door with a wide smile on her face.

"Hey! I didn't think I was going to see you tonight."

She's happy to see me.

She doesn't know.

Her smile fades as she takes in my expression. "Lucas? What's wrong?"

Chapter Twenty-Two

__Lucas__

I exhale roughly, dreading what I know I need to do. I have no idea how she's going to react to this, but I know losing her is a distinct possibility.

No. I will NOT lose her.

I can't.

She steps aside, motioning me in. I don't see Tim and Gabby anywhere. "They're at a concert," she explains when I ask. I frown. I don't like that she's alone with all this shit going on. But that line of thought only reminds me why I'm here.

"I need to show you something."

"Should I be sitting down?" she attempts a joke, clearly thrown off by my serious expression.

"Maybe," I admit.

Her smile falters, and gingerly she perches on the end of the couch. I'm far too agitated to sit and begin pacing the length of her living room.

"What's going on?"

My mouth opens and shuts in several false attempts as I try to organize my scattered thoughts into the right words. The ones that will convince her to stay with me despite everything. The irony hits me hard. I'd always assumed when I lost Ash, it would be because of my past, my fucked up family, not the one thing I thought may make me worthy of her. Not my career success. Not the show.

"Lucas? You can tell me."

I sit next to her on the couch, not touching but close enough I can smell her flowery scent. Lavender, she told me once. She uses lavender lotion when she's not at the hospital. The fact that I know what kind of lotion she uses just underlines how deep I've gotten with her. When have I ever known, even cared, what type of lotion the woman I'm sleeping with uses?

Never.

Never until Ash.

I will not lose her.

My chest is tight. I know this feeling; I need to hit something. Lately, the last few years, I've mostly experienced this when I've had to deal with my *family*, the Abbotts. What I wouldn't give to go to the boxing gym right now and work these emotions out on a bag. But I owe it to her to be here. She needs to hear this from me.

I lean forward, resting my elbows on my knees, stare at the floor in front of me and begin.

"We're not filming right now, so there isn't any crew around, and it's easy to forget, I mean, I actively *try* to forget about the show and just be normal on our time off, you know?"

I sneak a peek over my shoulder and see her nodding next to me.

"When we started filming, they installed cameras throughout the shop. The point was to catch stuff when the crew was on break, but also so we would kind of forget and act normal. So they could catch us being real, unguarded."

I sense Ash moving beside me, feel her settle right against me, and place a hand against my lower back. I tense but don't move away.

God, I hope this isn't the last time she ever touches me.

"Tanya got a call from a gossip show a few hours ago because someone had sent them a video from one of those cameras." I shift enough to pull out my cell phone and call up the clip she'd forwarded. I cue it up and then reluctantly hand it over.

"It's of us."

She starts the video. I can tell from her horrified expression she recognizes it immediately. She practically throws the phone back at me and leaps to her feet, stumbling away from me. Her arms wrap protectively around her middle. I want to kick my own ass.

"That's..." she swallows, "that's from when we...."

I gaze at her, hoping she can see my regret in my eyes. "I'm sorry, Ash. I don't know why it was recording. I don't know how it got leaked. But I will find out. I promise."

Her eyes are wide and wounded as she watches me. I want so desperately to go and hold her, but I'm not at all sure she'd welcome my comfort. Not when her first reaction was to leap away from me.

What if this is too much for her? What if she ends it because of this?

"What about...the things we said to each other? Did they...is that...?"

"It's muffled, but yeah. They've got some of it."

"Oh my god. And they're going to what? Put it on their show?"

Fuck. "Probably. But even if they don't tonight... it's already on their website."

Tears glaze her eyes with my announcement.

"According to Tanya, they don't name you. They were fishing for confirmation of your identity."

"But they will eventually. I mean. It won't be hard to figure it out. We were photographed together at the fundraiser just the other week. If they were paying attention, you came right over here. My last name is on the buzzer."

"Shit. I didn't even think about that. I just wanted to see you."

"So, they'll know. And my dad...and the hospital...." Her voice breaks, and she turns away. My fists clench against my thighs.

"What can I do?"

I feel miserable and helpless. She's hurting, and it's my fault. I really wouldn't blame her if she needed time. If she ended things. She hadn't signed up for any of this.

When I find out who the fuck was responsible, I am going to make them pay.

"Well, you could start by giving me a hug. This is kind of shitty, and I'd like my boyfriend to hold me."

Thankfully I'm still sitting down because I literally feel my knees go weak with relief at her words. Immediately I move over to her and wrap my arms around her waist as I pull her to me. She sinks into me, practically burrowing into my chest.

"I'm so sorry, baby."

"You didn't do it." Her voice is scratchy with unshed tears.

"It's my fault," I whisper. "If you weren't with me-"

Her head shakes and she pulls back slightly until she's looking me in the eye. "They did this to you too. They did it to both of us."

My heart warms at her words. That she's still got us on the same team. I love that, even devastated, she's offended on my behalf too. That fierce loyalty is rare and something I've never had from a woman I'm fucking.

Although, I think we're more than that. She's more than that.

She's returned to her spot against my chest. "So now what?" She asks.

I stiffen again. Feeling it, she steps back, and my arms drop to my sides. That sucks.

"It's up to you. If you want, I can get the show's press people to make some kind of joint statement. Or we can ignore it until it blows over, just no comment it. Or," I hate this next suggestion. It's what Tanya thinks we should go with PR-wise, but it's the last thing I want. I force the words out because Ash deserves all her options. I owe her that. "We can cool it a bit, not be seen together until the press gets bored and moves on."

She's watching me closely. "Is that what you want?"

"Fuck no. I want you to stay as close to me as possible. All the time."

Her answering smile finally soothes me. She gives me a quick squeeze, apparently liking that answer. The tension in my body finally starts to lessen. Maybe I won't need to visit the punching bag tonight after all.

"Then I think we should say something. Tell people I'm the one with you in the video, that we're together, that it was made without our knowledge, and we'd like our privacy. And that the creeps who did this are icky and gross."

"You want to go public with the fact we're a couple?"

Her eyes flick to my phone, still sitting on the couch where we'd dropped it. "I think that ship has sailed, don't you? Besides, the sooner your fan girls know you're off the market, the better."

I grin at that announcement. "Off the market, huh?"

"Yep." She confirms easily, and I'm loving it. "I'm the only one you have inappropriate back room, workplace sex with. Or any other kind of sex with."

Would some men be annoyed by this show of possessiveness? Maybe. But other men are obviously idiots because somehow I'm the lucky bastard that gets to be with Ash. The longer I have to make sure she's as addicted to me as I am to her, the better.

I lean in to steal another kiss.

"There's one other thing I think we should do," she tells me.

"What's that?"

"Well, if that video is going to be all over town, you should probably meet my dad."

I tilt my head back and groan. She pinches my side playfully, and I meet her gaze with a grin. Secretly I'm stunned and stupidly happy. I've never done the whole meet the parents thing. I've never mattered enough to anyone for them to ask me home. My chest fills with some emotion I cannot name and choose not to analyze.

"The things I do for you."

Her smile turns teasing, and she slips her arms around my neck, pressing herself along the length of me. "Let's spend some time focusing on the things you do *to* me. There aren't any cameras here." Her lips chart a path along my neck.

I groan again and move my hands to her ass, tilting her hips tightly against my quickly growing erection. "You're full of good ideas."

"I'd rather be full of you."

Lust surges through me, and I nip her earlobe lightly. My hand slips beneath the hem of her pretty blouse, caressing the smooth skin along her waist. "Damn. I've created a monster."

"You have," she agrees, stepping out of my arms and promptly stripping her shirt off. Before I even have a chance to appreciate this, she's got her jeans unbuttoned and slips them down her hips, stepping out of them.

She's like every one of my fantasies come to life, standing before me in skimpy scraps of pink and lace, and it takes everything in me not to pull her into my arms and take control. But she seems to have something to prove right now, and I'm content to let her take the lead. For now. Besides, I'm so relieved by her reaction I'd do just about anything she asked. This is not exactly a hardship.

Except for my cock, which is definitely hard and pulsing aggressively against my jeans.

She's eying the bulge in my pants appreciatively, which only makes it grow. "You were worried? About the tape and my reaction. You thought I might end this?"

I stiffen at the reminder and nod reluctantly. "I was afraid you might, yeah," I admit.

Her eyes raise to meet mine. "I'm sorry you were worried."

"I'm sorry you were hurt."

Hooking her fingers in my belt loops, she pulls me closer to her. "I know you would never hurt me like that."

I feel a pang in my chest. "You do?" I search her brown eyes intently.

Nodding, she presses her lips to the center of my chest, above my heart.

I don't know what I've done to earn her trust, but I hope like hell I never fuck it up. The look on her face when she saw that video... I never want to see her look that devastated ever again, and I absolutely never want to be the cause.

"Let's see what I can do to convince you I'm not going anywhere."

Slowly and deliberately, she sinks to her knees.

I curse under my breath. "Ash," I begin to protest. Shaking her head, she looks up at me, and I feel a kick in my chest at the heat in her eyes.

"Take your shirt off," she orders so sweetly.

I'm not an idiot. I grab the back of my shirt with one hand and pull it off over my head. I feel her gaze like a caress traveling across my chest and abs, and I've never been so thankful for a body women seem to appreciate. She's still kneeling at my feet, her hands gripping the waist of my jeans. My thumb traces her bottom lip bringing her eyes back to mine.

"You getting distracted, beautiful?" I smirk.

She bites my thumb playfully. "Behave."

A chuckle rumbles through my chest. "Not something I'm generally told by a naked woman. I thought you liked me a little naughty."

In response, she tugs my jeans open, relieving a little of the pressure. A sexy smile spreads across her face as she gazes at her prize. "My turn to be naughty."

"Fuck," I mutter. My head falls back on my shoulders, and I groan in anticipation. I move my legs slightly apart, bracing myself.

I'm never going to survive this.

Ash

I hook my fingers into the waistband of his jeans and briefs and gently pull them down until they pool at his feet. His erection springs free, and I wrap my hand around it, squeezing gently. His groan of approval is like a drug. God, he is so gorgeous. Every inch of him. Especially the inches currently throbbing in my hand.

I press a kiss to the head and hear him hiss in anticipation. I love that I can do that to him. Knowing my touch has such an impact on him is an incredible turn-on.

"Ash." His voice is hoarse and rough and sends goosebumps across my skin.

Gripping his erection, I let my tongue circle the tip. He groans, and I feel his hands in my hair.

I look up, the heat in his gaze makes my thighs clench. Keeping my eyes locked on his, I slowly take his length in my mouth. When I've taken as much of him as I can, I suck gently, and his eyes close, head falling back. His hands clench in my hair, but he lets me go at my own pace.

"So good," he mumbles.

I tongue the underside of his penis, and his thighs tense under my hands. His hips jerk and his cock hits the back of my throat.

"Sorry," he murmurs, tilting his head to look at me, his eyes molten.

But I'm not interested in apologies. I swallow him back down, humming in approval, and he watches for a few moments before again closing his eyes against the pleasure. I cup his balls, squeezing gently, and he moans. His whole body tenses signaling his coming release.

"Ash," he warns, but I'm not having it. I shake my head a little and shift on my knees, taking him deeper, urging him on.

"Fuck. I'm going to come. Don't stop, Ash. God, don't stop. I'm going to come so hard."

A moment later, he does, shouting my name hoarsely as his body goes rigid. And I stay with him through it. Loving it. Until the shudders stop and his hands gentle. He's breathing harshly when I finally release him, his eyes hazy with lust and desire.

My entire body is thrumming with arousal. I stand on shaky legs, strung so tight I'm sure the slightest touch from Lucas could set me off. "Lucas, I... I ...." I don't know how to voice what I need.

He must read the desperation in my eyes

"You need to come, beautiful?"

I nod drunkenly.

"I know. I'll take care of you."

He grips the back of my neck, pulling me to him roughly. His lips devour mine, and I sink into him, shivers of arousal still racking my frame. I feel his other hand tugging my nipples and can't help the cry of desire that escapes. He lifts me effortlessly, and my legs wrap around his waist, his hands on my ass holding me up. God, I love how strong he is.

He carries me to my bedroom, and I scramble onto the mattress as soon as my feet touch the floor. I don't think I've ever wanted anyone with this level of desperation. What is it about this man? If he makes me wait, I think I'll splinter into a million pieces. I need to feel him inside me, claiming me, owning me. I need to be his.

I want him to be mine.

He falls on top of me, settling between my thighs. Immediately I'm rubbing against him, trying to get the pressure and friction I need. He sinks on top of me and drags in a deep breath, his head nestling into the crook of my neck. I feel his harsh exhales against my skin as I'm mindless, caressing his back, his skin, everywhere I can reach.

Lucas takes another deep shuddering breath, his back expanding and contracting with the force of it, but otherwise, he doesn't move.

"Lucas?" I murmur.

He presses his face into my neck. I feel a hot kiss behind my ear.

"You okay?" I gentle my hands, soothing them over his shoulders and back slowly.

"I thought I was going to lose you," he whispers.

My hands run through his hair, nails gently scoring his scalp. "Hey," I pull gently, trying to see his face. "Look at me."

He does, his blue eyes grim. I cup his face and press a soft kiss against his lips. "You didn't. You won't." I whisper.

He groans. "I need to be inside you."

"I need that too."

He takes care of the condom, and I continue caressing him, admiring his hard abs. When he's done, he looks up at me, pressing a sweet kiss to my lips. I cup his face, returning the kiss as he lines us up. I feel the blunt head of his erection rubbing against my core, and I can't control my hips reaction, pressing against him, trying to take him deeper.

Lucas groans, "Always so ready for me. So wet."

"Lucas," I whisper, urging.

He doesn't make me wait; slowly, he slides inside me, groaning. "So fucking tight and sweet." When he's as deep inside me as he can get, I am so *full*, he pauses and seeks out my kiss.

What had been so frenzied just moments before was now achingly tender. So sweet, I feel tears form and blink them back.

And then he starts to move, pulling almost all the way out before slowing thrusting back inside. It feels amazing. He feels amazing. I raise my knees, notching them at his hips, and try to take him deeper. He rests his forehead against mine, his eyes intense on my face watching all my reactions. His breaths on my cheek become rougher as his thrusts increase in tempo. I stretch my arms down his torso, cupping his ass, urging him on.

"Lucas," I moan his name. His eyes spark, and he pauses his thrusting instead grinding his hips against mine. And just like that, I feel lightning spread through my limbs and my back arches as shivers spread through my body. I'm gasping for breath as my orgasm goes on and on. Distantly, I hear Lucas growling my name, his hips jerking against me. Slowly, I return back to myself. Lucas shudders on top of me, his forehead resting on my shoulder.

I don't want to move. I like this, the warm intimacy after. I caress a hand down the length of his back and back up into his hair. He presses a kiss to the skin behind my ear and levers himself off me. His eyes find mine as he cups my cheek.

"Ash."

That's it. Just my name. But there's a wealth of emotion in his gaze.

I trace his lips with my fingertips before cupping his chin and pulling him close for a sweet kiss.

He gives me a small grin as he pulls away, then he arranges us so I'm the little spoon and brushes a kiss across my shoulder.

I twist my neck until he can reach my lips, and he gives me a slow kiss.

I swallow the words I want to say. Something inside me knows he's not ready. But I am more sure every day that I love him.

Chapter Twenty-Three

Lucas

Ash's dad, Brent, is actually a pretty cool guy. And it's obvious that despite the physical distance they've had between them the last few years, they are close.

I'm not sure if she sensed my nerves, or had some of her own, or if she's just kind of perfect, but she had found a great 'neutral' territory for this introduction. Especially knowing at some point, we'd have to bring up the very awkward conversation of the video of us that was quickly becoming national gossip. I've gotten pretty good at ignoring the trolls and speculation on social media, but I know it's new for and hard on Ash. She's deliberately stayed away from any sites the last two days, which I appreciate, but it pisses me off that she has to and why. Anyway, she's invited her dad to join us at a great brewery with a huge outdoor beer garden. The weather is Chicago summer gorgeous, and it's early enough in the afternoon that it's busy but not packed. Our table is in a shady corner in the back.

He knows who I am, has seen the show a couple times but isn't a regular 'fan'. I don't know if that's a good thing or a bad thing. Apparently, he plays hockey with some friends on the weekends and shares funny stories from their most recent game. It helps break the ice. No pun intended. I share photos from work I did on one of Chicago's professional hockey players. Ash updates her dad on her work and her project.

"Excuse me a minute, I'm going to run to the restroom." Interrupting our laughter.

"He's a little more fun than that doctor guy you brought around." He tells her as she stands.

Ash's eyes widen in disbelief. "Dad!"

He laughs, and she wags a finger in his face. "Behave. I'll be right back."

Wait. He'd met Will?

I don't like that.

Turning his attention to me, he shrugs. "Eh. He was fine. The doctor. He was nice to my girl, so as long as she was happy, I stayed out of it. I learned that during the high school years," he says wryly, taking another sip of his beer.

"I've met him," I admit reluctantly.

"Have you now?"

I shift in my seat and reply, "He, uh, he operated on my friend. Jax."

"I heard about that. He's doing okay?"

"Yeah, he's finally out of the hospital, back home. Doing good."

"Good. That's good."

We fall silent, both sipping our beers.

"So, I'm guessing this family-friendly afternoon is so the two of you can try to smooth over the whole sex tape fiasco."

I sputter, choking on my beer. I was so not prepared to have this conversation without Ash. She knows her dad. She knows how to say things to him. I'm bound to get punched in the face if I try to explain anything about this.

His silence is a good indication he expects me to say something.

Taking a deep breath, I force myself to look him in the eye.

"I think she was hoping you wouldn't have heard about that until she could break it to you."

"A man's daughter has a sex tape out there, someone is going to let him know."

I grimace. "I'm sorry about that. We didn't...I mean...I would never intentionally disrespect or embarrass Ash. I care about her."

Ash seems to respond when I am honest and has been pretty unimpressed when I try to act tough; I'm hoping her dad is the same.

He nods, considering my words. "Being with you comes with a lot of attention, both good and bad. She's bound to get caught up in that."

I swallow. So far, it's been a lot of bad. I know that. I'm constantly worried Ash is going to decide it's too much. Too much trouble, too much hassle, too much ugliness. And bail. Since she's met me, she's had a gun held on her, her hospital has been vandalized, someone has followed and photographed her, scribbled out her face on a news clipping, and now this. Shit.

He sighs deeply and shifts on the bench across from me. "She's a lot like her mom," he seems to confide. "She cares what people think, but she makes up her own mind. It's this quiet stubbornness that makes arguing with her hell. But she's smart, so I don't argue very often. People always told me I should be more hands-on with raising her. After her mom died, I had no idea how to parent a daughter on my own. I never had many rules. But she makes good decisions. I trust her."

He puts just the tiniest emphasis on *her*. He doesn't trust me, I get it. Message received.

Ash takes this moment to return, plopping down next to her dad with a wide smile. "So, what did I miss?"

Her dad meets my eyes briefly before turning to her. "We were just talking about the unfortunate video. I'm assuming the reason behind this little outing."

I watch her cheeks pinken. I don't enjoy it today the way I usually do when she blushes.

"Lucas and I are together, Dad. I wanted you to meet him." She places her hand over mine on the table. That small touch releases some of my tension.

He remains silent, just watching us both steadily.

She starts again, "The video-"

Brent raises his hand, cutting her off. "I'm not an idiot, Ash. You're a grown woman. I know you have sex. I just prefer to ignore that fact. And I definitely prefer it when it isn't all over TV and the Internet." He grumbles through the last part.

"So do we. Believe me."

I nod a little more aggressively than necessary, agreeing with her statement.

Sighing heavily, Brent shifts forward and lifts his beer. "Let's never talk about this again, okay?"

The three of us toast. Never again? That would be great. The tension in my shoulders finally releases.

Ash doesn't mention any of the threats we've gotten or the vandalism, and I follow her lead. She'll let her dad know if and when she feels she needs to.

At the end of the afternoon, Ash gives her dad a hug with a promise to have dinner together later in the week. Brent turns to me and holds out his hand. I shake his hand, feeling him squeeze in an unspoken warning. I don't respond, taking it. I get it. He loves his daughter. And I'm the asshole having sex with her on camera.

"Good to meet you, Lucas. Be good to my girl."

"Yes, sir. I plan to."

He nods, gives Ash another quick hug and a kiss, and walks down the sidewalk to his car.

I survived my first Meet-The-Parents.

Ash

I exhale in relief. That went better than I thought it would. I hope Dad didn't give Lucas too hard a time while I was gone. I ask him, but he just smiles and says it was fine. I'll have to trust that. And he seems fine, so my dad must not have said anything that upset him.

My dad and I have always been close. My mom passing away just as I was entering my teen years wasn't easy, that's for sure, but we made it through. Plenty of awkward conversations but lots of laughter too. It means a lot to me that Lucas was willing to meet him even under these circumstances, and the fact that it seemed to go well is a relief. In general, my dad is pretty laid back, but I've also never introduced him to anyone thousands of people have seen ... doing the things Lucas was doing to me on that video. I still feel sick when I think about it. Who would do that? Why?

Melrose doesn't know for sure if all these things are connected. I don't know if I want them to be or not. Is it better to have multiple people harassing us in small ways or one person so fixated on us? Whatever it is, whoever it is, it feels like it's escalating. I know Lucas feels guilty like this is all his fault. I don't know how to relieve that guilt.

I feel his hand cup the nape of my neck, drawing me out of my thoughts. I turn and look up into his blue eyes and smile.

"You did it."

He chuckles. I love that sound. "I did. You okay?"

I nod. "He handled it better than I thought."

He loops his arms loosely around my waist and pulls me closer, resting his forehead against mine. Right there in the middle of the sidewalk.

"You want to come over to my place? Jax is coming over later to talk about some work stuff and have a couple beers."

I bite my lip, considering. I do, but.... "Jax won't mind?"

"He gets it. He knows I don't really want you to be alone right now. I feel better when you're with me with everything going on."

Honestly, I feel the same way.

"Okay. If you're sure."

We take the 'el' back to Lucas's. The lights are on when we arrive, and I hesitate seeing that.

"Looks like Jax is already here."

I relax. "He's got a key?"

Lucas shrugs, "Seemed like it made sense."

I nod. Right. Of course.

I feel Lucas stiffen beside me, and I get nervous all over again. God, I hate being so jumpy. I hope Melrose comes up with some answers soon.

But he's just eyeing the motorcycle in front of his condo with a frown.

"Fuck."

"What is it?"

"Jax rode his bike over. I don't think his leg is ready for that."

"Jax has a motorcycle?" I can't help my enthusiasm as I circle the bike.

Lucas is watching me with raised eyebrows. "You like motorcycles, beautiful?"

I nod. "Best way to get around Asia is on a scooter. I fell in love with them while I was there."

"Don't let Jax hear you compare his bike to a scooter," he laughs.

I make a face at him. "You know what I mean. Traveling on two wheels." I move closer to him, leaving the bike behind me. "You don't have one do you?"

He chuckles and shakes his head. "Sorry. I'm strictly a four-wheel man."

I sigh dramatically. "Well, I guess no one is perfect."

"Oh, that's it," he mutters and swings me up into his arms, tossing me over his shoulder. I'm laughing so hard that my protest is lost. I feel him smack my butt, and I retaliate in kind. He hesitates and then continues to move us through his front door. He dumps me onto his couch, I'm still giggling.

Jax emerges from the kitchen and takes in the scene. "What I miss?"

Without taking his eyes off me, Lucas informs Jax, "You're not allowed to ride your bike in front of Ash." Setting me off on another peal of laughter. Jax shrugs and disappears back into the kitchen. I'm clumsy with amusement as I stumble off the couch and wrap my arms around Lucas's waist. He pretends to scowl, but I see the teasing light in his eyes. I give him a quick kiss and a squeeze and follow Jax, Lucas right behind me.

"Hey, Doc," Jax greets as I slide onto a stool across the counter from him. He pops open a bottle of beer. "How's it going?"

I shrug. "Okay. We just met my dad to break the news about the video from *Vanished*."

He hesitates with the bottle halfway to his lips and changes directions, handing it to me. "Here. You need this more than me."

I snort but accept it. "Thanks."

He crosses the kitchen back to the fridge and grabs another one. "Luke?"

"Yeah, thanks."

Handing Lucas a beer, Jax gives him a once-over. "Well, you don't look like her dad beat the shit out of you."

Inhaling deeply, Lucas shakes his head. "Luckily, no."

"You hear anything from Melrose yet?"

He shakes his head. "Nope." He moves to sit beside me, and Jax leans against the counter. "Your leg okay? You need to sit?"

"I'm good."

"You're a stubborn ass."

Jax just grins and tilts his beer back.

"Well? Let's do this." Lucas slaps his hand on the counter. Jax shoots his eyes to me briefly and away.

"Do you guys want me to give you privacy? I can watch tv while you talk work stuff."

Lucas watches Jax, leaving it to him. He considers for a second and then shakes his head. "Nah. Be good to get your opinion." Jax grabs a leather portfolio and slides it across the counter to Luke. "I know you hate social media," he smirks, "so you may not know, but there are some memes that have come out of the show. Especially from Logan being snarky." As he's talking, Lucas is moving pages around, taking in Jax's prints and artwork. "I think we could take some of that and make merch. Shirts, hats, posters, stickers. We could even have each of us do some original artwork and sell it on stuff. I think people would buy it, and Krista and Tanya agree."

Silently, Lucas takes it all in. Jax starts to get fidgety and takes another swallow of his beer.

"These are great, brother."

I see Jax exhale, relaxing.

"How long have you been thinking about this?"

Jax shrugs. "I had a lot of time to think lying in the hospital."

They start discussing ideas, bouncing things off each other. Jax finally pulls up a stool and sits, getting off his feet. I order some pizza for us while they're busy. Their excitement is contagious, and I offer an idea without thinking. "You could have a special design each year and give the profits to charity. You guys do so much volunteer work. This could be another way to help."

They fall silent, looking at each other. And I realize I just volunteered them to give their profits away. I have a big mouth.

"That's a great idea." Jax looks at me with a grin. Then shrugs, "We could do something each month. It would drive people to the website more regularly, even off-season."

Lucas pulls me to him, so I'm standing between his legs and wraps his arms around me. "You got this. Run with it," he tells Jax.

Jax grins and holds out his beer to toast. "Well, sounds like Krista canceled Tanya's return to LA so she can deal with the, uh..." he falls silent.

"Mysterious sex tape?" I offer. Might as well own it. Also, I've had a lot of beer today.

He smirks and continues. "So she can help me get it all set up soon before we start filming again."

"You two good?" Lucas asks Jax, a serious expression on his face.

Jax shrugs, "Stop worrying, man. It's not a big deal."

"You're starting filming soon?" I ask, twisting in his arms so I can see Luke's face.

He frowns. "Yeah. I was going to talk to you about that." But just then, the pizza arrives, and we're all distracted. We laugh and eat and joke around. Lucas insists on Jax crashing here tonight, especially since he only has his motorcycle.

"Don't worry, I was planning on it. I've had too many beers to drive anywhere. And don't you worry." He turns to me with a devilish grin. "My room's in the basement, so I won't hear what the two of you," he gestures between Lucas and me, "get up to."

I blush but can't help my grin, and Jax laughs his ass off.

Lucas throws a pizza crust at him, but it only makes him laugh harder. "Good night, love birds." He waves as he walks away.

And those intense blue eyes focus all their attention on me. It's awesome.

Chapter Twenty-Four

Ash

Two days later, I get an email from the Chief requesting my presence in her office at the end of the day. The tone of the email makes me nervous. She's not usually quite so formal in our interactions. I'm worried about what it means. Unfortunately, I'm distracted by my nerves when a three-car accident is brought into the ER requiring all my focus for several hours.

Turns out I was right to be worried.

"Dr. Carrington." Chief Haywood has a grim expression on her face as she greets me. One that has all my nerves on edge as I take the seat across from her. She introduces the other person in the room as a representative from Human Resources.

This can't be good.

I sit silently, bracing for impact.

She inhales deeply, folds her hands on the desk in front of her, and meets my eyes.

"I'm afraid we have a problem. It has recently been brought to my attention that you have been involved in some... unfortunate publicity. Due to the nature of this publicity, some of our Board members have expressed concerns about how this could reflect on the hospital. You may recall in your contract, there is a morality clause-"

"I'm sorry," I interrupt, sitting forward. "Are you firing me because I'm being harassed?" *What the hell?* "I didn't ask for this publicity, as you call it, and I certainly-"

The Chief raises her hand, stalling my tirade. "No one is discussing firing you."

The HR rep shifts in his chair, and she shoots him a withering glance. "But there are individuals who have expressed concern about how this may reflect on the hospital and would like some assurances about how this is being handled to ensure that doesn't happen again."

I'm sure my face is flaming right now, but not out of embarrassment. I'm pissed. "Are *you* concerned, Chief?" Chief Haywood was instrumental in re-cruiting me back to Chicago with promises of support and compliments to my skill set and experience. If she doubts my commitment or benefit to the hospital, I'll be devastated and pissed. Frankly, I prefer anger.

She glances again at the HR Rep, who has remained annoying silent. Why is he even here?

"No."

Mr. HR shifts in his seat again, and the Chief glares at him. He clears his throat but remains silent.

The Chief moves her attention back to me. "No," she repeats. "But others have expressed concern." Her face softens a bit. "How can I help you? What do you need?"

I inhale sharply, pushing back sudden tears. "The police are looking into it," I finally get out.

I can tell my answers are not satisfying Mr. HR, and despite the Chief's assurances, I leave the conversation twenty minutes later, feeling very insecure about my position in the hospital. She wouldn't tell me who on the Board had *concerns.* I don't want to believe the Abbotts have anything to do with it, but I can't help the sneaking suspicion in the back of my mind. This has brought Lucas more press too, and more eyes on the name Abbott. Something they've never appeared to like very much unless they're controlling the narrative.

Gabby is furious on my behalf. She mutters all the way home, which is a little unsettling as the passenger in her car. I'm distracted, nauseous, and worried about what I'm going to do.

"I'll talk to my dad," she offers. "See what kind of legal options you have." Her dad is a lawyer in Milwaukee, although he's also licensed in Illinois.

"Thanks." I'll take all the help I can right now.

We get home in record time, thanks to her angry driving. When we approach, there's a box propped against the front door. We both hesitate, looking at each other.

What now?

"Expecting a package?" I ask hopefully. Gabby shakes her head.

"Maybe it's from Lucas?" she suggests.

"Maybe."

But I don't think either of us believes that. Wordlessly, we stare at the offending box another moment. Then Gabby takes a deep breath and straightens to her full height, which, unfortunately, is not really all that impressive at only 5'4". But she bravely powers forward and picks up the box.

"Cupcakes. At least I think they're cupcakes." She peeks into the cellophane.

"Weird." I frown, watching Gabby juggle the box of pastries and her other belongings.

"Agreed."

I unlock the door since she has her hands full. We get inside and place the box on the kitchen table. I do the honors, opening it up. WHORE stares back at me. It's impressive, actually. Someone has painstakingly piped the letters across a dozen cupcakes. So it really reads, 'W H O R E ! W H O R E !'. I hear Gabby gasp next to me, but she sounds far away. For some reason, I can't seem to tear my eyes away from the offending red frosting letters in front of me.

Gabby yells for Tim.

I go to the bathroom and splash some cold water on my face. I need to pull it together right now. I stare at my reflection. I look pale, but other than that, I look like I always look. Which is reassuring somehow. I'm still just me, despite all this craziness. And I'll figure this out. I make order out of chaos. That's what I do, remember? That's all this is. Prioritize the problems and fix them one at a time. Stop. Stabilize. Assess.

I take a deep breath and return to the living room, overhearing Tim's voice.

"...thirty minutes ago."

They turn to look at me, concern in both their expressions. Gabby's got her phone pressed against her ear but talks to me. "Tim just got home thirty minutes ago, and the box wasn't there then." Someone on the line must speak because she turns slightly away and says, "Lucas? It's Gabby. Can I get the number of that detective you know? Melrose?"

I stiffen. She called Lucas. Shit. He's not going to like this.

"No, we're fine. She's fine. We just, ah, got a special delivery, I guess you could say."

I sit down. Thinking. Processing.

Okay. Clearly, someone does not like the fact that I am with Lucas. That is not my problem.

What is my problem?

This person is jeopardizing my career.

This person knows where I live and where I work and has made threats against me.

This person is harassing my friends.

So, I need to shore up the support of the Chief and find a powerful ally on the Board of Directors. Some good press wouldn't hurt.

I need Melrose to find out who is doing this. I need to do what I can to increase security. I need -

Gabby interrupts my mental to-do list, shoving her phone into my face. "Lucas wants to talk to you."

Lucas

"I'm okay, Lucas, really."

I shove a hand through my hair and pace the back room. This is so fucked.

"I gave Gabby Melrose's number, but I'll call him too. Make sure he gets over there." Jax pokes his head in to see what's keeping me and stays when he sees the angry expression on my face. "I have another appointment yet tonight, but I can cancel-"

"No. Please. There's nothing you can do here right now. You're just getting things back on schedule."

I punch my fist against the wall. I hate feeling helpless like this. I've spent years organizing my life, so I didn't have to feel this way anymore. And now some asshole has come along and shaken it all loose.

"Lucas."

Ash's voice has only a mildly soothing effect on me. Nothing like usual. It doesn't stop this feeling of wanting to crawl out of my skin. Or wanting to be in two places at once.

"I'll be there as soon as I finish, okay? Call me if you need anything. And let me know when Melrose shows. Please," I add as an afterthought. I don't mean to be an asshole barking orders at her. She's had a rough enough day. But I hate that I can't be there for her right now.

This is so fucked.

She murmurs a promise, and I exhale roughly, forcing myself to relax.

The silence stretches between us, all the things I feel like I should say but can't hang in the void. "I'll be there as soon as I can." I end the call and toss my phone on the couch. Then I kick one of the chairs and send it skidding across the floor before it topples over. It's not enough.

"Doc, okay?" Jax asks, righting the chair and sitting his ass in it.

"This fuck knows where she lives. He left her a little gift when she got home."

"Shit. She okay?"

"I guess. She says she is."

Jax shakes his head. "Sorry, man. You need to take off?"

"No. I'll finish up and then head over. Have to call Melrose, though. Make sure he's on it until I can get over there."

Jax nods again. "Want me to call Mace? See if he can head over there?"

I shove a hand through my hair again, thinking. Do I? I'd definitely feel better knowing Mace was with Ash, but it's not his responsibility. Jax doesn't wait for my response. I see him texting when I turn to face him. He's always got my back.

It goes to voicemail when I call Melrose. I leave a brief message and not so politely ask him to call me back. Then I try to pull my shit together so I can do my job.

Ten minutes later, I get a call back.

"Sorry, man. Gotta take this."

My client nods. "No problem."

I accept the call. "Melrose?"

"Yeah. Assuming you're calling me about the little gift someone left for the good doctor?"

I grunt.

"I'm on my way over there right now."

"You got anything on this yet, Melrose?"

He swears under his breath. "Not enough. We traced the texts back to a disposable cell and found the location it was sold. Luckily, they have security footage, so I have someone going through it to see if we can ID anyone that also appears on the hospital security tapes."

I hesitate to ask my next question. Voicing it will make it clear to him just how vulnerable I am, and it's been a long time, years since I've put myself in that position.

But this is the first time in a long time ever, I've had something worth it.

"Is she...safe?" It takes a moment for him to respond. A space I fill with angry fear.

"I'll increase patrols in her neighborhood and the hospital. I can't do much more than that. I'm sorry."

I can. I can talk to Krista about hiring the security team we used while Jax was in the hospital. Jax, Macy, and I can help watch her back. Logan, too, if she's willing.

It's something, at least.

"I'll keep working on it. You know that."

"I know. Thanks, man."

"Thank me when we find him."

The two hours I spend finishing this tattoo are the longest two hours I've had in a long time. Except when we were waiting for Jax to wake up. Finally, I'm walking the client out the door. Jax started doing all the closing early, so we take off as soon as the door closes behind my client. I've got my car, and I drive us directly to Ash. I try to tell Jax he doesn't need to come, but he tells me to fuck off and gets in the passenger seat. I have to admit I breathe a little easier knowing he's here and knowing he'll look out for Ash even when I can't. Gabby opens the door when I knock and lets us in.

"Gang's all here."

I see what she means a moment later when I follow her back to the kitchen. Macy and Logan are sitting with Tim and Ash at the dining room table. Ash's eyes meet mine across the room. She's holding it together, but I can tell she's off. Her eyes are faded and sad.

Gabby offers us a drink, but I decline. Right now, the only thing I need is to feel Ash safe in my arms. But there's a lot of people around, and I doubt that's going to happen as quickly as I want it to. I stare at her, taking in every detail, reassuring myself she's okay. After a moment, she stands and crosses the kitchen, close enough I can finally pull her into my arms.

"You okay, beautiful?" I whisper into her neck, hugging her close to me.

She nods against my shoulder. I feel myself finally starting to relax now that I can hold her.

"Melrose left a little bit ago," Macy says from his seat. I inhale deeply before releasing Ash and turning my attention to everyone else in the room.

"Good thing too. Macy kept eying the cupcakes," Logan informs us, rolling her eyes.

"No reason to waste a perfectly good cupcake!" he argues.

"Are you serious? This guy probably poisoned them or peed in them or something."

"That's nasty," Mace grimaces, his expression causing the others to laugh, even Ash.

My biological family may leave a lot to be desired, but my chosen family is pretty great.

Chapter Twenty-Five

Ash

The next day I'm summoned back to the Chief's office. This is exhausting. I'm exhausted. I hardly slept last night, even after everyone finally went home. Lucas wanted me to go back to his place, but I refused. I will not let whoever this is scare me out of my own home.

Well, Gabby's home.

But I kind of felt if I didn't stay there last night, it would only get harder to come back. I could tell he didn't like it but ultimately respected my wishes.

He did text me bright and early this morning to check-in. Which did all sorts of things to my heart. He's such a good man.

When I walk into the Chief's office, I stop dead, realizing who the other man in the room is. Ethan Abbott. This can't be good.

Unaware of the tension I'm experiencing, the Chief has an excited smile on her face, which only knocks me more off balance. Her general vibe is much more upbeat than yesterday, and I wonder what has changed in the last twenty-four hours.

"Come in, come in! Take a seat. You know Mr. Abbott, I believe?"

"Ethan is fine."

I murmur a greeting and sink into the chair next to Ethan, across from Chief Haywood. I'm incredibly anxious and uncomfortable, having no idea what to expect.

She smiles at me and launches into an explanation. "As you know, Ethan's mother is on the Board, and the Abbott family have long been generous benefactors to the hospital. Senator Abbott was very impressed after our meeting a few weeks ago, and they've agreed to make a generous contribution to the Doctor Exchange and Training program you've proposed."

My heart starts beating with nervous excitement. This is amazing. It could actually happen! I feel a smile spreading across my face as my stomach flutters.

"My family has agreed to an initial contribution to fund your time in order to build the infrastructure and necessary commitments from fellow doctors and surgeons as well as other institutions, particularly in the countries with the largest need. I know you are personally most familiar with the needs in Nigeria, having spent time on the ground there, so we think this would be a good test case if you will."

"Absolutely. I know of several doctors I worked with and communities that I'm confident would be interested."

"Fabulous." Ethan looks at Chief Haywood. "How quickly can we get on the ground and firm things up?"

I'm stunned. Is this really happening? Just like that?

"Dr. Carrington and I will discuss her schedule and keep you in the loop."

Ethan nods, standing, and shakes the Chief's hand. I'm still in a daze when he turns to me and does the same, and then exits the room.

"Congratulations, Ash. I didn't imagine we would make things happen this quickly."

"I'm a little stunned," I laugh, shaking my head.

"I have to say, this is coming at the perfect time. With you overseas setting up this project, it will give everything else time to calm down and, I think, soothe some of the more nervous Board of Directors."

With you overseas...

Overseas...

Suddenly, I've come crashing down.

"When does she want you to leave?"

"In two weeks."

After work, I took the commuter rail to the nearby suburbs to meet my dad for dinner. I've just finished filling him in over fettuccine alfredo and wine. "Two weeks. Wow. How do you feel about that?"

I shrug, tapping the tongs of my fork slowly on my plate. "I'm thrilled, of course. This was always my plan. I just didn't imagine it happening this soon." I know I don't sound thrilled. I sound tired. And despite my excitement and pride in making progress on this, I've also got a small but persistent pit in my stomach.

"You don't seem that thrilled," Dad comments, echoing my thoughts.

I shrug. "I am. It's just...."

"You just got back."

I nod. "Yeah. I wouldn't be gone as long, obviously. Especially this time. But it would still be a couple months. And now...." I sigh.

"Now you're starting to have a life here again."

"Yeah."

"What does Lucas think?"

At the mention of his name, the pit in my stomach grows. "I haven't had a chance to talk to him about it yet."

He stands, picking up our empty plates, and walking them into the kitchen. I grab my wine glass and follow him. Rinsing off the dishes, he speaks over his shoulder, "That's probably a good thing. You should decide how you feel about it without his influence."

"I thought you liked him?"

"I do like him. More importantly, I like you together. But that doesn't mean it's going to be easy, honey."

I rub my forehead, thinking hard. This is what I wanted, so why am I so anxious? Why does it feel ... so intimidating and wrong? I should be happy.

"Long distance is never easy," my dad continues, "and Lucas has an...unusual life here." He dries his hands and turns to face me.

"I have to go." My voice cracks, and I look away, blinking back tears. Even after all these years, I hate crying in front of my dad. "My career...." I just leave it hanging out there between us.

My dad smiles softly, his eyes sad. "I'll miss you."

"I'll miss you too." My smile is watery and wobbles. It slips completely when he closes the distance between us and gives me a hug.

"Your mom would be so proud of you. She always said you were smarter than both of us combined. It made you a little shit to raise," he laughs and steps back, ruffling my hair like he used to when I was a kid. "Get some sleep, kiddo. Everything looks better in the morning light."

He's said similar things to me since I was a kid, and while I'm not totally convinced that is going to be the case here, his words are still reassuring. "Love you," I murmur.

"I love you too. Spare room is all made up for you."

"Thanks, Dad.

Lucas

My doorbell drags me from sleep an hour or so before I want to be. I groan but force myself out of bed and to my feet. I pull on a pair of sweats as the doorbell chimes again.

I'm glad I did when I open the door and see Ash on the other side. I smile sleepily and pull her inside, placing a light kiss on her lips and nuzzling into her neck.

"This is a nice surprise."

"Good morning," she chuckles at my enthusiastic greeting. She's soft and warm and smells amazing. I want to pull her back into bed and cuddle for an hour before sexing her. Her hands are smooth as they tickle down my bare torso. "I woke you," she murmurs.

"Best kind of wake up." I step aside and give her room to enter. "Everything okay?"

She nods. "Yeah, I just need to talk to you about something."

"Sure. Want some coffee? Sorry, I'm still foggy and need a caffeine hit."

"I'm okay," she says and follows me into the kitchen.

I get the coffee started and lean against the counter to face her. "What's up?"

She exhales roughly and shifts from one foot to the other. "I don't even know where to start."

I frown, taking all this in. This isn't like Ash. Usually, she's a great communicator, and I'm the one that never has the right words.

Ash takes a deep breath and starts. "The day the cupcakes showed up, I'd been called into a meeting with the Chief and HR. Apparently, some of the Board members were concerned about all the press around the video of us." I stiffen, already pissed even before I know the whole story. "There were some not-so-subtle references to my contract and the hospital's morality clause-"

"Are you fucking serious?" I burst out. That's seriously messed up. "You didn't say anything the other night. Are you okay?" I cross over to her and cup her elbows, looking down into her eyes. Their chocolate depths are worried, but she nods.

"Yeah. I mean, I was thrown for sure, but it seemed like the Chief was still on my side. And then the cupcakes happened, and that just seemed more urgent, and then after Melrose left, we all just needed to think about other things, you know?"

I nod and squeeze her arms reassuringly. "So, what does that mean? Are you in trouble at work?"

She lets out a nervous laugh. "Well, then yesterday I got called back in. We've got an initial donation that's supposed to help with 'proof of concept', I guess. It's enough to really get the project started in Nigeria and hopefully be able to expand in the future."

"That's great. Isn't it?" I'm confused. I thought this was what she wanted.

"It is," she agrees, but she doesn't sound convincing.

I press a kiss against her forehead and step back to pour myself a cup of the now finished coffee. This whole conversation is making me nervous. I'm obviously missing something, or Ash wouldn't be so anxious. I don't get it.

When I turn back, she's watching me with wide eyes. "The Chief thinks it's great timing. That the press will die down, and the Board members will calm down while I'm gone."

And there it is. I feel like I've been sucker punched and all I can do is repeat the words. "While you're gone."

She nods, her eyes shifting from me around the kitchen and back again.

I set the mug down and breath in slowly. Maybe this doesn't mean what I think it means. Maybe I'm still missing something. "You're leaving?"

"I'll need to be on the ground in Nigeria. Talking to my old colleagues, getting commitments, a sense of resources, everything we need to make this work."

Needing a minute, I turn my back to her and grip the counter. "Nigeria," I repeat. "That's...a hell of a commute."

Fuck. How could I have been so wrong? I feel a massive pressure building in my chest and clear my throat a couple times, trying to find some relief. It doesn't work. I still can't look at her. "When?" I ask.

She's silent for a beat, and then I hear her softly answer, "I leave in twelve days."

Holy shit. This is happening. She's leaving.

What did I really expect? I'm both stunned and resigned.

"So. I guess that's it then." My voice is flat. At this point, I just want her gone. I want to go numb and turn on autopilot until this doesn't cut me so ragged.

Fuck. How did I not see this coming? I start to replay the last few months, wondering what I missed. I thought things were good. But not good enough for her to stick around, apparently.

"Lucas, no, that's not what I'm saying. I-"

"Aren't you? You getting on a plane in twelve days and flying to another continent?" Finally, I release the edge of the counter and turn back to face her. Her eyes are bright with tears, and I steel myself against them.

"I have to go, but-"

"What?" I interrupt. "You'll write?"

And then another thought tortures me. "Who? Who donated the money?" I demand.

I know I'm right before she even answers me just by the look on her face. I feel the blood rush through my veins in a heated wave.

Fuck. Everything.

"Right. Okay. You should go. I'm sure you have a lot to do."

"Lucas, let me explain. I'll be back-"

"Go, Ash." I can't hear her right now. I've heard enough.

She's leaving me. And my family paid her to do it.

Chapter Twenty-Six

"**Y**ou're in a shit mood."

I grunt at Logan, not bothering to deny it. What I'd really like to be doing is to be sitting in the dark in my condo getting drunk, but I'm at least three hours away from being able to make that happen. After I chased Ash out of my place this morning, I texted Jax to meet me at the boxing gym. I needed to pound something. It helped in the moment but obviously didn't solve anything. Logan's right. I'm in a shit mood.

I know I was an asshole. I know that. But I can't listen to her justify letting the Abbotts pay for her to leave me. I thought she was better than that. I thought we were better than that. So being an asshole is kind of where I'm going to land for a while. Because I'd rather feed my anger than leave room for other emotions. I have a sick feeling when I stop being angry, all that's going to be left is the crushing weight in my chest I experienced this morning.

Thank God I'm not on the schedule tomorrow. I can get as drunk as I want and just sleep it off.

"Streaks! Come help me."

I hear Jax calling Logan over and appreciate him running interference for me. He doesn't know the specifics, but I'm sure he suspects something is going on with Ash. I'm not sure how long he'll wait for an explanation, and I don't know when I'll be ready to talk about it.

At the end of the day, I duck out as quickly as I can and head for home. I hop on the 'el' several stops before my usual one so I can walk through the city neighborhoods. Try to let the city work its magic. It doesn't work this time. When I finally get to my condo, I've barely got my first beer open when Jax walks through the front door. Stupid to think I could avoid him, avoid this for long. Wordlessly I open another bottle and set it on the counter in front of him. He's come with a six-pack. Reinforcements. I head out to the back deck and take a seat. It's excellent deck-sitting weather. Late summer, sun just starting to set. And I need air right now. We drink our beers in silence. Eventually, Jax stands and gets us another round. When he settles back into his chair, he stretches his legs out in front of him, crossing his ankles.

"So," he says.

We fall silent again, sitting in the dark side by side.

"I figure it's either something happened with Ash or something happened with the Abbotts."

I grunt, taking another sip.

"Considering I haven't seen you texting today with that dopey look on your face, I'm going to guess something with Doc."

"Even better," I say. "It's both."

Jax purses his lips and nods slowly.

"She's leaving. They gave her money for her project, and now she's getting on a plane." I lean forward, resting my forearms on my knees, beer in hand.

"Wow."

I rub a palm over my chest, annoyed by the tightness. And I see Ash's devastated face when I told her to leave this morning. Abruptly I stand up.

"I need something harder. I think I've still got a bottle of whiskey around here somewhere."

Jax follows me inside and watches while I find a half-full bottle and pour myself a glass.

"Want some?"

"I'll stick with the beer."

I down it quickly, savoring the burn, and pour another. We move to the living room, and I take the bottle with us, flopping onto the couch.

"Fuck!" I yell.

Jax lets me wallow in silence for several minutes before he interjects again. "When is she leaving?"

"Twelve days."

"How long is she going for?"

Ignoring the glass at this point, I take a drink right from the bottle. "Don't know. Last time she was there for three years."

He shifts in his chair. He doesn't admit it, but his leg still bothers him, I can tell. "You, uh, you didn't ask how long she was going?"

"Does it matter? She's leaving. Decision made. I wasn't even a fucking factor."

Jax studies me silently for a long moment. "This isn't like that, Luke. This isn't like when we were kids."

His words squeeze my throat. Really? Because it kind of feels *exactly* like that. But I stay silent, unable to form the words. Just another person moving on, leaving me behind, making decisions that impact my life without giving me a say. And the fact that the money is coming from the Abbotts.... Every time I think about it, it feels like acid in my veins. I told her there would be strings attached. I mean, look what they did to me when they offered me money. Will their money ever stop fucking with my life?

I take another drink. Jax sits with me, sipping his beer. I wish the whiskey would start to do its job. But I'm still thinking far more coherently than I want to be.

I see Jax frowning at his phone.

"What's up?"

He shrugs, shoving his phone back into his pocket.

I slouch down on the couch, resting my head against the back. "No, really. Distract me. I don't want to talk about my shit. What's up?"

He takes another sip, his face thoughtful. "Tanya's decided to move here. To Chicago."

What the fuck?

"I didn't think you two were serious."

Sighing, Jax says, "We're not. She says it's not because of me."

"You believe that?"

"I don't know. I think so? We've both been pretty clear this is just about passing some time. I don't even think she likes me that much."

"She seemed pretty worried about you when you were in the hospital."

I watch him grimace before he answers. "I'm sure she was. We're her meal ticket, after all."

"You think that's what this is? She's screwing you to keep you happy?"

He smirks. "I keep her happy too."

"I really don't want to know."

Jax starts laughing his ass off at the expression on my face. When he finally settles down, he says, "Whatever. Clearly, time to end it. This was supposed to be a short-term thing. Already lasted longer than I expected. If she's going to be living here...."

"Good luck with that." I hold up my bottle, toasting him.

He smirks and tilts his bottle at me.

"You should talk to Ash."

I lean my head back, resting it along the couch, and stare at the ceiling.

Maybe. But I don't see it changing anything. She's leaving me. Just like I always expected she would. I guess I just thought I'd have a little more time. Maybe long enough, it would be hard for her to go. And maybe she should go. If our being together is starting to fuck with her work, getting her called into HR, maybe it's for the best. And even as much as it kills me right now, it would only be worse six months from now. A year.

I take another swig of whiskey.

Ash

This sucks.

Obviously. No one likes getting dumped.

The worst part is I don't even really know if I was dumped. Although Lucas hasn't responded to any of my texts or voicemails for two days which seems to imply a dumping occurred. And the pain in my chest backs that up.

I'm going through the motions of my day. My mind is always somewhere else. There are moments here and there when I'm having a good conversation or getting a response from one of my former colleagues when I'm swept up in the excitement of what we're doing, watching my vision start to come together. Abeni is all over me, texting several times a day with random thoughts that pop into her head. There are moments I'm happy, flying high, proud of what we're going to do. But then I remember, and I lose my breath as my chest tightens and the pain returns.

It sucks.

My phone rings, and I sigh, leaning over to grab it off the table.

Lucas calling.

My breath catches in my throat, and I jump to my feet, quickly accepting the call.

"Hi."

Brilliant start, Ash.

"Hey," Lucas responds.

We both fall silent. I have no idea what to say, where to start. I'm so afraid I'm going to mess this up. My heart is racing, hoping this is a good thing and not just a more final version of our last conversation.

"I'm glad you called," I say softly. The silence stretches so long I begin to worry I imagined the whole thing, and he's not actually on the other end. "Lucas?"

"Yeah. I'm here." But he doesn't say anything else, and I sit nervously on the edge of my bed.

Finally, I hear him sigh and say, "I don't really know why I called. I'm not sure what to say."

I blink rapidly, feeling myself tear up. That pain in my chest is back, and now it's accompanied by a seriously nervous stomach.

"Lucas," I whisper.

He clears his throat. "How's Gabby?"

Confused by his change of subject but frankly willing to talk about anything to keep him on the phone a bit longer, I go with it. "Gabby's good. She and Tim have decided to do a long weekend. Get out of town, just the two of them."

"That's good. And your dad?"

"He's good. His hockey team is doing pretty well, so he's enjoying life. He's disappointed I'm leaving so soon."

Shit. I didn't mean to bring up the subject we're clearly trying not to talk about. But there it is. I suppose we might as well deal with it.

"Right. Yeah."

"I didn't really expect to leave this soon either," I explain.

"But you did expect to leave again, right? I don't know why I never really got that." His voice is hard edges, keeping me at a distance.

The nervous waves in my stomach start to congeal into one giant solid ball of dread.

"Yeah. I knew if this was going to work, I would have to go back. That was always my plan."

"But I wasn't part of that plan," he says flatly.

I clear my throat so I can speak. "I didn't plan on you. On us. I didn't plan on meeting someone." Or falling in love. But I am sure now is not the time to confess that bit. Not when I think he may be ending it for good.

"So, ten days." I don't say anything, not sure he expects a response.

"How long will you be there? I mean, is this for good? Is it another three years? What?"

"This trip will probably be three months." I hold my breath, waiting for his reaction.

"This trip. So, there will be others?"

"Yes. I'll need to go back."

"Right." I hear him exhale heavily and can practically see him shoving his hand through his hair in frustration.

"How exactly did you see this working, Ash?" he challenges.

"What do you mean?" I stall. Because the truth is I *didn't* think about it. I had these two things in my life I both really wanted, really cared about, and I just moved forward with them both separately, not really anticipating when they would collide and what I would do. And I realize now I should have. I should have prepared Lucas for the reality. I should have never gotten involved with him knowing I was going to leave. But I wanted him. I wanted this. And now I'm losing him, and the pain is unbearable.

"You and me. You in Africa. How exactly did you see this working?"

"It's only three months -" I start.

"This trip!" he interjects. "It's not going to be easier a year from now for you to leave for three years again. Unless you didn't think we'd be together a year from now."

Shit, he's angry. And I get it. But it's messing with my head, keeping me from explaining properly. Keeping him from ending things.

The truth is, I hadn't really thought about specifics. I was just doing what felt right in the moment. Doing what I wanted to do because it was what I wanted, maybe for the first time in my life. I mean, obviously, I wanted, want, to be a doctor, but because I want to help people and I'm good at it. I wanted to go to med school because I wanted to be a doctor. But Lucas, being with Lucas wasn't a means to an end. I just wanted to be with Lucas.

Want. Present tense.

But this is everything I've been working towards for three years. I can't not go. More than that, I want to go. I want to do this. I just don't want to lose Lucas.

I don't know what to say, and eventually, I hear him swear under his breath and say, "Goodbye, Ash."

Ten days later, I get on a plane. I don't admit to myself until I'm in my seat that part of me was still hoping Lucas would show up, tell me he'll wait for me, that we can make it work. That he loves me too. But that doesn't happen. Lucas doesn't show with any rom-com-worthy speeches or grand gestures.

It's really over. And now, on top of everything else, I have to figure out how to heal my broken heart.

Chapter Twenty-Seven

Getting back to 'normal' after Ash leaves is brutal. I'm a total asshole to everyone around me. Luckily Jax puts himself in my face on a regular basis, taking the brunt of it, so no one else has to. I know what he's doing, and I appreciate it, but it doesn't ease the constant rage I feel shimmering under my skin.

Two weeks after she left, one of my afternoon appointments cancels at the last minute. Normally I'd be pissed and charge the guy our cancellation fee, but his wife went into premature labor, so I just rescheduled him. But it leaves me with a free afternoon and nothing to do but think. Something I've been trying to avoid at all costs.

Logan wanders back to my station and plops into my chair.

"Tattoo me. Let's do it."

I must look at her like she's crazy, but she just grins at me. "What? You're going to deny me a Luke Abbott original? And I expect a discount." She shifts in the chair and lifts the hem of her tank top, revealing her ribs.

"Are you serious?"

"Yep. You're not worried you can't freestyle anymore, are you?"

"Fuck you." But I'm laughing as I say it. Fucking Logan. I take a few minutes, studying the space on her skin, deciding on an image. And I start to sketch it right onto her skin. "No veto power. I get full control."

She grins at me. "If it sucks, I'll make your life hell."

I laugh again. Damn, it's been a while since I've laughed. We spend the next few minutes bantering back and forth, eventually settling into a comfortable silence as I work.

"You gonna be okay, Luke?" she asks, breaking the silence. Startled, my eyes shoot up to hers. She's a tough bitch, Logan. It's one of the things I love most about her. She takes no shit from anyone and gives her fair share of it. But she's got a viciously protective heart for those she lets into it. And I know she doesn't let many people in, so I answer her honestly.

"Eventually. I think so. Yeah."

She nods, eyes serious. "It sucks when you're not with the people you love."

Love. I've been doing my best to avoid that word. For decades really, long before Ash. Love seemed like a luxury I was not allowed. I never had parents to love. Any girls I dated growing up, I knew I could be moved without notice at any time. No point investing much in that. And then, as an adult, I had so much to prove to myself and everyone else. Women just naturally became secondary, if a factor at all.

And then Ash walked in.

But she's gone now, and I have to deal with that. So, while I know Logan is trying to help, I don't really want to talk about it.

I don't think. But then I realize out of everyone, maybe Logan has the best chance of understanding what I'm feeling. And can help me understand it.

"You mean Bodhi?" She and Bodhi will go weeks, sometimes months, without seeing each other. I've always been kind of pissed about it, assuming he wasn't treating her right. That he didn't care about her or respect her the way she deserved.

She grimaces. "No. Not really." I turn my attention back to her skin and my design. "You know how I told you he was doing what we both needed him to do right now? And maybe someday I'd tell you about it?"

I glance at her again quickly. "Yeah," I remember.

"I love Bodhi. I do. But...." She sighs and looks over my head at the wall behind me. "I've known Bodhi my whole life. His little sister was my best friend. We did everything together. Everything. Then when we were sixteen, she started to change. She used to tell us everything, me and Bodhi, but all of a sudden, she had all these secrets. And then, on her seventeenth birthday, she just... disappeared. The cops said she ran away. Eventually, everyone just accepted she must be dead. Young. Runaway. Poor family.

"Except me and Bodhi. We've spent the last ten years trying to find her."

I stay quiet. Really there isn't anything to say except, "That's rough, Streaks. I'm sorry."

She nods and watches while I finish up.

"Finally. I've only been working here three years, and I can now say I've got a Lucas 'Winner of *Top Ink*' tattoo."

"Smart ass," I mutter.

Logan stands and straightens her clothes. "Anyway, I get it. It sucks not to be with the people you love. But I also know it should be a really good reason. If you're not going to be with them, it should be a really good reason, you know?" She turns and places a hand on my shoulder, looking me in the eyes. "Make sure this is a good reason. Because it's kinda obvious you're miserable. And you're miserable because you love her."

It's one of the rare afternoons when we're all actually in the shop, and after my talk with Logan, I'm trying to just enjoy being surrounded by people that matter to me. Logan and Mateo are sketching in the corner. Macy is doing a tattoo in the front station. Just a quick piece for a regular client, so both of them are yelling comments over as Jax is cutting up and joking around. I think he's relieved to see me smiling for a change.

The door chimes, and two police officers walk in. I stiffen, feeling the mood in the shop shift. This can't be good.

"Afternoon, folks. We're looking for Mateo Ortega. Told he was working here."

Shit.

I sense Mateo coming up behind me and stand protectively at his side. If they're here just to hassle him, they're in for a rough afternoon. Not for one second do I believe he's done anything to violate his probation. Kid's got his head on straight, and I'm proud of him.

"Yeah? I'm Mateo." His voice is shaky, and I put a comforting hand on his shoulder.

One of the cops steps forward. "Son, we need to talk to you about your mother." She looks up, acknowledging me. "Is there a place we could speak privately?"

"Not alone," I say.

"You can come if Mateo wants that."

He nods. I can feel him shaking.

The four of us move to the back room.

"I haven't seen my mom in nine months," Mateo states as soon as the door closes. "I don't know where she is."

The same officer says, not unsympathetically. "I'm sorry to tell you, your mother's body was discovered yesterday morning. She OD'd in a hotel room near Springfield."

"She's...dead?"

"We're sorry for your loss." The officer starts to say something else, but I interject. I can tell Mateo can't take anything else right now.

"You can contact Olivia Peters if any arrangements need to be made. She'll coordinate with Mateo and me."

She nods. Job done, she and her partner leave.

The silence crowds the room when they leave. Shit. I have no idea what to say to the kid. Ten minutes ago, we were all laughing at one of Jax's stupid jokes, and now....

"You okay?" Stupid question. Obviously, he's not okay. I'm so bad at this.

He nods but is swiping at the tears in his eyes as he does. He hasn't moved.

"Mateo?"

Not looking at me, he mumbles, "Yeah?"

"You don't have to be okay."

My tiny permission seems to be all he needs, and his skinny frame is suddenly racked with sobs. Awkwardly, I hug him, and it seems to help. He squeezes me tight while he cries. Eventually, the emotions lessen, and he's limp. I lead him to the couch and grab him a water. He gulps half the bottle down before gasping for air.

"Sorry," he mumbles.

"Nothing to be sorry for."

"She wasn't a great mom, ya know? But I still loved her." His voice cracks, and the tears well up again.

"Yeah. I get it."

Logan pops in and takes in the scene somberly. "What do you need?"

I walk over to her and leave Mateo in his grief. Quietly, I fill her in. "His mom OD'd. Can you call Olivia and let her know. Ask her to take care of funeral arrangements and let me know if she needs anything. And ask her to contact whoever she needs to about him staying with me for a few days."

She nods, casts one last look at Mateo, and goes to take care of business.

Jax goes to the group home and, with the help of one of the counselors, packs a bag for Mateo. Enough for him to stay for several nights until things settle down. I know they won't approve him staying with me for long, and frankly, I doubt my place is the best place for him long-term, but I want him to know he's got people who care about him. Due to the situation and his good behavior since his hearing, he's been approved to stay for three nights.

"He doing okay, you think?" Jax asks. The two of us are standing in my kitchen, able to see Mateo sitting on the couch watching television.

"I don't know. I think so. Fucking rough."

"Yeah." We're quiet, neither of us knowing what to say or how to handle this kind of loss. God, family is complicated. Rationally, I think we all know that Mateo is in a better place, a healthier place now than he would be if his mom were here, but, like he said, he loved her. Jax hasn't seen his mom in probably over ten years. Maybe longer now, whatever it's been, it's been a long time. And by his choice. His dad passed away even longer ago.

And me. Well, I still know next to nothing about my mother. Less about my father. Watching Mateo's grief is hard. For multiple reasons, including the fact that I've never really grieved my mother. I spent my early childhood imagining all kinds of scenarios, but it didn't take long for me to let go of fairytales. The Abbotts walking in my door only gave me more questions. So many questions.

"You mind sticking around for a while? There something I gotta do." I glance at Jax, asking for yet another favor.

"Sure, man. No problem. You good?"

"Yeah. I'm good. Text me if anything comes up."

"I've got it. Go do what you need to do."

"Thanks." I hold out my hand, and he grips it solidly, pulling me in for a quick hug and slap on the back.

I hop on the 'el' and head north. I watch the city pass by in a blur, my mind on autopilot. I've had the address for a while, but I've never used it. Never intended to either.

But it's time.

I take it to the end of the line and grab an Uber for the remaining 15 minutes.

There's a gate, of course. I should have expected that. I press the buzzer and wait for the crackling voice to answer.

"It's Lucas," I say. "Lucas...Abbott."

It's silent for a moment, and then I hear the mechanics of the gate releasing, and it starts to open. I slip between and walk up the longer-than-necessary driveway. Nerves creeping in with every step.

I've come this far. I'm about to knock when the door is opened from the inside. I'm expecting to see a butler or some shit, but instead, it's yet another of my cousins. Ethan's younger sister, Teagan.

Her wide eyes reveal her surprise.

"Hi." Her voice is soft. We've never actually met. But she obviously knows who I am, just like I know her.

"Hi."

She shakes herself loose and opens the door wider. "Come in."

"Thanks. Is, uh, Theo home?"

"He's in his study. I'll show you."

I stand awkwardly in the entry. And it is a legitimate entry. Shiny floors, a massive ceiling, a freaking staircase, and chandelier.

"Don't you need to announce me or something?"

"We don't announce family. We just barge in," she informs me. "Follow me. I'm Teagan, by the way," she calls over her shoulder.

I nod, although she isn't facing me to see it. "Luke."

She turns and grins at me, "I know. It's nice to finally meet you."

She leads me through the entryway and down a hall. Every step that I'm surrounded by the money obvious in every detail of this house, I feel more and more out of place.

Clueless to my nerves, she continues, "I've wanted to come and introduce myself for ages, but Ethan thought we should wait until 'you came to us'." She uses finger quotes and lowers her voice for the last bit, imitating her brother. Despite myself, I feel a small smile form. Finally, she stops in front of a closed door. "Which is ridiculous, of course. How are you supposed to know how awesome the rest of us are if you've only met Ethan?" She rolls her eyes. "But I'm just the little sister, what do I know?"

I can almost see myself liking this particular Abbott.

"Anyway, here you go." She opens the door and says, "Daddy, Luke is here."

And suddenly, I'm standing in front of my uncle, by choice, for the first time. He looks up from his desk, his expression mirroring his daughter's surprise. He sets his glasses on his desk and stands. "Lucas."

Now that I'm here, I have no idea how to start.

"Come in. Sit down," he gestures to the chairs facing his desk. "Teagan, please give us some privacy."

"You know I'm just going to listen at the door."

He rolls his eyes again, just like his daughter. These peeks at the family dynamic are disorienting. I've never imagined him as a dad. Just as the asshole who tried to manipulate me and buy me off. I try to focus on that barely buried rage, remember what he's capable of, and not be sucked in by his politician charm.

"Get out, Teagan."

She laughs and blows him a kiss. "Fine." Turning to me, she flashes a wide grin. "It was nice to finally meet you. Barge in anytime." And she's out the door.

"You'll have to forgive my daughter. She's...very determined."

"Is that what you call it?"

He laughs. "Among other things." I made my uncle laugh. This is getting weird.

I don't know if he reads something in my expression or just isn't interested in making small talk, but he turns serious again. "What can I do for you?"

"Tell me about my mother."

Chapter Twenty-Eight

It's been two weeks since my conversation with my uncle. Two weeks since we found out Mateo's mother was dead. Six weeks since Ash left Chicago. Nearly eight weeks since I've seen her.

The conversation with my uncle didn't answer all my questions, but it answered some. And gave me more new and different questions I don't know if we'll ever have answers for. But I'm glad I did it. If nothing else, I'm not as pissed off.

My mother's name was Elizabeth. Theo was several years older, he told me his brother Edward and my mother were closer if I was interested in talking to him. I'm still deciding on that. One step at a time, I guess. Anyway, he remembers her as stubborn and playful, and determined. Like Teagan, he said. She reminds him of my mother. Rebellious. She was the only daughter with three older brothers. Also, like Teagan. His parents had a particular and old-fashioned vision for their daughter's future. One she didn't share.

He was running for office for the first time when she started getting into trouble. His parents, my grandparents, told him everything was fine. Just normal teenage angst, but it was more than that. When she got pregnant, their parents wanted to send her away to have the baby, me, and give it up, but she refused. Instead, she ran away. And their parents, not wanting a scandal for multiple reasons, including Theo's budding political career, told everyone she was away at boarding school.

Even her brothers.

"I should have pushed more. But I was young and selfish and caught up in my own life. So, I just believed them when they said she was fine. I just accepted it. Of all the regrets I have in my life, that is one of the biggest. I should have been there for my sister, and I wasn't."

Despite everything, I believe him. His regret was written all over his face.

"We didn't know, Eddie and I, that she'd even been pregnant until years later. Not until my parents were gone. They'd confessed to us she had run away, of course, eventually. They could only make so many excuses for her missing holidays, never writing. We accepted them longer than we should have but eventually, even stupid twenty-something boys figure it out. By then, too much time had passed for the authorities to do much of anything, and my parents still refused to make it public, the scandal it would cause. Maybe Eddie and I should have done more against their wishes while they were still alive. I don't know."

"I am sorry it took us so long to find you, Lucas. I wasn't there for my sister, but I'd like to be there for you. If you'll let me."

And then he stood up and crossed the room to a wall safe, returning with a thick envelope that looked vaguely familiar. He studies it seriously as he slowly slaps it against his palm.

"I know you didn't want this. And although I wish you had chosen differently, I respect what you've accomplished over the last several years. This is your trust." He sets the envelope in front of me and returns to his seat. "I know you have very little reason to believe this, but once I learned of your existence, I have only wanted to keep you safe. For you to have the very best life. There are reasons for the things Ethan and I have done, and while I haven't yet earned it, I ask that you trust me. This is yours. It's always been yours."

"I won't give up the show. Or my shop."

He shook his head, a sad smile on his face. "I wouldn't expect so, no."

I looked at the envelope between us, still uneasy about taking it.

"Look it over. I'm sure you'll have questions. About many things, once you've had time to process. My door is always open."

Nodding, I tucked the papers into my jacket pocket and stood, preparing to leave.

"One other thing," he said, opening his bottom desk drawer. "I found this ages ago. I held on to it because I thought you'd like to see it. Maybe. One day." He hands me an ancient sketchbook. "It was Elizabeth's. She was a beautiful artist."

Then my uncle crossed the room and opened his study door for me, pretending not to notice the tears in my eyes.

Since then, I've had a chance to page through her sketches. It's weird knowing she was an artist in her way, just like me. It's weird knowing anything about my mother after all this time.

I'm at Jax's place Friday night, watching the hockey game and having some beers. Thank god he ended things with Tanya. I'm annoyed enough at life right now, I don't think I'd handle watching the two of them flirting all the time at all well. Not that they were a flirty couple but still. It helps that the *Vanished* crew are all single. People happily in love, even lust, right now put me in a bad fucking mood.

"I blew it, man."

"Told you never to bet against the Blackhawks," Jax mumbles around a mouthful of pizza, still staring at the television.

"Not that, you asshole. Ash."

"Ah. The hot doctor."

I roll my eyes, knowing he's giving me a hard time deliberately. "I'm serious."

He sobers, meeting my eyes, and hands me a beer. "Yeah. You did."

I lift my chin in thanks and take a drink.

"Doesn't mean you can't fix it."

"How am I supposed to do that when she's an ocean away?"

He shrugs. "Phones can do magical things these days. Not to mention airplanes."

"I can't just hop a plane. I have no idea how to find her."

"Bullshit. What's your real problem?"

"What the fuck are you talking about?"

"You could find her if you wanted to. You could ask Gabby. You could ask Will. You could ask your uncle to ask her boss. So what the fuck are *you* talking about?"

He's right. I know he's right. I could find out where she is if I wanted to. I mean, I do want to, but it's not that easy.

I still don't know how this whole thing would work. I don't want to move to Nigeria. I don't want to leave Chicago. This city, *Vanished*, these people, this is my home. I finally have a home and a life I'm proud of, and it's here. For the first time, it even seems like having a relationship with my biological family is a possibility. Something I didn't think I would ever have, and they're here too. Ash's passion, her project is there.

And it seems she and Tanya were right. The threats, the vandalism, everything has died down now that she's gone, and the press doesn't have anything to report or speculate about. Is it fair to drag her back into all that bullshit?

I admit some of this to Jax. He's still watching the game, but I trust he's listening.

He confirms it when he responds, "Seems like some of this is up to Ash, not you." The station takes a commercial break, and Jax turns his full attention to me. "Look, Luke. You are my best friend. I love you like a brother. And if what you need to hear right now is that you deserve a woman like Ash, then hear it. You are the best guy I know. Seriously. I know we've been through some fucked up shit but look at you, brother. Look what you've done. You just see how amazing Ash is, but you don't see how you make her better. Braver, more carefree. You don't see how she makes you better. Calmer, less defensive. You deserve her because you deserve each other."

The game flicks back on, and he settles into his couch cushion. "And I love you, brother, so if what you need to hear is that you're being a fucking coward, you should man up and tell the woman you love her because you're driving me fucking crazy with this mopey bullshit, then hear that too. I'm watching hockey."

Ash

"Dr. Ash, the van is pulling in."

I glance up at my friend in the doorway. "Thank you, Abeni. I'll be right out."

"Your friend arrives today, yes?"

I nod, smiling widely. "He's supposed to, yes."

She grins and ducks back out.

The past two and a half months in Nigeria have gone quickly. It's been a whirlwind, an insane amount of work I'm grateful for. We've been able to make some fantastic progress, including a local staff for our offices here in Yola and multiple hospitals and medical camps that are interested in participating in the training exchange. Several have already committed. Some of the larger and well-established camps will take longer if they ever participate. Many of them are connected to existing NGOs and have more bureaucracy in place. But that's fine. It's the others that really need more resources.

It's good. It's really good. And I've been busy enough to keep thoughts of Lucas and Chicago at bay. Until I go to bed. The minutes before I fall asleep, it creeps in, the pain of missing him. And every morning, it's one of my first thoughts, grief piercing through me as I drag myself out of bed. So I've kept busy. And I've managed to accomplish more than we originally planned. But today, I have a new, better distraction arriving.

I head outside to meet the van, arriving just as Sadiq parks and the passenger door opens.

I smile, seeing him climb out and wave him over. "Will!" I give him a quick hug. "Welcome! It's good to see you. How was your trip?"

"Long." He smiles wryly and sets his bags down. "Good to see you."

"I can't believe you're here." I laugh, feeling lighter than I have in weeks.

"Me either. Oh, this is Kent. He's here to do the publicity shots for the hospital."

We shake hands, and I introduce both of them to Abeni, as the Director of Operations, she'll be working with them closely while they're here. Then I show the two of them to their rooms so they can leave their bags.

"I don't have anything really planned for today. I assumed you'd want some time to rest and shower after your flight and the long drive. Dinner is at seven in the cafeteria. Tomorrow morning we can drive out to the closest site, and Abeni and I will introduce you. There are three camps I think we should visit while you're here. We should be able to get some great videos and interview some of the doctors and patients for the fundraising materials."

"That sounds great. I'm exhausted." Kent grimaces. "I may skip dinner and just crash until morning. What time do you want to get started?"

"Eight am, okay?"

"Sounds good. I'll see you then."

I turn to Will. "What about you? How are you feeling?"

"A little wired, actually. Any chance you feel like going for a walk?"

I smile. "Sure. That would be nice."

We walk in silence for a while, enjoying the light breeze and early evening sun and each other's company after all this time.

"Pretty different than Chicago, huh?" A group of women move down the sidewalk in the opposite direction, the vibrant textiles used to make their dresses and headpieces giving pops of color to the yellow and green landscape.

"That's an understatement." I see him sneak a glance at me from the corner of my eye. "You happy here, Ash?"

I shrug. "In some ways, I love it here. But I'm excited to go back to Chicago."

He nods as if he expected that answer.

"What about you? Excited to do a rotation here in a couple months?" Will was one of the first doctors to commit to a date to participate. I suspect the Chief helped 'convince' him to go sooner rather than later. Her attending physicians participating in the project make selling it to others that much easier. Will is well known in neuro. Having him as one of the first doctors to lead an exchange is huge. I'm incredibly grateful for his support. Not to mention the impact he can have here. We'll meet the Nigerian neurosurgeon trading spaces with him in a couple days.

"It doesn't feel real yet. But I'm glad I'm getting here for a couple weeks before the big move, you know?"

I nod. I get that, yeah. We turn a corner so I can lead Will down to the river. It's one of my favorite places when I'm in town. We sit on the bank for a few minutes, watching the handful of boats still on the water this late in the day.

When the sun is low in the sky, we head back and say good night, agreeing to meet up in the morning and get to work.

"Ash." Will's voice pulls me back, turning me around to face him.

"Mmm?"

He studies me in the soft light outside our building, his eyes serious. His silence is unnerving me, my stomach starting to flutter unpleasantly. Will moves closer, his eyes on my lips. I stiffen when I realize he's going to kiss me and twist away.

"Will-"

He turns his face away, exhaling a ragged chuckle. "I'm sorry. I thought maybe.... It's him, isn't it? You're not over him."

Over him. My heart squeezes in grief. No. No, I'm nowhere near over him.

Unable to speak the words, I shake my head.

"Right." He takes a step back, giving me space. "I'm sorry. I shouldn't have done that. Can we pretend the last five minutes never happened?"

I force a smile and nod. Yes, please. Let's erase this entirely.

He smiles sadly and turns, heading to his room. I do the same.

I climb into bed, the now familiar pang of regret and heartache settling into my chest. Seeing Will, having a piece of Chicago here, is soothing in so many ways. And it signals that I'll be returning soon. Will and Kent are here for two weeks to tour the facilities and camps that have already agreed to participate. Will to prepare him for his three-month rotation. Kent to do photos, videos, and interviews. Collect material we can use for additional fundraising materials. Two weeks and I'm going back home to Chicago.

I have no idea what waits for me there.

Chapter Twenty-Nine

Lucas

I'm too late.

There's a massive pit in my stomach as I stare at the newspaper in front of me.

I'm too late and suddenly, all of the petty shit I spent the last few months trying to figure out seems so pointless and stupid. Fuck.

The door chimes, and I shove the paper into the recycling bin behind me before Macy and Logan spot it. But getting rid of it doesn't erase the images from my brain.

Ash and Will. Laughing as they work together in Nigeria. *He went to Nigeria?* He's been with her. He went after her. Embracing as they landed at O'Hare. She's back. She's back in my city. *With him.*

Fuck. Fuck. FUCK.

I'm too late. Jax was right. I should have done something then instead of waiting. So stupid to wait. I should have told her as soon as I realized the mistake I'd made. But instead, I wanted to talk to her in person, look her in the eyes.

And now I'm too late.

Macy greets me with a slap on the back and moves behind the counter to check his appointments for the day. I head to the backroom, trying to get my head straight. I'm only slightly successful. I spend most the day avoiding people and conversation.

Wrapping up early, I leave Macy and Logan to close. I drive home mindlessly and somehow find myself on Ash's street. I sit in my car, watching her house. And yeah, I know that sounds creepy. But I'm just trying to get my nerve up to talk to her.

And then I see him. Will walking down the sidewalk. I glance at the light in the apartment window and back to him. Shit. I start the car, my skin burning with humiliation and anger. I pull out of my parking spot, and for a brief second, I think our eyes meet. Stupid asshole.

I'm not even sure which of us I'm talking about.

I walk in my apartment door and immediately change into workout clothes. The boxing gym is closed by now, but I can at least go for a run and try to exhaust some of this pissed-off energy out of me. Let the city at night soothe some of my anger. Before I make my escape, my doorbell rings. For a brief moment, I have a flash of hope that it's Ash. But even before I open the door, I know it's not. Can't be.

Tanya's on the other side.

"Hey, sorry it's so late. I tried to catch you at the shop, but you'd just left."

I grimace but open the door to let her in. "What's up?"

"Krista made some changes she wanted me to go over with you. It shouldn't take long."

We started shooting the next season a month ago. I'd rather be punishing myself with a long run, but at least this is something to think about that isn't a beautiful brunette and her ex. The ex that isn't me.

Tanya moves into my kitchen and pulls out a folder.

"I hope you don't mind, I grabbed some food and a couple beers on my way over. I figured if I was going to barge in, at least I could feed you."

I shrug. "It's no big deal. I was going for a run, though, so if we can bust this out, that would be great."

"Sure, it shouldn't take long. Where's your plates? Bottle opener?"

I point her to the cupboard with my plates and grab the bottle opener, popping two of the beers she brought open.

"Thanks." She digs out several containers of Chinese and serves herself a plate of food. I stand impatiently waiting for her but stay silent, not wanting to be a dick. And I'm pretty sure anything I say right now will sound pretty dick-ish.

Finally, she opens her folder and punches something up on her phone. We stand at the counter while she eats and goes through her list of urgent items.

When she's still going thirty minutes later, I finally interrupt. "Seriously, Tanya? You could have talked to me about any of this shit tomorrow. What's so important you needed to do it tonight?"

She blinks at me, eyes wide. Then slowly, she sets down her phone and pushes her plate away. She takes another drink of her beer and then turns to face me. "I saw the article about Ash in the paper today. I wanted to make sure you were okay."

I stiffen and fake a shrug. "Fine. Why wouldn't I be?"

She watches me for a second, then smiles and says, "Good. That's good."

I roll my neck, trying to loosen the tension in my shoulders, then turn to get a glass of water. When I turn back, Tanya is standing right in front of me.

Right in front of me. She takes a deep breath, her breasts brush against my shirt, and her hair tickles my chin and neck.

"What-"

The rest of my question is lost as she pulls my head down and presses her lips against mine.

I'm paralyzed with shock for a split second, and then I'm setting her away from me, moving several steps across the room until I can put the island between us. "Whoa. Whoa. Whoa. That's...that's not going to happen, Tanya."

For a brief second, I see something flash across her eyes, but then her face is just a mask of confusion. "Why not?"

Why not?

Oh, lady, let me count the reasons. Shit.

And then I remember how Jax thought she started sleeping with him to keep him happy after the accident. Jesus Christ, is this what I've become? Some charity case she's going to screw, so I'm not moping around again now that Ash is back in Chicago?

Pissed for a whole new set of reasons, I don't even try to play nice. "Go home, Tanya. You can call me tomorrow if there's anything else you need to discuss about the show."

She starts to protest, but I'm not inclined to listen.

"Get the fuck out."

Chapter Thirty

I can do this.

I can.

I want to do this.

I want to . . . see him again, talk to him, be with him.

What am I doing here?

What if he doesn't *want* to see me?

What if he doesn't regret the way we left it? What if he's perfectly happy?

What if he's with someone else now?

What if he's still too angry to listen to me?

I'm going to be sick.

No. I can do this.

I take a deep breath and lift my chin.

The door chimes as I walk through. Here we go.

"Damn, Doc! Where the hell have you been?"

I smile in relief at Jax's greeting. I wasn't sure what kind of welcome I'd get from Lucas, but I realize now I had also been nervous about the reaction of the others. We'd become friends, I'd considered all of the *Vanished* crew friends, but Lucas was their family. I knew their loyalty was to him.

He comes around the corner and gives me a solid hug.

"Hey, you."

He releases me, allowing me to take him in.

"You look good," I say with a grin.

"Back to normal." He winks playfully and pulls a complicated dance move.

I laugh at his ridiculousness. I'm intoxicated by relief and nerves. The silence stretches between us. My nerves are raging and overwhelming. I shift awkwardly from foot to foot. "Is he here?" I finally ask.

"He's doing a tat in back."

My stomach lurches. I can't tell if I'm disappointed he's busy or relieved I have a few more minutes to postpone the inevitable.

"Mind if I wait?"

He cuffs me under the chin. "I never turn down the company of a beautiful woman."

I attempt another smile but know it's only partially successful. "I'm sure you've had plenty of ladies offering to keep you company during your recovery."

He grins, basically confirming my suspicions.

I sit on one of the couches, my mind rewinding to the first time I entered this building. When Lucas Abbott was just a name and nothing more to me. I'd had no idea then how quickly he'd become a center of gravity in my world.

Instead of returning to his spot behind the counter, Jax sits perpendicular to me on one of the other couches. Grateful for the distraction, I ask him how the shop is going.

"Great. We launched that merch line. It's selling like crazy. Mateo may even create a design for one of the charity pieces like you mentioned."

"You're doing that? Mateo's an artist?" What else have I missed?

Jax grins. "He's more of a poet, but he and Logan are working on something together."

"That's amazing." It seriously is. "And the show?"

"Going good. Filming again. There's a crew in back with Luke right now."

Oh shit.

This was a bad idea.

I jump to my feet, stuttering excuses.

Jax watches me patiently, still reclining back on the brown leather couch. When I pause briefly to inhale, he interjects, "It's good you're back. He's been cranky as hell."

There's a pang in my chest at his statement, and I press my lips together, preventing any other words from escaping.

Before I can recover, Logan enters the lobby from the back and stops short when her shocked eyes land on me.

"Ash."

Oh god. This is such a bad idea. I shouldn't be here. "Hi, Logan."

"You're back."

I nod dumbly. Yep. I'm back.

"Does Luke -" her question ends abruptly as she looks from me to Jax.

Nope. No, no, no. This was not a good idea. I should have called him, or gone by his apartment, or...

Logan steps forward and hugs me. Actually hugs me, like she's glad to see me.

Stunned, I barely remember to hug her back. She steps back, looking almost as awkward as I feel, and gives me a lopsided grin. "Welcome back."

Wow.

Okay, my nerves are all over the place. But there's a teeny, tiny part of me that's starting to feel . . . Optimistic? Hopeful?

I mean, he can't have spent the last three months bashing me to his friends if this is their response to me showing up on their collective doorstep. That's promising, right?

And then I hear him. The low murmur of his voice signals his approach as he moves down the hallway toward the lobby.

Towards me.

I'm going to throw up.

Taking a deep breath, I brace myself.

A man I've never seen before slips into the room and pulls a camera to his shoulder, lens focused on the hall he just exited. And then he turns the corner, entering the lobby with what I'm assuming is his client. The two men clasp hands quickly in a casual handshake. Making small talk for the camera.

My stomach flips, a combination of nerves and desire. He's relaxed, smiling, and he's just so insanely, heart-stoppingly attractive. I've missed that smile so much. That thick hair with hints of red. He needs a haircut. I want to see him smile every day from now on. I hope he might still want that too. Want me.

His dark blue gaze takes in the room, flicking right over me.

Then returns, laser-focused, and widening in shock. He freezes, the smile falling from his face. Turning abruptly back to the crew member, he orders, "Turn off the camera."

Shit.

Lucas

I should be doing something right now.

I was doing something, I'm pretty sure.

Someone bumps into my back, and I blink.

But she's still there.

Ash is still standing in the middle of the room, looking as fucking gorgeous as ever. It's mid-November now, and the fall chill is in the air, but the sunny days are still beautiful. Today isn't a sunny day, and Ash is bundled up in a navy peacoat with a massive yellow plaid scarf wrapped around her neck. Her hands are shoved deep into her pockets while she shifts from boot to boot in front of me. I loved her tiny strappy summer dresses, but even this turns me on. She's a present I want to unwrap. But I don't think she'll ever let me do that again.

What is she doing here?

Had Will seen me last night after all and told her I'd been there? Was she here to tell me they were back together? That I should leave her alone?

RJ is looking around, clearly confused, but ultimately lowers the camera. Distantly, I hear Logan settling up with my client. He comes over and says something to me. I must respond appropriately because he grins, slaps me on the shoulder, and takes off.

The chime of the door as he exits finally snaps me out of my fog.

I tell RJ to take off for a while, I'm done filming for the day. He heads to the back room with a shrug.

"Hi, Lucas." Hearing her voice for the first time in months hits me hard. I have to clear my throat before I can respond.

"Ash."

Silence falls heavy between us, crushing the air in my lungs. I don't want to hear what she has to say. Do I?

Do I want to hear her say it's over? I know that. I know I did that.

After Jax's tough love talk, I've replayed that last conversation over and over and over again. I was an asshole. I knew that then, but time and space have only made it more glaring. I'd spent our whole time together waiting for the thing that would finally force her to realize I wasn't worth loving. Just like all the people who hadn't loved me before her. I'd just started to think maybe that thing was never going to come, and she hit me with leaving the country.

And that's all I'd heard. She was leaving. I wasn't enough for her to stay.

I didn't hear *three months*. I didn't hear *her career*. I didn't hear *her*.

I'd cut her out cold and clean, all my survival tactics from being yanked from foster home to foster home raging into place.

So no. I don't need to hear what she has to say. But I'll give her this if she needs it. If she needs some kind of closure my hasty exit didn't allow her.

Because the other thing Jax's verbal spanking and Logan's unusual vulnerability made me realize is that I would do just about anything for Ash.

Because I loved her.

Fuck. I love her, and I blew it. Guys like me, I'm pretty sure we don't get two chances at a happy ending. Ash does, though. She deserves a dozen happy endings. Hundreds. Millions.

And she's back with her ex now. Who I'm sure is more than willing to give her at least one.

I hate that dick.

Why the fuck should he get another chance with her? He blew it. She even said she didn't love him.

I guess I blew it, too, though. I'm the one that opened the door for him to try to win her back. But if she's willing to give second chances, I want mine. Screw that guy.

"Well. This is going shockingly well." Jax interrupts the growing silence. "Maybe you should take her out to dinner," he suggests. Jax turns to Ash. "Have you eaten yet, Doc?"

There's a brief pause before Ash responds, and I feel something suspiciously like hope rising in my chest.

"I have, actually."

Crushed. My throat is tight with disappointment. And still, I can't manage to say anything to her.

"I wouldn't mind grabbing a drink, though."

I can do that.

"Can you...? I mean, are you free? Do you have another appointment?"

I shake my head mutely and then finally find my balls and speak. "No. I'm done. I'm free if you want...."

She nods, smiling shyly. Those cheeks turning pink.

I point my thumb over my shoulder to the back. "Let me just grab my coat."

We don't go far, just to the brewery next door. I'm glad. I don't think the awkward silence of a long commute somewhere would have been good for me. I'd probably have ended up doing something stupid. Saying something stupid. Although that is still a strong possibility considering my track record.

Before, when Ash and I were together, she was surprisingly patient when I struggled with what to say. She was clear about what she needed, but she also was frequently okay with me saying nothing at all and letting my actions speak. I don't think that's going to be the case here. I'm going to have to be honest and upfront with her in a way that makes my muscles tense and stomach violent.

But if I want her, I need to meet her halfway. At least halfway. I may have some additional ground to make up.

Frankly, I may be getting way ahead of myself. If she's back with Will, she may not care what I have to say. Or not say.

We settle into a table and order a couple pints. I take my coat off, and she does the same, unwinding that massive scarf and then smoothing her hair back in place.

"Welcome back." It's a stupid thing to say, but something has to start us off.

She smiles that little smile again and murmurs, "Thanks. My timing was a little off, missing the best part of fall."

"True. Probably get snow in the next couple weeks."

Fuck are we really talking about the weather right now?

I shift forward and lean my elbows on the table. "How was the trip? Is that what you call it? Trip seems...vacationy."

"It was good. Really productive. We made a lot of progress."

We. Like her and Will 'we' or...?

"That's good, Ash. I'm happy for you. Really."

"Thanks. Jax says the show is good. He said you launched the merchandise line like you were talking about."

I nod. "Yeah. That's been huge, actually. He's doing awesome with it."

She smiles again, and we both fall silent. This is awkward.

Fuck it.

I'd rather just fucking know. This is freaking painful.

"I'm sorry about the things I said before you left. I was an ass. I know that." I shove a hand through my hair and exhale roughly. "This is important to you. I get that."

Her beautiful brown eyes widen at my words. "I'm sorry too. I should have been more clear about my timeline and plan. I should have talked to you about what it would mean for us. And I should have talked to you before I accepted the Abbott's money. I-"

Shaking my head, I interrupt her. "I told you to take their money if it would help. It wasn't fair for me to get pissed when you did."

"But still. You also said it would come with strings attached and me leaving.... It wasn't a condition per se, but it was implied. We all knew that would be the result."

I stiffen. "Is that why you went?"

She tucks a piece of hair behind her ear and shakes her head slightly. "No. I went because I had to. This is what I've been working on. My whole idea when I came back to Chicago. This is what I wanted."

Her words crush me, although I try not to show it. This is what she wants. Not me. And Will will be there, right by her side. That asshole.

I take a swallow of beer, trying to organize my thoughts into a sentence I can actually say out loud.

"Well, I'm sure the two of you will build it into something great."

She nods, and I can see the sparkle of excitement in her eyes. "We're starting the first rotation right after the new year. Will is going to lead the first group. Pretty amazing. We're both really excited. The hospital even sent a photographer out the last couple weeks to get images and video for a special fundraising campaign."

Well, that explains the article I read.

And then the rest of what she said sinks in. She's leaving again in just a couple months. This was a bad idea. Why did I agree to this? There's a fist squeezing the air slowly out of my throat. I rap on the table with my knuckles, preparing to exit. I can't do this after all.

"I just...I want you to be happy, Ash. And I want you to know I'm sorry for how I handled it when you first told me. I wish," I clear my throat roughly. "I wish I'd done things differently. Maybe then...." I gesture between the two of us. "Maybe then...." I don't know what I'm trying to say. I grab my pint and swallow greedily, desperately. Trying to finish, so it's not so obvious I'm running away.

Ash is watching me drink, a slightly confused look on her face.

I push back and stand, moving next to her on the other side of the table. Her face falls as she looks up at me and gets to her feet.

Because I am apparently a sucker for punishment today, I pull her into a loose hug and press my lips against her cheek. It all comes back in painful detail, how she feels, how she smells, how she is. "Be happy, Ash. I hope you and Will accomplish everything you want."

I force myself to pull back and release her. She's squeezing one of my hands, her mouth opening and closing soundlessly. I try to pull away and get my jacket so I can leave before I make an even bigger ass of myself. But she tightens her grip, refusing to let go.

I meet her gaze, those chocolate eyes killing me. "Ash?"

At first, her face is a maze of confusion, and then before my eyes, a veil of...determination? Resolve? Pissed-Offness? Whatever it is, I don't think I've ever seen this particular expression on her beautiful face.

"No. I'm not doing this again," she mutters, then more clearly, she speaks up again, "Lucas, what... what are you talking about?"

"You and Will. Moving to Nigeria. Building this exchange like you've imagined."

"Me and Will? I was talking about Abeni and me. She's the one that's championed me and this idea from the beginning."

"Oh."

She releases my wrist and puts her hands on her waist.

"I'm not dating Will again. Why does it seem like you think I am?"

I am stunned, stupid happy as her words start to sink in. "You're not?" *She's not.*

"No."

"I saw the article that he was in Nigeria with you. And then last night...."

"What about last night?" she asked, still with that same confused and determined look on her face.

I shuffle from foot to foot, awkwardly admitting. "I saw him at your place."

Now she looks really confused. "He wasn't at my place last night. Wait...you were at my place last night?"

"I saw you were back, and I...well...when I saw Will, I left."

"But he wasn't," she shakes her head. "Why would I be here if I was with Will?"

I shrug, feeling like an idiot. But also feeling a little hopeful. "I thought you might want some closure or something."

__Ash__

"I don't want closure."

This conversation has taken a very confusing turn. All the scenarios I imagined, all the ways I thought this could go, every conversation I played out in my head...none of them resembled the one we are actually having. But I refuse to leave this interaction with questions. I wanted to know, one way or the other, where we stood.

"Is that what you want? Is that why you agreed to come?" I asked, a sick feeling coming over me.

He looks at me in disbelief, his blue eyes boring into mine. "If the last three months have taught me anything, Ash, it's that I want *you*. So, I guess I should ask, did I blow it? Am I too late? I know I screwed up, but I promise you I will never be that stupid again."

My stomach flips, and I feel my pulse start to race, but I force myself to calm down and finish this conversation before I throw myself back into his arms. I press my lips together, fighting sudden tears. "I want you, too," I whisper.

He moves as if to pull me into his arms, and I take a quick step back, warding him off by raising my hand between us. His face falls. I motion to the table, and wordlessly he takes his seat across from me. I sit as well and take a deep breath.

"You kind of broke my heart, Lucas."

"Broke mine too," he admits.

Still nervous, I start absently playing with my napkin. Folding the corners, unfolding them, folding it in half. Now what?

Lucas covers my hands with one of his, stilling my nervous fidgeting. I look up from our hands and meet his eyes.

"I miss you," I confess.

"I miss you too, Ash."

"Now what?" I ask the question aloud.

He gives me a half-smile. "You're asking me? I suck at this."

It makes me laugh, relaxing us both. He leans forward, narrowing the space between us, and squeezes my hands gently with his. "Someone told me if I wasn't going to be with you, it should be for a good reason. And I know it won't be easy, but distance doesn't feel like a good enough reason, you know? I mean, I don't like that you're leaving again in less than two months, but how long will you be there this time?"

My heart warms a bit at his words. He's willing to meet me halfway, it seems. But he still needs to understand some things.

"I'm not going back in two months. Will is going again in two months."

"You're not?" his voice raises a bit in excitement.

I shake my head, smiling. "No. It was never my plan to go back permanently. I want to go back and work, but my dad is here. And Gabby. And... you."

The smile that breaks across his face is so beautiful my breath catches in my chest for a moment. God, I missed him.

"So...?"

"I will have to go back," I force myself to tell him, risking that smile. "But we're setting up some three-month rotations. So I could do that. Go for three months of a year. And the rest of the time, work with the local team from here. In Chicago."

"Yeah?" He's definitely excited about this idea if the sparkle in his eyes is any indication.

I nod.

"So, you'd be here for a year? And then only be gone for three months?"

I nod again.

He looks away, a thoughtful expression on his face. His blue eyes are serious when they turn back to me. "Maybe...." He clears his throat nervously. "I've been talking to Jax about taking on more with the shop. He's already doing great with this merchandising line, and I've been thinking about asking him to become a full partner. So, uh, I mean, I probably couldn't leave for three full months, but if it was timed right and we weren't shooting, I could maybe come for a month or so. Help out where I can. Go with you."

I'm stunned. My stomach is in knots. Shit, I'm going to cry. I don't know why I feel nervous; this is an amazing gesture.

"You'd do that?" I am. I am crying.

With a slightly panicked look on his face, Lucas stands and moves to sit next to me on my side of the table. He pulls me against his chest, and I bury my face against his shirt.

"Ah, shit," he murmurs, running his hands soothingly down my back. "I didn't mean to make you cry, beautiful."

Hearing him call me that after all these months only makes me cry even harder. But I also start laughing, the happiness bubbling up. I'm a mess but can't find any reason to care. I wipe my face and smile up at him.

"You'd do that?" I repeat.

"I'd do just about anything for you, Ash. I - I want you in my life."

It's not the full declaration I want to hear, but it's huge. It's a lot. It's enough for now. Because I know what Lucas does is often way more important than what Lucas says. Although, I'm really liking what he's saying too.

So I say the words I've held onto until now. I can't hold them any longer.

I wrap my arms around his neck and kiss his lips softly. "I love you," I say simply.

He squeezes me so tight I struggle to breathe, but his reaction thrills me. I don't need to breathe. And then he's kissing me, and my world rights itself. God, I've missed his kisses. His touch, his taste, his smell. Him. Everything.

He pulls away, breathing heavily. "Can we get out of here?"

I nod, laughing. "Yes, please."

Chapter Thirty-One

Ash

I'd like to say that Lucas and I went straight from that table to bed so we could tear each other's clothes off and spend the rest of the night making up for three months of lost orgasms, but...that's not what happens.

Lucas had left *Vanished* so abruptly when I showed up he hadn't thought to grab his phone or his keys, so before we can go anywhere, we pop back over there. And find all three of the others, not just Jax and Logan but Macy now, too, lingering in the front waiting area. Apparently, tonight it takes all three of them to close? Despite how eager I was to get Lucas alone a few minutes ago, it makes my insides a little warm and mushy seeing how much the three of them care about him.

Macy grabs me up in a massive hug when we enter, lifting my feet right off the ground while Lucas looks on with a soft smile. I'm laughing when he sets me back down and return to Lucas's side, slipping my arm around his waist.

"Hot damn. Doc's home! We should celebrate!" Jax declares. Lucas shoots him a death glare which only makes me laugh harder. I missed this crazy group.

Macy suggests we all head over to his parent's pub. Lucas looks at me with a question in his eyes, and I smile and nod. That sounds perfect. I'll tear his clothes off later. There isn't a chance in hell I'm closing my eyes tonight without getting him naked first.

We hop on the el and ride it to Macy's old neighborhood. His parents aren't working this late, but Macy knows the bouncer.

"Hey, man. Good to see you." They fist bump in greeting, and he smiles at the rest of us. "Jax, good to see you. No drunk redheads in tow tonight?"

Jax clears his throat and shifts nervously from foot to foot. He glances at Lucas before responding. "Not tonight."

The bouncer, his t-shirt says Tommy on it, chuckles quietly. "Too bad. She was a cute little thing."

Jax shrugs, clearly wanting nothing to do with this conversation. I admit I'm more curious about Jax's reaction than anything else. He's not usually so shifty, typically using barely appropriate humor or playing dumb when he doesn't want to talk about something. Or someone. Interesting.

Lucas also seems curious and pins Jax down as soon as we step inside. "What redhead?"

Jax seems like he's trying to ignore the question, but Lucas isn't going to budge. Finally, he rubs the back of his neck and finds Macy. "Uh. Riley. She, uh, showed up drunk one night after finding her fiance with another woman. We couldn't just send her out in the streets, so Macy and I brought her here."

"Riley."

"Yep, Riley." Jax raises a hand, signaling the bartender and deliberately not looking at Lucas.

"When was this?"

He shrugs, "About a month ago, I guess."

I'd never admit it to Lucas, but I'm pretty entertained by this whole conversation. Just when it looks like Lucas is going to ask another question, trying to pull information out of a reluctant Jax, Macy comes barreling up behind the two of them and wraps an arm around each of their necks.

"Yo! Hunter! We need a round. We're celebrating!" he calls to the bartender. A gorgeous blond with curves like a busty swimsuit model saunters over with a friendly smile. She seems vaguely familiar, but I can't quite place her.

"Hi, Mace. Guys. What's the occasion?"

Mace responds, "Luke got the stick removed from his ass."

Lucas jabs his elbow into Macy's gut and mutters, "Knock it off."

"Doc's back in town," Jax smiles at me and pulls me to his side. "Doc, this is Hunter."

I smile and shake her hand, "Ash."

"Sure, I remember you. We met at one of Macy's barbecues last summer."

I nod, it finally clicking why she looks familiar.

"Well, what'll you guys have?"

"What the hell? I'm being hustled!" Jax busts out after I hit another bullseye on the dart board. I'm laughing hysterically but manage to retrieve the darts and hand them over. I return to my spot between Lucas's legs. He's sitting on a tall barstool, and between turns, he wraps his arms around my waist, pulls me back into his chest, and keeps me close. I love it.

"Have to have a steady hand and decent aim in my work," I tease. Jax scowls good-naturedly and lines up his next shot. It's just outside the circle. I grin, feeling Lucas's chest behind me, moving with laughter.

Game over. Jax moves next to us, picking up his beer. Logan feigns sympathy but then takes the opportunity to insult his skills. He steals a handful of french fries off her plate.

"I'll accept that challenge," Macy says, sauntering over to the board and pulling out the darts. "You think you got another game in you?"

"You bet. You're not worried about being humiliated like your friend?" I taunt.

"I heard that!" Jax yells around a mouthful of fries.

"She meant you to!" Lucas tosses back.

Macy grins at me. "Bring it on, Doc. I'm not afraid."

Three rounds later, I'm the one being hustled.

He smirks and tells me, "You may have a steady hand, but I grew up in this pub. I haven't lost a dart game in years."

I look at Lucas accusingly, "You could have warned me!"

Shrugging, he smiles and says, "Where's the fun in that?"

I turn my attention to Logan. "No girl power? Women helping women?"

Logan shakes her head. "Everyone learns this lesson the hard way. Sorry."

We stay for hours drinking, talking, laughing, playing. It's a great homecoming and makes me feel even more excited about our future. The *Vanished* crew could have made things so hard or awkward for me, for us, but they didn't. They welcomed me back easily, supporting our reunion.

Toward the end of the night, I sense Lucas getting antsy. He snuggles into the curve of my neck, his breath hot. His lips press lightly against my bare skin and sends a shiver down my spine. When he pulls away, his eyes are hot and sexy. "Can I take you home now and do dirty things to you?"

My stomach flips with desire. "Absolutely."

Lucas

Finally.

Finally, I have Ash alone in my apartment. It's been way too long since I've held her. It took an insane amount of willpower to keep my hands off her the last several hours, and if it wasn't for the happiness on her face, I probably would have dragged her home a long time ago.

But we're finally here.

I pull her close, pressing a kiss to her forehead. She's still all bundled up, but now that I know we've got all night together, some of my urgency is put to rest. I breathe her in, just holding her. Letting it sink in that she's really here. We pass a few minutes like that, but eventually, I feel her shift in my arms, pulling away so she can take her coat off, and I do the same. Wordlessly, she takes my hand, and we move to my bedroom.

She seems nervous, which is not the feeling I'm going for. So, I pull her back into my arms and kiss her.

Someday maybe someone can explain to me why kissing Ash is so different than being with any other woman. Hotter. Sweeter. Sexier. She sighs against my lips and sinks into me. Her lips part, and I caress her tongue with mine, exploring thoroughly. I missed the little sounds she makes. Her breathless moans and soft sighs. God, I missed her.

And she loves me.

I'm a lucky bastard.

Ash stretches up, winding her arms around my neck, her fingers in my hair. I deepen the kiss. I grip her hips and pull her tight against me so she can feel how hard I already am for her. I feel her smile against my lips and break the kiss, squeezing her ass as I do. My eyes move down her body, taking in every detail. Remembering. Excited we get to make new memories.

"Take your clothes off." My voice is rough, and I see her shiver in reaction. My dick pulses against my jeans in eagerness.

She slips her sweater over her head, slowly letting it fall to the floor. She grins at me sexily, standing there in her bra and jeans, and says. "Your turn."

I grin and respond by peeling off my T-shirt, baring my chest. Her eyes are hot, leaving a trail across my skin. The pulse in her neck speeds up, and I experience a heady rush of lust, knowing I did that. When she meets my gaze, I raise my eyebrows in a challenge. She sits on the edge of my bed, unzipping her boots and pulling them off. Then she stands again and faces me. She rolls a finger in the air between us, a get-on-with-it gesture that makes me chuckle.

I toe off one shoe, then the other, and wait. Her move. She laughs and unbuttons her jeans, slowly lowering the zipper. Dragging it out. I growl impatiently. She releases her jeans and reaches behind her to remove her bra, and those gorgeous breasts spring free.

That's it. That's all I can take. I'm mesmerized by her bare breasts as I yank my own jeans off, kicking them away, and pounce. I take her down to the bed, landing on top of her and settling between her thighs. She's laughing at my impatience but sighs when I press my lips to the slope of her breast. I feel one of her hands gently fisting my hair while the other squeezes my shoulder. Our legs are tangled half on, half off the bed, but I'm too intent on my current goal to worry about that right now. I move down slightly and kiss her pert nipple, flicking it with my tongue. She gasps and arches beneath me, offering herself. I drag my eyes up to her face and lower my mouth to her other breast, pulling her nipple into my mouth and sucking. Her mouth falls open, her eyes squeezed shut, and she holds me close. I move between her breasts, making up for all our time apart until she's panting and squirming beneath me.

I slide down her body until I'm on my knees next to the bed, pressing kisses along her stomach as I go. Finally, I curl my fingers beneath her waistband, automatically, she arches her hips giving me room to pull her jeans and underwear down her smooth legs and off entirely.

"Damn, you're beautiful."

I look up from her body and see her watching me, a soft smile on her face, cheeks pink with pleasure. I stand and slip my boxers off, palming my aching dick.

"Look what you do to me," I murmur, stroking myself as she watches on, her eyes like melted chocolate. Her breathing speeds up, her chest rising and falling more rapidly.

"Lucas."

The need in her voice urges me on. I press one knee on the bed and help shift her higher up on the mattress. Then I settle between her thighs, groaning aloud when I feel her soft skin against mine for the first time in so long. My cock nestles against her core, and I roll my hips, torturing both of us with what we don't yet have. Her hands caress restless along my back and shoulders as she seeks me out for another kiss. I crush my lips down on hers feeling my control disappearing. My fingers tease her wetness, thrusting inside, making her breath hitch before she moans my name. My cock is weeping, it's so ready to be inside her. I curl my fingers, seeking the spot that drives her wild, and bring my thumb into play rubbing small circles against her clit. She starts to shake, her neck arching, hips thrusting eagerly into my touch.

"Lucas, please don't make me wait. It's been too long."

"No. No waiting. Come for me, Ash."

She strains against me, chasing her orgasm. I press my lips into the curve of her neck and suck, giving her the tiny push she needs to finally go over the edge.

So fucking beautiful. She cries out as she stiffens against me for a moment and then shakes, coming apart in my arms. When she's done, the shudders receding, she turns her wild eyes on me. I'm feeling like a fucking king knowing I gave her that pleasure.

"Hurry," is all she says.

Following orders, I quickly smooth on the condom and thrust home. She moans as I fill her, feeling her pulsing around me, hot and wet and so fucking sweet. I keep my hips tight against the juncture of her thighs, taking a moment to savor this. Ash raises her knees, digging her heels into the mattress, and moves her hips, trying to take me deeper.

"So good, baby."

And I start to move. She sighs and moans and moves her hips in concert with mine. Her breasts jiggle with each of my thrusts. I slip a hand beneath her and cup her ass, changing the angle, and she cries out.

"Oh god, Lucas. I love you. I love you so much," she groans and breaks apart again, triggering my own climax. Mindlessly I thrust my hips through the pleasure until I ultimately collapse on top of her, breathing heavily.

Ash

A couple hours later, neither of us seems particularly interested in sleeping, I'm sitting in the middle of Luke's bed wearing nothing but one of his t-shirts and paging gingerly through his mother's old sketchbook.

"These are really beautiful," I tell him. He smiles briefly, lying on his side next to me. I pause at one particularly striking image. It's an old lighthouse, cracks in the glass and foundation but still lighting the way for a small fishing boat being tossed by the waves beneath. So impressive for such a young woman.

One side of his mouth quirks up when he sees what I'm looking at. "I liked that one too."

I close the book, set it carefully aside, and turn my attention to him. "I'm really proud of you." I hesitate. "Is that a weird thing to say?"

That sad half-smile again. "No. Thanks."

"I am. I know that must have been really hard for you to go to your uncle like that. How do you feel now?"

He rolls fully onto his back and stares at the ceiling before answering. "I don't know. I'm glad I did it. I'm less... pissed at him. At all of them. But it's still hard to trust them."

"Of course it is. One conversation isn't going to erase everything that's happened. Even though it makes some of it easier to understand."

"He told me to come back anytime."

"Is that what you want?"

"Maybe. I don't know."

I lay down next to him, curling into his side. "Whatever you want."

I feel him press a sweet kiss on my forehead. "Thanks."

"Maybe start small. You said Teagan seemed okay. Or Riley. You don't have to invite Ethan out for beers anytime soon."

He chuckles beneath me. "Yeah, I still don't see that happening."

I give him a quick squeeze and press my lips to his heart, feeling it beating beneath me. "How is Mateo doing with everything that's happened?"

"Pretty well, actually. It's hard, but... he's in a better place now, you know? It was too much for him to take care of her. He's just a kid. Olivia made sure regular therapy was included as a condition of his probation, so he's got people to talk to."

"And he has you guys." He shrugs, dismissing the role they've all played in Mateo's short life. "I'm serious. He could have destroyed his whole life that night with his cousin, but instead, he's still in school, has a chance for a track scholarship. And is going to have his poetry on a *Vanished* poster raising money for charity."

"Logan's really taken him in. You'd never guess it, but she's great with kids. Even teenagers, apparently."

I prop myself up on my elbow to see his face when I tell him. "You know she hugged me? When I showed up today? Logan Dahl actually hugged me!"

Lucas laughs at my excitement, shaking the mattress. He pulls me down on top of him and wraps his arms around my waist so I can't escape. As if I would want to. Perfectly happy right here, thank you.

"She told me I was miserable without you. She's probably happy as hell I won't be such a mopey bitch anymore."

A warm feeling spreads across my chest at his words. "I missed you." My eyes trace over his face, taking it all in. Savoring. I shift my legs and press against his chest until I'm sitting astride his hips. Teasingly, I trace my fingertips along his tattoos. He watches with heat in his eyes as I glide over his chest and abs, reaching his hips and then changing direction. I can feel him getting hard against me, and a thrill of desire shoots through my system.

On my third pass below his navel, he bucks his hips, almost dislodging me from my perch. "You're playing with fire, woman."

I grin at him, undeterred. "Hush, and let me play."

He grabs my hips and squeezes but otherwise leaves me to it.

So much muscle and man, and he's all mine.

I lean down and press another kiss to his heart, lingering for a moment. Then I kiss his lips, teasing them with my tongue before he groans and lets me inside. His hands on my hips rock me against his growing erection. I'm sure he can feel how wet I'm getting, arousal building in my veins. Our kiss goes on and on, getting hotter and more frantic, until I finally pull away and start pressing kisses along the cord of his neck. His heart is beating faster now. One hand releases my hips so he can cup my breast, pinching the nipple lightly, causing me to cry out in pleasure. I arch my back, thrusting my breast against his palm, and urge his head up to suck on the other. And he does the tingles going straight to my core, and I rock my hips more urgently against him. God, I love the way he touches me.

"Ride me, Ash. I want to feel you come apart while I'm balls deep inside you."

Oh god, I want that too.

But I shake my head, determined to torture us both a little longer. Instead, I slide farther down his body, pressing kisses along the ridges of his abs as I go. He groans and curses when he realizes my intention. His hands urge me on as his breathing becomes harsher.

I grip his shaft, squeezing, marveling at the combination of hard and smooth. He groans, hips shifting beneath me. I love that I can do this to him. It goes to my head, lust, and power. I press a chaste kiss to the tip, and he moans my name, urging me to take more. My hand slides down and cups his balls, massaging them gently. Our eyes meet and my breath hitches at the blazing lust and affection I see reflected in his.

I love this man. He's it for me. And I think he loves me too, even if he hasn't spoken the words. I know they're more complicated for him, and I'm okay with that for now. He's willing to plan a future that has room in it for both of us and our dreams, and that speaks volumes for his feelings.

My lips part, engulfing his length, taking him as deep as I can before slowly coming back up and releasing him briefly.

His thumb traces my bottom lip. "What you do to me, beautiful." I nip at this thumb and smile naughtily.

"I'm just getting started."

He groans, his head falling back as I take him back in my mouth, working him in earnest. I feel his hands in my hair, urging me on. His voice in my ears, hoarse with pleasure.

"God, that's so good. I'm going to come."

I press my tongue to the underside of his shaft, sucking strongly, and he explodes. His cries of release make me shiver in anticipation and arousal. He pulls me up his body and holds me tight while his breathing calms down. And then he slides down my body to return the favor.

I never knew pleasure like this existed before Lucas. Shamelessly, I spread my legs, making room for him. His breath is hot against my sex, and I squirm, so ready for him.

"So pretty," he murmurs before teasing me with soft flicks of his tongue. "You gonna come for me?" I nod frantically, trying to urge his face back to my core. He chuckles. "Remember when you didn't like this?"

"Lucas!" I snap but then burst into laughter.

My laughter turns to groans when he slides two fingers inside me and begins to lick passionately. Randomly his tongue will move up and flick my clit, and every time my hips thrust up, intense pleasure racing through me. I'm so close. I'm... almost...there...

I cry out when the pleasure becomes too much, breaking apart inside me in wave after wave.

He slowly moves back up my body, pressing soft kisses as he goes. My hip. My navel. Between my breasts. My collar bone. Behind my ear. Finally, kissing my lips soft and slow.

He pulls me into his arms, and we finally sleep.

I love this man.

Chapter Thirty-Two

Lucas

Ash has been back for a week. And call me whipped, but it's been the best damn week of my life.

I haven't really even given her a chance to unpack, seducing her into staying at my place every night since our reunion. She finally insisted tonight she needed to go back home to Gabby's and Tim's so she could do laundry and get her stuff out of her suitcase. On my end, I'm thinking of asking her to repack immediately and move in with me.

Is it too soon for that? I don't know. I don't really care. It feels right. I want to spend as much time with her as I can.

She might care. Might think we're moving too fast. Especially considering we did just get back together. That's fine if she needs more time.

But I'm going to try to be persuasive.

I know she's probably going to want to hear me say, 'I love you' before she agrees to move in. I do. Love her. That becomes more obvious and real every day. Hell, every minute.

I know she needs the words. She deserves them. But I don't remember ever saying those words to another person, and for some reason, they aren't coming easily.

A text message pops up on my phone, and I grab it, grateful for a legitimate distraction. With Ash busy tonight, I'm still at *Vanished*, attempting to get some work done. I should be sketching up some concept ideas for my clients later in the week, but I'm having a tough time focusing tonight.

And any thought of work is immediately obliterated when I open the message.

I warned you.

Followed by a picture of Ash leaving my apartment this morning. Her face once again covered by a skull.

Fuck. I stand up so fast the stool I was on tips over and clatters to the ground. I yell for Jax, the only other team member here tonight. He pokes his head in, and I tell him to lock up. He takes one look at my face and ducks back out to do it.

I call Ash, swearing when it goes right to voicemail. I still don't know the number for her fucking work cell. I call Gabby instead. She picks up on the third ring.

"Hey, Luke. Thanks for giving me my roommate back for the night," she teases, totally unaware of the state of panic I'm in.

"Gabby, is Ash home?"

"Not yet. She said she'd be home around eight. She had to meet someone first."

Shit.

"Do you know who? Her phone is off."

"I don't. What's going on? Luke?" she prompts when I don't answer right away. I don't want to freak everyone out for no reason, but...this feels all kinds of wrong.

"I got another threat with a picture of Ash. I just want to talk to her and make sure she's okay."

"Oh god. I don't - I don't know where she was going."

"Okay. I'm going to call Melrose. Can you just keep calling Ash and trying to get through? And try her work cell. I don't have that one."

"Yeah, yeah. Of course. Keep me updated, okay? I'm going to be freaking out until we talk to her."

You and me both. But I don't say that.

I call Melrose.

"Lucas. I was beginning to think you'd forgotten all about me."

I wish. But he's right, it's been months since I'd called him. Since Ash left the country. And now...now she's back, and I did a shit job protecting her.

"I got another text, and I can't get a hold of Ash."

He swears. "Where are you?"

"At the shop."

"I'll be there in twenty minutes. Wait until I get there to do anything. Don't respond. Got it?"

"Sure, yeah. Just get here."

"I'm on my way."

He's actually here in fifteen, which is good because I'm about ready to tear down the walls brick by brick. Jax is by my side, always got my back. But he can't help me right now, and we both know it. Neither Gabby nor I have been able to get through to Ash on her phone. Even her work cell is going to voicemail which Gabby insists Ash would never do. She needs to be available to the hospital in an emergency. She was ready to come here too, but I told her to stay put until we heard what Melrose had to say. It's nowhere near eight o'clock yet, though, nowhere near the time Ash is supposed to be home.

He walks in, phone to his ear, mid-conversation. "I just got here. You ready? Okay." He hangs up. "Show me the text."

I hand my phone over. He looks at it frowning, then starts to type.

"What are you doing?"

"Responding. Trying to get them to engage in a conversation."

My heart starts to pound. "You think that's a good idea? If they know the police-"

"I'm pretending to be you," he says and continues his messaging. After a minute, he sets my phone down on the counter.

"Now what?"

"Now we wait."

It takes an insane amount of willpower not to physically grab Melrose and shake him. "Wait? What the fuck kind of plan is that? Can't you get an APB or a BOLO or whatever the fuck you do?"

He looks at me steadily. "Not yet."

"Not yet!?"

"Lucas. Trust me," he demands, cutting into the beginning of my unhinged rant. Jax walks over and puts a hand on my shoulder, squeezing in warning and support.

"We'll find her. She probably decided to meet a friend at the movies or something," Jax offers.

But none of us really believe that.

After that, we fall silent.

Waiting.

I can't lose her. Not now, after all of this. If something happens to her, it will be my fault. She was fine in Nigeria. No stalkers in sight.

Finally, my phone buzzes on the counter.

Melrose grabs it before I can and glances at the screen. "Fuck," he swears. He pockets my phone and picks up his own.

"What? What did it say?" I move as if to get my phone, but Jax, hand still on my shoulder, holds me back.

Calling up a contact on his own phone, he ignores me. After a brief pause, I hear him say, "We're out of time. Ash is missing."

The hell?

Melrose is silent, listening to whoever is on the other end of the line.

He looks back at me, his eyes somber. "Tell him I'm bringing Lucas."

Tell who what now?

Melrose pockets his cell. Immediately I demand, "What's going on?"

Grabbing my other shoulder, he turns me toward the door and starts us moving. "If we're going to get to Ash in time, then right now, I need you to trust me. So let's go. Jax? I assume you're tagging along as well?"

"I'm right behind you."

Ash

Surprisingly, Will and I have settled into an excellent professional partnership. The morning after the embarrassing non-kiss, we had a few awkward attempts at pretending it hadn't ever happened like we'd agreed. But remarkably quickly, we fell into an easy and productive routine. His growing excitement and commitment to the training and exchange program were inspiring to watch, and by the time we'd returned to Chicago, it felt almost like the friendship we'd had years ago before we had even tried dating.

Turns out he _had_ been on my street the night Lucas thought he'd seen him. I'd asked him about it a few days later, and he'd grudgingly admitted he'd been on his way over - to talk work. But when he saw Lucas, he decided to wait until we were back in the hospital. I haven't mentioned it to Lucas. I don't think he'd believe that excuse - I'm choosing to - and frankly, since he hasn't brought Will up again, I'm sure not going to do it.

The Chief and PR Person Jennifer Johnson practically drooled over the press shots and video that Kent pulled together. We're currently working on a targeted mailing, both brochure and email, they want to get out just before the first official rotation starts with Will. Two residents from the hospital have also applied and been approved to go.

It's actually happening.

Abeni is thrilled. Obviously, she would prefer people who would commit for longer than three months, but any trained medical help will make a huge impact. And frankly, she's counting on recruiting people to stay longer once they are there. Which I think is a distinct possibility. I fell in love with the work I was doing there, the people. It made me a better doctor, there is no doubt about that. And I imagine I'll return for years.

I just love something here more.

Someone.

Hey Ash, it's Logan. We're planning a surprise for Luke's birthday, and I was wondering if you wanted to help.

Apparently, I'm the worst girlfriend ever because I didn't even know Lucas had a birthday coming up. I respond immediately that, of course, I want to help.

Great. Can you meet me tonight at my place?

I agree, promising to head over around five, and she texts me her address. I'm still not quite used to the idea that Logan seems to like me. Obviously, I'm thrilled, but she's a tough nut to crack, and her sudden change of heart still makes me nervous. It feels tenuous like I could still blow it and go back to warding off her sharp tongue.

Turns out Logan lives in a garden-style apartment only a few miles from *Vanished*. I press the button next to the number she gave me at the entrance and hear the door buzz open. Her directions tell me to go through the lobby and out the back door, down the stairs on the right, so that's what I do. I find the apartment labeled 2B and see she left the door open for me. I step inside, calling out a greeting.

"Logan?"

The sun has set and the small windows don't let in much light. I blink, waiting for my eyes to adjust. "Logan?" I feel around until I can find a light switch and flip it on. Immediately I realize something is wrong.

Something is very, very wrong.

This is not Logan's apartment. This isn't anyone's apartment. There isn't any furniture, it's totally empty. I pull up the text message and press call, backing up towards the door.

Ringing echoes throughout the apartment, coming from a room down the hall. What the hell is going on?

Confused, I switch directions again and start to move toward the sound, flipping on lights as I go. I finally find the source in an empty bedroom. Except when I turn on the light, I realize it's not entirely empty. Logan is unconscious and sprawled on a bare mattress in the center of the room. Without thinking, I rush over to her side, dropping my phone next to her and checking for a pulse.

I exhale in relief when I find one, steady and strong. I gently pry open her eyelids, seeing only the whites of her eyes. I reach for my phone, so I can call 911.

And then my skin prickles with awareness just as I hear a rustle behind me. Stupid to let my guard down. I know better. But before I can correct my mistake, pain splinters across my skull, and everything goes dark.

Chapter Thirty-Three

Lucas

Melrose drives us downtown, just north of the Loop and a few blocks from the river and the lake. The city doesn't soothe me the way it usually does. I'm far too terrified and angry. I need to get to Ash. Stupid. Stupid to assume everything was fine because things were quiet while she was gone. And now it might cost me everything.

"Where are we going?" I demand, but Melrose continues to ignore me. Jax sits silently in the backseat.

He pulls into an underground garage showing a card to the security guard. A business card. Not his badge. What the hell is going on?"

"Melrose." I'm going to lose my shit, and my voice reflects that lack of control.

"We're here. Follow me."

"We're where? Why are you being such a cryptic fuck?" But Jax and I both climb out of the car and follow him to the elevators.

Melrose presses the up arrow and then says, "I've had some friends looking into your case. They've got information for us."

"They know where Ash is?" I demand, and for a brief second, the ball of anguish in my stomach shrinks.

"We'll know in a few minutes." The elevator arrives, and we all climb on. Melrose presses the button marked 41, and the doors close.

When the doors slide open again, we're on a floor with only one door. There isn't a sign anywhere indicating where the hell Melrose has brought us. If I don't get some answers in the next few minutes, I'm going to start inflicting violence on people. I can feel it bubbling up. He presses a buzzer and turns to me with a somber look on his face.

"I tried to keep him out of it. Just so you know. Out of respect. But after you started getting the texts, we had to be sure. And frankly, he has less bureaucracy and better resources than the department."

The door opens and a woman with wavy blond hair, dressed all in black, ushers us in. She nods across the lobby area to a white door on the other side.

Melrose leads us over and then hesitates, his hand on the doorknob. "Just listen to what he says and then tell me where we need to go. The less I know, the better." He twists the knob and holds the door open for us. I step through, still completely perplexed by what is going on.

"Oh, and Luke?" I turn back. "Don't be an ass, and don't let him provoke you, alright? He's actually our best shot to find Ash, and frankly, we don't have time for it right now." He shuts the door.

What.

The.

Fuck.

My cousin, Ethan Abbott, sits at a desk with multiple computer screens. Two men stand against the far wall, also dressed all in black. This is all so surreal I'd feel like I was in a movie if it wasn't for the constant fear for Ash bearing down on me.

"What the fuck is going on?" If Melrose won't tell me, then Ethan better because hitting a cop gives me far more pause than punching Ethan Abbott ever will.

"I'm trying to find your friend," Ethan informs me, never taking his eyes off the screens in front of him.

"Oh shit." I hear Jax mutter behind me. I turn and find him staring at one of the men against the wall. It takes me a second, but then I realize what he was surprised by. This was one of his security guards at the hospital. Peter or Paul or something like that. What the hell is going on?

"Why is one of Jax's security guards in your office? I'm assuming this is your office?"

"Is that really what you want to talk about right now?" Ethan asks, still not looking at me. "Here." He pushes back from his desk slightly and stands frowning at the screens in front of him. I am not a computer guy. I know enough to run my shop, and that's all I'm interested in knowing. But even I can tell there are tens of thousands of dollars of equipment in this room. Computer equipment and little else. It's like Dr. Evil's lair or something.

"What exactly do you do, cousin?"

"Cyber security," he mutters, barely acknowledging me. He bends down and hits a couple additional commands.

"Cyber security," I repeat.

"Among other things, yes." He points to a map of Chicago with various circles lit up across it. "Ash's phone is the white dots. These are all the places it's pinged throughout the last week. It last pinged here."

"Great." I'm hit with a sudden rush of adrenaline. "Let's go."

"Not so fast." He hits another key, and yellow lights overlay the same map.

"What is this? How do you have this."

"I hacked their phones."

"Whose phones?"

He finally glances at me. "Everyone's."

I clench my fists, still contemplating hitting him just for the pleasure of it. "You hacked everyone in Chicago?" my voice drips with sarcasm.

"Of course not. Don't be ridiculous. I hacked your employees, Ash and her roommates, and a handful of people from the hospital."

Holy shit. He's serious.

He points at the new round of lights. "Logan's phone last pinged here." It's right on top of where Ash last was.

"What are you talking about? Logan didn't do this. We need to find Ash."

"No. Logan didn't do this. But she's with Ash."

My stomach drops. Fuck. Immediately I pull out my phone and try to call Logan. Not surprisingly, it goes right to voice mail.

He hits another button on the keyboard, and yet another series of lights flicker to life on the screen. "This is where Tanya's phone last pinged."

"This fucker has Tanya too?"

"No. Tanya is the fucker."

Ash

My head. Oh my god, I've never felt pain like this before. I feel cold, rough cement under my cheek. It hurts too much to open my eyes and figure out where I am. How did I get here? What happened? Thinking causes stabbing pain to splinter across the front of my head. Clenching my teeth, I take a slow, long inhale, trying to organize my thoughts. I'm groggy, and my limbs feel heavy. I suspect it's from more than a concussion. I think I've been drugged.

Cautiously I assess my injuries. In addition to my head, my right shoulder throbs. I realize my arms are tied behind my back. My ankles are tied, too, but other than that, my legs feel fine. I shift my legs to make sure, relieved when there is no pain. I strain to hear anything, still afraid to open my eyes. I remember now, bits and pieces.

Someone hit me over the head.

After luring me to Logan's. My heart stutters in fear. Oh god.

No. After Logan asked me to come over. Or someone pretending to be Logan.

Logan! My eyes open in alarm. I remember seeing her on the floor just before I was hit. Before I was knocked out and taken...here.

It takes a moment for my eyes to adjust to the dim lighting. I hold my breath, listening for any sound, anything that would indicate I'm not alone, but I hear nothing. I force myself to calm down and think. Fight your panic; use your training. Practice until it's muscle memory. This is what I tell women in my classes. What I've been told over and over again. I can get out of this. Gathering my courage, I shift and rock until I manage to sit up and get my back against the wall so I can take in my surroundings. I'm in an unfinished basement, but other than that, I can't determine much. I don't think it's any place I've been before, though. It seems like the basement of a house. There are stairs to my right, but I can't see the door at the top. A deep wash basin on the wall to my left. A rickety old table and a couple wooden chairs in front of me. My shoulder throbs as I turn my head, trying to duck and see beyond the chairs. I think I see Logan in the shadows on the far wall.

We have to get out of here.

Breathe. Think.

"Logan?" my whisper sounds harsh and loud in the quiet, and I cringe, eying those stairs. The figure on the other side of the room moans softly but appears unconscious.

Shit.

My legs are bound with duct tape, which means I can get loose with enough time. I wiggle my wrists. Nope. Some kind of cord. I call Logan's name again but still no response. Distantly it occurs to me that whoever took us isn't concerned with us screaming because neither of us is gagged. Shit. How long have we been out? Where are we?

I take a deep breath, knowing this will hurt, and brace my feet on the floor in front of me, my shoulders against the wall. And using my feet, I shimmy up, my shoulder screaming in protest with every jolt. Once I'm mostly standing, I rub my ankles together until the tape loosens enough for me to get them almost crossed. And then I drop, letting gravity and body weight put pressure on the tape. It stretches but doesn't fully pop. My ankles weren't crossed enough. Dammit. I start to repeat the same process, but then I hear thuds upstairs and the door opening.

I sit again, resting against the wall and closing my eyes.

The steps are light down the stairs, and I peek, trying to get my first look at this psycho.

I see black boots crossing the floor.

Women's boots.

What the hell?

"You can stop faking. I know you're awake."

I recognize the voice but can't believe it. Not until my eyes fully open and I see her standing in front of me does it become real.

Tanya.

She smiles, but it's wrong. Creepy. Unhinged.

She takes a seat at the table in front of me and sighs.

"Why couldn't you just stay away?" Her voice is soft and sad. Conversational.

I stay silent, taking it all in.

"I never wanted this." She gestures between us. "I just wanted you gone. I tried. I tried to show him you were trouble. I tried to show him you were just a stupid slut like all the others. What makes you so special? Because you saved

Jax? I tried to show him I could take care of Jax too. But no. You were just always there. Always fawning all over him so he couldn't even see me!" Her voice rises on the last sentence, screaming it at me. She stands in a rush, kicks me in the gut, and then stomps on my thigh. I flinch and cry out, curling into a protective ball.

Tanya inhales deeply and smooths a hand over her curls, pulling herself creepily together.

"I'm the one that can help him. I can keep him relevant, keep him famous. Help his career. What can you do for him? NOTHING." She slaps me across the face. My lip stings, and I taste blood. She's losing it again and leans over me, breath heaving. I'm not sure if it's better for me to try to talk to her in her rational moments or keep her ranting and raving and hope she makes a mistake. Logan moans, drawing her attention.

"This one." She stands and crosses over to where Logan lies unconscious in a ball on the floor and kicks her viciously. "Always siding with you!" She was? That was news to me. Focus, Ash. Not the point here.

"And then you came back. Why did you have to come back? Now we're here. And I have to end this."

She's pacing now, on the other side of the table and muttering at the ground. I can't understand what she's saying but risk her distraction to continue working the tape at my ankles.

Logan groans again and rolls to her back. She stares at the ceiling silently for a moment and then turns her head. Her eyes meet mine as Tanya's legs pace between us. She sees me rubbing my ankles together and then looks at Tanya.

"You always were a crazy bitch," she says clearly. I suspect she's been awake longer than either Tanya or I realized. And now she's distracting Tanya so I can keep working myself free. Good job, Logan.

Tanya whirls and stomps over to her. "You shut up! You were supposed to help me! Not decide to be friends! Didn't even want me to call when you got in your bike accident. Some friend you are, letting this slut seduce Lucas instead of calling him home."

Logan manages to lever herself into a half-sitting, half-leaning position against the wall. "You mean when you rigged my bike so I would crash?" Tanya staggers a step and sits on the chair again. "Didn't think I figured that out, did you?" Tanya stares at her silently. "Melrose knows too. Might as well give it up, Tanya. He'll know who took us. Probably on his way right now."

"You're bluffing," Tanya accuses, but she sounds shaken and unsure.

Logan just smirks at her, and I finally, finally, feel the tape fully rip. Tanya stands up and glares at me again. I keep my ankles together, praying she doesn't notice.

"Then I guess I better hurry."

She turns and walks back up the stairs.

Chapter Thirty-Four

<u>Lucas</u>

S hit. And suddenly, it all comes together, crystallizing in my mind. Of course, it's Tanya. She must have seen Ash and me kissing that first time in the hospital. And trashing Jax's room; that was right after Logan called me out on dating Ash. Tanya canceled the security team. No one would have thought twice about her being in the hospital or going in and out of Jax's room. She knows all my numbers. All she would have needed to do is get a burner, and she could easily send me the text messages threatening Ash. The video of us leaking, that was right after Krista had called Tanya back to LA. She created a crisis so she could stay. Working with the production team, she totally could have learned how to access those video cameras. And just a few days ago, hitting on me even though I know she's slept with Jax.

Fuck. Jax. I risk glancing at him and see a ravaged expression on his face. Brother is never going to forgive himself for this. Even though none of it is on him.

"Anyway, like I was saying, this is the location the phones last pinged. But I doubt they're still there. No movement for an hour. The burner used to text you responded from this neighborhood several miles away. But it's gone dead. My guess is she tossed it."

I start to pace, shoving both hands through my hair. "So, you have no idea where she is?"

"I didn't say that." He pushes another key twice, and only the final set of lights remains on the map. "Tanya has been apartment hunting. But there are several spots her phone has been in the last week that are not neighborhoods she would want to live. Nice girl like that." He smirks and points to two spots far off the others. He's right. That's not a neighborhood even I would choose to live. "I checked the records of the leasing agency she's using, and they have three addresses in this area they are showing. My guess Tanya's got them in one of those buildings."

He hands me a list of three addresses. "Pick one and go with Melrose. My team will go to another, and whoever clears their address first will head to the last one. If we need to."

"Your team?" I ask incredulously. Once again, my life feels like a movie.

"Pick. And go."

I tell him we'll head to the first address. The two men standing by have apparently just been waiting for their cue because immediately, they head out the door. Jax and I follow them and find Melrose still in the lobby talking to the woman with wavy hair. Seeing us over her shoulder, he ends the conversation and approaches.

"Where we going?"

I hand him the address.

Ash

As soon as I hear the door snick close behind her, I scramble to my feet and move over to Logan's side. Between the pain in my head and my arms tied behind my back, I'm awkward and unsteady.

I drop to my knees next to her. "Are you hurt?" I ask.

"I don't think so. Just pissed off."

Somehow, I almost manage a laugh. "Was that true?" Between the two of us, we manage to get her to her feet.

"About the bike? Yeah. About Melrose? No." She winces as the rough cement wall scratches her bare arms. "Any idea where we are?" she asks.

"No. Pretty sure she drugged us." I nod at a small smear of blood on her shoulder, a possible injection site. "I'm not sure how long we've been out." I show her how to break the duct tape, and she does, tearing loose on the first try. I have her turn around so I can study the bindings on our wrists. I squint and bend at the waist so I can see better. It's some kind of thick cord. It'd be hard to cut through even if we had a knife, which we don't. We stand back-to-back and try to loosen the cords.

"I knew there was something wrong with that bitch," she mutters.

I wince as my shoulder throbs in protest when Logan pulls on my wrist, working the knots. I'm wracking my brain, trying to figure out a way out of this. I'm not sure anyone is even missing me yet. Gabby isn't expecting me until eight o'clock. What time is it? How long had we been unconscious?

And Tanya. Would anyone even suspect Tanya? I hadn't. I think we'd all assumed it was some unstable fan, a stranger. Not someone we saw on an almost daily basis. How did we all miss it?

I think I'm making progress on Logan's wrists when I feel her stiffen and look up. Tanya's back. I can hear her footsteps on the floor above us. I start pulling again more frantically.

"Ash," Logan whispers, and I turn to look over my shoulder at her best I can. "Do you smell that?"

My heart starts to race. I do.

Oh no.

"Gas," I say.

Chapter Thirty-Five

Lucas

The first address is an empty lot. The neighbor tells us the house was torn down just two days ago. I'm about to crawl out of my skin, the need to find Ash like a fire burning through my cells.

The three of us rush back to Melrose's car as he calls Ethan, leaving it on speaker. "We're heading to the third address. Any updates?"

"Nathan's team just arrived on site. So far, nothing. They'll meet you there unless something changes."

"Got it."

We tear through the neighborhood streets on our way to the final address. My last chance to find Ash. My stomach is tight with dread. What if she's not there? We have no other leads, no other ideas. What if Tanya's already hurt her? And Logan. I can't imagine never seeing that evil sparkle in her eye again.

We're here.

Melrose hesitates before getting out of the car. "Just so we're clear, whatever happens in there, I wasn't here. If we need to call in the police, I showed up after everything went down, and you called me. Got it?"

"Melrose, if we find Ash and Logan, I'll say whatever the fuck you want me to say."

Jax nods his agreement, and we burst out of the car.

Melrose breaks the door in with a well-placed heel and goes in first, his gun drawn. We go room by room. Finally, getting to the basement.

Nothing.

It's empty.

I punch the wall, leaving a fist-sized hole in the sheetrock. I'm going to be sick. *Where are you?*

Jax grabs my shoulder and ushers me outside onto the front lawn. The other team is pulling up just as we exit the deserted house.

"Anything?" The man, I'm guessing this is Nathan, asks us. Melrose shakes his head.

I explode in a yell, roaring into the night.

"Luke." Jax approaches me, the only one that dares.

"She's got to be here. She's got to be."

"We'll keep looking, brother. You know that."

"Where?" I yell. "Where will we look?"

I bend over, hands on my knees, and try to pull myself together. *Think.*

I take a slow, steadying breath. Think.

I straighten abruptly.

"Do you smell that?"

Jax tilts his head, thinking. He turns and looks out at the street. "I smell smoke."

Our eyes move up and down the street.

"There," I point across the street and down two houses. The flickering of light is all wrong. There's a condemned sign out front. So, there shouldn't be any light at all.

"Melrose!" I yell, continuing to point. "Fire! There!" This can't be a coincidence. It can't.

He follows my line, and suddenly he and the security team are running, a mad dash to the house. Jax and I follow right behind.

Ash

"That psycho!" Logan turns her back to me again. "Hurry!"

My heart is pounding in my ears, but I know from experience I can't give in to the fear and adrenaline rushing through my limbs. I need to stay focused on the task at hand and not let myself spiral, wondering what is going on upstairs.

Control what is in front of you, Ash. That's what you need to do. Focus on your training.

My fingers go back to the cord at Logan's wrists. I feel the knot with my fingertips and go back to pulling, tugging, and pushing until I feel them start to loosen. A few more tugs and Logan pulls one of her wrists free.

"Got it!" She turns around and works the rest of the cord loose. "Now you. Turn around."

The gas smell has gotten more pronounced. I don't think there's a fire yet, but the knowledge that it's likely to happen, could happen any second is horrifying. She's pulling at the cord. It's rubbing my wrists raw, and my fingers are beginning to tingle at being in this position for a long time.

She curses behind me. "It keeps getting tighter!"

She's losing it, I can tell. Her voice is tinged with desperation. We can't afford that right now, either one of us.

"Logan!" I say firmly, getting her attention. "Take a deep breath. Focus. One move at a time. You can do this."

I feel her behind me, hear her inhale deeply, centering herself. "Okay. Okay, I've got this."

"You've got it. One move at a time."

We both hear it at the same time. A whoosh of air above us. Immediately there's heat.

Tanya started a fire.

We have to get out of here.

I hear Logan sniffle behind me, but her hands are steady as they pull at the cord, and suddenly, I'm free.

Well, my hands are free. The rest of me still has some work to do.

I flex my fingers, letting the blood rush back in. My shoulder throbs even in this more natural position.

"See if there's another way out of here. I'm going to check the door." I run up the stairs. Smoke is starting to seep in under the crack in the door frame. I place my hand on the door, snatching it away from the heat radiating there. That way is going to be rough going. Last resort.

I run back down the stairs and see Logan struggling with a piece of plywood high on the far wall.

"I think maybe there's a window back here they boarded up. But this thing won't budge."

I turn around frantically, searching for anything we can use as a tool. Finally, I settle on the rickety chairs. Picking one up, I throw it as hard as I can against the cement block wall. It splinters apart, and I grab a leg. Giving it to Logan, I say, "Use this as a hammer. See if it can break through."

She does, swinging it with all her strength. I drag the other chair over.

"Will this hold you?"

Logan steps up onto the seat. This height gives her better leverage, and she continues to swing away. A layer of smoke is starting to hover along the ceiling of the basement. Frantically I try to rip off the sleeves of my long-sleeved t-shirt, eventually succeeding. I go to the sink and turn the water on, getting them wet. Then I return to Logan and tell her to wrap one around her nose and mouth, doing the same. She's managed to punch a hole in the plywood, enough for the cool November night air to whistle through. I take over, giving her a rest.

"Ash? Ash! Logan!"

I pause my pounding, wondering if I'm hallucinating. But I hear it again. Our names.

"Logan! Ash! Can you hear me?"

"Lucas!" I shriek. "We're here! We're down here!"

Logan starts screaming as well, together making as much noise as we can.

Suddenly I see a man peering through the hole we've made.

"Got 'em! Over here!"

Moments later, his face is replaced by Lucas's, and I've never seen such a beautiful sight in my life.

"Ash! Are you okay? Is Logan there?"

"Yeah! Yeah, we're fine."

As if to disprove my words, there is a crash from the floor above us, shaking the entire house.

"Hold on. We'll get you out."

He's pulled away, and the other man returns with a woman at his side. He lowers her down to the recess of the window, and using a tiny torch, she cuts a large square in the wood, big enough for us to climb out. She twists her body until she can kick it out. I hear Logan coughing behind me, and I make her go first. She grabs the woman's hand and gets pulled up and out. I'm next. As soon as my head clears the plywood-covered window, the man grabs my other hand and pulls me effortlessly to my feet outside.

A wave of dizziness hits me, and for a second, I'm worried I'm going to collapse, but suddenly Lucas is there. His arms wrap around me, holding me to his chest, and I take a deep breath.

We made it.

Chapter Thirty-Six

Lucas

T hank god. She's alright. We got to them in time.

I look over Ash's head and see Jax with his arm around Logan. They're both alright.

Ethan's *team* is circling the 'perimeter' communicating over their walkie-talkies or whatever the fuck they're called. Two of them go around the back, the other staying with Melrose and us on the front lawn. I hear sirens approaching in the distance. I guess someone reported the fire. Ash is shivering against me, and I hold her close, trying to provide some warmth.

"Noooooo! Get away from her!" We all hear the screech at the same time, and suddenly I'm flying back off my feet. I hear Ash scream at the same time I hit the ground, losing my breath.

Tanya is on top of me, a crazed look on her face. I feel a searing heat along my arm and see the light flash off a knife in her hand.

Shit.

"Drop it!" I hear Melrose yelling. Tanya doesn't even hesitate, her arm slashing down towards me, and I grab her wrist and twist. She screeches again, surprisingly strong, refusing to release the knife, and then I hear two loud explosions. Tanya jerks on top of me and then goes limp, falling to the side.

I see Melrose behind her, gun drawn. Ash rushes to me, inspecting my wound.

"It's fine. You're fine," she chants. Reassuring herself as much as me. She presses a cloth against my skin and orders me to hold it in place.

Then she moves to Tanya, placing her fingers against her neck. Melrose stands over them, his gun still trained on Tanya, her knife at his feet. A few moments later, Ash stands, looks at Melrose, and shakes her head. I sit up, and she returns to my side, helping me to my feet.

Melrose grimaces. "That's going to be paperwork."

"Thanks, man," I say. He nods.

The firetruck pulls up, followed by a black and white.

"Remember what I said," Melrose mutters in an aside.

I nod. I find Jax's eyes and motion to Melrose as he goes to greet the officers on the scene. Jax nods and leans down to whisper something in Logan's ear. I do the same to Ash. Getting our stories straight.

Hours later, Ash is curled up on my couch under a blanket. She looks tiny and fragile and sad, and I hate that I can't take away her pain. But I'm also so fucking thankful she's okay, and Tanya is dead. I'm probably an asshole for being glad another human is dead, but I am. I could have lost one of the most important people in my life and the love of my life tonight. Because of Tanya. I won't lose any sleep over her death.

We dropped Logan off at Jax's apartment. No one wanted her to be alone, including Logan. I hugged her tight before saying good night, so fucking thankful I can still look forward to her snarky attitude in my life.

It's late, or really early, depending on how you look at it, but neither of us has suggested going to bed. I called Gabby to tell her that Ash was okay and that we'd call her in the morning. I don't think Ash can take rehashing what happened one more time tonight, not even to her best friend.

I bring her some tea and slide onto the seat next to her, my arm along the back of the couch. She's showered, but it hasn't washed away all the evidence of her night. There's a bruise forming along the side of her face, and her arms and hands are covered in scrapes. The EMTs wanted her to go to the hospital and have her shoulder and head looked at, but Ash insisted she knew the signs of a concussion and would have a coworker look at her shoulder in the morning. I know more bruises are hidden beneath the sweatshirt and leggings she's wearing, and it makes me wish Melrose could shoot Tanya all over again.

I cup the back of her neck, my thumb rubbing gentle circles against her skin. I just need to touch her in some small way. Assure myself she's real and here and alive.

She takes a tentative sip of her tea. And before my eyes, her face crumples, tears running soundlessly down her cheeks.

"Hey." I take the mug out of her hands and place it on the coffee table before turning back and pulling her into my lap. She straddles me, her knees pressed firmly along the outside of my thighs. Her face tucks into the crook of my neck, and she squeezes me tight. I feel the first sob rack her body and hold her. Just hold her, rubbing my hands along her back soothingly.

"It's over now. You're okay. Logan's okay. It's over."

I lose track of time as she cries, letting everything out. This is the first time I've seen Ash really cry, seen her break. And I'm glad as hell I'm here to hold her through it. This woman, my woman, is tough, I know she'll pull through this, but I like being someone she can cling to when she needs it.

Eventually, she stills and sucks in a ragged breath. Leaning back, she wipes her eyes, averting them away from my face.

"I'm sorry. I'm such a mess." She sniffles, and I cup her face, my thumbs wiping away some leftover tears.

"Stop it. You're beautiful."

She gives me a rueful smile and finally looks me in the eye. "I am not. I'm such an ugly crier."

Her eyes are swollen and red, her face blotchy, nose runny. She's a mess, it's true, but I don't fucking care. She's still beautiful. And she's alive. In my arms. Exactly where she's supposed to be. I'll take any day of her like this over a day without her in it.

"I love you."

Her eyes widen and fill with tears again.

"I love you," I say it again, partly because she hasn't said anything, and I want to make sure she heard me. Partly because it turns out I really like saying it. Who knew? It had seemed so huge before, stripping myself, being vulnerable, but it turns out it's so easy.

She buries her face in her hands, her body shaking with new tears. And I hold her.

"You're telling me this now? When I'm such a wreck?"

Her complaint makes me grin. "I told you, you're beautiful."

She peeks up at me.

"Well, you could probably use a Kleenex."

A startled laugh bursts through her tears.

I chuckle and squeeze her to me, feeling so light and loose inside. Finally telling her how I feel lifted a weight off my chest I'd been smothered by for years. Maybe my whole life. I have no idea if I even have kleenex and have no intention of letting her off my lap anytime in the near future. Instead, I take off my t-shirt and hand it to her so she can clean up.

"Thanks," she mumbles, a small grin on her face.

"Better?"

At her nod, I give her a quick kiss. And tell her again. "I love you."

Her hands frame my cheeks and those dark chocolate eyes I adore so much look intently into mine. "Every part of you, Lucas. Even the parts of you, you think are hard to love. I love."

I have to squeeze my eyes shut briefly at the intense emotion that courses through me. She snuggles into me with another sigh, and I wrap my arms around her.

Fucking perfect.

Ash

He loves me.

I've known that for a while. Well, suspected. Believed.

But there's a difference between knowing and *knowing*. A difference between your head and your heart.

He loves me.

I snuggle against him, perfectly content to stay in his lap for the foreseeable future.

I must nod off at some point because the next thing I know, he's laying me on the bed.

"Don't leave me," I whisper, lifting my arms for him.

"Never." He has a soft smile on his face and crawls onto the bed next to me, curling himself protectively around me.

I roll and shift until I'm in his arms, facing him. "Make love to me."

I see the hesitation on his face. "You should rest. I don't want to hurt you."

"Then be gentle."

Cupping his cheeks, I press my lips to his. His protests melt away, and he returns my embrace, brushing his lips across mine again and again. Slowly he removes our clothes, his hands warm on my skin as they caress me everywhere. It doesn't take long until I'm begging for him, needing to be as close to him as possible.

Achingly tender, he slides inside me, making love to me slowly, carefully, completely.

"I love you," he whispers against my lips, and I feel tears leaking down the sides of my face.

"I love you, too, Lucas. I love you."

His breathing changes, becomes more urgent, but still, he moves with care. I gasp as I shatter into a million delicate pieces, so different than the orgasms he's given me in the past. His motions become jerky and uneven, and soon he's groaning his own release.

After, I lay on my good side, favoring my injured shoulder, and rest against his side. My head is on his chest so I can listen to the soothing beat of his heart.

I can't believe how safe and calm I feel when just hours ago, I was afraid I might die. But I didn't. We made it here.

We hold each other tightly, neither of us ready to close our eyes yet. He tells me how they managed to find us.

"So, Ethan was helping Melrose?" For whatever reason, I'm having the most trouble reconciling this part of the story.

Lucas shifts one shoulder in a shrug. "Melrose kind of makes his own rules. But yeah, Ethan helped. I guess he's some security computer expert or something."

"Wow," I whisper. His cousin helped save my life. "That's so crazy." Distantly, I wonder if I should feel offended or angry that Ethan Abbott hacked my phone and the phones of several people in my life. In any other situation, it would be an unforgivable violation. But now, here, tonight, I am nothing but grateful. I should encourage Lucas to be nicer to him in the future.

Releasing thoughts of Lucas's family, I roll into his side and look up at his face.

"I need to ask you a question."

"Anything."

"When is your birthday?"

He lifts his head so he can look into my face. "What?"

"When is your birthday? I love you, and you love me. I should know when your birthday is."

He chuckles, the sound sending a warm flush over my skin. "May 12th."

May 12th. I commit the date to memory.

Gabby comes over the following morning, as soon as I message her I'm awake. She squeezes me tight, and even though it hurts, all my sore muscles protesting, I return her hug. The guys, Tim is with her, leave us alone, retreating to the kitchen.

I asked her to bring the suitcase I'd yet to really unpack. Lucas asked me to move in with him last night, and I said yes. There's nowhere else I'd rather be.

Acknowledgement

This project has been a long time coming. And I'm excited about several more in the future. It would never have happened without the Happy Hour Crew – Mary, Megan, Allison, Jess – thank you for cheering me on and constantly demanding more chapters. I will endeavor to write faster in the future.

Mom, thank you for always being my biggest fan. It's awkward knowing you read all the scenes, but I appreciate your constant support.

The new friends that joined me on a rooftop in Antigua and heard I wanted to do this – thank you for celebrating women. The old friends that were shocked I even dreamed of doing this – thank you for embracing a wild left turn.

For so many that encouraged me along the way, Jenny, Emma, Jen, Mia, Ilysia, Maggie, Lucinda, Nikki, Leslie, Nicole, Charnds, Carly – thank you for embracing this project with so much enthusiasm and fun. And so many others, it's impossible to name you all. I'm truly blessed with an amazing community of women.

And Naja, thank you for always being so open and genuine with your compliments and gratitude. For wanting every woman to see their crown. This book may never have become real without you.

About the Author

Author, blogger, traveler, tea-drinker. I also like to take photographs. I like 80s dance parties. I love apocalypse movies. I tend to eat a lot of appetizers. I think Magic 8 balls are a valid way to make decisions. And I think the point of being an adult is the right to have ice cream for dinner if that's what you want. But I only do that occasionally. I dream of being multi-lingual. I am currently very far from this goal. I'm always on the lookout for new adventures. I think my child-like enthusiasm for life is endearing. Hopefully my friends and loved ones agree. I yoga on occasion. I feel Buffy the Vampire Slayer is the best TV show ever made. Veronica Mars a very close second. I was a closeted romantic for years, but recently came out. I frequently watch horror movies alone – and then regret it. I like beautiful oddities. Thundersnow is my favorite weather phenomenon. I consume a lot of wine and conversation. https://StaceyLynnHafner.com
FB: StaceyLynnHafner | **IG:** StaceyIsWriting | **Twitter:** StaceyIsWrite

Also by Stacey Lynn Hafner

COMING SOON IN THE VANISHED SERIES...

Tattoo My Love

SUMMARY: Jackson "Jax" Hall owes his life to his childhood friend Lucas Abbott and, more recently, to the love of Lucas's life, Dr. Ash Carrington. So even though he's drawn to Riley Abbott's kind gray eyes and wide smile, he's determined to ignore it. Lucas is slowly making peace with his family but dating his best friend's estranged cousin is not an option. But when Riley asks for Jax to help with her students, he can't say no. And the two of them spending more and more time together is weakening his resolve. Riley is moving on after a recent and devastating breakup. She's determined to follow her heart and her gut for the first time in her life. She knows Jax is attracted to her and is determined to explore the passion he makes her feel. When Riley is put in danger because of choices he's made, Jax knows he'll do anything to keep her safe. Even cut himself entirely out of her life.

Tattoo My Soul

SUMMARY: Logan Dahl is used to fighting for everything she's got. Working in the male dominated field of tattooing, she's worked her ass off to be taken seriously and it's paid off. She's now a member of Vanished, successful both as a tattoo artist and a reality star. She doesn't need pretty boy Connor Thomas coming in trying to smooth out her edges. But the MVP baseball player is sexy and sweet and every interaction with him lowers her defenses. Connor is intrigued by the stunning and snarky Logan. Her sharp tongue amuses him and he wants to know more about what drives her. When secrets from Logan's past resurface will Connor be able to convince Logan to let him in and let him help?

Tattoo My Life

SUMMARY: Macy O'Neill has watched all his best friends find love and their perfect match. He thinks he's finally found someone he can explore a future with when his entire life is suddenly and tragically turned upside down. Is it fair to drag her into the chaos his life has become? Hunter has known Macy practically her whole life and has had a crush on him nearly as long. Like something out of her fantasies, they have a hot and sexy night together but she knows he's going through a lot right now and doesn't want to be yet another responsibility or burden on him. But when her life and livelihood is threatened will either of them be able to stay away?

A Little Teaser

Turn the page for a sneak peek into Jax and Riley's story...

Tattoo My Love

Jax

What the hell is she doing here?

And why does she keep showing up unannounced at my door?

Granted, last time, I was lying in a hospital bed. And this is where I work. So not exactly my private space or anything. But still. This can't mean anything good.

I glance at Macy, still holding open the door Riley had just busted through, who seems just as confused as I am. Understandably confused. One, because we're closed, just locking up. And two, because Riley is an Abbott, and they aren't exactly on the guest list.

"Uh. Hi, Riley."

"Jax." She's unsteady on her feet but lifts her little chin as if lecturing in one of her classrooms. "I would like to speak with Lucas."

I stare at her dumbly, just blinking as I try to figure out what is happening.

When I don't respond, Macy informs her Luke isn't here. She spins at the sound of his voice and falls into him. Macy is chuckling as he reaches out to steady her, and I shoot him a look. He clears his throat, trying to disguise his amusement.

Riley is demanding we go hunt down Lucas so she can talk to him.

That is so not happening.

I hear Mace mutter something about Riley being feisty, and I am quick to deny it. "Not usually." Something is obviously wrong, and not just the fact that she's clearly drunk off her ass.

I cross the room to her side and lead her to the couch. "Mace, can you grab some water for her?" I toss over my shoulder.

"On it."

Riley is glancing around the room, taking in all the artwork. She's never been here before. Never visited our tattoo shop Vanished. Lucas isn't exactly a fan of his family. Although I think Riley is starting to chip away at some of his walls. I'd like to see him give them a chance. At least give her a chance. But I'd never tell him that. Not my place. My place is behind him, supporting him, having his back.

That's the way it's always been.

I crouch down in front of her. Despite her drunken determination when she stormed in, now she looks uncertain and avoids my eyes.

"Haven't seen you for a while," I offer, giving her a half smile. It's been about three months, actually. I haven't seen her since I got out of the hospital. She visited regularly when I was there, carefully avoiding Luke after one marginally brutal interaction. But she would come by and keep me company and smuggle me my favorite foods.

She finally looks directly at me, her eyes red and blurry. Shit. She's been crying.

"You look good," she whispers. "Better."

"Good as new."

Macy reappears with a bottle of water that he hands over and then leaves us alone again. My leg is starting to cramp, so I move to sit next to her on the couch. Making sure to keep a respectable distance. Luke may not like his family, but she's still my best friend's cousin.

Even if she is cute.

I don't normally do cute. Or sweet. And Riley, with her retro-style dresses, giant gray eyes, genuine smile, and enormous purse with KitKats, is both. She's a teacher. At a Chicago public school. If that doesn't tell you everything you need to know about her character, I don't know what will.

And I'd be lying if I said I hadn't thought about those gray eyes over the last few months.

But she's also an Abbott. So I keep my distance. Literally and figuratively.

Or at least I had been. But I'm not an asshole. I'm not going to turn her out on the street when she's drunk and obviously upset.

"So," I say, settling back into the leather couch. "What's new with you?"

Sniffling, she stares at her shoes.

"I finished work early tonight. One of my after-school meetings was canceled, so I thought I would bring Daniel some dinner. Surprise him. But when I got there... he was... he-"

Fucking hell. I glance at the rock on her finger.

"Wasn't alone?" I finish gently.

She shakes her head, silently starting to cry again.

Dammit.

Now, what am I supposed to do?

"Want me to have Mace go over and scare the shit out of him?" Macy is the largest of all of us, built like a fucking warrior. Luckily he usually has a smile on his face, or he'd be one scary dude. Now, he's just scary when he wants to be, which isn't very often. But I imagine he would terrify her skinny tax attorney fiance. Or ex-fiance. Cheating fiance.

Thankfully, this causes her to laugh, sniffling through her tears. She takes a sip of the water. Suddenly she jumps to her feet, swiping at her cheeks and the tears under her eyes. "Let's go dancing!"

My eyes widen in surprise. "You want to go dancing?"

"Yes! Let's go? Where should we go?"

"I don't think that's a good idea, Teach."

She crosses her arms and glares at me. "And why not?"

I open my mouth to explain, or at least try to explain without pointing out she's drunk, but before I can, her face falls. "Oh. Because of Lucas."

Surprisingly, I hadn't been thinking of him. Luke is suspicious of Riley, thinks she's often acting as an emissary for his cousin Ethan and his uncle, but she's growing on him. And he would definitely want her taken care of in this situation.

"That's not why," I tell her. "But if you go out to a club with Macy and me, there's a good chance some paparazzi will find us and take your picture. I can't imagine the school board would be excited about that."

"Oh."

She looks so disappointed I can't help but feel like I let her down somehow. I should just make sure she gets home okay. But I also suspect that's one of the last places she wants to go right now. And showing up at her uncle's house will lead to questions, I'm sure.

I shove a hand through my hair in frustration. I know what I'm about to do, and I know it's a bad idea.

I keep my distance from Riley. That's what I do. What I should do.

Instead, I find myself saying, "You want to go somewhere for a drink? I've got an idea."

The kick in my chest at her smile is further proof I'm making a mistake.

Too late now.

Macy

All I want to do right now is sleep.

Unfortunately, it's looking like that isn't going to happen for a while yet.

I was so close. *So close.* Literally turning the OPEN sign off and about to lock the door.

Instead, a blast of cool air hits me in the face as a blur of stripes and color blows by me.

I shoot a look of disbelief at Jax, who is behind the counter finishing the deposit.

"I want to speak with Lucas!" the tiny red-headed whirlwind demands. She seems a little unsteady on her feet.

Jax is wearing a surprised expression that I'm sure mirrors mine.

"Uh. Hi, Riley."

"Jax." She sways a bit and sniffs, importantly raising her chin. "I would like to speak with Lucas."

"He's not working tonight, darlin'," I offer when Jax remains silent, just staring at her with a bewildered look on his face.

She turns her attention to me and stumbles with the momentum.

My chuckle is cut short when Jax glares at me.

"Where is he? Let's go find him!"

"Well. She's feisty," I comment.

"Not usually," Jax frowns.

He rushes around the counter, wraps an arm around her waist, and guides her to one of the couches. He's murmuring something to her, but it's too quiet for me to make out what he's saying.

"Mace, can you grab some water for her?"

"On it."

I'm man enough to admit I grab a bottle of water and promptly make myself scarce, letting Jax deal with the drama out front.

I'm allergic to drama. Something more than one woman in my past has abruptly discovered. Unfortunately, she's family, slightly removed, so while I don't feel the need to jump right into the fray, I'm also not inclined to totally bail. I don't know Riley well, and the Abbotts are basically persona non grata, but Riley's never shown up on our doorstep drunk before, either.

Eventually, Jax comes to find me in the break room. He's rubbing one hand over his hair, a concerned expression on his face.

"She caught the fiancé cheating," he informs me.

"Damn. That's rough."

"Look, she's not ready to go home, and I don't think she should be left on her own. But she can't stay here, obviously." Jax winces, running a hand through his hair again. "We need to take her somewhere the paps aren't going to find us. The last thing she needs is to be all over the gossip sites drunk and jilted."

"We? When did I get dragged into this? Doesn't she have a girlfriend she can call?"

Jax just glares at me silently.

I sigh, resigned to my new plans for the evening. "Fine." He knows I've got the perfect place.

We finish closing up and then hail a cab across town. If we're in for a night of helping to drown some sorrows, it seems wise not to have a car with us.

Riley is a chatty little thing, at least when she's a little wasted. According to Jax, who has had more interactions with her than I have, she's usually kind of shy and sweet. His word, "sweet". I roll my eyes. That's a shitstorm waiting to happen.

We pile out of the cab in front of my family's pub, O'Neill's. It's trivia night, so it should be busy enough for us to blend in, but mostly full of regulars. People who know my family and me won't feel the need to call any paparazzi. Hopefully. Most people here find it amusing that I've somehow achieved tangential celebrity status and would much rather give me a hard time than feed into that nonsense.

They keep me grounded.

Mostly.

Tommy's working the door and grins when he sees me. "Hey, man. How you doing?" I left my chin in greeting, clasping our hands as if we're going to arm wrestle and slap him on the back.

Riley's still talking non-stop, although I'm starting to get this is half the alcohol and half nervous energy. She smiles widely at Tommy and starts peppering him with questions, some of which seem relevant, questions about the bar, how long he's worked here if he likes it. But others make my head spin with their random landing pads. Does he prefer hockey or baseball? Has he seen the new James Bond movie? Has he ever done a walking tour with the Chicago Architecture Foundation? Apparently, they're great. Really informative.

I smile apologetically at Tommy, but honestly, she's growing on me. And watching Jax try to distract her from Tommy and keep her at a respectable distance is quickly turning my night around.

We finally make it inside, and I see a flash of familiar honey-blond hair behind the bar. I tell Jax to grab one of the open tables, and I'll grab a pitcher of beer.

It's about the crowd I expected, slowly clearing out for the night. I rest my elbows on the bar, eyes following the gorgeous blond working behind it. I'll be honest, mostly, I watch her ass. Hey, I'm a guy. And Hunter has a fantastic ass. Lush and curvy, encased in a pair of well-worn jeans. Years ago, she let me tattoo that ass. Back in her wild child days.

"Hey, Super Star. What brings you to this side of town?" She grins, finally turning her attention to me.

I smirk. "Got sick of all the Cubs fans up there."

"Damn right." She nods. Then laughs out loud. "What can I get for you?"

"No kiss? What the hell? What kind of service is this?"

She laughs again, placing her palms flat on the bar, and jumps to reach across, giving me a loud smack on the cheek. "Your dad's going to be bummed he missed you. He took off early tonight."

"What are you doing here anyway? Slumming it?"

"No, I just told your dad I could help out for the night. Brandi was feeling a little tired."

I stiffen at the mention of my sister. Hunter covers my hand with one of hers. "Just tired."

I blow out a deep breath. My sister Brandi was diagnosed with breast cancer several years ago. She's been in remission for a while now, but it's still terrifying, at least for me.

"Besides, it's fun to help out once in a while. I won't be able to much longer."

I grin at her. "Yeah? You opening your pastry shop soon?"

"Two weeks, we have our soft opening." Her smile could light half of Chicago. She inherited the bakery from her grandmother, but it's been closed for over a year as she sorted out the bills, debt, and zoning crap. Grandma May was an incredible baker, but she wasn't detail-oriented. If she hadn't been such a fixture in the neighborhood for decades, she probably would have been shut down years ago.

"Congrats, sugar. That's awesome. Make sure you send me an invite."

She nods. "So. Drink?"

"Right. I'll take a pitcher of Goose Island. Three glasses."

"You got it."

Hunter steps away, and I scan the bar spotting Jax and Riley at one of the pool tables in the back. She seems a little more steady on her feet now. Adorably focused on lining up her shot, then squealing in excitement when the ball bounces into a pocket. She draws the eyes of several folks in the bar, but Jax doesn't even seem to notice a soft, indulgent expression on his face I've never seen before.

Well. That's interesting.

She was cute, sure. Especially drunk off her ass like now. But she didn't seem like the type Jax usually.... I guess Jax didn't usually do much with the women in and out of his life.

I grab a beer and cross the room to join them. I half lean, half sit on a nearby stool. In the middle of the next 'game,' Riley decides to check out the jukebox, claiming she's got mad song-choosing skills. I laugh at her antics, but Jax seems to be veering wildly between being his typical flirtatious self, unnecessarily protective, and just plain baffled.

Despite the drama I see coming, I've decided I'm rooting for Riley. While she's across the room proving her skills, I have a little fun.

"So, cheating fiancé, huh?"

He nods, eyes never leaving Riley, and sips his beer.

"What a dick. They live together?"

A flash of annoyance crosses his face. "I don't think so. I'm not sure."

"If they do, she's going to need a place to stay tonight," I continue on.

He's silent.

"Hell." I grin. "She can come home with me. Cute little thing." Truthfully, Riley is not at all my type, which Jax is well aware of. Little sprites like her make me feel like I'm going to break them.

"She's not going home with you, Mace."

"Why not? I got a perfectly comfortable bed."

"She's Luke's cousin," Jax growls. Dude literally growled at me.

Smirking, I point out, "She's a grown-ass woman."

Jax stiffens beside me, finally turning to face me full on. "She's not for you, Mace."

I stand up, deliberately keeping my movements slow and relaxed. "Oh, I know she's not for me." I stretch my arms above my head, then reach for the remainder of my beer. "I'm not the one that keeps sneaking glances down her shirt."

I'm still laughing when I reach the bar.

"You need another round?" Hunter asks. The bar is pretty empty at this point, but there's still a good forty minutes before last call.

"No thanks, sugar. I'm going to head home. Kick those two out whenever you need to, okay?"

"They need to crash in the apartment upstairs?"

I shake my head. "No. They'll grab a cab home. Jax isn't drunk."

"Fair enough." She tilts her head, her ponytail swinging. "Good to see you."

"You too. I'll see you in a couple weeks for your opening, right?"

It's hard to tell in the dim lighting, but I think her cheeks get a little pink. She nods.

I stare at her for another minute before pulling myself away and heading out. Finally, I'll get to sleep.

Going home alone isn't as appealing as it was a few short hours ago.

Riley

Oh god. What did I do?

My head is pounding, and I cringe, squeezing my eyes tight against the light.

Reluctantly, I blink open and realize I am not where I am supposed to be. I don't recognize the bed I'm in or the industrial-style loft it's located in. I sit up in a rush but have to grab my head when the sudden movement clashes through it painfully.

And it all comes back in a rush.

Daniel. Alcohol. Lots of alcohol. Vanished. Jax.

Oh god.

This is so embarrassing.

I am not a drinker. I hardly ever drink. And I haven't gotten drunk in years. Not since college.

And Lucas's best friend witnessed the whole thing.

I bury my face in my hands and shake my head in denial.

I'm still in my dress from yesterday. My mouth is dry and stale. I can only imagine the state of my hair. But somehow, I have to gather what's left of my dignity and get out of here.

And I should probably thank Jax for taking care of me last night. I'm sure it was not on his To Do list.

Gingerly, I move to the edge of the bed, testing the sturdiness of my stomach. I notice a glass of water and some aspirin on the nightstand, and I swallow them down gratefully. Then chug the entire glass of water. I am so dehydrated.

Well done, Riley. Way to handle your life like a champ.

Now that I've managed to get to my feet, I take in more of my surroundings.

The loft is huge and largely unfinished. The concrete floor is polished, exposed brick makes up three of the four walls broken up by giant, nearly floor-to-ceiling windows. He's divided the 'bedroom' from the rest of the space with a large screen. Peaking around, I see a cluster of couches in the center with a TV and gaming console. The far side is separated by another large screen hiding whatever is behind it.

One of the couches has a pile of blankets, indicating where Jax spent the night, but he's nowhere to be found. I can't decide if I'm relieved or disappointed he's not here.

I can never really decide what it is with Jax. Uncertainty shrouds every interaction I have with him.

Except, apparently, when I'm totally intoxicated.

The sudden silence is startling. I didn't even notice the sound of the shower until it turned off. A moment later, Jax emerges from the only door in the loft wearing a pair of jeans and nothing else. His hair is still wet, finger-combed back from his face.

I swallow. He's wearing jeans and nothing else.

To keep myself from staring at all the muscles and tattoos on display, I force myself to step forward.

"Morning." My voice is hoarse. I feel my cheeks heat.

He tosses me a look over his shoulder. "Hey! Teach! You're up. Want some coffee?" To the left is the kitchen, appliances lined along the wall with a large island and stools defining the 'room'.

"Coffee sounds good." I awkwardly slide onto a stool, trying not to stare at his back as he starts the coffee brewing. "Sorry about last night. I don't usually-"

He chuckles. "You think I don't know that isn't your usual MO?"

Silently, I drop my eyes to the island in front of me.

Jax turns, facing me, crossing his arms, and leaning his hip against the counter. "You don't need to apologize, Riley. It's not every day you walk in on your fiancé cheating. You're allowed to act a little crazy."

"Still, I disrupted your whole night."

He grins at me, causing my stomach to flip. I push a hand against my abdomen, pretending this is also a reaction to my drinking. "I didn't have any plans. We had fun, right?"

I nod reluctantly. From what I remember, we did have fun. We played pool and danced to the jukebox, and chatted with friendly strangers.

"Macy must think-"

"Macy doesn't think anything. Other than you needed a night out. He's not like that. He's not going to judge you for something we've all done."

I smile ruefully. "I liked his folks' bar."

Jax nods and turns back to pour the coffee. "Yeah, it's a good spot. It's great when we're looking for a place to just chill, you know?"

He sets a mug in front of me.

Gratefully, I take a fortifying sip.

I hear him take a deep breath, and then he asks, "So what are you going to do? About the cheating asshole?"

Tears sting my eyes, and I blink rapidly to fight them off.

What am I going to do?

Instead of answering, I look around suddenly. "Do you know what I did with my phone?"

He walks over to the couches and grabs my purse off the center table. "I shut it off last night. It kept beeping," he explains, handing it over.

Smiling my thanks, I grab my phone out of my bag and turn it back on. I cringe when I realize it's nearly 11am. But I have a vague memory of us not returning to the loft until nearly four last night. This morning. Whatever.

Sure enough, I have dozens of missed calls and unopened texts from Daniel.

I can explain.

Please talk to me.

I'm sorry you saw that.

Riles, I'm getting worried.

Don't do anything stupid.

Where are you?

And then **Please talk to me** again.

I text him, letting him know I'm alive but not ready to talk, and turn my phone back off. I force the images of him in bed with someone else from my mind. I wish I could erase them entirely, but I know that won't ever happen.

And if I'm being completely honest with myself, beneath the pain and betrayal and confusion, I'm also the tiniest bit... relieved.

I don't want to marry Daniel. And now, it seems pretty obvious he doesn't really want to marry me.

So, I have no idea what I'm going to do. But I know what I'm *not* going to do.

I'm not going to get married.